The
Night
Swimmers

BOOKS
by Betsy Byars

Novels

After the Goat Man
The Cartoonist
The 18th Emergency
Good-bye, Chicken Little
The House of Wings
The Midnight Fox
The Pinballs
The Summer of the Swans
Trouble River
The TV Kid
The Winged Colt of Casa Mia

Picture Books

Go and Hush the Baby
(Illustrated by Emily A. McCully)
The Lace Snail
(Illustrated by Betsy Byars)

The Night Swimmers

by BETSY BYARS

ILLUSTRATED

by Troy Howell

DELACORTE PRESS / NEW YORK

Published by
Delacorte Press
1 Dag Hammarskjold Plaza
New York, N.Y. 10017

Manufactured in the United States of America

First printing

Library of Congress Cataloging in Publication Data

Byars, Betsy Cromer.
The night swimmers.

SUMMARY: With their mother dead and their father working nights, Retta tries to be mother to her two younger
brothers.
[1.   Single-parent family—Fiction.   2.   Brothers
and sisters—Fiction]   I.   Howell, Troy.   II.   Title.
PZ7.B9836Ni   [Fic]   79–53597

ISBN: 0–440–06261–6
ISBN: 0–440–06262–4 lib. bdg.

Typography by Jack Ellis

For Sloane and Cole

The
Night
Swimmers

When the swimming pool lights were turned out and Colonel and Mrs. Roberts had gone to bed, the Anderson kids came out of the bushes in their underwear. They moved silently over the moss-smooth lawn, across the Moroccan tiled terrace.

At the edge of the pool they stopped. Retta, the girl, said, "See, I told you it was beautiful." She stared at the shimmering water as proudly as if she had made the pool instead of just discovered it one day.

"But what if somebody sees us?" Roy asked. He hiked up his underwear uneasily. The elastic was sprung, and he wasn't sure the safety pin was going to hold.

"No one's going to see us. It's too dark." She

shrugged as if it didn't matter anyway. "The shallow end's down here. Come on."

She led them to the end of the pool, and together the three of them started down the steps.

"It's cold," Roy said. He clutched his underwear tighter, pulling it toward his chest.

"You'll get used to it."

Abruptly Johnny pulled away. "I want to go down the ladder," he said. He started around the pool.

Retta frowned slightly. Lately Johnny had started doing things his own way. "All right," she called after him, belatedly giving permission, "but then you swim right over to the shallow end, you hear me? I don't want to have to come in and save you."

"You won't." As Johnny took hold of the smooth metal ladder, an adult feeling came over him. He entered the water slowly—it was cold—and then pushed off. He dog-paddled to Retta and Roy, turning his head from side to side in a motion he thought made his dog paddle look more powerful.

"Now you two play here in the shallow end while I do some swimming," Retta said when Johnny joined them.

"I don't see why *I* have to stay in the shallow end," Johnny said.

"Because only one can go in the deep water at a time. That's a rule, and you already had your turn."

Beside them Roy was pretending to swim. He had one hand on the bottom of the pool and was lift-

<2>2</2>

ing the other arm in an elaborate swimming stroke. Then he put that hand on the bottom and lifted the other. "Want to see me swim, Retta?"

"That's nice, Roy," she said. She moved toward the deep end and began to swim silently. She was aware that Johnny was watching her, hoping to find fault, so she moved with deliberate grace. She copied the movements she had seen the Aquamaids do on television. She turned on her back. Then she swirled and dived under the water. Her bare feet rose, toes pointed, and shone in the moonlight.

Johnny was both impressed and irritated. Since he could find no fault with Retta, he looked down at Roy and said meanly, "You aren't really swimming."

"I am too!" Roy paused in the middle of the stroke to look back at Johnny.

"Your hand is on the bottom."

"It is not," Roy said. "Here's my hand right here."

"The other one is on the bottom."

Roy made a quick switch. "It is not. See, here's the other one."

"You aren't fooling anybody."

Johnny turned back to watch Retta. She was under the diving board now. She reached up and grabbed the board with both hands. She glanced around to see if Johnny and Roy were watching. When she was sure they were, she skinned the cat and dropped into the water without a sound.

She swam to the side and pulled herself out of the water without bothering to use the ladder. Then she got the inflated mattress that Mrs. Roberts always used. She carried it to her brothers at the shallow end of the pool. "Want a ride?"

Roy paused in the middle of a swimming stroke; one arm was raised as high as if he wanted to be called on. "Is it all right if we use that?" he asked, peering at Retta from under his arm.

"Sure, get on."

The boys crawled onto the mattress and stretched out self-consciously. Their arms were stiff at their sides.

"I'll push you around the pool." Retta began to move the float into deeper water. "Doesn't it make you feel elegant?"

Johnny nodded. He was shivering in his wet underwear, chilled with the excitement and the evening air. He tried to relax, to feel the elegance Retta mentioned. He tried to imagine that he was a movie star in his own swimming pool. It began to work. He relaxed. He pantomimed smoking with a long cigarette holder.

"Aren't you glad you came?" Retta asked, spitting water out of her mouth. She was now in the deep water, kicking silently, moving the mattress under the diving board.

Roy reached up and touched the diving board.

4

Retta smiled. She had a wonderful feeling of belonging tonight, as if it really were her pool.

"Want to go around again?"

Without waiting for an answer, she turned the corner. Retta considered herself a sort of social director for her brothers. She often told them, "We're going to do all the things rich people do." Then she usually added, "Only we have to do them at night, that's the only difference."

Both of the boys were relaxing now. In the brief time they had been at the pool, they had come to associate the smell of chlorine with elegance. They breathed deeply as their sister pushed them through the water. Johnny had his hands folded behind his head, a pose he associated with famous people. Roy was waiting, arm lifted, to grab the diving board again.

Suddenly a light went on in the upstairs of the Roberts's house. The Anderson kids froze. All three faces turned to the window. Retta stopped kicking and waited, froglike, in the shimmering water.

"Retta!" Roy wailed. He turned to her. In the moonlight his twisted face revealed his fear. He was the youngest and the most sensitive to being caught.

"It's all right," Retta assured him. She reached forward and put her hand on his trembling shoulder. "That's just the bathroom light."

"How do you know?"

"I *know*. If you'd shut up, you could probably hear the toilet flush."

"I'm getting off this thing," Johnny said. He felt exposed. If somebody looked out the window, he thought, the first thing they would see would be him. The water was safer. He rolled off the mattress with a splash.

"Be quiet or they *will* hear us," Retta warned.

"Don't topple me!" Roy cried. He struggled to get in the middle, but the mattress tipped. With his arms clutching Retta's neck, he plopped into the water.

His head went under, and he came up sputtering. "Don't let me drown!"

"Shut *up*!" Retta said.

The three of them were at the side of the pool now. Johnny was holding on to the mattress; Retta was holding Roy. Their faces were turned up to the square of light above them.

"I'm scared," Johnny said. He was shivering hard now. His teeth began to chatter.

"There's nothing to be afraid of."

"Let's go home."

"Not yet."

"I *hate* it when people run us off," Johnny said.

"Me *too*," Roy said. He always spoke in a loud, positive voice when he was agreeing with his brother. "And I want to go home too!"

"Look, the reason people run you off is to *make* you feel bad," Retta explained. "They figure they'll run you off and you'll feel so bad that you won't come back. Only that is not going to work with us. We are going to swim here every night this summer."

While she was saying this, the light in the upstairs of the Roberts's house went out.

"See, I told you," Retta said. "It was the bathroom."

"I'm cold. I want to go." Johnny was the thinnest of the three and felt the cold most.

"We'll make one more lap of the pool and then we'll go. Come on, we'll all hang on to the mattress. Kick, everybody."

"I want to go. I'm cooooold," Roy wailed.

"Not yet," Retta said firmly. It was her policy never to leave at once. Even if the colonel had appeared in person and had yelled at them in a military voice, she felt she would still insist they make this one extra lap.

They kicked their way around the pool without speaking. Johnny was kicking with all his strength in order to get the swim over with. The only sound was the chatter of his teeth.

When they were back in the shallow end of the pool, Retta straightened. "*Now* we'll go home," she said.

She pulled the mattress out of the pool and set it

where she had found it. "Come on," she told her brothers.

Together they ran across the lawn and got their clothes from the bushes. They pulled on their jeans as they walked under the trees. Retta had come to like the feel of dry clothes pulled over chilled wet skin.

"Didn't that make you feel good?" she asked.

Roy nodded. He was hopping on one foot, trying to get the other foot into his pants leg. His wet underwear sagged, and he yanked it up. Retta held on to his elbow to steady him.

Then they moved together across the lawn, past the rose garden, past the orchid greenhouse, past the lemon trees from Florida, over the wall made from stone from Mexico.

As she walked, Retta wore a faint, proud smile, as if she were being cheered by an invisible crowd.

The Anderson kids entered their house noisily.
They called to each other. They snapped lights on and
off as they moved to their bedrooms. Roy paused in
the living room and turned on the television, but as
soon as Retta heard *The Tonight Show* she came back
and turned it off.

"Why not?" Roy whined.

"Because it's late. Now get to bed." She pointed
with one hand to his bedroom. Her other hand was
on her hip. When she stood like that, like a real
mother, Roy knew there was no point in arguing.

"I never get to do anything!" he yelled. He
stomped out of the room.

There was no reason for them to be quiet because the house was empty. Shorty Anderson, their
father, was a country-western singer who worked at

night. Their mother had been dead for two years, and Retta was raising the three of them.

"Want me to get you something to eat?" Retta asked. The success of the evening had made her feel more maternal than usual.

In the hall the sound of Roy's stamping feet stopped. "Peanut butter sandwich," he said quickly.

"Okay."

"*With* bananas."

"You want anything, Johnny?"

Johnny mumbled, "No," sleepily. He was already in his pajamas. He got in bed, rolled over, face to the wall, and fell asleep.

Beside him Roy was getting ready for his sandwich. He smoothed the sheet over his body as carefully as if it were a tablecloth. He wiped his hands, front and back, on his T-shirt. He loved to eat. The thought of the unexpected sandwich—Retta usually did not allow them to have bedtime snacks—made his face glow with pleasure.

"Kool-Aid too, please, Retta," he called out in a polite voice.

In the kitchen, in the bright light over the sink, Retta was humming under her breath. She was slicing the banana, placing the slices in neat rows on the peanut butter. In the window she could see her reflection, her long wet hair swinging about her face. She smiled at herself.

Retta was happier tonight than she had been in months. She had been taking care of her brothers all her life, but this summer, since they had moved to this neighborhood, it had become a lonely task. Tonight, however, they had had fun. She and her brothers were like friends now, she decided, doing things together. The summer vacation stretched ahead as one companionable, fun-filled day after another.

Retta finished making the sandwich, set it on top of a glass of milk, and carried it into her brothers' bedroom. "No Kool-Aid," she said firmly as she handed the sandwich and milk to Roy.

"Thank you." Roy was polite when it came to food. He said "please" and "thank you" without even knowing he was saying the words. In kindergarten he never had to be reminded by Miss Elizabeth, "Now, what do you say to Mrs. Hartley for the cupcakes?" because he gasped out, "Thank you," at the first glimpse of a white bakery box.

He turned his sandwich carefully, like a dog circling a bone. When he made his decision and took his first bite, an expression of contentment came over his face.

As usual, he began to eat the crust of the bread first. He nibbled around the sandwich, trying to be dainty. He believed that you got more if you ate daintily.

Retta leaned against the chest of drawers,

11

watching him work his way around his sandwich. Just when he finished the last of the crust and was ready to sink his teeth into the peanut butter and banana, she said, "But, tomorrow, Roy, I'm putting you on a diet."

He was so startled that he almost dropped his sandwich. He looked at her. In the soft bread remained the horseshoe print of his teeth. "What?"

"I'm putting you on a diet tomorrow."

"Why?" It was a cry of pain. "I'm not fat."

"You have to wear Chubbies now. Before long you'll be in Huskies."

"I won't!"

"We'll talk about it tomorrow."

"I won't be in Huskies. I promise!"

"We'll talk about it in the morning," Retta said in the mature voice she had gotten from TV mothers.

"I promise I promise I promise—" He went up on his knees in a beggar's position. "I promise I promise I—"

"Will you shut up and lie still?" Johnny rose up on one elbow and gave Roy a look of disgust and anger. "I'm trying to sleep!"

"Well, I'm not going on a diet no matter what!" To emphasize his point he began to take huge bites of his sandwich, gnawing at the bread like an animal, poking stray bananas into his mouth with his finger. When his mouth was completely filled, a solid mass of

banana, peanut butter, and bread, he folded his arms over his chest. He stared defiantly at Retta. He smacked. He chewed. He kept on working his jaws long after the sandwich had been eaten.

Then he sat, arms folded, staring at Retta. "Drink your milk," she said.

He drank it without pausing, eyes always on Retta.

"Now, good night," she said.

"Good night, *Lo*retta," he called after her, wanting to hurt her and knowing how much she hated to be called by her full name. She alone resented that she had been named for a country singer. "*Lo*retta *Lynn!*"

She turned. "Good night, Roy *Acuff!*"

"*Lo*retta Lynn!"

"Roy Acuff!"

"*Shut up!*" Johnny yelled. He sat up in bed and glowered at them both.

Roy lay down. "Johnny Cash," he said, just mouthing the words, silently taunting his brother.

He smoothed the covers over his stomach. It was nights like these, he thought, when he missed his mother most. Suddenly Roy imagined her coming into his room in one of her country-western outfits, the white satin one with the sequined guitars on the skirt.

In the daytime he could never remember what

14

his mother looked like and stared at her photographs in vain. But on lonely nights he could remember every detail. Tonight she surprised him by bringing with her a tray full of tiny cakes with lighted candles on top. She was still coming to his bed, smiling, when he fell asleep.

In the living room Retta was sitting on the sofa. She picked up the evening paper. Usually she went through the paper at night to check for possible outings. She circled them in Magic Marker, things like free Cokes at McDonald's, a wedding reception at the Catholic church.

Tonight, however, she had no interest in such minor events. Now she had the pool. And it was only five blocks away—that was the best part—just on the other side of the park.

Tomorrow, she thought, I'll get some inner tubes at the filling station. Suddenly she sat up straighter. And bathing suits! I'll get us bathing suits!

The picture of them crossing the colonel's lawn in bright new bathing suits was so clear, so beautiful, that she was determined to make it real.

She got up and went into the kitchen. Her father kept household money in the breadbox. She opened the lid and counted. Seven dollars and thirty-nine cents. She would need at least—she paused, estimating—at least seventeen dollars.

She left the kitchen. As she passed her brothers' room, she glanced in. The boys were both asleep: Johnny, a long, thin line under the sheet; Roy, a round ball.

"We," she told them quietly, "are going to have inner tubes *and* bathing suits." And she went into her room feeling as satisfied as if they already had them.

It was ten o'clock in the morning, and it was raining, a hard, solid rain, the kind that could go on for days unless the wind shifted and the southwest weather moved in.

Retta sat on the top step of the porch, eating a piece of toast. She finished, licked her fingers, got up, and went slowly into the house. She eased the screen door shut behind her. Her father was asleep in the front bedroom, and he did not like to be awakened by slamming doors, loud television, or shouting children.

She stood for a moment in the doorway. The living room was a mess. The furniture was faded and worn. Newspapers and letters, some crumbled into fist-sized balls, lay on the rugless floor. The corner with the plastic leather armchair, her father's corner, was littered with plates piled with cigarette butts, half-filled coffee cups, and empty beer cans.

Retta was beginning to realize what a mess the house was, but she didn't know what to do about it. "We need a vacuum cleaner," she decided suddenly and felt better. She sat on the floor, cross-legged, and began to leaf through the newspaper.

"What are we going to do today?" Roy asked. He was standing in the doorway of the kitchen. He was happy because there had been no further mention of diets. Retta had even fixed his favorite, peanut butter toast, for breakfast. He pulled his jeans up higher on his hips and walked into the room.

"I'm looking for possibilities now," she said. She paused to work out her horoscope.

"We can't go swimming tonight because it's raining."

"I know that."

"So what are we going to do? I want to *do* something." He forgot his good fortune about the diet and broke into a whine.

"What you're going to do, if you don't shut up, is wake Dad and you'll be very, *very* sorry."

"But what are we going to *do*?" he whispered.

"Maybe we'll go to Sears and play TV ping-pong."

"The salesman's too mean."

"We'll wait till he's on his coffee break or something. Is Johnny up?"

"I'll wake him."

Roy loved to wake people. He had his own method, which he considered kind and considerate. He simply breathed on them until they opened their eyes. He hurried from the room, the legs of his jeans brushing together as he ran.

He went into the bedroom and leaned on the bed. It sank with the pressure of his elbows. He bent over Johnny.

Johnny stirred with irritation. "Get away from me," he said without opening his eyes.

"It's me—Roy."

"I know it's you, peanut butter breath," Johnny snarled. He turned over. "Now get off my bed."

"It's my bed too!"

Roy hesitated. He was disappointed. He remained with his elbows on the bed, staring at Johnny's back. A breeze blew in the window, and Roy glanced over at the billowing curtains. A heavy, sweet smell filled the room.

The Bowlwater plant, Roy thought. His frown disappeared. A slight smile came over his face.

To Roy, the Bowlwater plant was the most enormous bush in the world, something out of "Jack and the Beanstalk." Any plant that could produce such a strong, fascinating smell, a smell Roy associated with the Orient, *that* plant had to have leaves as big as bed sheets and flowers like tubas. No one had ever explained to Roy that the Bowlwater plant was a factory that made chemicals, and when the wind blew from the southwest, it brought the smell of chemicals with it.

Roy's ambition was to see the Bowlwater plant, climb on it, slide down the leaves, and later—when he got a piece of paper big enough—to draw a picture of it.

He looked at Johnny again. He said, "Want to smell the Bowlwater plant? Open your eyes and you can." He spoke in the voice he used in kindergarten when Miss Elizabeth said, "Let's use our *indoor* voices, boys and girls."

Johnny yanked the sheet up over his head. He flopped over, writhing with irritation.

Roy was irritated too. He abandoned his gentle methods. He said, "You better get up if you want to go with me and Retta." He stood up and waited, hands on hips.

"Where are you going?" Johnny asked without removing the sheet.

"We're going to Sears and play TV Ping-Pong."

"Go ahead."

"All right, we just will." He started from the room. "But don't blame me if *we* have a good time and *you* don't."

"Get out of here."

"I'm going. I just don't want you to blame me if—"

"Get *out*!"

Roy was discontent. Even the mysterious scent of the Bowlwater plant could not soothe him now. "He won't get up," he told Retta. He waited in the doorway, watching Retta hopefully.

Retta had always been his daytime mother. Even when his real mother was alive, it had been Retta who looked after him. He admired her most when she acted like the mothers he saw in grocery stores, mothers who shook their kids and said things like, "You touch another can, and I'll can *you*!" *That* was mothering.

He wanted Retta to put her maternal skills to use now. He wanted her to pull Johnny out of the bed by his ear. "You'll play Ping-Pong or I'll Ping-Pong you!"

Retta remained on the floor. She began to tear a coupon from the newspaper. "Hey, there's a merry-go-round at the mall. With this," she waved the coupon in the air, "and a sales slip from Murphy's you can ride free."

"But do we have a sales slip?" Roy took two steps into the room.

"We'll fish one out of the trash can, if we have to."

21

Roy's excitement rose. "Let's don't tell Johnny, all right? And when we get home you can say, 'Listen, you wouldn't get up when Roy called you,' and he'll say, 'I didn't know there was a merry-go-round,' and you can say—"

"Come on. The rain's stopping."

They walked out the door and paused on the top step. Roy inhaled deeply. "I smell the Bowlwater plant," he told Retta. Visions of the plant rose again in his mind, the trumpetlike blossoms blowing out odor like music. "Can you walk to the Bowlwater plant?" he asked.

"No, it's too far."

"Can you go on the bus?"

"I think so."

"Someday," he promised himself, "I'm going there."

Johnny lay in bed. He heard the front door slam, and he threw back the sheet as if he were going to get up and run after Roy and Retta. Instead he lay staring up at the ceiling.

He felt a deep resentment at Retta and Roy for going off without him. Even though he had said he didn't want to go, they should have begged him. The thought that if he hurried he could still catch them made him even angrier.

He got up slowly and walked into the living room. He could see Retta and Roy waiting at the edge of the porch. "I thought you'd gone," he said, drawing his mouth into a sneer.

Retta turned. "The rain's stopped. You want to come to the mall with us? There's a merry-go-round."

"But we've only got *one* coupon," Roy said importantly. "So only one of us gets to ride and that's me, isn't that right, Retta?"

"We can get another coupon if—"

"Only *babies* ride on merry-go-rounds," Johnny said.

Roy's mouth fell open. He was stung by the insult. He turned to Retta. "That's not true, is it? He's just saying that, isn't he, because he doesn't have a coupon and I do?"

Johnny started into the kitchen. He was aware that Roy was probably making a face at him through the screen door but he did not turn around.

"We'll be back soon," Retta called.

"I don't care if you never come back," Johnny grumbled. He opened the refrigerator door, took out the milk, and drank directly from the carton, something Retta did not allow them to do. Then he walked into his father's room.

He looked down at his father. Shorty Anderson was lying on the bed in his underwear. There was a faint smile on his face.

"Dad?"

Shorty Anderson did not move. He was half asleep and he was dreaming about the new song he had written and recorded the week before. It was called "You're Fifty Pounds Too Much Woman for Me." In his dream he was singing the chorus at the

24

Grand Old Opry. "When you get eatin' off of you mind, I'll get cheatin' off of mine. I don't want no extry woman in my aaaaaaarms," he sang to himself.

"Dad?"

Shorty Anderson heard Johnny's voice, and the Grand Old Opry began to fade away. He was not there on the stage in a red satin cowboy shirt with the lights picking up the glitter of the rhinestones. He was here in bed in his dirty underwear. He let the air out of his lungs in a long sigh.

"What's wrong?" he asked without opening his eyes. Usually he played a game when the kids came into his room in which he pretended to get their voices mixed up. Roy would become so agitated when his voice was mistaken for Retta's that he would pry his father's eyes open to prove his identity. Shorty Anderson wasn't up to games this morning.

"Nothing," Johnny said. "I was just wondering if you were going to get up."

"In a little bit."

Johnny continued to stand beside his father's bed. "Retta and Roy went to the mall."

"They did?" Shorty Anderson said without interest.

"Yes, they didn't want me." Despite Johnny's efforts to keep his voice normal, a tremor of self-pity ruined the sentence.

"They wanted you."

"They *didn't*. They *hate* me, and I hate *them*."

Shorty Anderson's eyes were still closed. He was thinking about his song again. He wanted a hit recording more than anything in the world. The closest he had ever come to success was with a song called "My Angel Went to Heaven in a DC-3," which he had written and recorded just after his wife died.

His wife, Mavis Lynn, had been a singer too, and she had been killed in a plane crash on her way to a state fair in Kentucky. Shorty wrote the song the next night, and within a month it had risen to number thirty-seven on the country-western charts.

Shorty Anderson had been much in demand during that time, and he had had a black satin cowboy outfit made up for his appearances. Within another month the song went off the charts, and Shorty went back to wearing the reds and pinks and purples that he preferred. People still remembered the song, however, and every time he started singing it, there would be a little applause of recognition.

Watching "My Angel Went to Heaven in a DC-3" move up the charts had made him happier than anything else in his life. In his opinion "You're Fifty Pounds Too Much Woman for Me" could go all the way.

Johnny noticed the faint smile on his father's face, the same smile that had been there when he first came into the bedroom.

"Dad!"

"What's wrong now?"

"You're going back to sleep. You aren't even listening to me."

"I'm listening. What's wrong?"

"*Nothing!*" He stamped heavily out of the room.

"Johnny!"

Johnny paused in the hall. "What do you want?" he asked in a dejected voice. He did not bother to turn around.

"Is there any coffee?"

"*Retta* drank it all," he said in a hard, accusing voice.

"Well, would you make some more?"

There was a long pause. "I guess," he said. Shoulders sagging, he went into the kitchen.

Behind him Shorty Anderson began to sing aloud. "If you get eatin' off of your mind, I'll get cheatin' off of mine. I don't want no extry woman in my aaaaaaarms."

He sat up and swung his feet off the bed. They did not touch the floor. "Hey, Johnny-Oh! Make me a piece of toast while you're at it."

In the kitchen Johnny let his shoulders sag even more. With his mouth turned down as sad as a clown's, he reached for the instant coffee.

Roy was sitting at the kitchen table making men out of Pillsbury refrigerated dough. He had worked over them so long that they had a gray look. He was now rolling a piece of dough between both hands.

"This man's going to have a tail and it's going to be soooo long that you won't believe it."

The dough was hanging out the bottom of his hands, swinging back and forth.

"Well, don't make them too funny looking or Dad won't want to eat them." Retta glanced at him. "Roy, did you wash your hands before you started?"

"Yes, I washed my hands before I started," he said, imitating her tone and wagging his head from side to side.

With great care he attached the tail to the dough man and curled it upward. When the angle of the tail was perfect, he rubbed his hands proudly on his shirt.

"I get the one with the tail," he said.

He was still looking at his dough men with a fond, pleased smile when Johnny came into the kitchen. "Want to see what I'm making?" Roy asked.

"Nope."

"I'm making dough men."

"I'm not going to eat any of them. They're filthy." He crossed to where Retta was working at the stove. "What's for supper?"

"Spaghetti."

"You call what you make spaghetti?" Johnny asked. "It's nothing but tomato soup poured over noodles. Real spaghetti has meat in it and onions and a lot of other stuff."

Retta was never hurt by criticism of her cooking because she herself was always pleased with the results. She got a lot of her ideas from the school cafeteria and from Kraft television commercials.

"Where did you go?" Retta asked. She took a sip of soup to check the flavor, then turned to Johnny. "We came back to get you and you were gone. We found an extra coupon and—"

"*And,*" Roy broke in, wanting to tell the important part himself, "since you weren't there, I got your ride too." He patted his dough men happily. He wished they wouldn't keep rising. "Now, stay down," he told them.

"I went out," Johnny said in a casual way.

"On *my* ride I got on a giraffe," Roy said, "and on *your* ride I got on an elephant."

Johnny remained at Retta's side. He wanted her to ask him exactly where he had been because he was eager to tell her.

She glanced around him. "Are those ready for the oven?" she asked Roy. "Have you now made every single one as dirty as possible?"

"Want to know where I went?" Johnny asked.

"They're *not* dirty," Roy said defensively. He gave each one an extra pat.

"They are too. They're gray."

"They're supposed to be that color, aren't you, you guys?" He leaned over them.

Retta said, "If you start kissing them, nobody's going to eat them."

"I wasn't going to kiss them," Roy lied.

In the pause that followed, Johnny said, "In case anybody is interested in what I did this afternoon, I went to the park and helped a boy set off rockets."

Roy looked up. His mouth fell open. He could not bear it when Johnny or Retta did something without him.

"*And* he also makes and flies model airplanes."

Roy's mouth formed an O. He was suddenly so jealous of Johnny's afternoon that as he straightened, he pressed down on one of his dough men, flattening it, and didn't even notice.

"He flies these airplanes with"—Johnny paused to give importance to his next words—"radio controls." He now had both Retta's and Roy's attention. It was the most satisfying moment he had known in a long time.

"And next time I go over there, he's going to show me how to work the controls."

"Johnny," Roy wailed. "Why didn't you wait so I could come too?"

Johnny shrugged. Smiling slightly, he turned and started for the door. Even his walk was new and important.

Roy had been kneeling on the kitchen chair so that he could work more efficiently on his dough men. Now he scrambled to the floor. "You'll let me go next time, won't you, Johnny?" He followed Johnny to the door. "You'll let me see the airplanes and the rockets, won't you?"

"Roy!" Retta's voice was suddenly sharp. "I thought you wanted to watch your dough men cook."

Roy paused in the doorway. His face was twisted with indecision. Retta was putting his dough men into the oven. He had intended to press his face against the oven window and watch the entire process, but now he abandoned the idea. This was more important. He ran after Johnny.

"Roy!" Retta called.

"Not now!"

Roy followed Johnny to the front porch. His excited pleas floated back through the house to where Retta stood at the stove. "Please take me, Johnny. And if you do, you can have the dough man with the tail."

Retta slammed the oven door shut and leaned against the stove. After a moment she began to push at the noodles with her spoon. The water boiled up around the edge of the pot. Retta felt as if her mind were boiling too.

Her change in mood had been seesaw quick, so abrupt she couldn't understand it. A moment before she had been happy and satisfied with her day, contentedly letting Roy ruin the biscuits. Now, in some odd way, a balance had shifted and she was down.

She slapped the spoon against the noodles. She felt her bad spirits deepen.

This had nothing to do with the fact, she told herself, that Johnny had gone off and made a new friend. And it was not that Roy was out on the porch, begging and pleading, turning Johnny into some kind of supreme being just because he had a friend who made airplanes. It was that she wasn't appreciated, she decided abruptly. No one in the whole family appreciated her.

On the porch Roy was making one of his solemn promises. "I'll do anything in the whole world if you'll just take me with you."

Retta lifted a spoonful of noodles and let them fall back into the water, not noticing that they were done. It seemed like a long time since Roy had begged *her* for anything other than food.

Shorty Anderson came into the kitchen doing a clog step. In his high-heeled boots he was two inches taller than his daughter; without them, an inch shorter.

"Supper ready, honey?"

"Almost," she said in an unhappy voice.

"Mmmmmm, looks good." Shorty Anderson was always cheerful in the evening when he was shaved, showered, dressed, and ready to go to his job at the Downtown Hoedown. He opened the oven door and glanced at Roy's dough men. "What are them things?"

"Dough men."

"Hooey! How many dads in this whole world are lucky enough to be having dough men for supper?" He danced around her.

She did not answer. Holding the pot with dish towels, she carried it to the sink. As she drained the water, she spilled a few drops of boiling water on her hand. Her throat swelled with tears.

Shorty Anderson looked over her shoulder. "I could eat that whole thing," he said.

"You always say that—"

"I mean it too."

"—and then you take about three bites and get up and leave."

"I have to, hon. Short people can't eat like other people."

Retta dumped the noodles in a bowl and poured the tomato soup over them. She stared at the dish disgustedly.

Shorty watched his daughter. He knew something was making her unhappy, just as he had known that morning that Johnny was unhappy. However, he never interfered. After all, he hadn't interfered with Johnny, and now, only eight hours later, Johnny was on the porch, problems solved, happy as a bug. Besides, if he asked Retta what was wrong, she might tell him.

"Dish me up a great big plateful," he said, hugging her. "Even if I can't eat it all, it makes me feel good to have a lot."

He sat at the table and began to spread paper napkins over his purple cowboy suit to protect it from spills. It took eight napkins. If he only used seven— he knew this from experience—he would spill something on that one uncovered spot.

"Boys," he called cheerfully, "soup's on!"

Retta slammed the bowl on the table. The noodles trembled. "It's not *soup*!" Retta said. The tears moved up from her throat to her eyes. "It's *spaghetti*!"

Shorty looked up in surprise from the safety of his paper napkins. "I know that, darling." He began to serve himself, taking more than he wanted. "Hmm-mmmmm," he said as the steam reached his face. He tucked his napkins more securely around him and began to eat.

"And what's more, I need *seventeen dollars*!" Retta said, leaning over the table toward her father.

"Well, hon, you can have it. I get paid tomorrow."

At that Retta burst into tears, ran from the kitchen into her room, and slammed the door. The door didn't catch and opened again, banging against the wall.

Through the open door she heard Shorty Anderson say, "Clean your plates now, boys. Retta's touchy tonight."

This time when she slammed the door, it stayed shut.

"Somebody's spying on us," Johnny said in a low voice. He reached across the water for Retta's arm.

It was the next night. The Anderson kids were in the Roberts's swimming pool. They were floating in the black inner tubes Retta had gotten, and they were holding on to each other so that they made a three-leaf clover in the center of the pool.

"Isn't this fun?" Retta had been saying as they turned in formation. "Don't you like your inner tubes?" She was trying to be especially bright and cheerful tonight to hide the fact that she was miserable. Also she wanted the evening to be a special success because Johnny hadn't wanted to come. "Aren't you having a good time, Johnny?"

"It's all right," Johnny had answered. He *was*

enjoying himself, but he was not going to let Retta know that. For the first time in his life he felt superior to his sister. He had *consented* to come—that was the way he thought of it.

He certainly was not going to jump up and down like Roy, screaming, "Inner tubes! Inner tubes!" After all, inner tubes were just old tires.

"Do you like your inner tube?" Retta had asked.

"I said it's all right."

Johnny could hardly believe that just getting a friend—even a fascinating friend who made rockets and airplanes—could make such a difference in his life.

Johnny had been seven years old when his mother died, and he had mourned her more than anyone. He would go into her closet and sit for hours hunched among her high-heeled boots, his face buried in the folds of her western outfits. He would dry his tears on her skirts before he crawled out.

After those first terrible weeks he had started clinging to the only person available—Retta. He had clung as tightly as a person in a storm, but now, somehow, he felt the storm was finally over. He felt he was stepping out into a world that actually welcomed him.

It was while he was enjoying his inner tube and this new security that he had noticed a figure by the garage. With his words, "Somebody's spying on us," the good feeling left him. He was, once again, a skinny kid in a patched inner tube, swimming illegally in the colonel's pool.

"Where?" Retta asked. She glanced up immediately at the darkened windows of the house. "I don't see anybody."

"Not there. There!" He pointed with one dripping arm to the garage.

"I still don't see anybody," Retta said.

There was a light that burned over the garage doors, casting a pale light on the driveway and bushes. Moths, drawn by the light, flitted around the bulb.

"Well, somebody was there a minute ago," Johnny said. "I saw them."

"Let's go home," Roy wailed. Being spied on, something he had never even thought about before, suddenly became the scariest thing there was.

"Oh, Johnny's just seeing things," Retta said. "Let's go around in our inner tubes again, want to? And this time—" She broke off because she, too, saw the figure moving behind the shrubbery. She paused in the water. Her long legs, which had been trailing behind her, sank like weights.

She had expected, had been prepared for the fact that some night the colonel might come striding out in his bathrobe. She had been prepared to shove her brothers to the opposite ladder and have them out of the pool and across the lawn in seconds.

But this strange figure, passing behind the bushes, this she had not been prepared for.

"Yes, I see him," Retta said in a low voice.

Roy struggled in his inner tube. "Where?" His round face was twisted with worry.

"He's gone now."

"I want to *see*!"

Retta turned and started swimming for the side of the pool. "I'm going to find out who it is," she said.

"Retta!" Roy grabbed for her but got only water. Kicking desperately, getting nowhere, he tried to move after her.

"I'm coming too," Johnny said.

Now Roy grabbed for Johnny, but Johnny was out of his reach too. "Wait for *me*!" he cried.

Retta was at the ladder. She pulled herself up and, dropping her inner tube, moved toward the garage. Johnny reached the ladder too. Roy struggled harder.

Retta and Johnny ran across the lawn. They paused at the garage and glanced around uneasily. Then they looked at each other.

Roy, fighting the water and the inner tube, reached the side of the pool at last. He flopped out like a seal.

"I want to go home," he wailed as he ran dripping across the lawn.

"Hush up! You want to wake the colonel?"

Roy was less afraid of the colonel than he was of the spy. "I don't care. I want to go home."

"Oh, all right!" Retta said. "I guess whoever it was is gone anyway." Now that she was at the garage, in the light, the desire to pursue the spy had left her. She, too, was ready to go home.

"I'll go back for the inner tubes. You two get the clothes," Retta said.

She was cold now, shivering. As she ran for the pool, she felt an unfamiliar weakness in her knees. She gathered the inner tubes and, holding them in both arms, ran to join her brothers.

Roy and Johnny were already running for the fence, their clothes clutched to their chests. Roy glanced back over his shoulder to make sure only Retta was behind him.

Roy had never enjoyed being scared the way some children did. He put his hands over his eyes during the scary parts of movies. He put his hands over his ears when Retta told that fearful story, "I'm on the first step. I'm on the second step. I'm on the third step." He could not bear that final *"Got you!"* Now that it seemed about to happen to him, he was moving the way he moved in his dreams—so slowly he could never get away.

He glanced back over his shoulder again. This time he stumbled over a bush and fell, dropping his Chubbie jeans in the darkness.

"Rettaaaaaa!" he wailed.

41

She was there instantly. She yanked him to his feet in one swift movement. "There." She swooped up his clothes. Holding the inner tubes awkwardly on one hip, she led him to the fence. As they scrambled over, Retta glanced back at the garage.

The figure was there, watching as they ran away.

"Let's *go*!" Retta said.

5

"**D**on't bother me now," Retta said. She was pretending to watch television.

"But I want to know if we're going swimming again or if we're not," Roy persisted. He was worried. He wanted Retta to promise that they would never, ever go swimming again because he was afraid. All night in his dreams he had run without getting anywhere.

"Of course we're going again. No stupid spy is going to keep us from experiencing things."

"But there's some things people don't want to experience," Roy said earnestly. He was remembering not only the evening before at the swimming pool but a long painful story a boy in his kindergarten had

43

once told during Show and Tell about having his tonsils out.

"Look," Retta said, straightening, "I'm not going to allow us to grow up ignorant."

"I *know* that."

Roy sighed. Retta was already a stricter teacher than Miss Elizabeth. Once Retta had slapped Johnny when he was reading aloud and pronounced island "*is*-land" for the third time. The worst thing Miss Elizabeth ever did was shake you by the arm.

"*Why* do we have to go swimming again though?" he asked. The thought of having to climb down into that cold, dark water while spies waited in the bushes made his voice tremble. He blinked back tears.

Retta gave Roy a serious look. "Listen, Roy, life's more than just school stuff."

"I *know* that."

"I mean, reading and arithmetic are important because you don't want to go to a fancy restaurant and count up the bill on your fingers, do you?"

"No."

"But other things count too." She was looking at him so sternly that he temporarily forgot his fear. "Swimming in a nice pool, for example—that's important. I mean, when you grow up and are invited to a nice pool, you want to know how to act, don't you?"

"Yes." Roy inhaled deeply. He imagined himself

44

as a grown man, floating in a pool in a black inner tube while onlookers admired his style. The frown on his face eased.

"And when we get to be grown-up and important," Retta's voice softened because this was one of her dreams, "when we're grown-up and have pools and nice houses and cars, what will we do?"

Roy struggled with his memory.

"We'll share our stuff."

Roy nodded. He imagined himself smiling from an upstairs window of his mansion while poor kids swam below in his pool. It was a pleasant picture. He said sincerely, "Retta, anybody who wants to swim in my pool can."

Retta smiled.

Encouraged, Roy went on. "I don't care how many kids get in my pool. They can even make the water run over and I won't care." He made a solemn promise. "Every kid in the world can get in my pool and I won't say one single word."

He paused. He was awed by the scope of his own generosity. In his mind kids from all nations jumped into his pool. The water rose. More kids arrived, many in native dress. They jumped in too. The water flooded his lawn.

Above, in his window, he smiled a benevolent smile. He made a papal gesture of welcome. "Jump right in, kids," he said grandly.

45

"I'm going out," Johnny said. He crossed between Retta and Roy. He could have gone out the back door, but he wanted to make sure they knew he was leaving.

Roy stopped smiling. "Where are you going?" he asked, taking one step forward.

"To see my friend."

"The one with the airplanes and rockets?"

"You got it."

"Johnny, can I go too?"

"No."

Roy paused. Then he said slyly, "I don't believe you've really got a friend!" This kind of thing always worked on him. If someone said to Roy, "I don't believe you've got a friend," he would say, "I do too, I'll show you!" He could see at once it wasn't going to work on Johnny.

Johnny sat down and began to retie his shoelaces. "I don't care whether you believe me or not." He got up, stretched, and started for the door.

"Why can't I come?" Roy whined. He followed Johnny to the door.

"Because."

"Why!"

"You really want to know? All right. You can't come because, one, you're a pest. Two, you whine. Three, you have peanut butter breath. Four, you touch things. Five, you act stupid."

"Tell me *really* why you don't want me to come," Roy persisted.

Johnny gave a snort of disgust and turned away. At the door he paused. He looked back at Roy, and then he glanced at Retta on the sofa.

"Oh, all right," he said. "You can come if you want to."

"Me? I can come?"

"Yes, if you don't act stupid and if you keep your hands off Arthur's stuff and if you don't act like a pest."

"I won't. I promise."

They went out the door without glancing back at Retta. She sat without moving. She could sense the excitement that joined them and fenced her out. She turned back to the television.

On the porch Roy was saying, "I'm going to act so intelligent you won't even believe it's me."

"If you act intelligent at all, I won't believe it's you. Now keep up."

"Don't worry, I'll keep up. Look how fast I'm walking, Johnny." He ran down the steps.

Retta sighed. On the television a woman had just won a fur coat and a trip to Mexico and she was jumping up and down in the enormous coat.

Suddenly Retta got to her feet. She turned off the TV and walked to the door. Her brothers were at the end of the block, turning the corner. Then they moved out of sight.

Retta went out on the porch. She went down the steps slowly, idly, as if she weren't going anywhere important. But at the bottom of the steps she turned and started down the hill after her brothers.

She paused at the corner. Her brothers were crossing the street. Slowly, keeping a long distance between them, Retta followed.

Shorty Anderson was sitting in his corner of the living room with one leg slung over the arm of the chair. He had gotten up after Retta and the boys left, and he was now working out a new song on his guitar. His foot swung with the rhythm.

Ideas for songs were coming faster these days than he could write them down. This one, he hoped, would be the follow-up song for "You're Fifty Pounds Too Much Woman for Me." The title of this one was "You Used to Be Too Much Woman, but Now You Ain't Enough."

He was hunched over his guitar, strumming a chord, singing. "You used to be too much woman. You filled up lots of spaces."

He paused, his eyes looking up at the ceiling. He

strummed the chord again. "And now you lost your fifty pounds, but you lost it in all the wrong pla-a-a-ces."

He broke off as Retta came into the house. He gave her his not-now-I'm-composing-a-song look. She stood in the doorway watching him. Her face was as red as if she had gotten too much sun. She was breathing hard.

Shorty began to sing the chorus, playing to Retta as if she were an audience.

"Your hair's got thin, but your head's still thick.
Your feet stayed big, but your legs are candlewicks.
Your hips ain't round, and your ears weigh fourteen
        pounds.
Oh, you're not the right woman for meeeeee."

He grinned at Retta. She pulled herself away from the doorway and started for the kitchen.

"How you like it?" Shorty called after her.

"Fine."

"Want to hear the second verse?"

No answer.

Undaunted, Shorty began to sing.

"Your teeth thinned down, but your lips swelled out.
Your nose got fat and your chin's a waterspout.
Your cheeks they flap, and your eyelids overlap.
Oh, you're not the right woman for meeeeee."

Retta sat down at the table. The kitchen was big and old. The cabinets had old-timey glass doors that showed the unmatched dishes. The table was covered with oilcloth in which Roy had poked holes with his fork.

In the living room Shorty Anderson started over. He liked the verses, but he wasn't satisfied with the opening.

"You used to be too much woman," he sang. He paused, waiting for an inspiration. When none came, he started over. "You used to be too much wooooooo-man . . ."

Johnny came into the kitchen by the back door, and Retta glanced up. Johnny was walking in his new, important way. His hands were in his pockets. He made a point of not looking at Retta.

Behind him Roy was babbling about the afternoon. "I didn't really believe you about the airplane. I'm not kidding. I didn't really believe it was true!" His face, red with heat and joy, shone in the sunlight from the window.

Roy was happily amazed because, as of late, his world had been drying up like a raisin.

"I didn't believe it was true," Roy told the cabinets, the refrigerator.

Once Roy had believed anything was possible. For example, he had had high hopes of digging to China. He had envisioned going down through layers of earth and popping up in front of startled Chinese.

He had drawn a picture of the event in kindergarten, of the world with a line right through the middle—his tunnel—and a bubble at the end—his head. He was getting ready to draw the startled Chinese when Miss Elizabeth took up the papers.

Once, too, he had thought he would fly, not in airplanes like other people, but by flapping his arms. There was a certain spot on his body that he would press and he would rise into the air as easily as a bird. As soon as he found that spot, he intended to fly straight to another planet.

But lately his world, once as magical and enchanting as a fairy tale, was becoming narrowed by rules and laws.

The sight of that yellow airplane in the sky had somehow given him back a faith in the world's possibilities. He had reeled with pleasure and grown dizzy from turning his face upward.

He had forgotten his promise to be intelligent, and Johnny had had to tell him to shut up twice and to get out of the way a dozen times. Still, the afternoon had been a great success.

Johnny moved through the kitchen, still walking in an important way. He opened the refrigerator door. Retta watched him with wary eyes. "Don't eat the hard-boiled eggs," she snapped. "That's supper."

Johnny did not bother to look closely. He was not really hungry. He just wanted to come in and let Retta hear Roy babbling about the afternoon. He wanted her to know the afternoon had been a bigger success than any she had planned.

He slammed the refrigerator door in disgust. The bottles and jars rattled.

"We never have anything to eat around here," he complained. "Come on, Roy."

"Yeah, we never have anything to eat around here."

The two of them went out the door, leaving Retta alone at the table. Roy's voice saying, "I really, honestly, and truly didn't believe it was true!" floated back to her through the window.

Retta put her chin in her hands and slowly exhaled. She thought about the afternoon. It had the long, unreal beat of a fever dream.

She had followed her brothers all the way to the park, keeping a good distance away. And at the park she had sat alone under a tree and looked down the hill at the field where her brothers waited.

Staring down at them with slitted eyes, she had hoped, first, that their friend would not appear, hoped even that there was no friend. But then he came, a tall, skinny boy laden down with a yellow airplane. Her bad feelings swelled. She began to will misfortune upon them. She hoped the plane would not start, then that it would crash into the ground. She had felt like an evil witch made suddenly powerless to cause the trouble she wanted.

When it was obvious that the flight was success-

53

ful, Retta had gotten up and started for home. Halfway there she began running, stumbling over the sidewalk even though she knew every crack and buckle. She had come into the house, flushed, out of breath, to find her father with his guitar. Her harsh look had continued, piercing Shorty Anderson in his red cowboy shirt. It seemed that all her life, at every vital moment, Shorty Anderson had been composing a song.

She had stood there, heart pounding so hard she couldn't hear the words he was singing. And she had suddenly felt as if she were seeing her father so clearly that her image of him might be damaged forever, the way one's eyes are damaged by looking directly at the sun.

She remembered the night after her mother died. Retta had come into the living room to be with her father. It was late, but Retta had not been asleep; indeed, she was so troubled she thought she would never sleep again. She had drawn close to her father.

"You can stay in here," Shorty had told her, "but you have to be quiet."

"I will."

It was three o'clock in the morning, and Shorty was playing his guitar. Retta lay on the sofa, nightgown wrapped around her thin body, eyes on her father.

Shorty Anderson was bent over his guitar, intent. His voice rose, then fell. The phrase, "Yes, my angelllll went to heavennnnn in a D . . . C . . . three!" filtered through her unhappiness.

"Are you writing a song about Mama?"

He nodded without looking up. She turned her head away. That was her last memory of that night. But the unswallowed, unspoken pain of her mother's death stayed in her throat so long that sometimes she thought she would die of it.

Retta sat at the kitchen table without moving. She stared down at her hands. Everything was clear to her now. Her father's goal—becoming a star, achieving a place where his voice made people laugh and cry, his clothes made people stare, where his life itself became the daydreams of ordinary people—that goal was so powerful that everything else, even his family, became a mere interruption.

If I died, she thought, Shorty Anderson would just write a song about that too. She put her face in her hands and sighed. In the silent kitchen her sigh had the slow, dangerous sound of a snake's hiss.

The Anderson kids came out of the bushes slowly, shy even though they were in their new bathing suits. They glanced, not at the pool shimmering in the moonlight, but at the bushes and trees, the shadows where somebody might be hiding, spying on them.

"Do you see anybody, Retta?" Roy called quietly. He was standing close to the bushes. Out of habit he held up his bathing suit with one hand.

"No, I do not see anybody," Retta said firmly, "and that is because nobody is here."

She had had a hard time getting her brothers to come tonight. Roy was afraid to come and admitted it, but Johnny had pretended he had better things to do.

"What?"

"Things!"

"Oh, both of you are *scared*. You make me sick."

"I'll show you who's scared!" Johnny had said then, throwing open the front door and going outside.

"Well, don't forget your bathing suit!"

And now here they were, moving so slowly across the lawn that they still had not left the shelter of the shrubbery. Retta felt as uneasy as her brothers. All the pleasure of swimming in the colonel's pool was gone, but she was determined not to let that stop her.

She glanced over her shoulder and saw that Roy had not moved. "Are you just going to stand there all night like the Pillsbury dough boy?"

He shook his head. His eyes rolled fearfully to the garage. His plump toes curled down as if to clutch the grass and hold him in place.

"Come *on*," Retta said through her teeth. Her eyes shifted to Johnny. "And for someone who isn't *scared*, you certainly are sticking close to the bushes. You remind me of a weasel."

She looked at her brothers critically. For the first time she was struck by their physical shortcomings. The new bathing suits, she decided, made them look even worse. Johnny's was too big and Roy's too little, so that in their matching striped suits they accented each other's faults.

"All the trouble I went to getting those bathing

57

suits and then you act like this!" Retta had spent that whole morning walking to the shopping center, picking out the suits, walking home.

"I wanted blue," Roy had whined as she pulled his out of the bag, and Retta had thrown the suit at him so hard he had put up his fat arms in defense.

"I don't know why I even bother with you!"

She frowned at them. She wanted to make them presentable, the way mothers change a child by tugging a collar, yanking a belt into place, smoothing hairs. It would, she decided, take a lot more than that to make these two presentable.

The intensity of her dislike for her brothers surprised her because she had never really hated anyone before. She thought she had. She thought she had hated her third grade music teacher who criticized her singing, and two girls in her homeroom who whispered about her clothes, and the neighbors who disapproved of her family. That, she saw now, was only mild dislike. This was hate.

"All right, stay there and rot, chickens!" she taunted. "*I'm* going swimming!"

She strode toward the swimming pool, taking big steps, swinging her arms boldly. She did not glance behind her because she was certain Johnny would follow.

"I'll show you who's chicken!" Johnny yelled suddenly.

Retta turned.

Johnny came running toward her. He passed her so quickly that she felt the breeze. His skinny arms pumped. His legs, long pale sticks in the moonlight, scissored over the ground.

"Johnneeee!" she warned. He did not even glance in her direction.

Retta stepped back. Her hands rose to her chest, covering the flowers on her new bathing suit. Her mouth was slightly open.

Johnny reached the edge of the patio. He didn't pause. He headed for the forbidden diving board. "Even *I* can't go off the board," Retta had told them. "Even *I* would splash."

"Johnneeeee!" Retta's voice rose with her concern.

Johnny was on the diving board now. He ran to the end, bounced once, and then threw himself into the air, making a ball of his body. As he hit the water, the splash seemed to cause sound waves in the air. It was like an explosion, loud enough to mark the end of something. In the after-silence, water sprayed lightly onto the patio tiles.

"Oh, Johnny," Retta said in a flat voice. She stood like a lawn statue with her arms over her chest. With the moonlight upon her, she was as pale as marble.

There was a moment of calm. Moonlit shadows flickered over the lawn. A bird called.

Then everything happened at once. A light went

on upstairs in the house. A solid square of light shone on the pool. In this square of light Johnny's head bobbed to the surface. He struggled to the side of the pool.

The colonel was at the window now. He peered down through his Venetian blinds at the pool. He turned abruptly and disappeared from view.

Retta ran forward a few steps. "Johnny!" His head appeared over the side. He pulled himself out and flopped onto his stomach. He got to his feet and began to run.

The downstairs lights went on in the house. The patio lights went on. The pool lights. Johnny was spotlighted as he scrambled to his feet in his new red-striped bathing suit.

He slipped on the wet tile, went down on one knee, and got to his feet. He was running again, heading for the bushes.

The door to the house was flung open. The colonel stood in the doorway in his shorty pajamas, glaring out into the brightly lit yard. He put one hand up to shield his eyes.

"Who's out there?" he yelled. His voice boomed through the silent night. "What's going on?"

Johnny was on the grass now, zigzagging across the lawn like a soldier trying to avoid gunfire. He passed Retta, spraying her with water.

With a start, Retta joined him. She scooped up

her clothes and Roy's and grabbed Roy's arm as she came out of the bushes. The three of them ran for the fence.

"Stop! This is trespassing!" the colonel shouted.

He was striding across the patio now. Outrage made him look like a military man even in his shorty pajamas.

"Stop or I'll call the police!"

Roy, Johnny, and Retta were at the fence now, crawling over. Even Roy with his short legs was moving like an athlete. They dropped into the ditch and ran for the road. The only sound was Roy's hard breathing.

"Keep running," Retta gasped.

She was dividing up the clothes as they ran, handing Roy his T-shirt, pulling on her own blouse. She broke stride to put one leg into her jeans, then the other.

Beside her, Roy refused to pause even to put on his pants. As a concession to modesty, he held his pants in front of his bathing suit so that anyone who saw him from the front would think he was fully clothed.

At last they reached the house, entered, and slammed the door behind them. Retta threw the lock into place, something she had never done before. She leaned against the door, weak with the narrowness of their escape.

She looked at Johnny, who had sunk onto the sofa. His clothes were in a bundle on his lap. His skinny chest rose and fell as he tried to get his breath.

"Why did you do that?" Retta asked.

"Yeah, Johnny," Roy gasped, "we could have been arrested."

Johnny looked up at them. Water ran down his forehead from his dripping hair. He wrapped his clothes tighter and put them under his arm like a football.

"Now who's chicken?" he said.

Roy was connecting dots in a puzzle book he had given Johnny for his birthday.

"You're going to ruin Johnny's book," Retta said. She was sitting on the sofa watching him critically.

"I am not."

He connected the next two dots with special care and drew back to view his work. He nodded his approval.

"You don't know your numbers," Retta went on. "How can you connect *numbered* dots when you don't know your numbers?"

"This happens to be a picture of a pony and I *do* know ponies. I rode on one one time."

He bent over the book again. He loved to connect dots. He considered becoming a dot connector when he grew up. He liked the thought of himself at a desk, connecting dots while his secretary sharpened pencils.

"That's no pony," Retta said in a disgusted voice.

Roy jerked the book up and hid the half-finished picture against his chest. "It is too."

"It's a *zebra*. You're supposed to be going up and down making stripes instead of plodding on around!"

Retta got up and went to the kitchen. When she was gone, Roy lowered his book and looked critically at his picture.

"I was *going* to make the stripes," he explained to the empty doorway, "only I was doing the outside dots *first*, so *there*!"

Retta did not answer.

"You think you know everything."

He connected two dots, one at the top of the zebra, one at the bottom. He regarded his work with pleasure.

"Well, you *don't*!"

He heard the sound of water in the kitchen. He began nodding his head for emphasis. "You don't even know who was spying on us night before last."

The water stopped running. There was a silence in the kitchen and in the living room.

Roy realized what he had said. His fingers, fat as

sausages, flattened his mouth. His eyes rolled to Retta as she appeared in the doorway.

"What did you say?" she asked in a quiet voice.

"Nothing."

Retta crossed the room as quickly as the mothers in the supermarket rushed to keep their children from toppling toilet paper pyramids.

"I want to know what you said."

"Nothing!"

Her fingers closed around his arm. She was the grocery store mother he had admired and feared and loved to see grabbing other children. He found himself doing exactly what those other children did—twisting to get free. "You're hurting me," he whined.

"Do you know who was spying on us?"

"Ow!"

"Roy!"

"I can't think when you squeeze my arm like that."

"All right!" She released him. "Your fat arm is free. Now think."

He rubbed his arm. He couldn't even remember the question. Tears of self-pity welled in his eyes.

"Do you know who was spying on us?" Retta asked in an unnaturally calm voice.

"Yes."

"Who?"

Roy's arm still bore her fingerprint marks. He

regarded his arm closely. "Look," he accused, "you *squeezed*."

"And I'm squeezing again if you don't tell me right this minute." She reached toward him.

"All right!" He drew back. He hesitated. He had promised Johnny he would not tell Retta, and he now weighed Retta's anger against Johnny's. The deciding factor was that Retta was here, threatening pain now.

"It was Arthur," he confessed quickly.

"What? Who's Arthur?"

"Johnny's friend—you know, with the airplane?"

"*He* was spying on us?"

"Yes, but he wasn't doing it to be mean. Johnny said so. Arthur happened to see us walking down the street one night with our inner tubes and he wondered where we were going. He just moved here, see, like us, and he didn't know where people swam. That was all. He and Johnny laughed about it later. Johnny said not to tell you because he wanted you to be worried."

"*Did* he?"

Retta was cold now. She seemed suddenly taller, an adult. Roy looked up at her. He hesitated for a moment. Then he surprised himself by saying, "Anyway, *you* spied on *us*."

The tone of his voice made it an accusation, and Retta looked down at him in surprise. "What?"

"You did too spy on us. At the park."

"I did not *spy*."

"Johnny said you did. He saw you. He said you were sitting under a tree and as soon as we finished flying the plane you got up and ran home and sat down at the table so we'd think you'd been there the whole time."

Retta straightened. She tried to regain the powerful, adult feeling she had had only a moment before, but the room seemed to have tilted and left her off-balance. "That was different," she said.

"No." Roy shook his head back and forth. "It was the same."

"It was different," she explained, "because I was looking after you guys, making sure you were all right."

"You were spying," Roy said.

"If you are so stupid that you can't tell the difference between looking after someone and spying on someone—well, you're just hopeless, that's all."

She turned abruptly and strode into the kitchen. There was an explosion of sounds. Water rushed into the sink. Pots rattled. Dishes spun on the table. The refrigerator door slammed.

"Spying is spying," Roy said wisely.

He went back to his book. With great care he connected the dots on the zebra's tail. He had been saving that till last, like dessert. As an added personal touch he drew seven hairs on the end of the zebra's tail. He was so pleased with this original touch that he wanted to rush out the door and show it to the world.

Head shaking with admiration, he paid the picture his highest compliment.

"You," he said, "should be put in a frame."

Retta sat on the back steps with her arms over her knees. She lifted her head idly and looked at the house behind theirs. A face at one window moved out of sight. Retta closed her eyes.

She had felt isolated ever since her family moved to this neighborhood. It was a neighborhood of old people, and Retta knew that none of them approved of the Anderson family. When Shorty Anderson went out at night, rhinestones gleaming, high-gloss boots clicking on the pavement, yelling, "Be good!" to his children on the porch, Retta saw the older women on their porches look at each other and shake their heads. They also disapproved, Retta knew, of the Anderson children who "ran loose at night like dogs."

If we still lived in our old neighborhood, Retta thought, where we had friends . . .

"Well, what are you doing out here all by your-self?" a voice asked behind her.

Retta glanced over her shoulder at the screen door. "Oh, hi, Brendelle." Brendelle was Shorty Anderson's girl friend.

"I just stopped by and Shorty invited me to stay for supper. You going to have enough?"

"We're just having grilled peanut butter sand-wiches," Retta said without interest.

"Oh, listen, grill me two. I love them things."

Brendelle stepped onto the porch and let the screen door slam behind her. She sat on the steps be-side Retta. She stuck out her left foot and pulled up the leg of her pants. "Look at that," she said. "I'm supposed to clog tonight at the Downtown Hoedown and my ankle is swollen up like a football."

"What happened?" Retta asked, still looking across the fence.

"I was getting in the car over at Foodland and this new boy was carrying out my groceries and he puts the groceries in the back seat and then he goes, 'Have a nice day, ma'am,' and slams the front door right on my leg. My leg was sticking out, you know, like it does when you're getting in the car. I wanted to hit him over the head. I mean, honey, I got to clog tonight and you got to have two good legs to clog. You think anybody's going to notice?"

"No."

Brendelle turned her leg and looked at it critically from another angle. "Is it getting purple on this side or is that my imagination?"

"It is purple."

"Maybe I can wear some real dark hose."

Brendelle lowered her foot and her pants leg. " 'Have a nice day, ma'am.' Bang!" She re-created the incident, imitating the carry-out boy perfectly. "And the bag of groceries wasn't any bigger than that." She sighed. "The only reason he wanted to help me was because behind me was a woman with great big bags of flour and potatoes, and he didn't want to help her." She straightened. "Hey, where are the boys? I want to see them."

"I don't know where they are."

"They'll be here for supper, won't they?"

"I guess."

"Why, Retta, I thought you ran herd on those boys. I thought you knew where they were every minute of every day."

"I used to. They got a new friend, though, and I never know where they are now."

"Well, that's nice—the boys having a new friend. All three of you ought to get out more."

"His name is *Arthur*." Retta made the name sound as ugly as possible.

"I used to know an Arthur," Brendelle remembered. "Arthur Lee Gribble."

"I hope he was better than this Arthur."

"Well, he wasn't. He asked me out one time and I didn't want to go because he was bald and in those days I went for looks. Well, he wasn't *real* bald," she conceded, "but he had to part his hair low on the side and comb it over the top of his head to hide his bald spot, and the least little wind would ruin it."

Brendelle shifted as if trying to get comfortable on the wooden steps. "Anyway I didn't want to go out with him but finally I ran out of excuses and said, 'Oh, all right. Pick me up at eight o'clock.' I got all dressed up and I sat and waited and, would you believe it, he never showed up?"

"But if you didn't want to go out with him, why wouldn't you be glad he didn't show?"

"Because it don't work that way. No matter how much you don't want to go out with *them*, you want them to want to go out with *you*."

"I wouldn't."

"Later I saw Arthur Lee Gribble on the street and he goes, 'Don't I know you from somewhere?' and I go, 'No, I never forget a bald head.' " She straightened. "Hey, this Arthur—the boys' new friend—he's not nice?"

"I don't know. He spied on us once, I know that," Retta said.

"Spied on you?"

"Yes, while we were swimming."

"Where was you swimming at?"

Retta looked up at the pale summer sky. "Oh, nowhere," she said casually.

"Come on, I'd really like to know. I mean, if you got friends with a private swimming pool, don't keep it to yourself."

"I don't have any friends with a swimming pool."

"That makes two of us."

Shorty Anderson opened the door behind them. He was dressed in his red cowboy suit with white satin cactus plants on the yoke. "Is this girl talk," he asked, "or can anybody jump in?"

"I was just telling Retta that I used to go for looks in a man," Brendelle said, grinning slyly, "but now I just go out with any old ugly thing that asks me."

"I'll pass the word along," he said, "if I run into any old ugly things." He nudged her in the back with his knee, and she got to her feet. She stretched.

"I—" She broke off as she saw Roy coming onto the porch. "Well, look who's here. Come here, Roy, I haven't hugged you in two weeks."

Roy came willingly. He loved to be hugged. Brendelle was the best hugger he had ever known because she put a lot of extras into her hugs. She swayed and patted him and scrubbed his hair and pretended to spank him. Then, just when he thought

76

she was through, she would say, "One more time!" and start all over again.

"And where's Johnny?" she said. "I want to hug him too." She glanced over her shoulder at Shorty. "Way I'm acting, a person would think I'm half starved for masculine affection." She grinned. "Johnny, where are you?"

She had a hard time with Johnny because he didn't like to be touched. Sometimes Brendelle had to chase him for five minutes before she caught him. And then he would stand as stiff as an oar in her arms, hands at his sides, eyes closed tight.

Brendelle saw Johnny in the doorway. "I can't chase you tonight," she called. "A carry-out boy at Foodland crippled me. Look at that."

She held out her discolored ankle. Johnny hesitated for a moment and then came forward dutifully. Hands stiff at his sides, he walked into her arms.

She had both of the boys now. She hugged them together. It was as if she were trying, by squeezing them with all her might, to make the three of them into one huge, complicated package.

Johnny suffered the embrace with his eyes shut. Roy swayed with Brendelle, taking advantage of every aspect of the hug.

"I'll start the sandwiches," Retta said. She passed the three huggers, turning sideways so as not to disturb them. She went around her father in the same careful way. "Excuse me," she said.

"Put lots of peanut butter on my sandwich,"
Brendelle called happily. She grinned down at Roy
and Johnny. "And put lots of oleo on the grill. I love
goo."

She bent and kissed the top of Roy's head. "And
so does Roy." She smoothed his hair back from his
forehead so she could kiss his brow. "He wants the
same thing, don't you, Roy? Lots of goo."

Roy lifted his head. His face shone. His answer
had the earnest ring of a marriage vow.

"I do," he said.

"If you want to see Arthur, now's your chance," Roy sang at the window.

Retta glanced up from the television set. She had been watching television all day, but she didn't really know what she was seeing. The soap operas, the game shows, passed like one long, boring dream before her eyes. "What did you say?"

"Arthur's in our yard, so if you want to see what he looks like up close, you can."

"No."

"*I* had to come in the house," he said, his voice losing its happy lilt. "Arthur and Johnny were talking about something *secret*."

Roy stood at the window with his hands in his pockets. He was hurt. He hated to be left out. Once in kindergarten he'd accidentally colored his George Washington face mask green and had not been allowed to march in the Parade of Presidents with the other kids. He had waited in the classroom with Miss Penny, weeping with the pain of exile, vowing never to be left out of anything again.

He glanced at Retta. He sensed that she really wanted to see Arthur up close but didn't want to admit it. Out of kindness he began to describe Arthur to her.

"Well, he's got on blue jeans with a patch in the back and a yellow T-shirt. There's writing on the shirt, but I can't read it. There's a Band-Aid on his elbow and a watch on his arm. He's got a—"

"Will you shut up? I am trying to watch television."

"That show's no good. It doesn't even have good commercials." Roy believed the quality of TV shows could be judged by the commercials. The most boring programs had commercials for false teeth glue and toilet paper.

"I'm not watching the commercials," Retta said, giving him a cool nod. "I'm watching the program."

Roy glanced out the window. "Arthur's leaving now," he reported. "He's walking down the sidewalk."

"Good."

"He's pausing, scratching his head, he's turning,

he's—" Suddenly he broke off. He drew in a long, shuddering breath. "I smell the Bowlwater plant," he said happily.

"Maybe you smell *Arthur*," Retta replied, making an ugly face as she said the name. She did not take her eyes from the television set.

"No, it's the Bowlwater plant. I'd know that smell anywhere."

In his mind the plant was growing, reaching for the sky, shading the countryside with its huge leaves. The enormous flowers were swelling on stems thicker than his arms and sending out their magical fragrance, today, luckily, in his direction.

"I wish they'd close that plant down," Retta said suddenly.

Roy looked at her. He was as astonished as if she had proposed doing away with the Atlantic Ocean. "They would never do that."

"They should."

"Anyway, why did you say *close* it down?" he asked, puzzled. "You can *chop* down a plant, maybe, or pull it up, but you can't *close down* a plant."

Retta turned her eyes from the television. She looked interested in Roy for the first time. "What do you think the Bowlwater plant is?"

"A plant."

"What kind of plant?" she quizzed.

"A big plant." He was careful not to commit

himself. Sometimes he got trapped that way and people laughed at him.

"Well, you got it," Retta said. "That's what it is—a big ugly plant."

"It's not ugly."

"Have you seen it?"

"In my mind," he said with a dignified nod. Roy felt as if he were moving toward something unpleasant. He felt himself on the edge of a step—one slip and he would descend into a world that was even less magical than it already was. He willed himself not to look down, willed the Bowlwater plant to be as he imagined.

"Somebody told me they make army chemicals there," Retta went on in a conversational tone. "That's chemicals that kill people and leave the cars and buildings so that the army can use them."

Roy didn't hear her. He had closed his mind. He was now interested only in what was happening in the yard.

"Arthur is leaving again," he said. "This time he's really going." Roy moved to the door and was waiting when Johnny stepped onto the porch. "What was so secret?" Roy asked.

"Nothing."

Johnny crossed the room, taking his time. He plopped down in his father's chair and slung one leg over the arm as his father did.

"If it wasn't secret, then why couldn't I hear it?"

"Don't bug me," Johnny said.

There was a silence. Retta tried to concentrate on her television program, but she felt herself being drawn into her brothers' conflict. She looked at Johnny.

"I know you and Arthur are going to do something," Roy was saying, "and I want to know what it is."

"It's none of your business."

"I want to *know*! Are you going to fly the airplane or are you going to shoot the rockets?"

"Neither."

"Then what *are* you going to do?"

Retta said, "Don't beg him. That's exactly what he wants you to do."

"I do not," Johnny said. He sat up straight in his father's oversized chair. "What makes you think I want to be begged?"

"Because you're sitting there like the king of Arabia with that I-know-something-you-don't-know sneer on your face. You're disgusting."

"You're the one that's disgusting. You can't stand it, can you, that I have a friend and you don't?"

Retta stared at him as if he were an ugly, offensive stranger.

He got up slowly and walked toward the hall. At

the doorway he paused and looked back at Retta and Roy. "I'll tell you one thing," he said, "whatever I'm going to do, I'm going to do it without the two of you." He disappeared into his room.

Roy hit his fist against his leg. "I *knew* they were doing something secret." He turned to Retta. He sensed her helplessness, but he had nowhere else to turn. "Retta, make him tell me!"

Retta looked at the empty doorway. "I can't seem to make him do anything anymore," she said.

Roy rarely played with his food because he was always in a hurry to eat it. The one exception was mashed potatoes. Tonight he was making a volcano of his potatoes, smoothing the sides up to a pool of melted margarine in the middle.

A trickle of margarine ran down one side, and he quickly repaired the damage. He wished they were having green beans so he could plant trees on the side of his volcano—that way the eruption would be more dramatic. But tonight Retta had only fixed one thing —mashed potatoes.

The volcano was almost as tall as his cup of milk now, a really spectacular display. "Look," he said to Retta and Johnny.

He waited until he had their attention. Then,

making sound effects with his mouth, he erupted the volcano, sending margarine spilling down the sides, creating destruction on one side and then the other until the entire volcano was a flat mess of potatoes that covered his entire plate.

Satisfied at last, he picked up his spoon and began to eat. "Want me to make something out of your potatoes, Retta?" he asked.

"No."

"I can make anything—boats, rivers, planets—"

"No."

"I won't make anything for *Johnny* because he won't tell me the secret."

"Good," Johnny said.

Johnny and Retta were not eating. Neither was hungry. Johnny was too excited to eat because he and Arthur were going on a secret mission that night. Retta was too suspicious to eat. She knew Johnny was up to something—she could tell from the nervous energy that caused him to dig at his food, shift in his chair, pull at his clothes, and dig at his food again.

She watched Johnny with eyes sharp enough to penetrate his thoughts.

"Quit staring at me," he said finally.

"I'm not staring."

"You are too."

She looked down at her plate and shifted her potatoes with her fork. She lifted the fork and sipped the potatoes on it as if she were taking medicine. Her eyes rolled to Johnny.

"You're staring at me *again*!" he accused.

"Well, you're staring at me too!"

"All right, everybody," Shorty Anderson said, coming into the room with a square-dance step. "Everybody can stare at me!" He had on his hot-pink velour outfit with the rhinestone lapels, his favorite. He danced around the table in his matching leather boots.

"Supper's cold," Retta said.

"I don't believe I'll have anything, honey. I'll just get something at the Hoedown. Looks mighty good though." Shorty never took chances eating in his pink suit. It cost twenty-two dollars to have it cleaned.

"We had mashed potatoes," Roy said, "and I made a volcano."

"I used to do that when my mama wasn't looking," Shorty Anderson said. "But my mama wouldn't let us play with our food. That's the only bad thing I can say about her." He put one hand on Retta's shoulder. "You're lucky to have a sweet sister who lets you do what you want."

"Oh, Dad," Retta said through her teeth.

"Well, they are." He turned away. "You kids behave yourselves now."

"We will," Roy called happily.

87

Retta, Roy, and Johnny continued to sit at the table after their father left, even though they had finished eating. Retta kept her eyes down, but her thoughts were on Johnny. He's slipping out tonight, she said to herself.

Finally Johnny broke the silence. He stood up, stretching. "Well, I'm tired. I'm going to bed."

"It's only eight o'clock," Retta said.

"So—I'm tired. All right?"

As Johnny left the room, Retta looked up, eyes burning. She watched him until he disappeared into the hall. Then she got up and began to wash the dishes. Over the hot, steaming water, her face was set.

They all went to bed early. Roy fell asleep quickly, but Retta and Johnny lay wide awake, eyes staring at the ceiling. From time to time Johnny smiled slightly in anticipation, but Retta's face remained hard, unyielding.

She knew the exact moment when Johnny got out of bed because she heard the creak of his bed springs. She lay without moving, eyes shut, while Johnny slipped out of his room and into the hall.

Johnny paused in the doorway of Retta's room. He wanted to make sure Retta was asleep. If she stirred, he was going to pretend he was on his way to the bathroom. She did not move. Breathing a sigh of relief, Johnny moved quietly into the living room.

Johnny had always felt that the one thing he was really good at was not being noticed. Indeed, he sometimes thought he must be invisible. One day last fall, in school, his teacher, Miss Lipscomb, was passing out papers, matching pupils to papers, and then paused with one paper left in her hand.

"Johnny Anderson?" she had said. She had looked as puzzled as if the name were foreign. He raised his hand.

"Are you new?"

"No'm."

School had been going on for six weeks. He had not been absent a single day. Miss Lipscomb had shaken her head, smiling at herself. "Well, Johnny Anderson, you and I are going to have to get better acquainted."

"Yes'm," he had said, shifting so that he was, once again, hidden by the boy in front of him. In the spring, when he moved away, she said, "I really don't feel like I got to know you at all."

"No'm," he answered.

Now Johnny walked across the living room, opened the screen door, eased it shut, and went onto the porch. Leaning against the banister, he put on his shoes.

Inside the house Retta was getting out of bed. She was already dressed in her jeans and shirt, and she slipped noiselessly into the hall. She waited a moment in the darkness until she heard Johnny going down the steps.

As he turned onto the sidewalk, he began to pick up speed. Retta moved quickly onto the porch. She went down the steps and stood in the shadow of an elm tree. It was eleven o'clock, and the moon was full and bright, weaving in and out of the clouds.

Down the street, her brother was at the corner. A car passed on Hunter Street and Johnny waited, then crossed quickly and broke into a run.

Retta glanced right and left to see if any snoopy neighbors were watching. All the houses on the street were dark. Keeping to the shadows, Retta moved quickly after Johnny.

Roy woke up and knew instantly that he was in bed alone. His side of the mattress was lower than usual. He flipped over and said, "Johnny?"

In the light from the living room he saw that the other half of the bed was empty.

"Johnny!"

He got up. He hated to be alone and he sensed that Johnny had not just gone to the bathroom or the kitchen. He stumbled into the hall, eyes alert, mouth worried, body still clumsy with sleep.

He staggered into Retta's room and turned on the light. When he saw that her bed was empty too, he began to yell for either of them. "Retta! Johnny! Rettaaaaa!"

There was, as he had feared, no answer. He went

out onto the porch and sat down on the steps. He began to cry.

"Why did they leave me?" he asked mournfully. "People shouldn't go around leaving people."

He paused to wipe his tears on his pajama top. "I wouldn't have left them."

Each statement made him feel worse. He began to cry harder. "Next time I'm going to leave them and show them how it feels."

Even the thought of this just punishment did not cheer him. He could not bring into focus the picture of Retta and Johnny sitting on the steps, weeping, while he went off to some good time.

His tears came faster. Being left behind was a terrible feeling. He had always had a special feeling for anyone left behind. The night before he had seen a television program where the pioneer family left their old dog behind while they went west. He had wept real tears for that dog.

Later in the show the dog followed the family and saved them from a surprise Indian attack by barking. "I don't care how many Indians attack Retta and Johnny," he said wetly, feeling a closer bond with the pioneer dog, "I won't let out one single bark."

The thought of Retta and Johnny going down under Indian attack while he waited in the bushes, lips sealed, was pleasant, but it didn't make him feel any better. He continued to weep quietly in the moonlight.

Suddenly he sat erect. He remembered that Johnny and Arthur had had some kind of secret. He licked at a tear on his cheek. He tasted the salt. And Retta had to be in on the secret too, he thought. Everybody was in on it but him.

"They've gone swimming," he said abruptly.

He remembered that Retta had told him they could never go to the colonel's again, but that was probably just to throw him off the track. He got to his feet. The tears were drying on his cheeks. He went slowly down the steps.

As he stood on the last step, scarcely breathing, a wonderful plan came to him. He would sneak up to the colonel's house and spy on Retta and Johnny and Arthur. He was, it seemed to him, the only one who had not done any spying. They would see him in the shadows, he went on, and be terrified. He would feel no mercy. Abruptly he strode down the sidewalk in his striped pajamas.

At the edge of the street he stopped, struck dumb with an even better idea. When he got to the colonel's and saw that Johnny and Retta and Arthur were in the pool, he would run forward, whooping and yelling as Johnny had done, and dive in with them.

The picture of Johnny running across the lawn,

not caring about anything or anybody, had impressed him deeply. It had seemed the kind of grown-up thing that he himself had never been able to do. If he lived to be a hundred, he would never feel more awe and respect for anyone than he had for Johnny as he launched himself off the diving board in that perfect cannonball.

The brilliance of his own plan washed over him. Arthur and Johnny and Retta would be in the pool, swimming quietly, trying not to splash. They would hear the sound of running. They would look up, mouths open, as he dashed forward. Before they knew what had happened, he would be launched off the diving board in the same fearless cannonball.

He hurried down the sidewalk. He no longer felt the twigs and stones beneath his bare feet.

"Ro-oooooy," Retta would say. He could hear her in his mind. He mimicked her as he walked, wagging his head from side to side. "Ro-ooooy!"

And Arthur—Arthur would be especially impressed because Arthur would not know he was copying something Johnny had done.

The pleasant dream continued. Retta would herd them all out of the swimming pool, and the four of them would run across the lawn, bonded together in their escape. Behind them the lights would be coming on in the colonel's house.

"Faster!" he would call back to the others. He himself would be in the lead at this point. "Come *on*!"

94

The thought of being in the lead for the first time in his life made him shudder with pleasure.

The colonel's house appeared in the distance, big and white in the trees. Roy began to walk slower. He moved closer to the fence. There was a little smile on his face. His heart was beating so hard that he put his hand over his chest to make swallowing easier.

He climbed the fence by the trees as Retta had taught him to do. Overhead, the moon was hidden by a cloud, and he waited in the darkness, so tense and expectant that his knees were trembling. He swallowed again.

Bending, he began to creep toward the pool, a short stooped figure in wrinkled pajamas. He paused, lifted his head. He could not see what was happening in the pool, but he could hear the faint sound of splashing.

Still stooping, he ran forward. He crossed the clearing and paused by an azalea bush. He peered through the foliage with one hand over his eyes.

They *were* in the pool. He could hear them swimming. He straightened and drew in his breath. He moved his feet back and forth on the lawn, like a cartoon character getting ready to run.

Surprise is everything, he told himself. It's *got* to be a surprise. He leaped out from behind the bush and started running for the pool.

Running across the lawn was wonderful. He felt powerful for the first time in his life. He didn't care

95

about anything or anybody. He surprised himself by leaping up and letting out a whoop of joy.

He crossed the tiled patio, taking smaller steps now. He didn't want to slip. He headed for the diving board. He had a rush of panic as he ran to the end— he had never even been on a diving board before— but by taking tiny steps he managed not to fall off the side. His excitement carried him to the end of the board.

He had intended to bounce at least once, but he didn't have time. He fell immediately, curled forward like a shrimp. He hit the cold water and sank.

Roy came up struggling. He sputtered and reached out for Retta. In the excitement of his plan he had forgotten the crucial fact that he did not know how to swim. "Retta," he gasped. He choked and went under again.

Water went up his nose. He struggled for the surface, pulling desperately. He felt as if he were at the bottom of the sea and would never reach air. He bobbed up. He screamed Retta's name, choked, and went under again.

Suddenly he felt an arm grab him and pull him to the surface. He gasped for air. He turned blindly, wrapped himself around the arm, and crawled up to clutch the attached shoulder. He gagged on the water he had swallowed and held on tighter.

He felt himself being drawn to the side of the

pool. He was lifted out and stretched out on the patio tiles. He was shivering violently. He gagged and began to cry.

"Retta!" He clutched the empty air, wanting her to hold him again. "Retta, I almost drowned!"

He looked up through his tears and saw that it was not Retta standing over him. He wiped the water from his eyes and saw the stern face of the colonel.

"Where's Retta?" Roy asked. His voice quivered on the night air like a bird's.

"Who is Retta?" the colonel asked.

And Roy turned over and gagged so hard that he lost not only the swimming pool water he had swallowed, but his mashed potato volcano as well.

Retta had been following her brother for four blocks. Her eyes were as intent as an eagle's on its prey.

She was breathing deeply, but she did not smell the scent of night flowers in the air. She was filled with the satisfaction that came from doing right. She was, at last, the mother she should have been all along —strong and purposeful. And it was not easy these days, she told herself, to be a strong and purposeful mother.

She lost Johnny as he went around the corner and she felt a quick anxiety. She walked faster. When she caught sight of him again, hands in his pockets, head up, she let out her breath like a horse.

She was walking quickly now, out in the open,

forgetting that she might have to slip into the shrubbery and hide. Then suddenly Johnny turned up a walkway, and she stopped. She moved silently into the neighboring yard, pausing in the shadows when the moon came from behind the clouds.

When she was safely behind a hedge, she stopped. Johnny was waiting at the foot of the steps. He shifted impatiently, glanced up at the house, wiped his hands on his shirt. When the front door opened, he moved back into the shadows, then he came forward as he saw Arthur step out.

Arthur. Retta's mouth drew into a sneer as she said the name to herself. At that moment she hated her brother and Arthur equally. The boys spoke to each other quietly, heads together. Arthur must be slipping out too, she thought with the same sense of disgust.

Suddenly the boys started walking away. Arthur shifted a bag of equipment from one arm to the other. Johnny offered to carry it. Arthur shook his head.

Retta was so intent on not losing her brother that she plunged through the hedge, coming out on the other side with swimming motions. She barely felt the scratches on her arms and legs. She scrambled to her feet.

Ahead, Arthur was talking and Johnny nodding in agreement. They won't get away with this, Retta promised herself. Now Arthur was explaining something in a low voice. Johnny lifted his hand and waved it in a wide arc. He was almost skipping with excitement. He laughed.

Every movement, every word, made Retta angrier, and the more excited Johnny became, the more Retta wanted to ruin that excitement. It was all she could do to keep from running forward, grabbing his arm, and shaking away his joy.

"I'll teach you not to slip out at night," she would say. "I won't have this kind of behavior!" She forgot that it was she herself who had taught him to slip out in the first place.

Johnny and Arthur did not glance back. Johnny was walking sideways now, facing Arthur so he wouldn't miss anything Arthur said or did. Retta was moving through the yards, keeping close to trees and shrubbery even though she felt Johnny would not notice her even if she walked openly in the street.

The street came to a dead end, and the boys cut through a vacant lot. Retta moved closer. Without the street lights it was harder to keep them in sight.

Retta stumbled over a child's lawn mower that had been left in the weeds. She fell forward. She remained face down for a moment, afraid they might have heard her.

When she raised her head, she saw they were moving up the hill, unaware of anything but themselves. "I could have broken my neck and they wouldn't notice," she muttered as she got to her feet. Her eyes were hard, her lips set.

Up the hill the boys were now in the clearing. They moved to the top of the hill and paused. Retta stooped and began to crawl toward them. There were few bushes and no trees, and she was determined not to be noticed until she was ready. Still stooping, she moved around the hill and came up behind them.

Arthur and Johnny were bent forward, backs to her, when she came over the crest of the hill. She eased herself onto her stomach and lay watching them.

Their backs hid what they were doing, but Retta did not dare move closer. They had some sort of plastic dry cleaning bag—she could see that—and Johnny was holding one end in the air.

"Is that right?" he asked.

"Yes."

Arthur was kneeling, striking matches, shielding them from the evening breeze with his hand. He was lighting something. Retta got to her knees. She had to see what he was doing.

In the opening of the plastic bag was a wire circle with narrow strips of wood across it. The strips of wood were covered with little candles. Arthur lit the candles quickly, lighting new matches from the burning candles. When all the candles were lit, the bag began to fill with hot air.

Retta stood. She was glad they were playing with fire because that was something no mother allowed.

The bag was filled now. The candles glowed eerily in the night. "It's getting ready to go," Arthur said. Johnny stepped back, hands clasped together with excitement.

Retta took one step forward as the bag rose into the air. Her shoulders were straight. The fact that what the boys were doing could be dangerous gave her extra strength. With her hands on her hips, she started across the clearing.

The bag was rising rapidly now, shooting up into the cool night air. Both boys' faces were turned skyward.

Retta moved toward them. She was not running. She had all the time in the world.

"Look how high it is!" Johnny cried. At that moment Retta reached him. She paused a moment, watching him. His hands were clasped beneath his chin, his face turned upward.

Abruptly Retta grabbed him by the upper arm and spun him around. "What do you think you're doing?" she snapped.

Johnny's mouth fell open. He drew back instinctively. Retta clutched his arm tighter.

"I said what are you doing?"

Johnny had no answer. His mouth had gone dry.

His knees were weak. He drew in a long, shuddering breath as if it were his last.

Retta pointed to the hot-air bag. It was descending now down the hill. It hovered over a tree and then rose as the candles reheated the air. Retta had a renewed flash of anger that the candles had not set the tree on fire. That would have really proved her point.

Arthur moved toward them then, and Retta turned back to her brother. She shook him as fiercely as an animal shakes its prey. Johnny did not struggle. He allowed himself to be shaken.

Suddenly Retta wanted to make his actions look as bad as possible. She leaned forward, including Arthur in her dark glance. "What are you trying to do?" she yelled. "Burn down the whole city?"

"**I** don't see what you're so upset about," Arthur was saying. The three of them were walking down the sidewalk with Retta in the lead. "We didn't do any harm."

"You almost caught a tree and a house on fire," Retta said. "You don't think that's harm?"

She had been determined at first not to speak to Arthur at all in order to show her contempt for him, but she had not been able to do that. She was condescending to answer his questions now, but over her shoulder, as if he were a servant.

"I don't get it," Arthur went on. "It's all right for your brothers to slip out at night with *you*, but—"

"*I* don't start fires," she said.

"I don't either. Did I start a fire?" When Retta

106

did not answer, he directed the question to Johnny. "Did we start a fire?"

He turned to look at Johnny, who was trailing behind them, but Johnny did not look up.

"You did not start a fire," Retta said in what she considered a mature voice, "because you were fortunate enough to have the candles burn out in the air."

Johnny was walking slower now. With each step he fell farther behind. His head sank forward in misery. The backs of his legs had a weak feeling that made walking difficult.

Retta's appearance at the very moment of his triumph had been as shocking and sudden as that of a wicked witch. Indeed, she had been so witchlike in her actions and voice that it had seemed a remake of that scene in *The Wizard of Oz* when the Wicked Witch of the West appears in a puff of red smoke.

He had a helpless feeling. It was as if he were a puppet, and his sister would always be there, pulling the strings, spying on him, waiting for just the right moment to leap forward and spoil his life.

Ahead, Arthur was saying, "I don't see why you have to treat your brothers like prisoners!"

"*You* wouldn't," Retta said over her shoulder. Then, realizing she had made a mistake, she added quickly, "Anyway, I do *not* treat them like prisoners."

"Yes, you do."

"I do not!"

She swirled suddenly to face him. Caught off-guard, Arthur almost bumped into her.

"I happen to be in charge of my brothers," Retta said. Her hands were on her hips now. She felt strong enough, mature enough, to be put on a Mother's Day card. "I cook for them and I wash their clothes and I see that they go to bed and I even do their homework for them, and they are not prisoners!"

"And do you think for them too?"

Retta turned abruptly. She began walking rapidly down the sidewalk.

"Look, I didn't mean to upset you," Arthur said.

"You couldn't upset me."

"It's just that we really weren't doing anything wrong."

"Huh!"

"Anyway, what we were doing wasn't any worse than swimming in somebody's pool without permission."

"That's *your* opinion."

Johnny was lagging even farther behind. As soon as he had heard Arthur use the word "prisoner," he had realized that was what he was. Tears stung his eyes, and he was grateful for the dark and for the distance between him and Arthur.

He realized that his friendship with Arthur was

ruined—it had been too good to be true anyway—but he did not want Arthur to see him cry. To see him treated like a baby was bad enough. He began to drag his feet on the sidewalk, pausing every now and then to stand, arms hanging, and look at the ground.

"Isn't that your house?" Retta asked Arthur over her shoulder.

"Yes."

"Well, shouldn't you go in? We would like to walk home by ourselves, if you don't mind."

"I do mind. I'm not one of your brothers, you know. You can't boss me around."

Arthur stopped and waited for Johnny to join him. Johnny, head down, said, "Go on in. You don't have to worry about me."

"Well, I just don't feel right about what happened," Arthur said, lowering his voice.

"Me either."

"If only your sister would listen to reason."

"She won't."

"It's not like we did anything wrong."

"I know, but that's the way she is."

"Stop talking about me," Retta snapped. She was standing apart from them, waiting. She kept her back to them as if they were too unimportant to notice.

"Well, that *is* the way you are," Johnny said. Arthur's presence at his side made him feel stronger.

He glanced up at Arthur for the first time since his sister's arrival. "Everything always has to be her way. She always has to be the boss."

"I got that."

"Nothing we want matters."

Arthur glanced at Retta's unyielding back. He said, "Well, maybe she really cares about you guys, only she just doesn't know how to—"

Retta spun around, eyes blazing. With the moonlight shining on her, she looked taller than either of the boys. She looked at Arthur with such loathing that he moved back a step.

"Don't you dare say anything nice about me!" she yelled.

Retta knew something was wrong as soon as she rounded the corner of her block. The porch light was on, and a strange car was parked in front of their house.

"Something's happened," she said. She began to run up the hill toward the house.

Behind her Arthur and Johnny sensed something too. They moved faster, closing the distance between them. The three of them reached the porch steps at the same time, but Retta beat them through the front door. It was she who saw the colonel first.

She stopped so abruptly that Johnny bumped into her and shoved her to the center of the room. Then Johnny saw the colonel too and drew back, leaving Retta standing alone. He had only had a brief look at the colonel before—and the colonel had been wearing shorty pajamas at the time—but he knew this was the colonel. He let out his breath in a long, uneasy sigh.

The colonel sat with his hands on his legs in a pose that looked military. Beside him, crumpled into a ball, lay Roy. He had cried himself to sleep and now lay still, wrapped in one of the colonel's flannel shirts, drawing an occasional shuddering breath.

Roy had been, from that first illegal swim, afraid of the colonel. It was the kind of unreasonable fear usually saved for ghosts and wolves and two-headed giants. And in his one dramatic meeting with the colonel tonight, the colonel had seemed to live up to expectations.

The colonel had been so big, so stern, so all-powerful as he stood above Roy that Roy had quivered with fear. His hands, reaching for him, had looked as big as hams, and his eyes seemed to glow red.

At the same time Roy himself seemed to be shrinking. It was as dramatic a sensation as something out of science fiction. He could actually feel himself getting smaller. He half expected to disappear.

This miracle had not happened, however, and he found himself forced into the colonel's house, forced into dry clothes (that was how he thought of it), forced to tell his name and address. Then—this was worse than being arrested—he was driven home.

As the car had pulled up to the curb in front of his house, Roy had had a brief hope that the colonel would let him go with a stern warning. He tried to get out of the car with a strangled, "Thank you for the ride," but politeness did not work.

The colonel unbuckled his seat belt. He got out of the car. On the way up the walk the colonel said the most terrible words Roy had ever heard in his life: "I want to talk to your father."

Now Retta looked from the colonel to Roy. When her eyes met the colonel's a second time, she straightened her shoulders. "What happened?"

"Are you his sister?"

"Yes. I take care of him."

"You weren't taking very good care of him tonight. He almost drowned."

"What?"

"He came swimming alone. He jumped into the deep end of the pool and he can't swim. If I hadn't been there, he would have drowned."

"Oh, no."

Retta stood in the center of the room. She felt as if the middle part of the room had suddenly shifted, leaving her off-balance. She reached out for something to steady her, but she felt only air.

"I called your father," the colonel said. "He should be here any minute."

Retta stepped back. She put up one hand as if to stop whatever the colonel was going to say next.

The colonel turned to Johnny. "Who's in charge of you kids?"

"*She* is," Johnny said.

Retta closed her eyes. When she opened them, she saw Roy lying on the sofa. Suddenly she realized how young, how vulnerable, he was. She looked at Johnny, who was standing shoulder to shoulder with Arthur. She felt as bewildered as a child whose dolls have come to life and are demanding real care and attention.

"I don't know how all this happened," Retta said, more to herself than to the colonel.

"Well," the colonel said, "it happened because—" He broke off.

There were footsteps on the porch, and Shorty Anderson appeared in the doorway in his hot-pink cowboy suit with the rhinestone lapels. Tears sprang to Retta's eyes, turning Shorty into a glittering pink circle. As she watched, her father seemed to swirl away like a Frisbee, moving far out of reach in an eddy of glittering lights.

She blinked and he was, once again, there in the doorway. Just as Roy had looked younger than she remembered, her father now seemed older. The pink velour suit looked a little tight, worn at the seams. Tears came to her eyes again, and this time they spilled onto her cheeks.

The colonel moved to the doorway. "Mr. Ander-

114

son?" he asked. The colonel was so tall he could have been Shorty Anderson's father. Shorty Anderson took three steps forward in his high-heeled boots.

Johnny and Arthur pulled back the way bystanders in cowboy movies retreat to safety. Arthur groped for the doorknob behind him.

The colonel put out his hand. "I'm Colonel Roberts. The kids have been swimming in my pool at night."

Shorty Anderson took the colonel's hand. "At night?" he asked. He looked blankly from the colonel to his children. "Aren't they in bed at night?"

The colonel shook his head. "They've been coming over and swimming in our pool after we go to bed. It's not that we mind them swimming there, but it's dangerous and we're responsible. Tonight the little boy almost drowned."

"You kids have been doing this?" Shorty Anderson asked Retta.

She nodded, unable to speak.

"Johnny?"

"Yes."

Shorty Anderson looked at his youngest son on the sofa. Roy stirred. He opened his eyes and saw that he was no longer alone with the colonel. Indeed, the room seemed to be filled with people.

Blinking with sleep, Roy struggled to sit up. He remembered why he and the colonel were here—to

have a talk with his father. The horror of the evening washed over him again. He stood up on the sofa, tottering on the uneven cushions. He clutched the colonel's wrinkled shirt tightly, as if to give himself extra support.

Then, in a voice trembling with self-pity, he announced, "It was her fault." He pointed at Retta. He had spoken without thinking, but he saw suddenly it was the truth. Unwittingly he had hit on the real reason they were all standing here. He summed it up in three words. "She left me!"

Retta stepped back. Everyone was looking at her. She made a gesture with her hand and knocked over Shorty Anderson's lamp. In the silence that followed the shattering of glass, Shorty Anderson sighed. He looked around him like a man who has just discovered the sun rising in the west. He glanced up at the colonel, down at his broken lamp.

For a moment he seemed to get even shorter. Then he straightened. "Maybe we better sit down and talk," he said in a tired voice.

"**N**ow, honey, it's not all that bad," Brendelle said. She had arrived as the colonel was leaving, and she now sat in the kitchen with Retta.

"Yes, it is," Retta said. She began to pull at one of the worn spots Roy had made in the table cloth.

"No, it's not. Now, listen. Nobody got drowned. Nobody got hurt. Nobody's been arrested." Brendelle began to tick off their blessings as if they were the lyrics to a song. "And best of all, maybe now that sorry father of yours will take better care of you. You hear me, Shorty?"

"What?" he called from the living room.

"I was just saying that, well, now maybe these kids' sorry father will take better care of them. Did you hear me?"

Silence.

"What these kids need is a mother. You hear me, Shorty?"

Silence.

"You ought to find yourself a nice girl and get married," Brendelle suggested.

Silence.

"Though I don't guess they'd be a whole lot of nice girls who'd want you. As a matter of fact," she winked at Retta, "I can't think of but one!" She waited; when there was no answer, she reached out and put her hand over Retta's. Retta looked up and Brendelle said, "It *is* going to be all right."

"I just don't know what I did wrong."

"You didn't do anything wrong." She shook her head. "Okay, you went swimming where you weren't supposed to. But, honey, look, everybody does that. Why, when we were graduating from high school we had this dance and afterwards we all climbed over the fence around the municipal pool and went swimming in our evening clothes."

"Did you?"

"My mom almost killed me because I had on a new pink formal that cost thirty-five dollars and it was ruined. One boy had on a rented tuxedo and he wouldn't go in so we threw him in. And that tuxedo —they don't use good dye on them or something— that tuxedo turned the swimming pool water *purple*. Would you believe it? And when he got out, every-

where he stood he made a purple puddle and nobody
would let him ride home in their car.

Retta was picking at the tablecloth again. She
said, "I just don't see how mothers do it."

"What?"

"Oh, I don't know. Take care of kids and have
them turn out right. I mean, I can see how you can be
a good mother if you're there all the time saying,
'Stop that,' and, 'Don't do this.' But when they get
away from you, well, I just don't see how mothers do
it."

"I don't know either, hon. When it comes to
mothering I'm as green as grass. But I do know one
thing—you can't hold on too tight. As soon as you
start holding on so tight that somebody knows they're
being held—well, then you're in trouble."

Retta sighed. "You know something? I've been
hating my brothers all week."

"You didn't really hate them, hon."

"Yes, I did."

"Let me tell you something. My sister Rhonda
and I, well, we are really close now. We talk on the
phone three times a week and she lives in Ohio. Anyway, last year we were going through some old stuff
at Mom's and I found a diary of mine. The whole
diary was how much I hated Rhonda. Rhonda got to
do everything. Rhonda had the good clothes. Rhonda
this. Rhonda that. 'I hate Rhonda,' was on every
page. Honey, I wrote the word 'hate' so hard that

fifteen years later the page was still dented." She took Retta's hands across the table. "You'll get over it."

"I already am over it, I guess." Retta smiled for the first time that day. "Everything I say, you say the same thing happened to you."

"That's because everything has happened to me. Everything but one thing." She raised her voice, grinning at Retta. "Nobody ever asked me to marry them. That's the only thing that hasn't happened to me. You hear that, Shorty?"

"I heard."

"You think anybody ever will, Shorty?"

"Maybe. There's a lot of fools in this world."

"It don't take but one."

Retta looked at Brendelle. For the first time she understood that Brendelle and her father might really get married.

"What's wrong?" Brendelle asked. "I turn away and you look all right and I turn back and you've got a funny look on your face."

"It was just something I thought of."

"Something bad?"

"No."

"Well, that's good because we have had enough bad thoughts around here for one night." She turned back to the door. "Shorty, come on in here with us. I'll fix something to eat."

There was no answer.

"Shorty?"

Shorty Anderson was sitting in the living room. The evening had been so upsetting that he had not taken off his pink velour suit. The telephone call from the colonel, summoning him home from the Downtown Hoedown, had frightened him. And the sight of his children—who looked smaller, somehow, paler than he remembered—had not made him feel any better.

It seemed to him that every time his life started getting good, something bad happened.

His song, "You're Fifty Pounds Too Much Woman for Me," was on the charts, and now, just when he wanted to devote his full time to making it a hit, the burdens of fatherhood fell upon him. It made him feel so low he didn't even want to write a song about it.

"Shorty, did you hear me calling you?"

"I heard." He got up slowly, walked into the kitchen, and opened the refrigerator door.

Brendelle watched him. "I hope you're not planning to eat while you've got on that suit," she said. "You know how you spill stuff. One spot of mayo and that pink velour is ruined."

He stood tiredly at the refrigerator.

"Now you go take off that suit and I'll fix you a sandwich. What kind you want?"

"Fried egg." Obediently he started for his room.

123

"Coming up. Retta, you want one too?"

"No, thanks."

"Then you go on to bed. Somebody's got to start giving orders around here."

Retta nodded. She got to her feet. "Good night, Brendelle."

"Good night, hon." She hugged Retta to her. "And you sleep late in the morning. That's another order. I'll fix a bunch of fried egg sandwiches and put them in the fridge. You can have them for breakfast."

"Do they keep?" Retta asked. Suddenly she began to feel her own fatigue.

"Hon, they get better. The grease goes right through the bread and when you toast them—well, you just wait till in the morning and see."

"All right."

Retta left the kitchen and paused in the hallway. Her father was standing in his room, in front of the mirror, having one last look at himself in his pink suit before he took it off. He turned sideways. The sight of himself in velour, a star's material, made him feel a little better. His fatigue began to ease.

Watching himself, he sang, "When you get eatin' off of your mind, I'll get cheatin' off of mine. I don't want no extry woman in my aaaaaarms."

He caught sight of Retta watching him and said, "Did I tell you 'Fifty Pounds Too Much Woman' is number eighty-nine on the charts?"

She nodded. "I hope it goes all the way for you."

"Oh, hon, me too." He came out into the hall. His energy was returning. Grabbing Retta, he square-danced her into the living room. He steered her through the dining room, into the kitchen, around the table, back into the hall.

Brendelle called, "Shorty, you are supposed to be changing and Retta is supposed to be going to bed."

"First things first," Shorty Anderson called back. "I'm dancing with my daughter."

He swung Retta around in the hall, turning her until she was dizzy. Then, still humming to himself, he released her, danced alone into his bedroom, and began taking off his pink velour suit.

Standing in the hallway, still slightly dizzy, Retta had a funny feeling. Everything had changed and yet nothing had changed. It was like those stories where a person is whisked away to a different time zone, lives a whole different life, and then returns to find that no time has elapsed at all, that everyone is still in exactly the same place.

She glanced into her brothers' room. They were asleep. She walked softly into the room. Roy stirred and lifted his head.

"Is that you, Retta?"

"Yes."

"What are you doing?"

"Nothing. Just standing here."

"You can get in bed with me if you want to."

This was Roy's peace offering. He could not imagine anything lonelier than having to get in a bed by yourself.

"All right. For a minute."

Roy wiggled to the edge of the bed, and Retta crawled over the foot and slid between Roy and Johnny. She turned onto her back. The mattress springs rattled comfortingly.

"What will we do tomorrow, Retta?" Roy asked sleepily, more out of habit than because he wanted to know.

"Oh, I don't know." She swallowed. "I imagine Johnny will go play with Arthur and you'll go play with somebody. I don't know exactly." She paused. "Is there anything really *special* that you'd like to do tomorrow?"

There was something final about the way Retta asked the question. It was as if what they would do tomorrow, this special thing, would mark the end of something.

He looked at Retta. She was staring up at the ceiling. In the light from the hall, her face had a strange, still expression. For a moment she looked so much like his mother that he held his breath. He noticed for the first time that Retta had the same nose, the same full bottom lip, the same statuelike eyes as his mother. And the hall light almost seemed to be a spotlight, highlighting her features.

The last time Roy could remember actually see-

127

ing his mother, she had been on the stage, lit up so that everyone in the audience could see her while he, in the wings, looked at her profile. He blinked, and abruptly he was back in his bed, acutely aware that Retta was just his sister.

"*Is* there something you'd like to do?" Retta asked.

"The Bowlwater plant," he said almost without thinking.

She looked at him and he shifted his head. Now it was he who was staring at the ceiling. "Retta?"

"What?"

"The Bowlwater plant—is it a great big plant with leaves and giant flowers and stuff?"

"No."

He took a deep breath. The wind wasn't blowing in the right direction, but he thought he smelled the Bowlwater plant for the last time. He exhaled.

"It's a factory, isn't it?" he asked.

"Yes."

"And there aren't any giant plants with giant leaves, are there?"

"Maybe in the jungle, Roy. I don't know."

"Yes, in the jungle, or maybe on other planets. There could be giant plants on other planets."

"That's right."

"But not around here."

"No."

A satisfied feeling came over Roy as he lay there. It was as if, by swallowing a hard truth about life as willingly—this was the way he saw it—as Popeye swallows spinach, he had become stronger. "There are no giant plants around here," he said again, feeling better every time he confirmed the unhappy fact.

Retta rose up on one elbow to look at him, remembering his hopes for the Bowlwater plant as a kind of recreational facility, a natural Disney World where everything was real instead of plastic. He seemed almost pleased as he lay there with the covers pulled up to his chin. Maybe each of us, she thought, had been off into that strange time zone that changes a person while keeping the rest of the world the same.

"Well, I better go to bed," she said. "It's three o'clock in the morning." She hugged Roy. "Good night."

She turned over and hugged Johnny. Johnny stirred. He was drawn out of a dream in which he and Arthur, grown men, were sending rockets off to planets as yet unnamed. He squirmed with irritation and said, "Let go of me."

"I have," Retta said.

"Retta, you can hug me all you want to. I don't care how many times you hug me," Roy said.

"Thanks."

She climbed off the foot of the bed and started for her room. In the hallway she bumped into her father, shorter than she now, without his cowboy boots. "Doesn't anybody ever go to bed around here?" he asked.

"I'm going."

She went into her room and got under the covers without bothering to take off her clothes. She sighed. She was as tired as if she'd been working in the fields.

She could hear Brendelle talking in the kitchen. "Here's your sandwich."

Shorty Anderson said, "You know, that's not a bad line for a song."

"What? 'Here's your sandwich'?"

"No, what you said earlier when you were hollering at me in the living room. I said, 'There's a lot of fools in this world,' and you said, 'It don't take but one.'"

Brendelle said, "Now, look. Aren't you glad you changed? You already got egg yolk on your shirt. If that had been velour, well..."

Shorty said, "Hand me a napkin." There was the sound of rustling as he tucked it into his shirt collar. "Now, listen to this, Brendelle."

"I'm listening."

He began to sing. "It don't take but one fool and you got a fool in me. It don't—"

"Shorty Anderson, didn't anybody ever teach you to hold your hand under a fried egg sandwich while you're eating?"

"I'm sorry, hon, hand me another napkin."

130

"Here's two."

There was more rustling. Then Shorty said, "Wait a minute. Would this be better? Something like 'You Got Sixteen Kinds of Fools in Me.'"

"That's not bad."

He began to sing again. "You got a fool who loves you and a fool who'll let you go." A pause. "You got a fool who needs you but who don't want it to show. You got a fool who'll be around through good times and through bad, and a fool who'll—"

He broke off. "I'm going to get my guitar."

"I'll get it, hon," Brendelle said.

And in the comfortable silence that followed, Retta fell asleep.

About the Author

Betsy Byars is the author of many books for children. Among them are *The Summer of the Swans*, awarded the Newbery Medal in 1971; *The House of Wings*; *The Cartoonist*; *The Pinballs*; and *Good-bye, Chicken Little*.

DATE DUE

39/89

Margaretha Zelle Aug 7, 1876
md Rudolph Mac Leod July 11, 1895
   Norman John Mac Leod Jan 30, 1897
(Non) Jeanne Louise Mac Leod May 2, 1898

   Von Jangow - young. head of German Police
                foreign minister of
                              Germany

   General Missimy - French Minister of War

Ladoux

Eye of Dawn

Also by Erika Ostrovsky

Céline and His Vision
Voyeur Voyant: Portrait of Louis-Ferdinand Céline

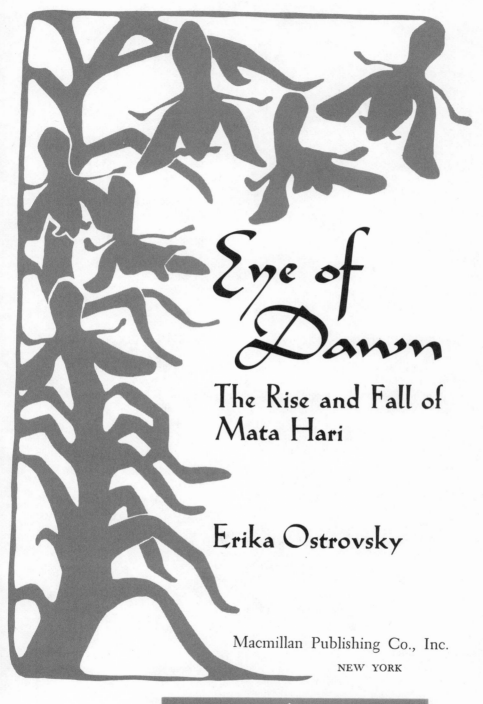

Eye of Dawn

The Rise and Fall of Mata Hari

Erika Ostrovsky

Macmillan Publishing Co., Inc.

NEW YORK

Macmillan Publishing Co., Inc.
866 Third Avenue, New York, N.Y. 10022
Collier Macmillan Canada, Ltd.

Library of Congress Cataloging in Publication Data
Ostrovsky, Erika.
    Eye of dawn.
    Bibliography: p.   MAY - 4 1978
    Includes index.
    1.   Zelle, Margaretha Geertruida, 1876-1917.
2.   Spies—Europe—Biography.   3.   European War, 1914-1918—Secret service—Germany.   I.   Title.
D639.S8Z466   940.4'87'430924 [B]   77-17391
ISBN 0-02-594030-9

First Printing 1978

Printed in the United States of America

Contents

Prologue

The soul of the spy is somehow
the model of our own.
—Jacques Barzun

The Woman in the Menagerie

Paris, February 13, 1917

It was one of the bleakest days in a grim year. The Great War had been raging for 920 days. France was at the point of exhaustion. Trench warfare had drained her; Verdun was a recent, agonizing memory. The morale of the armed forces was ebbing fast. A new malady, diagnosed as "espionitis," had been infecting entire populations. Suspicion, fatigue, and despair—sharpened by the severe and unusual cold—hung in the air. An unexpected wave of harsh winter weather had hit Paris in the previous few weeks; snowstorms and icy winds bombarded the city, usually spared such extremes. A growing fuel crisis added to the already dismal state. It turned houses into inhospitable abodes; forced shops, restaurants, and cafés to close their doors; drove people into the streets in the vain hope of diversion or warming exercise.

The great panoramic views of the city were marred by the swirling snow. Morose-looking pedestrians scurried across the exposed bridges, leaning against the wind, the collars of their worn coats upturned. Sharp gusts swept over the balustrades and howled in the sculpted stones. The waters of the Seine were without color.

Jagged sheets of ice moved with menacing slowness or ground against each other with a grating sound.

Here and there the figure of a soldier added some color to the scene, but the face had such a weary and desolate air that it belied the vividness of the uniform. Civilians eyed him suspiciously as he passed. Hadn't the Senate just voted new laws to deal with deserters and members of the armed forces guilty of insubordination? A soldier away from the front might easily fall into one of these categories! A sailor would not escape scrutiny, either. The Germans had begun to wage unrestricted submarine warfare, and five ships had been sunk on this day alone. Mutiny might spread, plaguelike, from trenches to the high seas. Nor was it safe in these days of strife to trust one's neighbor, mistress, barber, waiter, or shopkeeper. Hadn't they recently arrested a woman on charges of espionage for sending crates of laxatives to Brazil? And what of that waiter who drew plans of fortifications in his order book? Who knew if that harmless-looking old man in the Luxembourg, ritually surrounded by flocks of pigeons at dusk, did not wire code messages to their feet?

It was a winter not only of discontent but of distrust on every side.

The pleasure-loving Parisians were in a vile mood. Their patience —not to speak of their appetites—was being sorely tried. They had only to glance at their newspapers when they awoke to be instantly assailed by a list of new deprivations. The front pages listed them all. The latest headlines read like a parody of the Tables of the Law:

RESTAURANTS SHALL NOT SERVE MORE THAN TWO COURSES AT A MEAL.
PASTRY SHOPS SHALL NOT BE OPEN ON MONDAYS AND WEDNESDAYS.
CHOCOLATE SHALL NOT BE SOLD ON TUESDAYS AND THURSDAYS.
AN ADDITIONAL TAX SHALL SHORTLY BE LEVIED ON BUTTER.

Where were the banquets of yesteryear? Their mouths watered in vain. Tempers grew shorter as menus did. Diners watched their neighbors suspiciously in restaurants, counting the number of courses served, ready to pounce at the sight of one contraband raspberry or an additional sliver of Coulommiers on a favorite's plate. The lines in front of the pastry shops were held with as much valor and savagery as those of the Somme or the Chemin des Dames. Mourning over the coming loss of butter occupied more space than the long lists of war dead.

It was not the palate alone, however, that suffered. The other senses were equally deprived. The Ten Commandments of restriction continued in the headlines:

THEATERS SHALL SHUT DOWN TWICE A WEEK.
NEWSPAPERS SHALL NOT EXCEED TWO PAGES.
MARRIAGE IS IN A STATE OF CRISIS.
THE COAL SHORTAGE IS CRITICAL.

There was decidedly not much left to delight either body or mind. Except, perhaps, a few brief hours of escape—among the *"Grandes Horizontales,"* while watching Mistinguette at the Casino de Paris, "The Good Luck Girl" at the Olympia (where Mata Hari had once played), or *"Le Laboratoire des Hallucinations,"* now presented at the Grand Guignol. But the harvest of illusions was meager. And one always had to retain one's overcoat.

Decidedly, it was not a vintage year, and the French were in no mood for clemency.

Xenophobia returned. Old specters were revived. It occurred to some (as many times before) that scapegoats were the epitome of Biblical wisdom and that there was solace and unity in hate.

If spectacles were limited, executions were not. The firing squads worked overtime at Vincennes. The guillotine did not long remain dry; Deibler was much in demand. It was the season for manhunts. Military tribunals judged behind closed doors. If the morale of the citizens could not be improved by offers of victory, plenitude, or the return of fair weather, perhaps some old-fashioned bloodletting could turn the defeatist tide.

On this bleak day of winter the old Saint-Lazare prison was hardly visible. The street signs were so obscured by snow that it was almost impossible to make out the letters that spelled "Boulevard Sébastopol." Its high gray walls were lashed by sleet; the barred windows were covered by ice flowers.

Inside, rats scurried for shelter in the long corridors. The heavy tread of jailers echoed on the stones. Now and again a door clanked shut as if a trap had been sprung. Then there was silence once more, and only the shrieking wind prevailed.

Somewhere in this labyrinth of passageways a gate swung open. Iron hinges creaked. A tall woman was roughly thrust into a cell.

Among the initiated this cell was known as "The Menagerie." Hidden in an obscure wing of the prison, it was reserved not for exotic wildlife but for spies and public enemies. Madame Steinheil, accused of having been the death of one of France's presidents, and Marguerite Francillard, the dressmaker executed as a spy, had dwelt here.

Its present occupant, though listed simply as Number 721 44625 in the file of new prisoners, was far more illustrious and her list of titles as lengthy as that of any aspirant to the royal throne: Margaretha Geertruida Zelle, a/k/a Lady Gresha Mac Leod, a/k/a The Red Dancer, a/k/a H 21, a/k/a Mata Hari. And the crime of which she stood accused was far more formidable (as the voice of the police commissioner indicated when he pronounced the dread formula at the moment of her arrest):

The woman Zelle, Marguerite, also known as Mata Hari, residing at the Palace Hotel, of Protestant faith, a foreigner born in Holland on August 7, 1876, five feet ten inches tall, able to read and write, is hereby accused of espionage, attempts at intelligence with the enemy, and efforts to assist in enemy military operations.

The door of the cell swung shut and was double-locked. The prisoner would be left there alone to spend the night before interrogation. In order to prevent attempts at suicide—which happened not infrequently—certain precautions had been taken: The walls were padded, the gas jet was out of reach, the only furnishing consisted of a straw pallet on the floor.

Like some great beast just captured, the woman peered wildly about. Her jewels flashed. A veil half covered, half revealed the proud outlines of her face. Furs, silks, and fine leather encased her body from head to feet.

She tossed her head (now freed of its ornaments), and the hair spread into a thick mane. Her hands resembled claws. She paced about the cell with the long strides of a tigress, stopping short at each wall. Then suddenly she stood still. The head rose, the nostrils dilated. She surveyed the terrain: a cube of empty space, one high barred window, a gas jet located outside, a cagelike door, a Judas window for the jailer's eye, padded walls, traces of vermin everywhere.

The woman's hands rose and covered her face. She slowly sank down on the pallet and for a long time lay motionless in this pose.

What thoughts were circling in her mind? The image of a spinning roulette wheel in which certain numbers continued to show— and lose: 13, the thirteenth, Room 131, 103 Champs Elysées, the thirteenth Arcana of the Tarot? The sign of Leo, whose pride would now be broken by fear, humiliation, and captivity? Or her famed body (tattooed with serpents, serpentine in motion), which would grow pale, fat, and slow as a slug? Perhaps it was her chosen name that, like the sun, its ascent followed by decline, was now past its zenith, moving into night.

She seemed to be sleeping now, but fitfully. Her hands clutched at the air or scratched at the stones.

What did she dream of in those long hours? Her daggers, the sharp jeweled pins, the curved, inlaid *kriss* with which she had danced? The basket of figs, in which the deadly asp lay coiled, that sent the Queen of Egypt to her grave? The witch's chariot that carried Medea high above the palace roofs? Perhaps it was only an old half-forgotten memory, a child's cart drawn by a pair of horned goats—the *bokkenwagen*—that, as dawn came, gave her face its enigmatic look of repose.

Part 1

If the world should perish, I would
go to the Netherlands: there, everything happens fifty years later.
—Rainer Maria Rilke

1. Childhood's End

Frisia is an ancient land. It already existed in the days of Tacitus and has not changed its name since then. This harsh and desolate place, lying north of the Hook of Holland, is covered by mists and is so ambiguous in nature that it made one of the Romans exclaim: "It is difficult to say whether the region belongs to land or sea, since the tides wash over it twice daily. The inhabitants dwell on mounds or platforms, appearing as sailors at the floods and castaways at the ebbs."

These inhabitants were a fierce Nordic race, fair-haired, blue-eyed, extraordinary in strength, independence, and bravery. They rebelled against the Romans and defeated them; they defended their pagan beliefs ferociously against invading missionaries: St. Amandus, who converted all Flanders, was by them "much abused and once thrown into the river"; St. Boniface fared worse, for he was murdered. The warlike Frisii defeated Charles Martel, and even the great Charlemagne had to agree to a treaty, for they would submit to his rulers only if promised that they would be governed in accordance with Frisian laws. Only the Vikings ever succeeded in plundering their lands.

They tilled these lands despite their unyielding nature. Marshes and dunes, *kelders* along the icy coast, some meager plots of soil reclaimed from the sea, peat bogs, and flat windy planes were all that they could count their own. But they kept sheep on the *kelders*, spun "frieze" cloth of international renown, painstakingly extracted salt from the sea-soaked peat, built great tublike *kogge*, and developed a profitable shipping trade. With tenacious pride they clung to their region, their customs, their tongue. Frisian (a cross between Anglo-Saxon and Old Norse, often closely resembling English) was preserved into modern times and is still spoken in the countryside, as it was at the time of the Romans in the first century.

When Margaretha Geertruida Zelle was born in Leeuwarden, the ancient capital of the Frisians, much had changed there with the passage of time. True, the town was still located on artificially raised *terpen* (because of the low-lying and water-logged nature of the ground), surrounded by peat fields and pasture lands. But by the late nineteenth century it had about 30,000 inhabitants, considerable trade in cattle and agricultural products, a condensed-milk factory, a strawboard plant, and a new railroad line that linked it with larger Dutch cities and the steam ferries that crossed the Zuiderzee. It sported the typical Hofplein and Stadhuis, as well as a Weighhouse and a Gothic tower. Its gold and silver wares were widely renowned, as was the beauty of the Frisian women, which travelers were advised, in guidebooks, to notice in the marketplace.

It was into this world and with this heritage that Margaretha was born on August 7, 1876. The second child of Adam Zelle and his wife Antje van der Meulen, an only girl in a family of boys (Johannes, the oldest; Ari and Cornelis, the twins), she was her father's favorite and, it appears, much indulged by him. Tawny-skinned, dark-haired, with flashing black eyes, Margaretha contrasted with the blonde, blue-eyed natives from an early age. Her warm coloring distinguished her so sharply that she seemed almost alien: "an orchid miraculously dropped into a bowl of buttercups," as one observer said, while others hinted at Jewish blood on her father's side or a strain of illicit Javanese genes.

Margaretha (or M'greet, as she was more familiarly called) was blissfully unaware of such tongue wagging during her early years. She lived in ease and comfort, for Adam Zelle was a successful burgher of considerable means. True, he was only a hat maker by profession, but his shop on the *Kelders* was so fashionable it could compete with elegant boutiques on the Continent, and its tall, handsome proprietor always sported a top hat and flowered waistcoat. The natives considered him arrogant, a social climber and spendthrift. They criticized his pretentions, his lavish expenditures, his rash temper, and jokingly referred to him as "the Baron." Many concluded that his one moment of glory, when he was chosen as standard-bearer for King William III's horse guard of honor (recorded in a portrait that hangs in the local museum with the unlikely name of *Friesch Gennotschap, Oudheid, en Taalkunde*), had gone to his head. But Mijnheer Zelle continued to be arrogant, and successful.

So much so, that by the time M'greet was five, his speculations permitted him to purchase a splendid patrician home at 28 Groote Kerkstraat, one of the loveliest old streets in Leeuwarden. And, for her sixth birthday, to give his daughter a present she never forgot:

It was the height of summer. The town was bathed in warm light. The gray mists of spring had dispersed; the sun was at its zenith. There were no shadows anywhere. At noon, the landscape seemed to doze. The *grachts* were flat and still in the glare. Not a barge, not one mast or sail broke the glassy expanse of water. Hardly a leaf stirred in the low, overhanging trees. The streets were empty. The fair-skinned inhabitants evidently feared the noonday sun and preferred to remain in the shelter of their homes. The town seemed deserted, totally devoid of animation. Only at the gates of the Zelle mansion did something stir. It was a curious spectacle: a team of horned goats, hitched to a miniature coach. They pawed the ground and bleated joyously. Their delicate hoofs, the bright leather seats, the polished wheels, all gleamed in the summer sun.

Suddenly the gates flew open, and M'greet emerged. She ran swiftly down the landscaped path, looking back triumphantly at her three brothers, who hovered in the doorway, joined by her father now. She clapped her hands with joy, shouting: *"Een bokkenwagen . . . een bokkenwagen!"* Then she blew an ecstatic kiss in the direction of her father, shook her black curls, and leaped into the carriage as though it were the royal coach. Seizing the reins, she urged her team on. The goats were as high-strung and sensitive as the finest thoroughbreds. Their eager hoofs struck the ground; the cart almost flew through the quiet streets, clattering across the cobblestones. M'greet's tawny face gleamed. Her hair streamed behind her as she rode, standing, in her chariot.

The town seemed to awaken at her approach. Faces appeared at the neatly curtained windows. Children ran out on the stoops but were hastily pulled back indoors. The stolid citizens frowned at the audacious vehicle, which disturbed the orderly monotony of the day. Some muttered under their breath that "the Baron" had gone too far; some uttered adages to their offspring having to do with pride and fall. A few crossed themselves to ward off the evil that cloven-hoofed beasts are said to bring; others simply gaped open-mouthed at the strange spectacle.

But she drove on, triumphant, aloof, her red dress a garish spot in the noon haze. Beyond the mocking or angry eyes. She raced her goats so swiftly now that they appeared to fly, their hoofs barely touching the ground. A passing stroller was almost knocked into one of the canals by the speeding team. He raised his arm and cursed the rich hatter, his ancestors, his pretensions, his elegance, his horsemanship, his fine shop, his flock of servants, his offspring, but most of all, this witch of a girl.

And still the cart sped on, drawn by the golden-eyed goats, carrying M'greet in her vivid dress far beyond the narrow confines of the town.

When she entered school that fall, her classmates all knew of the *bokkenwagen.* Although Miss Buys' school, on the Hofplein opposite the Stadhuis, with its renowned halls and archive rooms, catered to the children of the well-born families of Leeuwarden who gathered in these refined surroundings to learn French, calligraphy, and the writing of poetry, M'greet stood out even in such select company. While most girls of her age were dressed in demure, rather prim dresses, she wore flamboyant clothes (preferably in reds and yellows); while they came from a solid line of respected burghers with no other distinction than generations of affluence and civility, she announced with grandiose gestures: "I was born of illustrious ancestors. My cradle stood in Caminghastate." Although some whispered that she had invented all this, and others suggested that she told outright lies, they were nevertheless intrigued by M'greet and her astonishing ways.

She turned out to be a gifted student, with a fine talent for languages and a flair for writing. At a time when relatively few children in Holland received much schooling, and girls were even less frequently educated, M'greet enjoyed all the privileges of her class and her father's predilection for his only daughter.

The carefree schooldays continued until she was nearly thirteen. She was a tall young girl now, her body almost nubile, her hair darker and glossier than before. Her older brother teased her about her vanity, her newly acquired habit of walking with the upper part of her body thrust forward to emphasize the budding breasts, her furtive visits to the washerwomen in the cellar at certain times of the month. She cried easily, flew into wild rages, had spells of melancholy, composed a great deal of poetry, which she carefully burned, and otherwise exhibited all the usual symptoms of oncoming puberty.

She was so absorbed in the changes within her own body that she hardly noticed the tension that had lately gathered in the house. There were often great quarrels between her parents; her father frequently came home late at night and stormed into his study, slamming the door. Letters were constantly brought to the house; the servants of merchants stood in the hall, holding folded sheets of paper to be delivered in haste. Once or twice she heard tradesmen utter angry words and saw her father's face convulse with scorn. But she paid no attention to the cause of these happenings, considering that the center of the universe was located somewhere between her shoulders and her knees, confident that the pleasure and ease of her life was destined to go on into the far-off and assuredly rosy future.

Until the dreadful day in July 1889 when it all vanished. When she saw her father stand at the door of their grand house, his face dark and fierce, his beard jutting out defiantly, while someone uttered a word she had never heard but which had the sound of doom: "Bankruptcy." And she saw their home invaded: Creditors swarmed through the gracious rooms, seals were put on every door, burly men carried off the china, crystal, and silver, rugs were snatched by auctioneers, her father's proud portrait was lifted off the wall, their childhood games hauled out of the attic and carried away. And all the while he stood mute at the door, his thumbs hooked into the armholes of his flowered vest, and haughtily surveyed the wreckage below.

Then he also vanished. He tipped his hat to his family and walked out of their lives, while they remained at the top of a strange house, alone among the smug burghers, whose looks implied that they had been justly punished for their pride.

The family now lived on the Willemskade, not far from the railroad station and the cattle market, in a section far less lovely than before. Summer had gone. The trees looked parched and were beginning to lose their leaves. The canal they faced sent up odors of stagnation and decay. It seemed to M'greet that all the hallways smelled of boiled vegetables and insecticide and that her mother had grown smaller, as if shrunken into herself with grief and shame, perhaps in an attempt to disappear. There had been some news that her father had gone to The Hague to try his luck there, which she received with a shrug of the shoulders and her mother with a bitter smile.

Autumn came and with it one of the hardest days in M'greet's young life. She had to attend the Camingha State School now instead of Miss Buys' charming establishment in which she had spent such happy years. She now carried her schoolbooks in a satchel on her back; the dress she wore was still extravagant in color but showed signs of wear and had been outgrown. She saw her brothers come scuffling along the hall, trailing their books, dragging their feet. They looked dejected and stood, as if undecided, on the stoop. The window under the eaves opened, and their mother, looking faded (like an old photograph, somehow), called down: "Ari . . . Cornelis . . . Johannes . . . don't stand there! Be off to school!" They shrugged and sauntered slowly down the street. M'greet looked back at the window. Her mother waved with a forlorn air and withdrew.

She walked toward a distant part of town, tossing her long black hair, attempting to look indifferent to the neighbors' stares and the snickers of the schoolmates she met on the way (who surely remembered the stories of royal birth she had once told). Whenever a tall, bearded man passed, she glanced in his direction but each time swiftly lowered her head again and walked on. Once, when passing a certain show window on the *Kelders* that had been cleared of its display, she stopped, stared at the empty space, and bit her lip fiercely as she turned away.

Finally, the Camingha State School came into view. It looked even more forbidding than when she had passed it on a summer day. The gray walls suggested a prison, the recreation area the exercise yard of a jail. She composed her face and, with a fixed smile, joined the long line of students who filed mutely through the main gate.

How long ago it seemed to her that she had ridden, like an empress, in her *bokkenwagen*. The cart rusted at some ironmonger's now. Her rams had surely been slaughtered.

While she walked in thick, ugly boots along the grimy corridors. Toward childhood's end.

The true end came somewhat later: the day that her mother died. She had been ailing for over a year, but it was hard to tell whether she suffered from their near poverty, her husband's legal separation from his family, the shame of being thus abandoned in a society in which conformity, domesticity, and fidelity were extolled, or whether it was mere physical illness that brought her to her grave. Johannes and M'greet, being older, could see their mother becoming more feeble and silent each day. They watched helplessly as she faded from their life, uncomplaining, discreet as a cat that knows it is doomed. Until one day in May she simply did not rise from her bed. And they knew from the way she lay there that she was dead.

The day of the funeral arrived:

Black crepe framed the doorway of No. 30 Willemskade, forming an arch on which the initial Z appeared. Since it was not a first-class burial, the trappings of mourning had been kept to a minimum. A few wreaths, placed against the front wall, bore streamers expressing grief in banal formulas. The funeral coach, a large black box with glass sides, had driven up to the door. A pair of dark-plumed horses shook their sleek heads and pawed the ground. The coachman tipped his tricornered hat as the gate opened and the mourners appeared.

They moved through the narrow door, slightly swaying under the weight of the coffin (although it was small, almost puny in size). The minister followed, his face expressionless and his movements wooden. Adam Zelle (who had returned from Amsterdam for the occasion) led the procession. He was followed by his four children, all adolescent now. M'greet, nearly fifteen, appeared tall and willowy in her mourning clothes, almost a woman.

As the cortege wound its way through the cobbled streets, past the cattle market, smelling of dung and sweat, past the Stadtuin, in which band concerts would soon be held, men doffed their hats, women crossed themselves hastily, children looked frightened or bored. One or two spectators joined the procession but soon dropped behind and disappeared into one of the taverns on the way.

Past the outskirts of town, the road grew narrow. It was now a country lane, cut between the flat pasture lands, full of ruts and holes. The wind blew sharply here. The funeral coach lurched. Because of the recent rains, its wheels moved with difficulty across the muddy ground.

The mourners struggled to walk with dignity. Some looked in disgust at the state of their boots. One woman drew up her shawl with great indignation when she noticed that its fringe had trailed in the mire. Adam Zelle strode forward with a haughty air, holding his silk hat to keep it from being blown away. His sons controlled their faces with difficulty. M'greet's lithe body strained forward, as though joined to the coffin by an invisible cord.

At a designated spot in the cemetery a hole had already been cut in the ground. It formed a sharp and perfect rectangle in this landscape of mist and blurred outlines. Roots had been severed, their delicate network destroyed. The rich surface loam gave way to grayish sand toward the bottom of the pit. Broken pebbles lay covered with a film of slime (as though the sea had already seeped in). The truncated body of an earthworm had begun to turn black, while another, though hacked in two, continued to writhe.

Two men in leather aprons (vaguely resembling butchers or executioners), stood waiting at both sides of the grave. The coffin was laid before them.

The mourners formed an uneven circle around the gaping earth. The minister, looking dour, began the ritual, composed of litanies and prayers. The mourners repeated his words and gestures with mechanical exactitude, as if they had long rehearsed this ceremony. Even the clods of earth that dropped into the grave had a measured rhythm as they struck the lid of the coffin with a hollow sound. Only M'greet broke the chain of prescribed motions. She tore loose from the circle, threw a red flower into the open pit, then turned and hid her face in her father's coat.

When she turned back, there was only a slight mound to be seen. The gravediggers had filled in the earth and evened the ground. A rough wooden cross, with the year 1891 at the end of the scrawled inscription, marked the burial place. It looked naked and ugly, without grass or growing flowers. The other graves formed soft protuberances on the plain, but the new ground seemed like a gash torn in the tranquil fields, not yet scarred over like the tombs whose headstones and shrubs spoke of the slow passing of grief.

The empty funeral coach, ornate and futile now, still waited. The horses grew restless; the coachman yawned. The mourners, casting furtive glances at the new grave, began to slink away. They gathered at the cemetery gate and at a sign from the minister began the return journey to town. No longer proceeding in orderly fashion as on the way out, they broke into groups. Their gestures grew animated, their faces flushed, their voices boisterous. They might have been returning from a country fair, a harvest feast, a wedding even. No one seemed to notice the young girl, walking as though she had suddenly grown old, who trailed behind.

A mist rose, shrouding the pasture lands and the dunes that stretch all the way to the Zuiderzee.

That evening, when the funeral meats had all been eaten and the last guest was gone, M'greet sat in her mother's room under the eaves, musing. Grief mingled with foreboding in her thoughts. She knew that the family would now be dispersed. Her father had mentioned her godfather, Mr. Visser, who lived in Sneek, a small town nearby to which she might go. The twins would probably be taken to Amsterdam and Johannes to Franeker, where her maternal relatives lived. They would no longer even have the solace of each other's company. From the way her father looked at the women at the funeral feast, a stepmother would soon arrive on the scene.

M'greet leafed through the poetry album that her mother had left her as a legacy; it contained mostly religious verses, copied in her neat, simple hand; but one poem that spoke of love (which must have been composed long ago, for she had lain alone in her narrow bed in the years before the end); a few dried flowers, so shadowy that they could hardly be identified. A pitiful summary of a life.

M'greet put down the album and moved toward the piano in the corner of the room. Her fingers touched the keys caressingly at first, then struck chords with growing intensity.

The inhabitants of Leeuwarden heard music stream into the streets that night. A strange sound, coming from a house in mourning, although the melody was grave and slow. The notes swelled until they seemed one long cry. "It was the pain I felt," a friend later remembered her saying about the way she played.

The neighbors looked at M'greet, uncomprehending, perhaps concluding that drama had always been her forte; recalling the flights of fancy of her youth. They could not guess that she would, one day, transfigure her mother's memory but that for now she could only mourn her by playing. No one could see, when she stopped, her blind stare or the disconsolate pose of the feet. Nor did they see her weep as the wind blew in from the Frisian fields.

2 The Bride Wore Yellow

Life in Sneek proved to be as dull and puny as its name. The small town, seventeen miles from Leeuwarden, was even more provincial and staid. Its only distinction consisted of maintaining a considerable butter and cheese trade. For those who do not find excitement in dairy products, Sneek offered little to do. The women sat for hours at their windows watching the endless stream of bicycles—the offspring of the wooden velocipedes of past decades—move along the narrow streets with the regularity of sheep going to pasture. Everything here was "nice, neat, sensible, prosperous, and respectable"; designed, it seemed to M'greet, to make her feel like an intruder, an oddity. The very size of the place, which, as one traveler observed, looked "like a toyshop . . . its living rooms about as tiny and airy as birdcages," made her feel cramped, awkward, and gigantic by comparison. She had already attained her full height of five feet ten inches and towered over the girls of her age. Her clothes were old; her hair was of a noticeably different hue; her father was rumored to be leading a dissolute life.

She felt like a charity case in her godfather's house. True, Heer Visser did his duty. But she felt barely tolerated; obliged to efface herself when visitors came; a poor relative who had no real family claims, somehow always in the way. So that she was rather relieved when he suggested she'd better prepare to earn her living and think of a suitable career. It seemed there was a school at Leyde that trained kindergarten teachers, a profession fit for women—safe, proper, not too badly paid. There was no question of whether such work interested her. Tastes mattered little in a case such as hers. The head of the Visser household had decided. She would be enrolled as soon as it could be arranged.

Thus, Margaretha set out once more. Still in her mourning clothes, a tall slender figure with all her belongings in one small suitcase, she boarded the train. Men moved to make room for her; the conductor smiled as she handed him her fare. The black dress made her look older. Although still not quite sixteen, she was obviously considered a young woman by those who saw her for the first time.

Which she became instantly aware of when she was ushered into the office of the headmaster of the school, Heer Wybrandus Haanstra. He appeared flustered as he explained the establishment's rules and kept his eyes fixed on the inkwell when he saw that she had caught him staring in the direction of her thighs. While it pleased her to be thus appraised as a woman, she was frightened by the look of his fleshy hands, with carefully tended nails that stroked the rounded gold watchcase as he spoke.

The routine of the school was tedious, and the living conditions Spartan, to say the least. The girls spent long hours in the study halls, at prayer, taking pale children, whose noses seemed to be forever in need of wiping, on walks through the chilly countryside. M'greet discovered that she had no aptitude for the work. She was not good at discipline; it bored her to sing endless nursery rhymes or recite the alphabet. She could not bear to bring the switch down on their palms when they failed.

She often encountered Heer Haanstra in the halls. He always detained her on some pretext, and as he spoke, his eyes traveled over her body as if to ferret out each contour beneath the stiff school uniform. In class, he sometimes pretended to inspect her work, bending over her until his paunch touched her back and she felt his hot breath against the nape of her neck.

And yet, in these chaste surroundings, there was nothing to excite sensuality. The walls were constantly whitewashed. The sheets were rough and so stiffly starched that one had the impression of sleeping between layers of cardboard. Even the paintings were prim: cool interiors, maidens pouring spring water from glazed blue pitchers, staid burghers posing with their wives—all fully dressed, of course. As one observant traveler said: "As regards the Dianas and Venuses, it was perhaps . . . the Dutch climate which kept them away; such damp and rheumaticky surroundings are not exactly in the interests of nudity."

But Heer Haanstra did not seem to agree. He pursued Margaretha into the garden, the study rooms, even the dormitory one day. What happened behind the white curtains that shrouded the overseer's alcove from view is not known. Whether M'greet lost what French girls call their *petit capital* (and for which Dutch girls probably have a more prosaic term), no one can say.

But scandal erupted in the quiet establishment. The sedate old maids were horrified. The girls turned on M'greet (perhaps feeling slighted at not having been singled out in the same way). Everyone was outraged that this impoverished orphan had the audacity to cling to her pride and refuse to comment or answer the questions of her inquisitors.

The result was that she was asked to leave the school in a state of disgrace.

She could not return to Sneek. Another relative had to be sought; perhaps her uncle, Heer Taconis, in The Hague could deal with her better than her godfather, and at least her behavior would not cause so much comment in a bigger town. It was decided that her next stop would be The Hague.

Life there was much more exhilarating. Lately, this city had become the favorite place for officers of the Dutch Colonial Army in the East Indies to spend their leaves. The streets were filled with colorful uniforms and suntanned faces; medals gleamed in the sun, sabers rattled, rowdy voices were heard at night. While most girls watched all this with coy reserve, M'greet openly glanced in their direction as she went on errands into town. When the weather grew warmer, she took the steam tramway to the beach at Scheveningen three miles away.

Scheveningen was a crowded, fashionable resort to which about 20,000 visitors came annually. The Grand Hotel des Bains, with its spacious verandahs and its richly adorned *Cursaal*, which could accommodate nearly 3,000 persons for its spectacles, was the main rallying point. Equally famous were its beaches, spotted with bathing coaches (with awnings for ladies; without, for gentlemen), which had a reputation for great daring in those days. For while there were separate bathing places for the sexes, as in most resorts, a warning in a current travel guide read: "The custom of promiscuous bathing has lately been observed here."

M'greet's full young figure, clad in a modish 1890s' bathing costume, appearing on one of these "promiscuous" beaches caused many an officer to pause admiringly. At a time when the glimpse of a shapely calf constituted a daring feat, not far from voyeurism, her appearances at Scheveningen made numerous members of the Dutch Colonial Army wish they could bring her back to the East Indies to while away the long tropical nights, but they had to content themselves with whirling her along the dance floor of the *Cursaal*.

One of these officers had returned to Holland on August 14, 1894 (a week after M'greet's eighteenth birthday). He was Rudolph Mac Leod, who, having seen more than sixteen years of uninterrupted service in the colonies, was now here on sick leave. Having begun his military career at sixteen, colonial duties at twenty-one, he had participated in the great Atjah War, gained an officer's cross, and become a hardbitten, ruthless warrior. Alcoholism, diabetes, rheumatism, and a long stay in the tropics had undermined his health to such an extent that he had to be carried on a stretcher from the ship that brought him home on leave. But he preferred to be thought of as a conquering hero. Coming from an old Scottish family that traced its origins back to Olaf the Black, claimed Dunvegan Castle as its ancestral home, boasted of several vice-admirals, generals, a captain of infantry, an adjutant to King William III, a mother who was a baroness, Mac Leod at thirty-eight was both proud and slightly weary.

It was perhaps this weariness that caused him to cross Margaretha's path. For while he was in no shape to appear at Scheveningen, his morose mood was the cause for a stag-party joke that would have far-reaching consequences: One day, while sitting in Amsterdam's Café Américain on the Leidsche Plein with De Balbien Verster, a journalist friend, some officers remarked that Mac Leod looked down in the mouth and Verster jokingly suggested that what he needed was a wife. Mac Leod tried to dismiss the matter with one of his usual, coarse oaths. De Balbien Verster smiled slyly and said no more. But the next day he inserted two ads in the newspapers:

Officer on home leave from Dutch East Indies would like to meet girl of pleasant character—object matrimony.

Captain from the Indies, passing his leave in Holland, seeks a wife to his liking, preferably with a little money.

(As if pleasant character and a good dowry could not possibly be found in one prospective bride).

Margaretha had been living with relatives who considered her of marriageable age, foresaw no career for her, and probably found her something of a burden besides. She had begun to read the matrimonial ads in the newspapers, mostly as a joke, being somewhat restless and bored of late. Most of them were laughable: sturdy burghers desiring buxom wives who would prove to be good breeders; elderly widowers seeking unpaid nurse's aides; pimply youths offering chaste correspondence with virtuous maids.

Until she came to Mac Leod's offer. The words had an exotic ring. "Captain" . . . "Indies" echoed through her mind. She seized a pen and dashed off a note (not forgetting to include a photograph).

An answer soon arrived. It was obvious from his tone that he was a man of the world, experienced both in love and war. She began to dream about him, to make plans for an exciting life but also to worry about competitors—girls with large dowries or reputable families. She would simply have to trust to her good looks and seductiveness to win him. And so she wrote him such passionate letters that he said she "seemed to be quite a girl" and asked her to meet him in Amsterdam.

She prepared feverishly for the rendezvous, trying out clothes and hairdos for hours in her room. But that first meeting had to be postponed. Rudolph had suffered a sudden and severe attack of rheumatism (a slight drawback for an ardent admirer).

Finally, on March 30, 1895, they met, as agreed, at the Amsterdam Rijksmuseum.

The Rijksmuseum was an imposing building that covered nearly three acres of ground—erected from 1877 to 1885 in the so-called Dutch Renaissance style, a passing tour guide explained—surrounded by pleasure grounds and wrought-iron grill work. The principal façade was surmounted by a statue of Victory, and above the archway there were allegorical figures of the Netherlands, surrounded by Wisdom, Justice, Beauty, and Truth. It seemed an intimidating array of virtues to Margaretha, who was hurrying to her place of assignation in the east court of the main floor.

She saw a large hall covered with a glass roof through which the sun filtered obliquely, illuminating trophies, weapons of all kinds, and brilliantly colored banners. She bent to read the inscriptions, which informed her that this was the Military, Naval, and Colonial Collection of the Rijksmuseum. It seemed a fitting setting for the officer she was here to meet.

Trying to look unconcerned, like a casual visitor in search of culture, she brushed a feather from her fashionable suit, fixed a stray tendril of dark hair (piled high on her shapely head to make her look more mature), and walked about the room, refraining from

glancing at the door. Out of the corner of her eye she spotted someone in uniform. It could only be he. She looked up and saw a man
in his middle years, heavy-set, erect and powerful, his chest covered
with medals, sporting a long sweeping mustache and saber to
match, his officer's hat shading his eyes and partly concealing his
baldness. He seemed to be appraising her also.

There was an imperceptible sign of recognition on both sides.
They walked toward each other, she with her lithe gait, slightly
swaying at the hips, he with somewhat halting steps, as though
still rather stiff in the joints.

After that, neither threw a glance at the paintings that lined the
walls. They studied each other with far greater interest than art
lovers devote to obscure Rembrandts or a little-known Vermeer.
He saw only her svelte body, rounded in all the crucial places (he
was an old hand at such matters), a wealth of black hair, almond-
shaped eyes, a mouth that promised sensuality, and decided that
her photograph had not lied, except that she was even better in
the flesh. She saw a mysterious and virile stranger, burnished by the
sun, who had traveled distant lands in which one commands barbaric tribes and partook of exotic rites—a man as close to a knight
in armor as one could hope to find in the nineteenth century.

He offered her his arm and paraded her across the marble floors.
Soon they were engrossed in talk, banter, and in the contact of
their bodies as they moved. By the time they had strolled through
the last of the halls, Rudolph Mac Leod and Margaretha Zelle
walked in unison, the rhythm of their steps attuned. She knew then
that she would soon be his bride.

And indeed, six days later he asked for her hand.

Their engagement should have been a blissful period, but it was,
in fact, full of tribulations. Rudolph had another attack of rheumatism, so severe this time that his sister Louise had to write the letters to his fiancée. Then his family, worried by his sudden move,
insisted on inspecting the bride. Margaretha had to submit to being
scrutinized by Rudolph's uncle, Norman, an impressive old man

and a retired general. True, she passed muster (the ancient soldier evidently still had an eye for the ladies) when he muttered gruffly: "Young, but good-looking, damn good-looking." But Louise, Rudolph's sister, seemed less enthusiastic in her estimate.

Then there was the matter of Margaretha's father. She had told Rudolph she was an orphan, being loath to produce an impoverished traveling salesman living in a decrepit part of town as her progenitor. But when she found that by law a woman could marry at sixteen with parental consent but only at thirty without it, she had to admit that Adam Zelle was alive and well in Amsterdam, residing at 148 Lange Leidschedwarsstraat with his recently acquired wife. And they had to visit him to obtain his permission. To make matters worse, Adam Zelle seemed to have kept some of his old arrogance, for he demanded a visit from the betrothed couple and specified that they arrive in a large carriage, not a simple one-horse cab (undoubtedly, to impress his cronies).

There were also raised eyebrows on both sides to contend with when they announced that they would marry in July, only three months after their already shockingly swift engagement. Evil tongues whispered that such speed suggested necessity rather than ardor; many suspicious glances were thrown at Margaretha's waistline.

Finally, however, the wedding day arrived. On July 11, 1895, Rudolph and Margaretha became man and wife in a quiet ceremony at the Amsterdam city hall. It was a standard wedding, quite routine, in fact, except for the startling detail of the bride's brilliant yellow wedding gown.

After the civil ceremony, the boisterous festivities began. A wildly cheering mob, composed mostly of Adam Zelle's cronies who were hoping for a free drink, followed the bridal party along the canals. They finally reached the Café Américain (where it had all started, as a joke, just a few short months ago). The guests assembled, the summer sun beating down on their heads. Some wiped their brows carefully under the brims of their hats in an effort not to disarray their hair; others dabbed at the drops of sweat on their bosoms with embroidered handkerchiefs; a few attempted to shift their position to move into the shade. But none seemed to want to lose sight of the bridal pair—a perfect picture, they all agreed, and well worth being roasted in the July sun.

Photographers arrived and crept under the black hoods of their cameras, waving instructions with their arms. The couple posed. The bride's father was conspicuously absent from the scene. (Someone suggested that the groom had sent him on a wild goose chase.)

No one bemoaned his absence, however, for the feasting was about to begin. From the kitchens vast platters appeared. Artfully arranged to please the eye before the palate, they were paraded before the guests as if to flaunt their plenitude. Finally, all were seated and fell to with enormous appetite: they speared, dismembered, and devoured the food. A whole barnyard in carcass form was soon only a heap of bones. Fields of ripe vegetables, orchards laden with fruit, dairies overflowing with milk, butter, and cheese, all spilled their riches unto the tables and were swallowed up. Liquor flowed unendingly into glasses and mugs. The servants ran back and forth, pouring, replenishing, sweating in the summer sun.

The guests now belched with gusto, caressed distended bellies, mingled the last morsels of food with coarse jokes. By the end of the meal some dozed heavily where they sat, while others grew increasingly boisterous and obscene.

The groom laughed heartily as he surveyed the scene. The bride drew herself up and looked with revulsion at the ruins of the feast.

He turned and seized her brutally, his fleshy face inflamed. His breath reeked of alcohol as he whispered in her ear: " 'Do whatever you want,' that's what you said, remember, 'rather ten times than once,' remember?"

Although she yielded to his embrace, she shivered slightly in her yellow gown despite the sunny afternoon.

3 Love's Labors

The honeymoon was soon over. They had a brief stay at Wiesbaden, the famous German spa, but its *Kursaal* did not appreciably differ from the *Cursaal* at Scheveningen. While the latter catered to the so-called German "lemmings" that rushed to the sea during their holidays, the former was their natural habitat. Arrogant young Teutons crowded the restaurant and dance floor instead of Dutch officers; they eyed Margaretha more openly than her compatriots.

Rudolph was visibly irritated by men's attentions to his young wife. He blustered and puffed himself up like a turkey-cock, but this did not keep their eyes from following her wherever she went. It seemed to him that she encouraged their advances, and he began to make violent scenes. He probably wished now that he had married some nice bourgeois girl who knew only the homey Dutch art of *geselligheid* instead of this German brand of distinctly non-domestic *Gemütlichkeit*.

Perhaps a stay at his sister's house would tame her down and teach her the rules of family life. Upon their return to Holland, they moved into Louisa's home at 79 Leidschekade. It was around the corner from the Café Américain, and Margaretha threw longing glances at the place as she passed by on her shopping trips or the visits to relatives she was expected to make. It seemed a long time ago that she had sat there in her wedding gown, full of naïve girlish dreams.

Now her life was full of bitter feelings. Her aging, widowed sister-in-law seemed to resent her youth, her looks, her brother's desire for a woman who had answered a matrimonial ad. Rudolph had actually not abandoned any of his bachelor ways. He often stayed out late at night, offering no explanation for his whereabouts, taking for granted his rights as the male of the species. Margaretha spent long, lonely evenings at home, playing the piano, fretting over her embroidery, knowing all the while that her husband was out wenching somewhere. He frequently came home drunk, his eyes full of rage, and took her with rude force. In the early days of her marriage she had taken such moods for passion. Now she knew what it meant to be possessed. She felt disgust at her slavish submission and hatred for her body's desires.

Months passed thus. She was just beginning to think of a way out when a new form of servitude began. A few unguarded seconds in bed, and suddenly she had fits of vomiting, dizzy spells, and the strange feeling that changes were taking place in her body that she could not understand. Its svelte lines began to disappear; her waist thickened; her breasts grew heavy and sore. She realized that she must be with child.

Soon she could feel (with a mixture of wonder and fear) something flutter in her entrails like a captive moth, then a weight that grew heavier with each passing week and forced her to walk with a waddling gait, rise slowly from armchairs, change her posture while sleeping. The long months of waiting continued. She felt movement inside her, as if an unknown creature were struggling in those confines. Her navel grew flush with her skin and then began to protrude. She wondered where it would all end. Old wives' tales pursued her wherever she turned: a boy if you carry high; a girl if quickening is early; a stillborn babe if you see lightning strike; a hunchback if you trip on the stairs.

She dreaded the moment of delivery. Her mother was not there to comfort her. She tried to turn to her relatives, but they were of no help. Louisa only looked at her mockingly. The others spoke in half words, as to an imbecile or a child. Older women smiled knowingly (and with some malice, it seemed), then spoke of God's will, of woman's lot, of bringing forth in pain. Men snickered or treated her like an invalid. The midwife announced that her time would soon come. Rudolf was out late more than usual.

On January 30, 1897, while she sat at the piano, her hands idly wandering over the keys because the fullness of her body prevented her from bending forward to read the notes, she felt a heavy pressure in the small of her back. It gathered force, reached a climax that made her wince with pain, then subsided again. She was afraid but continued to play, hoping that the feeling would not recur. But it did, with increasing strength and at shorter intervals. When she cried out, the women of the household came running toward her. She was led to a bedroom in which everything was already prepared:

The curtains were drawn. In one corner, mysterious objects were covered by a towel. A wash basket, lined with lace, stood near the door. The fire burned brightly, warming a kettle of water hung over the flames.

The women gathered around her. They held her hands and feet. Suddenly, the room seemed to grow dim. The old midwife murmured some unintelligible words while M'greet groaned. There was a crack in the ceiling. She watched its twisted line as her womb contracted in waves that lifted her whole body and let it fall back upon the sheets.

Between pains (she had heard someone say) it was best to think of pleasant things. The past year or so offered few such memories. She searched her mind frantically. All that appeared was the reception at the Royal Palace given by the queen. She tried to recall how she had danced in her yellow gown, spinning till dawn across the polished floors; tried to reincarnate the figures of the dance, the flow of the silk, the firm clasp of her partner about her waist. But it changed into the heavy pressure in her womb; her body was wracked with labor pains once more.

The midwife hovered over her. She now ordered, now cajoled:

"Bear down, my pretty! . . . once more . . . harder . . . The head is crowning!"

She heard a long scream and felt torn in two. Then, in a flow of warm liquid, something moved, passed out of her, lay in alien hands between her thighs. They lifted a bleeding bundle before her eyes. A voice (far away) called out: "A son . . . a son!"

The new father strutted into the room. The midwife held up the infant. He inspected the son presented to him, now washed and wrapped in swaddling clothes. Although he hardly glanced at the mother, he seemed to approve of the offspring he had produced.

"He shall be called Norman John," he announced, "after the most illustrious members of the Mac Leod family."

Margaretha took the infant and without a word put him to her breast.

4 A Passage to the Indies

The spring passed in languorous ways. Margaretha, recovered from the delivery, spent long, dreamlike hours looking at her son, watching the wrinkled newborn face fill out, the downy scalp become covered with silky hair the color of her own, the slate-gray eyes turn a warm shade of brown. She delighted in seeing the small hands reach for a beam of sunlight, the toes curl when she touched the soles of his feet, in hearing his lusty cries when hunger drove him to her breast.

For a while she was altogether absorbed in this new life that turned to her as a plant to the sun. She hardly noticed Rudolph. And he, strangely enough, seemed almost diffident before her in her motherly role. But before long he grew restless. His home leave was drawing to a close. By summer he would have to return to the colonies once more, and it was already late spring. In April, he heard that he would be stationed at Ambawara, in the center of Java, and knew that he would have to inform Margaretha of their imminent move.

To his surprise she seemed delighted. Of course, to her, it seemed like an enchanted place. She had heard the islands referred to as "Insulinde," a graceful and musical name that she found much more to her liking than the Dutch *"Oost-Indisch Archipel."* The term "Spice Islands," which the region was often also referred to, seemed equally pleasing. It evoked odors, tastes, and colors never experienced before, a garden of earthly delights such as Hieronymus Bosch had dreamed of in his paintings. She began to picture herself in this island paradise, clothed in splendid native robes, striding among exotic fauna and unknown flowers.

And then there was, of course, the danger of volcanoes to add excitement to this strange world. Krakatau—the fantastic cataclysm of a decade or so ago—remained vivid in her mind. Although she had only been seven at the time, she remembered the stories of the island's annihilation, the flames that spread over adjacent lands, the clouds of vapor five times as tall as Mont Blanc, a tidal wave eighty feet high that engulfed the coastal regions of Java and Sumatra, the strange red glow over the Pacific for thousands of miles.

She could hardly wait for their journey to begin. The preparations seemed endless. It seemed as if the day of departure would never come.

But finally, on May 1, 1897, they boarded the S.S. *Prinses Amalia,* which had stood waiting in the harbor of Amsterdam. It was a memorable sight:

The tall ship stood majestically in the port, ready to depart. On the decks, wet with spray, ropes lay uncoiled, sailors ran to and fro performing a multitude of tasks: They climbed the masts, hoisted and lowered flags, loaded casks into the hold, guided embarking passengers along the swaying gangways.

Excitement ran through the waiting crowd, the bustling porters, the travelers who stood at the railings readying their handkerchiefs for the farewell. It seemed most evident in the figure of a tall young woman who held an infant in her arms—Margaretha, who surveyed the drama of the scene with gleaming eyes, as though the whole port were her audience. Rudolph, appearing stocky beside her, seemed to be used to the proceedings and either affected boredom or was truly indifferent to his whereabouts.

The boat horn blew, majestic and slow. A shudder ran through the crowd.

Now the moorings were cut. The ship swung gracefully around, its prow pointed toward the open sea, then headed east, beginning the long journey to the Indies, halfway around the globe.

Margaretha remained alone at the rail. Norman had been taken inside because the sea air had grown chill. Rudolph had become increasingly bored and wandered off in the direction of the officers' bar. She watched the shore recede, the coastline grow indistinct, and Europe slowly vanish in the mist. All her childhood seemed to disappear as if dissolved by water and dispersed by the wind. She stared for a long time at the waves, although it had grown far too dark to see.

She began to dream of her new life, the fabled Indies she had never seen. Gray Holland faded before odors and colors unknown; a world seemed to be unfolding with each wave. The ship swayed softly. A vessel of transfiguration, she thought, upon a sea so vast that it might wash away the stains on the sheets, the blood of afterbirth, soiled dreams, and the debris of the wedding feast.

The prow was turned toward the Orient. The swell caused the decks to rise and fall with a heaving motion. The masts trembled; the engines labored; spray flew to the topmost deck. But nothing could impede the vessel's course. It traveled due east, as if aimed straight into the dawn.

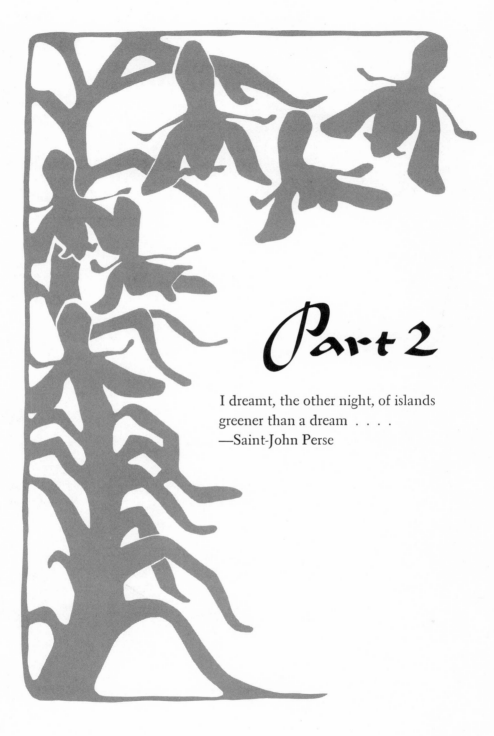

Part 2

I dreamt, the other night, of islands
greener than a dream . . . .
—Saint-John Perse

5 Scorpions and Birds of Paradise

The beauty of Java is probably unsurpassed by any other country on the globe. Dazzling to the senses, charming the beholder with their exotic strangeness, its scenic splendors are unending in their variety. Driving along its winding roads, where *sawahs* in varied shades of green alternate with graceful coconut palms or are arranged on terraced grounds that give the plains the appearance of a carefully cultivated garden, the traveler is shaded by Canarien, *djati*, or *vandoe*, trees, or by magnificent *waringen* groves so ancient that no one knows who planted them. There is a profusion of orchids, ferns, mosses, and Javanese "edelweiss" everywhere. The hills are covered with tall bamboo; the tough *alang-alang* grass grows in clearings; *lianas* cover the trunk of every tree in a sensuous, deadly embrace. The valleys are full of sugar cane and coffee plantations, fields of tobacco and acres of rubber trees. In the distance, there are always the mountain chains, which are like the spine of the island— numberless volcanoes whose truncated summits give the country-side its characteristic aspect.

High on these slopes, tea grew in vast groves, and young girls delicately pinched the precious leaves with their tapered fingertips. In the peaceful landscape below, small brown boys drove their *caraboes* to the watering places or sat dreaming on their broad backs while they grazed. Graceful farmers plowed, planted, and irrigated the rice fields; by these crops they traditionally counted their age and measured the passing of the seasons. Here and there in the countryside stood the *dessas*, in which the inhabitants lived, with their stately *aloen-aloen*, or public gathering place, in which the home of the *weddana* stands, in which their women in multicolored *sarongs* and *kabayas* adorned with gold coins gather, and in which, in the evening, the erect, graceful maidens stand in long rows before their houses, stamping the paddy to husk the rice while singing their melodious native tunes. In some of the fishing villages, the huts were built on stilts, and during the hot afternoons one could see the women sit in their shade, nursing their infants or doing their weaving on huge frames. And everywhere—in the fields, on the paths, along rivers, at the edge of the road—played the children of Java, naked, barefoot, their small bronze bodies as lithe as vines, as agile as gibbons, as full of laughter and chatter as the tropical birds in the trees.

Then there were the *pasars*, those teeming markets in which Chinese, Malays, Javanese, and Arabs sold their wares, bartered, and haggled in a variety of tongues; in which one saw an undreamed-of array of produce displayed: damar, sago, ratongs, ebony, hatuloes, cassava, indigo, peanuts, kapok, teak; fruits, with unknown names and tastes, such as kalapa, pisang, mangosteen, djerok, pompolo-moes, tamarind; skins of the bird of paradise, cages of rare birds, peacock feathers, captured wild beasts, batik and jewelry, yards of fine woven cloth in colors that vied with the fauna and flora of the isle.

It seemed impossible to exhaust the beauty of the place. At each turn of the road another spectacle of unsurpassed splendor awaited the beholder: fish ponds, in which in a series of artificial lakes, each separated from its neighbor and planted with palms, a multitude of colored fish swam among the reflections of the swaying leaves in clear and limpid waters; temples of such great magnificence and antiquity that cathedrals seemed mere toys in comparison—Djokjakarta and Boro-Budur, among the greatest Buddhist monuments in the world, wonders to which pilgrims traveled over thousands of miles.

Margaretha felt as if she had landed in paradise. Aside from the incredible loveliness of the place, the weather was perfect when she and Rudolph arrived. It was the dry season; a sea breeze refreshed one from the heat. In the center of Java, because of its higher altitude, the days were sunny and the nights delightfully cool. The natives seemed full of a flawless courtesy, a natural grace, which contrasted sharply with the brusque manners of her countrymen. She could not seem to get her fill of all the delights this country appeared to hold for one from the old gray world from which she came.

Rudolph was far less rhapsodic than she. He saw Java as an overpopulated isle, with natives who must feel fear to be useful to their colonizers, full of the vicious habits that Orientals acquire with their usual facility. He spoke of the need to keep them uneducated if the whites were to retain the upper hand as well as of their filthy habits (in such sharp contrast to the renowned cleanliness of the Dutch). He also warned her that scorpions hid in the bed linen, shoes, and flowerpots; that there might be invasions of moths, termites, and flying ants; that typhus, malaria, and other diseases often struck.

But she remained under the spell of the place. She sat for hours on the verandah of their house, watching everything shimmer in the intense light: the lush jungle growth, the wild peacocks strutting through the underbrush amidst other birds whose brilliant plumage rendered them indistinguishable from the most exorbitant blooms; even the mosquito netting shrouding the bed, the hammock swaying beneath the giant leaves, the fan that rhythmically cooled her face, seemed to her magically transformed into objects of ritual use.

Margaretha herself had blossomed on this isle; her beauty ripened as if she had found the climate suitable to her growth. Never had her skin seemed so radiant, her hair so glossy, her movements so languorous. The native sarongs she had begun to wear seemed designed to enhance the lines of her body; their colors brought out the golden glow of her arms, the blue shadows in her hair.

Men's eyes followed her wherever she went: at the club in which officers and planters gathered; in the gardens in which the coolies toiled; in the village square that she crossed on her way to the *weddana*'s house; at the performance of a *wayung* play at the *kraton* of a Javanese nobleman; even when she sat on the verandah and brushed her long hair.

"*Ushas*," the natives murmured as she passed.

"*Délicieuse*," a Frenchman exclaimed at a café in Malang.

"*Eine Schönheit*," his German neighbor concurred.

"Filthy bitch," her husband hissed as she whirled past him on the arm of a young officer at the regent's ball. For Rudolph did not delight in the beauty of his wife to the extent of the other men. Her youth contrasted too sharply with his decline. The tropics were aging him visibly, while she thrived in these climes. His old illnesses all returned.

As did his drinking. And his vile temper (which had been somewhat calmed by northern latitudes). He watched her suspiciously all the time, drinking more and more heavily during his vigils. The alcoholic haze made her appear doubly beautiful and desired, while he seemed doubly exposed to cuckoldry and ridicule. He cursed and raged, then began beating her savagely.

If she expressed any desire to stir from under his watchful eye, he became nearly insane. One day she mentioned that she would like to visit the temple of Boro-Budur, which was supposed to be the depository of the sacred ashes of the first Buddha and, if one climbed the various terraces by moonlight, offered a spectacle never to be forgotten, rivaled only by a visit at sunrise when the warm tropical rays lit up the eastern side with successive and ever-increasing waves of soft radiance, revealing in all its pristine beauty the ancient carvings in the volcanic stones. His response was to lash at her with his riding whip, accusing her of craving a night of heathen debauchery.

She learned to cringe as soon as he approached. Often she thought that he had lost his mind. She feared the weapons he kept around the house, especially the revolver, which was always loaded and which he had waved at her in fury during several of his tirades. Her island paradise had turned into an inferno. The wild beasts that the natives captured to sell to menageries were more fortunate than she.

Then the monsoons came and with them thunderstorms and high winds that lashed the palms and bent the boughs of the most ancient trees. The cart road, paved with pebbles from the seashore and clay, became one long stream of mud and could no longer be traveled. The pack horses slipped; the water buffaloes stood desolately in the downpour; only the rhinoceros' thick hide seemed impervious to wind and rain. It seemed to her that she was marooned on an island that would soon be washed into the sea. At times, the crash of the thunder was so loud that she thought one of the many volcanoes had erupted and that she would be buried in lava, consumed by a flow of liquid fire.

She felt imprisoned by Rudolph, by the season, by this land surrounded on all sides by a raging sea. And, with terror, she realized that she was also a captive of her body. For she was once again with child.

The rains lasted from November to January. Long months passed in which she almost never left the confines of the house. Time went by so slowly that she stopped looking at the calendar. Distinctions between night and day were obliterated by the contant, steady downpour. As her body grew heavier, she began to feel more and more like some giant snail and turned to see if she had not left a viscous trail behind her as she crawled from room to room. She knew that she had only a tenuous hold on sanity and began to search wildly for something to tide her over until the end of her confinement and the close of the rainy season.

She found that some previous owner had left a collection of books in the storage room. She plunged herself into the pages with the intensity of one possessed. Anything to hide from the horrors of nature and the domestic scene. The books contained accounts of Javanese history. She discovered that the island had been known to the Western world since antiquity, that Ptolemaeus had called it Jabidore and that merchants from Hindustan had visited this land during the first centuries of the Christian era; that Buddhism had flourished and left its imprint in those great monuments of which she had recently heard the natives speak. She read about the most famous Javanese epic, the *Ardjuna Wiwaha,* and the forerunners of the *wayungs* of Hindu origin, performed in the forest by the *"Sjamaan,"* in which the spirits of dead ancestors were represented by the shadows on the screen and their great and noble deeds portrayed for posterity.

And secretly, since Rudolph violently disapproved, she began to learn Malay, practicing on the servants and a few native friends. She found that she learned quickly. The acquisition of each word (melodious, unlike any of the languages she spoke) delighted her as it would a child. One word especially echoed through her mind: *matahari,* "eye of dawn," which meant the sun.

Despite all her efforts, she grew wearier every month. It sometimes seemed to her that spring would never come and that she would never bear this child. Yet it affirmed its life each day, moving more animatedly in her womb than her son. She felt pity for this unborn infant, fathered in hate, destined to live in an atmosphere of fear. For Rudolph continued to impose his fierce rule upon the house. He terrorized the servants and did not spare his wife brutal attacks even in her present advanced state. Although it was common knowledge that he kept a native concubine (as was the custom, she was told), she was not safe from his vicious form of lechery. He liked to drag her to bed by the hair and seemed to derive satisfaction from her weeping.

She caught the pitying glances of those around her and knew they must wonder why she did not murder him. Poisons were easy to obtain and much used in this land; it would suffice to attribute death to a scorpion bite, insulin shock, or one of the many tropical diseases so difficult to diagnose. She preferred to hope that one of his men would kill him: one of those petty officers drawn from the dregs of Dutch society, the younger son of some virtuous burghers gone wrong, or one of the rank and file, composed of miserably paid, badly housed, and discontent natives. His tyranny certainly gave them all sufficient cause. She decided to bide her time; he was aging so rapidly that he could not last very much longer.

She was too centered on the life inside her to devote herself to bringing about his death. Her confinement was nearing. The child would be born in late spring.

Just at the start of the dry season, when nature was radiant once more, a daughter was born to her. May 2, 1898: a year, almost to the day, since the old world had vanished and Margaretha had set out for the East.

The delivery was easier than that of her first child, perhaps because of the deft way of the native women who attended her, so used to bringing forth their children between harvests in the rice fields; perhaps because they had mixed some opium with the beverage they held to her lips between pains.

"*Nonah*," the midwife whispered in her ear as soon as the child was born. Margaretha smiled as she sank back into the pillows. A girl, born on this jungle soil at the outset of the most splendid season. She would be strong and fortunate. And be called "Non."

Rudolph scrutinized his new offspring and seemed somewhat put out because it was not a boy. He then decreed that the child was to be named Jeanne Louise, after his sister (whom Margaretha would have been the last to choose as a namesake).

Despite his decree, however, the child was known as Non from that day on, as if her true heritage were Javanese.

6 The Dead of Summer

As the rice stalks ripened, so the children seemed to grow. They thrived on this fertile soil, surrounded by flowering shrubs and wild peacocks, tended by the slim hands of native girls, fanned with palm leaves, bathed in cool spring water. Margaretha, watching them, remembered her own early days, which had been as carefree as theirs, if not as filled with sunshine and living toys. For they chased gigantic, unbelievably brilliant butterflies, saw the young rhinos drink at the watering hole, touched the eggs of the bird of paradise.

But summer passed, and the rains inevitably came. With them, days as dark and threatening as the monsoons. Rudolph became irritable once more, as if in tune with the weather. The children, whom he had doted on, now irked him when they fretted or cried. The house began to echo with his shouts. The nurse or Margaretha swiftly whisked them out of the way when he arrived. He thundered at the women, claiming they were spoiling his offspring and that, at this rate, Norman would never learn military discipline. But the future general, at the age of two, only pulled a face at his father's outbreak and fled into the outstretched arms of his *baboe*.

It was rather a relief when Rudolph announced that he would

shortly leave for Sumatra, where he would be stationed next. The possibility of living in Medan intrigued Margaretha and seemed a welcome change from this rural life. What she had not expected, however, was the manner in which he set out to change their place of residence.

In January, at the bleakest time of the year, he suddenly announced that he was leaving for Medan. Their house was abruptly invaded (as once before, long ago in Leeuwarden) by auctioneers who carted off the furniture, the household goods, the books she had accumulated, even the cradle in which she had rocked Non to sleep in her infancy. It was much simpler, Rudolph brusquely stated, than moving everything to Medan. Then he proceeded to deposit Margaretha and the children at the comptroller's house with no more ado than if they had been household pets. They were to wait there, she was told, until he sent for them. With those orders, he rode off on the road to the coast.

The spring went slowly. Letters took a long time to travel from island to island. Rudolph seemed in no hurry to send money to provide for their keep. Margaretha, despite everyone's assurances that hospitality among colonialists made her stay at the comptroller's quite usual, felt wounded in her pride for being a financial burden on her hosts. She attempted to be helpful by copying the long lists of accounts, of goods for export, that read rather like an alchemist's catalogue: dammer, gum benzoin, tripang, bird nests, tiger's eye shells, dragon's blood, birds of paradise . . . and played the piano to amuse the comptroller's wife. She also went to numerous dances at the officers' club.

Finally, the day for her arrival at Medan came. It was summer once more, and Margaretha felt the exhilaration of a new life rush to her head.

The city thrilled her. Its houses of several stories seemed marvels of architecture after the thatched huts she had become so accustomed to. There were paved streets instead of cart roads, fine shops in lieu of the primitive marketplace, splendid horsedrawn carriages in place of rickety carts or worn-out beasts of burden. Most miraculous of all, there were myriads of electric lights, which transformed the thoroughfares into glittering jewels at night.

She remembered that someone had once called the East Indies "a girdle of emerald, flung round the equator" and thought that it was indeed a fitting comparison. Their new residence stood in the midst of all this splendor. And it was an imposing place. Rudolph had been named garrison commander, an extremely important post, and his home was the site of all the official receptions in the area, the place in which visiting dignitaries were habitually entertained.

Margaretha was in her full glory. The house was filled with festivities, servants, diplomats, members of colonial high society, officers, native princes, traveling scholars, captains of foreign fleets. In their midst, she could reign like a queen. Dressed in the latest fashions imported from Amsterdam, a paragon of beauty and elegance, she conversed with visitors in their native tongue—whether Dutch, German, English, or French—gave instructions to the servants in Malay, played the piano most musically, danced with unusual grace. Garrison Commander Mac Leod could indeed pride himself on his wife. The women imitated her clothes, her gestures, her smile, but could not achieve her poise. Men surrounded her in droves. She accepted their homage as naturally as if it were hers by divine right. Stooping now to caress her children before they were taken off to bed by the nurse, now to accept the arm of a rheumatic general as dinner was announced, she seemed equally in her element. She basked in the glow of their adulation and grew more beautiful.

Rudolph seemed glad of her presence. Her successes were a great help to his career. The children, also, he considered more presentable than before. He liked to parade Jan Pik and Fluit (as he had nicknamed them, in true Dutch style), proud of the offspring he had produced at his advanced age. Moreover, the boy already showed an interest in military affairs and seemed sure to follow his footsteps to a glorious career; the girl promised to have her mother's good looks.

Rudolph Mac Leod, the chief military officer of the Netherlands, strutted about, the undisputed king of the Sumatran hill. Margaretha seemed to stand at the summit of colonial glory.

And then horror struck the house with the swiftness of lightning:
On June 27, 1899, in the dead of night, a groan came from the nursery. It grew louder and more shrill as the minutes passed. Lamps were lit. Voices called. Running figures scurried through the house.

Margaretha leaped from her bed. Up the stairs. In the direction of the sound. When at last the door of the nursery was thrown open, it revealed a hideous sight.

The two children writhed in their beds. The sheets were covered with black vomit. Their groans had turned to shrieks now. Their bodies were wracked with convulsions that lifted the small bodies and threw them back in grotesque poses across the beds.

Norman's face was almost unrecognizable, so contorted were the features by agony. Non's screams no longer sounded human, but more like those of a small animal in its death throes.

Rudolph ran like a madman from the house in search of the Dutch doctor in town. Margaretha clutched both children to her as she sat on the floor of the nursery, peering ferociously about, as if to defend them—tooth and claw—from approaching death.

By the time the physician arrived, Norman was dead. Non still moved feebly, but there seemed little hope. "Poison, . . . those rotten, murdering natives," he murmured as he wrenched the child from her mother's hands to rush her to the hospital.

The silence was so great that it seemed to throb. Margaretha sat staring into space in the empty nursery.

7 Rites of Initiation

Nothing now seemed to matter. Neither the transfer back to Java which had been ordered by Rudolph's superior officer, nor the monsoons, not even the dismal base of Banjoe Biroe, so different from the glitter of Medan. The tragedy had marked the Mac Leods so deeply that external events had hardly any weight or reality.

Their house stood in a desolate region. There was nothing to see except the mountains, whose timeless face reflected the meaninglessness of human suffering. The days dragged on in deadly torpor. The night were terribly still. Nothing disturbed the silence except an occasional bird cry. The black expanse of trees was unbroken but for a swaying lantern that created a twilight zone at the crossroads.

Margaretha sat always in the same chair, rocking endlessly to and fro, with a blind stare that did not seem to register the details of the scene—the ramshackle barracks and native huts, the swarms of insects, fruit rotting, snakes coiling. Her pose did not change except when her body stiffened at the sound of a bird call that sounded like a child's dying scream.

Then her face contorted. She mumbled phrases to herself, toneless and hoarse, seemingly incoherent: "The nurse . . . the nurse's

lover . . . the servant's wife . . . the children . . . why the children?" The questions continued. She shook her head as if the
answers rattled inside it and, by this act, might fall into place but
soon gave up and sank back into her torpor once more.

If a leaf stirred, she started. Her eyes glowed like those of a mad-
woman. She stared fixedly at a clump of trees, as if the murderer
had emerged from them, then sprang up from her chair, to stab,
choke, disembowel the figure she seemed to see, only to find that
she was attacking the empty air.

At those times, nothing could calm her. Not even the sight of
Non—miraculously saved—playing in the garden with her dolls.
She felt as if one half of her body had been ripped away. The other
reached out to the living child. But each of her gestures came from
a great hollow space and fell short of its destination.

Rudolph had turned into an old man overnight. He roamed
about with faltering steps. At night, she heard him rave in his room,
suffering from delirium tremens or apparitions of ghosts. He complained that something was cracked inside him and had violent
pains in his chest whenever a certain military march was played.
She saw his ravaged face as he wandered about the house in the
evenings and felt a momentary rush of tenderness for him. But
he suddenly turned on her, shrieking: "Bloodsucker . . . filthy
beast! Norman is dead because of you!"

She froze. The consoling gesture stopped in midair, as though
her arm had been suddenly paralyzed. She returned to sit motionless in her chair.

Months passed. Or years. For time seemed impossible to measure or define. Rains came and went. The rice grew tall and was
cut down. Clouds swept the craters of extinct volcanoes. The jungle steamed or was obscured by storms. The cycle of the seasons
took its course.

Slowly, Margaretha's gaze began to encompass the world around
her once more. It fell on books that were lying about: sacred texts,
as timeless as this place; legends that had survived the centuries.

Strange names floated before her eyes; disembodied figures arose, shrouded in mist: *Puranās* . . . *Anangaranga* . . . *Kokashāstra* . . . *Rahasya Kalolini* . . . *Kamasūtra* . . . *Devādasis* . . . *Apsaras* . . . *Suyra* . . . *Kali* . . . *Shiva* . . . *ūrdhvalinga* . . . .

She read on, partly because the words had the effect of an opiate, stilling the pain with their sound, partly because the very strangeness of the tales echoed the estrangement she felt from life. And as she read, she felt something within her change. It was as if old voices were being silenced and new ones had begun to speak. She began to muse about holy pleasure groves, divine afflatus, a god who danced to create the universe. And began to think that perhaps it was not impossible to find the route to another world.

One night, in the spring, as she read, the figures seemed unnaturally vivid, and the words danced before her eyes. Also, she felt so hot that her cheeks burned, and alternately, so chilled that she might have been immersed in an icy stream. It occurred to her that she might be gravely ill.

By the time the doctor arrived, she was delirious. "Typhoid," he said, and looked concerned. Not uncommon in these parts, what with the primitive notions about sanitation these natives had. Why, he had seen one of them wash his face in the same stream in which, above him, another performed his natural functions with great nonchalance. A serious illness, he added. One could only wait and see.

Margaretha was so weak she could not turn her head. She only heard people walk in and out of her room, speak in whispers, stir liquid in a glass, draw the shades. Toward nightfall the fever always rose. It was then that the visions began. They covered the walls, clung to the mosquito net, flew across the ceiling. She saw monsters and deities, fabulous beasts—half elephant, half snake—worshipers who revered the genitals of a goddess, couples endlessly entwined, heroes and dancers, divinities with a dozen arms. Most often she dreamed of Shiva's shrines in which the sacred *lingam* was worshiped, with offerings of rice, flowers, incense, and lights, anointed with melted butter and milk. Once, Rudolph's harsh voice cut into the dream and said: "It's an expensive business, this illness of hers—five bottles of milk a day at one guilder each. . . ."

She went on to dream that she was an Apsaras on the heaven bands of a temple and that a hero from the *Ramayana* addressed her as she passed: "Where are you going, beautiful hips? For whom does the sun rise who will enjoy you? Who will mount into your broad secret parts, like a great golden wheel adorned with a golden band, and which are the embodiment of heaven?" The ardent words were interrupted by a harsh, familiar voice that said: "She's getting worse and worse . . . nothing but skin and bones!"

She drew herself up in her dream and became Kali, the Great Destroyer with a necklace of human skulls, whose womb is Time and to whom mortals and gods alike must bow and submit. (The nurse noticed that the sheets were twisted beneath her and that she was gnashing her teeth.)

For months she lay thus struggling with the dread illness. Only at the beginning of summer did the fever subside and she begin on the road to recovery.

When a pale and gaunt Margaretha returned to the living, she seemed to have undergone a great change. Despite her physical fragility, all those around her could sense a hard, distant strength. It was as if, by an alchemy of suffering, she had emerged tempered and purified.

She wore a triumphant but absent smile and hardly seemed to notice what took place in the world. When Rudolph addressed her, she did not seem to hear. If she answered, it was as if she spoke from a great distance. He did not know how to deal with her. It seemed as though she had sloughed off her former self like an outgrown skin and assumed a new form that remained unknown.

Then she began to disappear for entire days. No one dared to ask her where she went. But rumors began to spread; people began to whisper that she partook of native rituals, studied sacred dances and erotic arts, and joined the temple celebrations. Perhaps she had been hypnotized by the slow, trancelike movements of this dance, the complex rhythms, the magnificent costumes, the music of the *gamelang*, the rituals performed for days in the open air, mingling the splendor of the dancing with the spellbinding beauty of the crowd.

It was impossible to know, for she had become so secretive and aloof that no one dared to pry. They only overheard the natives refer to her as *"Matahari"* among themselves; and saw her respond as gravely as if it were her rightful name. They shook their heads and decided that this strange behavior was the aftermath of the fever and the loss of her son, concluding that it would pass in time.

They could not know that in the crucible of pain a lasting transformation had taken place: Margarethe Zelle Mac Leod had vanished and the Java-born Mata Hari had emerged.

8 Farewell to Sindaglaja

The century had turned. It should have been a new beginning; instead, it seemed like the end. Rudolph had retired from the army in the fall. They now lived in a remote mountain village, Sindaglaja, which some considered idyllic but which, to Margaretha, seemed more like a retreat from life. It might have been a perfect spot for a sanatorium or a home for pensioners, but she, at twenty-four, longed for adventure, risk, and exhilaration. Money was short, activities almost nil. She saw herself chained to an aging, bitter man, weary except for sudden flashes of ill temper, which only increased with the advent of the climacteric years.

Europe welcomed the new century as though the millenium had arrived. General euphoria, prosperity, and a spurt of creation marked the arrival of the modern age. It seemed that everything was brilliantly alive and possible. Although Nietzsche had died at Weimar and Wilde in Paris, a man named Freud had found the key to the interpretation of dreams, and another, named Planck, had discovered the quantum theory.

Paris, quite naturally, was the center of celebration. In the past year, its International Exposition had attracted fifty million visitors, who marveled at the newborn Eiffel Tower, the miracle of the Pont d'Alexandre, which spanned the Seine in a single sweep, the grand new Métro, the "Fairy of Electricity," the *trottoir roulant*, the Palace of Science, the byzantine splendor of the Russian pavilion with its Trans-Siberian railway, the Viennese fantasy in *Art Nouveau*, the glory of Javanese dancers, the paintings of Gauguin, the banks of the Seine transformed into replicas of Venice, the newly finished Sacré Coeur, which stood like a gigantic wedding cake on the hill of Montmartre, where frenetic gaiety reigned at the Chat Noir and the Lapin Agile and Lautrec rubbed elbows with La Goulue and Miss Tinguette.

It was a triumphant moment in history. But the reports of it seemed to come from another planet. How remote it all seemed. How inaccessible! Margaretha devoured the descriptions in the newspapers, which took weeks to arrive. It seemed to her that these were glimpses of the Promised Land. All that was needed was to cross the sea. Alas, there were no plagues of Biblical proportions to convince Rudolph of the inadvisability of her servitude—only his chronic diabetes and rheumatism, which were not sufficiently excruciating to have such an effect—no manna from heaven, no pillar of fire to point the way. Nothing. Only his enraged screams at her enthusiasm: "Hell! If you want so much to go to Paris, well, just go and leave me alone!"

Which was much easier said than done. She had no means of livelihood or transportation. Nor miraculous powers to walk on the waters that separated her from the other side of the world. She wrote to her father but received no help. She fared no better with her sister-in-law. Everyone just advised patience, submission, or compromise.

There was no choice but to bide her time. To wait in silence, exile, and cunning. For she had youth on her side. Rudolph seemed to be rapidly waning and would soon have to leave the tropics once more. They had been here for almost five years now, and his poor health would demand that he be repatriated.

Their battles continued. The village resounded with their shouts, for Margaretha had now begun to retaliate. Non, who had grown into a beautiful child in her fourth year, was usually on her mother's side. She clung to her hand and made faces when her father raged, so that he had to confront two allies, which he found rather disconcerting. He finally wearied of the struggle, and Margaretha began to see signs that he would capitulate.

By early spring he gave in to her clamors, announcing that they would return to Europe. She was triumphant, knowing she had won.

To bid farewell to Sindaglaja was cause for rejoicing, not for tears. In March 1902, the westward journey began. To Margaretha it was more exciting than the voyage East half a decade ago. Europe beckoned. At the start of a new century. And she was returning, a survivor from death, isolation, slavery, with the wealth of the Orient stored in her mind and her senses like precious contraband.

On the horizon, Europe beckoned. Somehow, in an intuitive way, she knew that one day she would have that continent at her feet.

Part 3

I am a lie that always speaks
the truth.
—Jean Cocteau

9 Toward the City of Light

Paris, during *la belle époque*, resembled a great stage on which—though the foundations slowly sank—a fabulous performance was taking place.

The spectator was instantly struck by the splendid décor. Haussmann had designed wide, tree-lined boulevards that opened new vistas, cleared spaces for the great monuments, created a harmonious whole through which the Seine flowed between banks of books, adding color by its barges and *bateaux-mouches,* its sailboats and *bateaux-lavoirs* filled with washerwomen. The perspectives were multiple and revealed marvel after marvel: From the Louvre one saw the new Opera House, from the Pont d'Alexandre the Grand Palais and the Place de la Concorde, from the Champs Elysées (then a huge bridle path flanked by elegant mansions) the Etoile and the Arc de Triomphe. Above the Madeleine, Montmartre rose with its farms and windmills. Far in the distance, one caught a glimpse of the Bois de Boulogne, that "Garden of Woman . . . [where] like the myrtle-alley in the Aeneid, planted for their delight with trees of one kind only [there was] the *Allée des Acacias* . . . thronged by the famous Beauties of the day."

Nor did the costumes fail to equal the magnificence of the stage set. The men wore frock coats with bowlers or top hats, whiskers and boutonnieres; the women, corsets, whalebone and lace, velvet and satin, muffs, bustles, leg-of-mutton sleeves, and voluminous hats. There were street cleaners in striped denim; butchers in leather aprons; grooms in a variety of flamboyant uniforms; gendarmes in smart capes; *chasseurs* in plumes, gold braid, and shining boots; artists with flowing bows and soft berets; skating instructors in "caviar toques and milliner's boots." And in the spotlight stood the *grandes cocottes*, accompanied by wealthy admirers with monocles, gaiters, and white mustaches; envied by the *demi-castors* laden with Lalique jewels in the form of "peacocks holding amethysts in their beaks, cornflowers entwined together, snakes twisted round each other . . . ingenious fauna and flora" in enamel and precious stones.

At the very center of this stage moved the *monstres sacrés:* de Max, Duse, Réjane, and the great Sarah Bernhardt, who, "like some Venetian palace sank beneath the weight of necklaces . . . painted, gilded, engineered, propped up and covered with flags."

Their grandiose gestures were mimed by the general populace, whose actions resembled a series of theatrical flourishes: duels arising from *affaires d'honneur;* murders considered *crimes passionnels;* melodramas at the races at Longchamps; carefully staged entrances at Maxim's; outings on a ten-man bicycle christened *la Décuplette;* feats of daring in flying machines; bon mots uttered by boulevardiers; orations at state funerals; histrionics at banquets and openings of art shows. Noted personalities joined this drama, resulting in the conquest of Paris by Edward VII "le Roi Charmeur"; the social tragedy of the Dreyfus affair; the antics of Alfred Jarry; the poses of the great dandies of the day; the tragicomedies of the demi-monde; the initiation ceremonies of the elite salons—down to the figures traced by the fashionable skaters at the Palais de Glace.

Even the minor actors were a dazzling troupe, from which stars would soon emerge: Rousseau, Modigliani, Picasso, Matisse, Toulouse-Lautrec, Picabia, Klee; Jarry, who had made his literary debut "like a wild animal entering the ring"; Proust, with "his strangely luminous, omnivorous eyes"; Anna de Noailles, seen by Maurice Barrès as "the most sensitive spot in the universe"; the young Colette, in Jean Cocteau's words, "thin, thin . . . a sort of little fox dressed up for cycling, a fox-terrier in skirts"; Cocteau himself, the fair-haired boy, Apollinaire, who had just written "La Chanson du malaimé" but not yet loved Marie Laurencin; Satie, silently walking about with a lit clay pipe in his pocket; Debussy, Ravel; Mistinguette, with "her big cheerful mouth, her animal-like eyes which never smiled, her chestnut curls and silken legs . . . [a] voice that had studied in the school of street cries and newspaper sellers, this voice made for laments"; Yvette Guilbert; the great Otéro, whose face was "a masterpiece of convexity," according to Colette; Emilienne d'Alençon; Cléo de la Mérode, "in her golden cuirass"; Liane de Pougy; Isadora Duncan, who "wanted to live massively, beyond beauty and ugliness, seize hold of life and live it, face to face, eye to eye"; Loïe Fuller, who "discovered the dance of the age"; the clowns Footit and Chocolat; Rastelli the juggler; Blériot the aviator; les Frères Lumière of the cinema; "Wild Miss Barney"; Ida Rubinstein, "thin, long, glaucous," discovered by Diaghilev in a Russian ghetto; Renée Vivien and the rest of the Amazons; Emma Calvé, Henri de Rothschild, Mme Kiréevsky, Emile Guimet, and other patrons of the arts.

The stage lighting had switched from candles to electricity; the music from waltzes to the cakewalk and something new, wild, and exhilarating known as jazz.

Altogether, it was a never to be forgotten spectacle.

Far from these footlights a small figure struggled in the wings, advanced, and was driven back, appeared vanquished yet would not retreat: Many miles away, in Holland, Margaretha found a setting far less glorious than she had imagined while in her Javanese retreat. She had not reckoned with stolid Dutch society, which did not seem to have changed with the turn of the century. Old rules still held. A husband was the undisputed ruler in his house. Rilke's judgment of Holland seemed full of truth to her. It was a bitter defeat after the triumph of the homecoming.

A few weeks after their return to the Old World, Margaretha found herself alone, beaten and deserted by Rudolph, who took Non with him. She was stunned for a day or so, the blow had been so sudden and complete. Then her newly resolute self took over; in a daring gesture of revolt it was *she* who demanded a legal separation before the Amsterdam tribunal (an unheard-of audacity in those days).

Much to her amazement, she was almost instantly vindicated. The separation was granted in her favor. The court ruled that Rudolph was to return Non to her mother and pay 100 guilders a month for their support. She rejoiced over her victory and embraced Non so fiercely that the child almost began to cry.

For a short time she relished the feeling of revenge and superiority and decided to revise her estimation of Dutch society. Perhaps she had been too rash in her condemnation; justice was possible even in these hinterlands of Europe. But when September and the first support payment came around, she realized that the distinction between the law and its application was great indeed. Rudolph refused to pay, claiming poverty, and got away with this lie. And she was powerless to insist on the court's ruling being enforced. It all looked very equitable on paper, but, in fact, she was left penniless with a young child. Without a personal income, a profession, or a husband, a woman in her country was as good as lost, she knew.

To make matters worse, Rudolph (as once before in very different circumstances) placed an ad in all the Amsterdam newspapers that read:

I request all and sundry not to supply goods or services to my estranged wife Margaretha Mac Leod-Zelle . . .

To add injury to insult, he informed everyone he knew that she had deserted him and thereby broken his heart.

Thus branded publicly as an outcast and a menace to decent

men, Margaretha had little hope of surviving. She tried to find work but had no skills that were marketable. For a while she tried to study acting at the Toonel School, but it seemed hopeless to begin such a career at her age. Driven farther and farther into the shadowy outer reaches of society, she went to live in the Van Woostraat, the red-light district of Amsterdam.

She could not properly care for Non with her way of life. It was dreadful to see the child hungry and cold. Margaretha thought, with something resembling nostalgia, of the warmth and plenitude of the Javanese soil. At least there poverty had a far less sharp sting, for one could live on the fruits that fell to the ground and lie in the shadow of coconut palms, accused of no greater crime than indolence and sloth. It cut her to the quick to see Non eagerly look forward to visits to her father's house in which food and fuel could be had in abundance, and no one made snide remarks when one turned into one's hallway.

When Non did not return from one of these visits, Margaretha felt too broken to insist, knowing that the child could only end in shame among these outlawed or fall ill as a result of so much deprivation.

She was utterly alone now. Since she was also homeless, she began to wander from relative to relative: her uncle Taconis at The Hague (where she had stayed before reading that fateful ad in the newspaper); another uncle—by marriage—at Nijmegen; even, as the last resort, her father's house. It was hateful to be reduced to a state akin to alms taking. Whatever remained of her pride rebelled against such humiliation.

Perhaps it would be best to try her luck elsewhere. She remembered the accounts of Paris she had read in the Indies: the splendid theaters, the prosperity, the freedom of artistic life, the appreciation of beautiful women. It certainly sounded better than braving public opinion on Dutch soil.

Having scraped together the fare, she decided to risk the trip to the French capital in 1903. It was with pounding heart that she saw the train pull into the Gare du Nord and the voyagers descend like bees flying straight to the hive. She felt small and insignificant as she hung back from the crowd, about to enter the splendid metropolis she had so long imagined but must now encounter face to face, alone.

The city dazzled her but paid her no heed. She wandered from one theatrical agency to another, becoming discouraged as she was repeatedly turned away. She tried modeling for painters but was forced to stand without moving in icy garrets, pawed and ill paid. There remained nothing to try except brothels and third-rate music halls. It was a far cry from what she had imagined. She realized that here also she would only sink into poverty and degradation.

Besides, threats from Rudolph pursued her wherever she went. He swore to sue her for desertion, to have her committed to a state institution for incorrigibles and to take Non away permanently, unless she returned instantly. The law appeared to be on his side. She knew that she had no recourse against him and remembered the vicious lengths he had gone to before.

And so she returned, her hopes and spirit broken.

It was in the winter that she thought she had reached the bottom rung of the ladder, and despair. She was exiled in the desolate province of North Brabant, watched over by Rudolph's relatives like a dangerous criminal. If she complained, he jeeringly offered to let her enter a convent as an alternative and threatened her with lawsuit if she made the slightest move. She wrote letters to her relatives, pleading for help, but without faith in their efficacy. In one especially she described her sense of exile and humiliation:

Behold me then, condemned to remain here, here where there exists only the shadow of a gray and humid hearth in which only the copper pots have a right to shine in the pale sunlight. Where there is only the silent, grave, hostile street, in which an alien footstep calls the audacious housewives to windows shrouded in lace curtains. Here, where a small tulip shudders in the winter winds. Here, where the fog, the soft fog, veils everything and blankets to a silvery chime the strokes of the municipal carillion. Here, there is the incessant overseeing of beldams and matrons who have vaguely heard reports of a flight to Paris and dances in theaters. Here, in fact, is shame . . .

Suddenly, without warning, she broke out of her prison. It was a desperate move, burning all bridges behind her, allowing no chance of return; a leap into nowhere, with the risk of mortal injury. But it led away from the silence, the hostile eyes, the fog, the righteous beldams, the long humiliation.

Penniless, childless, unknown, unskilled, at the end of her youth and virtually at the end of her strength as well, she landed in Paris once more.

She had half a franc in her pocket, a revolver in her handbag, and a brazen smile on her face as she sauntered into the Grand Hotel during one of the last days of the winter of 1904–1905.

In the shadowy wings of the great theater that was Paris, this obscure character was about to take the plunge that would land her stage center in a blaze of lights.

10 Among Buddhas and Amazons

The spring of 1905 was an exciting season. The German crown prince took a bride; in Moscow, the grand duke was assassinated; the Dreyfus case was once again reopened; a man named Einstein wrote his doctoral thesis on a new theory of relativity; Jules Verne died; John D. Rockefeller was cured of a stomach ailment by means of electricity; the Salon des Indépendants opened; there was mutiny on the *Potemkin*; Gabriel Fauré was named director of the Paris Conservatory, and Anatole Deibler official executioner; Richard Strauss fought to preserve the necrophilia of *Salomé*; Baron Alphonse de Rothschild was buried; the *Fauves* shocked Paris, making the critics feel they had wandered into a "wild animal cage"; Chaliapin was at the Opéra; Otéro starred in *La Dominicaine*; Sarah Bernhardt was publishing her memoirs; de Max played in *Le Talisman*; Duse was returning with her troupe after the great success of Gorki's *Lower Depths*; the Comédie Française was rehearsing *L'Espionne* of Sardou; the double bill at the Grand Guignol featured *La Dernière Torture* and *Un Début dans le monde*.

Another debut was about to take place: On March 13, 1905, the halls and staircases of the celebrated Musée Guimet were crowded with *"le gratin"* of Paris's artistic, scientific, and literary world. Ambassadors rubbed elbows with aristocrats, industrialists with orientalists, millionaires with maestros, poets with panders, amateurs with "Amazons." Monsieur Guimet had sent out over 600 invitations, and to judge by the crowd, there were few who had declined.

The culture buffs and the culture seekers jostled each other in the lobby. The ladies emerged from their silken wraps as from cocoons. The men handed their top hats gingerly to the *vestiaire*, who arranged them in long rows on her shelves. A low murmur of civilized discourse filled the hall; it swelled with each new wave of arrivals and ebbed as they took their positions in the crowd. Now and then, all heads lifted, as incense came wafting down the stairs and the guests sniffed the air like hounds on the scent of a prey.

The anticipation grew greater as the hour of the performance approached. Ascending the stairs, the crowd strained forward, eager to reach the upper level, where the spectacle would take place. When they reached the dome-shaped hall, a splendid sight awaited them:

The rotunda had been transformed into an Indian temple. Its eight columns were garlanded with flowers, stretching up towards the round balcony on the floor above . . . The light of candles deepened the atmosphere, while one of Monsieur Guimet's most prized eleventh century statues, a three-foot high, four-armed Siva Nataraja from southern India, surrounded by a circle of flames and crushing a dwarf with one of its bronze feet, emerged floodlit from the background . . .

When the audience was settled, Emile Guimet stepped from among an array of buddhas and introduced the performance of sacred dances from the East that was about to take place. A hushed tremor ran through the crowd, as if already under the spell of an exotic ritual.

[Then] sounds of a strange music were heard . . . In the mysterious light there appeared a silhouette of a woman. As the eyes became accustomed to the semi-darkness, the silhouette took on a more definite form. It was that of a tall, handsome creature with a heavy mass of black hair . . . A golden collar round her throat and several strings of pearls on her arms and legs . . . almost naked, she began to "dance." Slow, voluptuous movements wove into the pattern of the strange music; as the rhythms quickened, so quickened her movements.

Her undulating body floated with infinite grace among the disarray of veils and the intoxicating odor of perfumes. Her look contained all the *fauve* languor of a true Oriental.

The audience appeared spellbound. It was as if all their senses had been aroused, and "the spectators—both male and female—led to the very limits of interest permitted by decency." Their hands joined in thunderous applause, mingled with exclamations of desire and curiosity. Whispers ran through the crowd, eyes searched the darkness for the woman who was the source of such intense enthusiasm. Who was she? From what far-off place? What magic rites had she performed?

Emile Guimet stepped forward again. The woman emerged from the shadows and stood beside him in the candle glow. Wrapped in a sari now, which hid the curves she formerly had revealed, she remained silent while he spoke, introducing her as Mata Hari, Hindu dancer, who had "come to honor the museum and the Parisians with the dances of the Devadasis and present the sacred art of expressing, by harmonious gestures, the far-off mysteries of vanished cults."

The audience again broke into applause, entranced by the explanation, which added a cultural justification for their sensual response and raised it above the instinctual level that they might have been somewhat reticent to advertise.

Mata Hari bowed, heaping erudition upon eroticism as, in a low musical voice, she chanted:

My dance is a sacred poem in which each movement is a word and whose every word is underlined by music.

The temple in which I dance can be vague or faithfully reproduced, as here today. For I am the temple.

All true temple dances are religious in nature and all explain, in gestures and poses, the rules of the sacred texts.

One must always translate the three stages which correspond to the divine attributes of Brahma, Vishnu, and Shiva—creation, fecundity, destruction . . . By means of destruction towards creation through incarnation, that is what I am dancing—that is what my dance is about.

She further dazzled the spectators when she graciously translated her speech into English, Dutch, German, and Javanese, as easily as she had given it in French.

Everyone concluded that the event was truly phenomenal.

In the days that followed, all of Paris spoke of the beautiful woman named Mata Hari (even if they frequently misspelled her name) and of the exotic art she practiced. In the newspapers, exuberant (although not always grammatical) descriptions appeared:

Tall and slender, she carries a marvelous neck, supple and the color of amber, a fascinating face that makes a perfect oval and whose sybilline and tempting expression strikes everyone at first sight. The mouth, firmly outlined, traces a mobile line, disdainful, very alluring, under a nose, straight and fine, the nostrils of which quiver above two shadowy dimples. Her magnificent eyes, velvety and dark, are slightly slanting and set with long curving lashes—they are enigmatic, seeming to look into the beyond. Her black hair, divided in two bands, makes for her face a dark and wavy frame. The effect is voluptuous, possessing a magic beauty and an astonishing purity of outline.

The fashionable papers also revealed that Mata Hari had been born in the south of India at Jaffnapatam on the Malabar coast; that she came from a Brahmin family; that, by reason of his piety and pureness of heart, her father was called Assirvadam, which means "The Blessing of God"; that her mother, a dancer at Kanda Swany, died in giving her birth when she was only fourteen years old; that the priests who adopted the child gave her the name of Mata Hari; that from her earliest youth, she was shut up in a great underground world in the temple of the god Shiva until the high priestess consecrated her to his service and taught her the mysteries of love and faith one spring night in the Sakty-Pudja.

They also quoted her pronouncements on her antecedents:

My mother was a glorious temple dancer who died on the day I was born. When I reached the threshold of womanhood, my foster mother saw in me a predestined soul and resolved to dedicate me to Shiva . . . It was on the purple granite altar of Kanda Swany that, at the age of thirteen, I danced for the first time, completely nude.

It would have been impossible to guess that this mysterious stranger who suddenly appeared in the limelight of the Paris scene was, in reality, Margaretha Zelle Mac Leod.

To those who witnessed her birth as a star, it was as miraculous as Aphrodite's rise from the sea foam. They knew nothing of the long years of gestation that produced this phenomenon, a metamorphosis in which the dismal events of her past life were, as by some sleight of hand, changed into legend.

They did not see the defiant resolve with which she had attempted every possible use of her talents: seductiveness, dancing and horsemanship. She had made efforts to become a circus rider and as a result met Ernest Molier (the wealthy owner of the Cirque Molier) at his home on the rue Benouville. He had asked to see her dance and, when she had done so, exclaimed: "This is different from anything we have in Paris. The only thing resembling it are the Annamite dances performed some years ago by Mlle Cléo de la Mérode!" And he strongly advised her to dance. Margaretha took his advice and began to experiment with appearances in various elegant salons, changing her name to fit the occasion to Lady Gresha Mc Leod and letting it be known that she had been born in Java of European parents and married to Sir George Mc Leod, a colonel in the Dutch colonial army, now unfortunately deceased. One hostess vied with another to have her perform. She danced at the home of Lalique, for the Countess T————, for Mme Kiré-evsky. It was after a performance at the latter's house that she met Emile Guimet, the museum owner, and his director Monsieur de Milloué. Both appear to have been convinced of the authenticity of her Hindu dances, and it was decided that she should make her first public appearance at the Musée Guimet of Asiatic Arts on the Place d'Iéna, which housed a treasure of objects from the East and functioned as a center of study for orientalists. For the purposes of this debut, a change of name seemed indicated since one suggesting Scottish origins was certainly less fitting than one that would invoke a sacred *bayadère*. Thus, Mata Hari was born.

To those who had observed the evolution from Margaretha Zelle Mac Leod to Mata Hari, it might have looked simply like an unerring instinct for showmanship, a clever publicity stunt, the exploitation of a current fad for oriental dance, but to those who had some insight into her life of the past decade, the change of name had a more fundamental meaning and spoke of an alteration of identity that would have far-reaching consequences.

At this moment, however, it seemed that with the advent of a new name, a new life had begun. Her luck appeared to have turned. In the space of one night, she had become the sensation of the season. The owners of the most exclusive salons vied for her presence. She was asked to appear at the Baron Henri de Rothschild's and at the home of Cécile Sorel (the celebrated actress of the Comédie Française), at Arthur Meyer's, at the mansion of Menier (the chocolate king), at Emma Calvé's "before a portable altar that she used as a backdrop, supported by a group of musicians . . . snakelike and enigmatic . . . causing dithyrambic raptures," in the house of Mme de Loynes, who had requested that she be less dressed than at her last appearance and perform "for women only."

She made one of her most memorable presentations of the season, however, in the garden of a villa at Neuilly before a group of "Amazons" on May 5, 1905, which was remembered by one of the guests, Colette:

Suddenly, from behind a screen of foliage, a naked woman appeared on a white horse whose trappings were studded with turquoises, a dancer whose name was already famous among her followers—: Mata Hari—. The fashionable public had seen a supple torso, a proud and agile back, muscular loins, long thighs and slim knees . . . In the May sunshine, at Neuilly however, despite the turquoises and the black loose mane of hair, despite the diadem made of tinsel, despite, above all, the long thigh against the flank of her Arabian steed, she disconcerted one by the color of her skin which was no longer brown and luscious as in artificial light, but a dubious, uneven purple.

But despite the sharp eye of this observer (and her even sharper tongue), Mata Hari triumphed among the "Amazons," just as she had among the buddhas of Monsieur Guimet. Miss Barney, the "Wild Girl from Cincinnati," invited her to another garden party at her house on the rue Jacob, in which the famous Temple de l'Amitié stood (which Proust, in a Freudian slip, referred to as the Temple de l'Amour) and a select band of liberated women artists met.

The triumphs multiplied. She danced six times that spring at the Trocadéro Theater, in a setting approximating that of the Musée Guimet. During the summer, Gabriel Astruc (the impresario of Chaliapin and Diaghilev) had taken her under his wing and booked her at the Olympia, where she appeared in the sumptuous production of "Le Rêve." Her wildest dream had indeed been realized.

Only six months after her debut, Paris lay at Mata Hari's feet.

11 The Conquest of Europe

In the space of nine months France was entirely conquered. Victory followed victory. Foreign correspondents and domestic journalists thronged the luxurious apartment to which Mata Hari had moved from her shabby rooming house, crowded around the carriage in which she drove; photographers caught her image in every possible pose: at the piano, in her dressing room, at the fashionable restaurants, the races, the galas, the benefits. Her portrait was being painted, her handwriting analyzed, her every wish and whim gratified. She could boast of victory over her rivals, of lucrative contracts, and of cultist adoration.

And her empire seemed to be expanding constantly. London sent its emissaries. St. Petersburg, despite the Bolshevik Revolution, offered to open the city gates to her. Berlin and Vienna welcomed her triumphal entry into the Austro-Hungarian Empire. Beyond the Alps, Milan and Rome lay waiting for her arrival. Monte Carlo was preparing for her appearance.

The conquest of Europe had begun.

The first campaign, after Paris, was Madrid. In January 1906, during the coldest time of the winter, she appeared in the capital of a country in which children dance as soon as they walk and aficionados watch the movements of a dancer's feet with the same intensity as the twirls of a bullfighter's cape. It was not an easy audience to conquer, she knew. Her performance that night must outdo her usual act. She felt as though she were stepping into an arena as she moved toward the footlights.

When she had stopped dancing, the thunder of applause rose to meet her. Applause sounded different here, perhaps because of the hollow the Spaniards created between their palms as they clapped. It continued to swell each time she bowed, with a sound like that of a thousand castanets.

Spain was conquered. Victory was hers once more. The audience was on its feet now. Flowers covered the stage. Unknown figures paid her homage from boxes decorated with varied crests. Guttural cries voiced their adulation. The applause followed her long after she had left the stage and the curtains had been drawn.

But in her dressing room, among the cosmetics and face creams, the jewels, the magnificent costumes, surrounded by wardrobe mistresses, makeup artists, *masseuses,* and vast displays of flowers that contained discreetly attached cards with coats of arms, messages of amorous capitulation, offers of titles, treasures, and territories, assurances of eternal servitude, kudos by artists of renown, Mata Hari sat, reclining in an armchair, musing.

She had a pensive look on her face that might have passed for sadness. "This spoiled darling, upon whom destiny had showered gifts, grace, talent, fame," the portrait painter Namur said, "rarely lost the expression of inmost sadness . . . I cannot recall that I ever saw Mata Hari smile." True, she had everything she could have dreamed of a few short months ago when she was only an obscure figure in a Paris railroad station. So rapid had been her rise to fame that it seemed, to outsiders, that she should reflect her good fortune in a permanently radiant smile.

But she continued to sit in her armchair, musing.

Perhaps the past still clung to her in moments of calm after the tumult of the stage. Perhaps she wondered what the future could hold. Most probably, however, she was preoccupied with present cares (of which her audience had no indication, preferring to see its idols as two-dimensional as tinseled paper dolls): the lawyer who had recently appeared in Paris to induce her to divorce Rudolph, who was ready to remarry; the fate of Non, whom she had seen for an instant between trains at the Arnheim station and who had hardly recognized her in her chic clothes; reports of her father's sudden interest in her, now that she had achieved fame; Rudolph's rankling remark, "She's got flat feet and can't dance"; or the harsh graphologist's analysis of her handwriting:

The striking thing about this handwriting is the excessive, impulsive strength of the lines and their contrasting nature . . . All these contradictory impulses reveal a tumultuous, chaotic inner life which affects the worth of all the subject's activities . . . One cannot trust such a changeable, agitated, restless nature which is always ready for extreme moves. Nothing can hold back this impetuous, fearless character which does not measure obstacles and is overly confident of its destiny . . . One of the most marked characteristics of this personality is exaggeration: it is a dangerous tendency, for it obscures judgment, results in a lack of foresight, produces blind rages, hasty resolutions, an inability to measure the consequences of actions . . . This personality is characterized by great *sang-froid* and terrifying resolve, based both on courage and blindness . . . The motives of the subject's actions are: egotism, calculation and pride . . . The handwriting reveals a strong need to please and to be visible, as well as a lot of self-confidence . . . a taste for luxury which leads to excessive spending and a harsh, inflexible desire to acquire wealth . . . these passions, together with a blinding tendency toward exaggeration, expose the subject to all temptations . . . There is evidence of very refined taste and originality, a cultivated appreciation of the harmonious and the beautiful, a remarkably alert mind . . . It is the exalted, excessive nature of the subject which obscures reality, and leads to lies . . . This nature is in constant conflict, alternating between equally passionate expressions of imprudent truthfulness and the most monstrous lies . . . An extremely complex personality, of rare vigor . . . one which could undertake the most surprising actions, due to the intensity of its passions, its penchant for excess, and its blindness . . . .

It was indeed an analysis (or an augury) which gave one much to think about. And very little cause for smiles.

During the months that followed, despite her triumphs at the Nice carnival, where she rode in the invisible garb of Venus through the flower-decked streets, in Monte Carlo, where she received the homages of Puccini and Massenet while dancing in *Le Roi Lahore*, in Vienna, where all the newsboys shouted "Isadora Duncan is dead. Long live Mata Hari!," proclaiming her the new queen of the Austrian empire, she continued not to smile and mused for long hours in her dressing room.

It hardly seemed to matter that in "the heart of Europe" they agreed that the Vestal was dead and Venus had triumphed; nor that she had, upon her arrival, started a war that divided the city into two camps as hard to reconcile as the Capulets and the Montagues (and all that, simply because she had danced naked at her first appearance and subsequently had donned tights). Despite her vanquished rivals; despite entering her second triumphant season; despite having launched—if not a thousand ships—dozens of news items, she appeared pensive and somewhat melancholy off-stage. Her mind was certainly preoccupied with the part of her life that, to her audiences, remained unseen: Rudolph had succeeded in getting a divorce, with all the "wrongs" on her side ("debauchery" . . . "adultery") and had almost instantly remarried, a woman almost thirty years younger than he; Non had already been sent to live with another family, obviously at her stepmother's request, a bitter lot, as she remembered from her own past; her father had published a book that was supposedly her biography, which had been countered by a hostile exposé from the pen of Rudolph's lawyer, both cashing in on her fame, or infamy.

The only amusing news at this period in her life was that a Dutch tobacco manufacturer had put out a "Mata Hari" cigarette containing only "the best Sumatra and choice Turkish tobaccos." She would relish smoking this homage to herself in her exotic cigarette holder.

On the threshold of a new year she mused more than ever about the past, appraised the present (already somewhat weary of her easy triumphs), and restlessly surveyed the future for challenges yet untried. Perhaps she should explore new lands.

Egypt was tempting, with its age-old dances, its art treasures un-equaled for magnificence, the stillness of sphinxes half buried in sand, the Valley of the Kings . . . .

The year 1907 was one of many travels for Mata Hari. The first voyage took her from Marseilles to Alexandria (—a sea crossing quite different from her last one when she had been only an obscure colonialist wife returning to Dutch soil). Journalists pursued and devoured every word she uttered; her whims were no sooner ex-pressed than immortalized in print. Once weary of forever being classified as the "famous Hindu dancer, the exponent of the sacred dances of the East" and feeling badgered about her Indian snake number (in which supposedly, she appeared on stage with a huge, living python, moving her body "in a rhythm more serpentine than anything that had ever been seen,") she pouted and said the first thing that came into her mind, only to find her mood of the moment instantly recorded in the newspapers: "She has renounced Shiva and his cult . . . she has adopted Berlin and speaks German without the slightest oriental accent . . . she hopes to settle on the banks of the Spree." Mata Hari only shrugged at the foibles of the publicity hounds and continued her travels.

Alexandria . . . Assuan . . . a voyage along the Nile (in the wake of Cleopatra's barge) . . . the Sphinx of Giza . . . the land west of Thebes . . . Karnak . . . the great pyramids; nomads and grave robbers; men with lips as chiseled as those of the sculpted figures; women in black outlined against the desert. And everywhere the colossal statues of the impassive gods.

She felt renewed by this ancient land. Time had a different dimension here. And human cares seemed puny against the serene backdrop of thousands of years.

When she returned to tour Europe, it was in a different frame of mind. Success continued to follow in her footsteps wherever she danced—Berlin, London, Rome, Amsterdam, Monte Carlo—but she felt somehow above it all. It was lovely to be back in Paris once more. She settled at the elegant Hotel Meurice, which suited her taste extremely well; made an appearance frequently at Longchamps to see the races; let herself be photographed in her sumptuous wardrobe by the top fashion magazines, as well as by the famed Reutlinger; did charitable works by dancing at benefits; shone at the Trocadéro with Sasha Guitry and Cécile Sorel. She was now the undisputed "Star of the Dance," of greater magnitude, it appeared, than her rival luminaries Isadora Duncan, Mme Otéro, Cléo de la Mérode, Loïe Fuller, Lola Montez. Admiring audiences hung on every word, as she explained her favorite "Sacred Flower Dance":

It is the legend of the Goddess who has the power to incarnate herself in the flower which is burned as an offering to her . . . The prince enters the temple with orchids, burns them before her and, becoming filled with ecstasy as he breathes in the smoke, he rises and begins to dance . . . He implores the Goddess who sits on the altar like a bronze statue . . . The priestess who personifies her rises, incarnates herself in the flower and speaks the prophesy whose fundamental meaning is this: "You shall die, as everything must die. Live for the beautiful and glorious moments. It is better to live on earth for a few short and intense instants and to pass away, than to drag about through old age without beauty or joy."

And sometimes Mata Hari wondered whether she herself would fulfill this prophesy.

But at the moment, she was more concerned with dancing the role of Salomé. It had preoccupied her for several years now, ever since the time of her debut when one critic had written of her: "She danced like Salammbô before Tanit, like Salomé before Herod." Now that Strauss had written a work of sinister beauty that did justice to the words of Wilde, and it had been refused performance in London, Berlin, and Vienna on grounds of sacrilege, she was especially eager to undertake the role. What intrigued her most, of course, was the scene central to the controversy, the one in which "Iokanaan's head, made up in realistic pallor of death with appropriate gore, was held in full view, and Salomé's seven veils were ritually discarded one by one while Herod leered." It seemed custom-tailored to her talents. She could see herself as "Salomé pouring out her hot erotic pleas to the eyes, the hair, the limbs, the body and the love of Iokanaan," followed by a "voluptuous dance to excite King Herod's lust and win her ghastly desire." She had to have that part.

Astruc had served her well in the past. She wrote to him about the role while in Rome. And to make doubly certain, to Strauss himself. But she received no replies. She fumed and raged, finding no solace in dancing Cleopatra in Monte Carlo and Paris. The Egyptian queen's powers of seduction suddenly seemed like mere child's play to her when compared to the lethal charms of Salomé.

Moreover, Antoine, the director, complaining of her "pride," had had the presumption to fire her. Never before had she endured such an effrontery. She instantly resorted to lawyers, bringing a suit against him for breach of contract. But although she won the case and was awarded 200 gold francs for the performance in Monte Carlo, the role of Cleopatra was spoiled for her. Let Ida Rubinstein do the part. She had heard that she had already been shown to Antoine, "wrapped in a bunch of rugs, which they put in the middle of the stage . . . then unrolled, unwrapped . . . and Madama Ida Rubinstein appeared, with legs so slim that she resembled an ibis from the Nile."

The temptress in her clamored for Salomé. But she would have to wait a while for that desire to be realized.

In 1910, she disappeared mysteriously from the Paris scene. It was rumored that she was living in a castle, riding horses in the idyllic French countryside. When she returned, in 1911, she had a villa of her own in Neuilly. The stables were stocked with splendid thoroughbreds; a new motorcar stood before the gate. She gave soirées in her garden and on those evenings the lawns overflowed with *"gros légumes"* of every variety to watch her perform her celebrated dances, accompanied by her own orchestra of Indian musicians, led by Inayat Khan. The audiences particularly appreciated those dances which, Mata Hari announced, were traditionally performed "in the temple of Vishnu during the festival of the

Moon, mother of earthly Fecundity" and that she gave "on those beautiful nights at the end of summer when the pale gold crescent reigns and magnificently evokes the eternal symbol by which they are inspired."

But she had other symbols to evoke as well. Gabriel Astruc had arranged for her to dance the role of Venus at La Scala in Milan. The magnificent opera house to which all the greatest stars aspired suited her dreams of splendor. The opulent audience, arriving for performances clad like royalty, the sumptuous appointments of the hall, the grandiose production in which she portrayed the most powerful and irresistible of the goddesses, were a fitting tribute to her, she felt. The fluttering attentions of the director, who whispered "creatura adorabile . . ." each time he perceived her, the thunderous applause of the effusive Italian audience, the enthusiastic acclaim of the critics, were simply a fitting recognition of her glorious endowments. Everyone proclaimed that this was the greatest triumph of her career. She did not like to think of it this way for to have reached the summit implied that a descent must follow. She preferred to dwell on other peaks still to be conquered.

One of these was her appearance in *Salomé*, which was finally arranged. True, it was not to take place in one of the great public halls of the continent, but she thought it even more fitting that she should dance this orgiastic, trancelike incarnation of lust and bloodlust in the land of the Borgias, at the home of Prince di Faustino, the magnificent Palazzo Barberini. As she danced, portraying the role of woman as seducer and betrayer, she felt she reached the culmination of her desires and, in some intuitive way, the revelation of her true self.

For some reason she began to think almost constantly of her daughter. In 1911, Non was thirteen. At that age, Mata Hari had been abandoned by her father and would soon lose her mother. Non, also, was as good as orphaned, living in miserable straits in Velp, a small town in the dismal Dutch countryside, her mother in some distant land, seemingly lost.

Mata Hari began to plot how to have her daughter abducted and to take her to live in splendor, sharing all her triumphs. Most of all, she wanted to hold her as she had done on that dreadful night in June so many years ago. It was a complicated plan, involving an old and faithful servant who would go to Velp, wait for Non as she came out of school, and board the next train with her to Paris.

But Anna, the servant, came back from Holland alone. The kidnaping attempt had misfired, for Rudolph had arrived at the school that afternoon and intercepted Mata Hari's agent. Non was hastily taken away by her father, unable even to receive the gift that had been meant to lure her to the railroad station.

The dream of regaining her daughter was shattered. The joys of motherhood were evidently not in the cards for Mata Hari.

Another dream, however, came close to being realized, so close that she loudly announced its successful outcome: to dance with Diaghilev's Ballet Russe. She had been watching this fabulous troupe "in which all the fever and fecundity of the hour seemed captured," its leading dancers Pavlova and Nijinsky, and especially "the barbaric and gorgeous talent of Léon Bakst . . . [his] voluptuous physical spectacles and intoxicating colors." She remembered their first sensation, *Cleopatra*, in which the "sorceress of the Nile . . . Ida Rubinstein . . . [was] borne on a palanquin surrounded by a whirling bacchanal of veils and rose leaves arranged to conceal the fact that she was as yet barely trained as a dancer" and others that followed, equally magnificent, for which Bakst designed the sets and costumes of "houris of the Sultan's harem, bacchantes from Greek vases . . . forest creatures in green and gold suggesting the sparkling beauty of spotted pythons." It seemed to her that only he could clothe her fittingly, for the world of his imagination was peopled with the kind of creatures she preferred to incarnate.

In 1912, the Ballet Russe was preparing *L'Après-midi d'un Faune*, in which Nijinsky would dance the title role "in skin-fitting tights painted in animal spots, with a tiny tail, a wig of tight curls made of gold, and two little curling horns." It was rumored that he would mime sexual consummation on stage. She also heard that, during his dinners at Larue with Diaghilev, Bakst, and Cocteau, he moved his head as though he were suffering from a stiff neck. Diaghilev and Bakst worriedly interrogated him, without being able to get any answer. They only learned later that he was practicing to carry the weight of the horns.

The whole troupe fascinated Mata Hari. Their colorfulness, their eccentricities, their daring, were what her restless spirit craved. Besides, they were a sensation. She was determined to become one of the group.

It was arranged that she should meet Diaghilev, Fokine, Nijinsky, and Bakst in Monte Carlo. Her first view, in 1912, of Diaghilev, whom she had been attempting to meet for quite a while, was rather disconcerting: "He seemed to wear the smallest hat in creation, for his head was so large that every hat was too small for him. His dancers called him 'Chinchilla,' because of an isolated white lock in his very black dyed hair . . . He wore a tightly fitting fur coat with an opossum collar . . . buttoned up with safety pins." It was certainly a surprising get-up for a man of his fame.

He did not seem much impressed with her fame, either. For he received her in the theater in which his dancers were rehearsing without any ado. For a while she was too nonplused to speak and simply watched him as he ground one tooth on the edge of his mouth, "seated in the back part of the loge from where he watched his artists to whom he handed on no advice . . . his wet eye looking downward." This was the man who had discovered some of the greatest stars of the century! He seemed laconic in his appraisal of her, which was also unexpected. She was not accustomed to such indifference, having had only adulation for many years and expecting that he would immediately pay homage to her great talents and engage her on the spot.

It was an angry and surprised Mata Hari who swept out of the theater. She would not be outraged in this manner again but deal only through intermediaries. Let her manager do the negotiating.

She learned that Diaghilev was reticent about her and not at all inclined to sign a contract without having seen her dance. It was outrageous to suggest such a thing, with her reputation. She fumed.

But he continued to stall. And she flew into rage after rage. To make matters worse, Bakst asked to examine her to see what costume—or lack of costume—would suit her figure and the role she was to incarnate. Not that she minded undressing before an audience; it was certainly something she was accustomed to. She wrote to Astruc in a tone of outrage: "I undressed *completely* before Bakst in my room, which is sufficient." But Bakst did not seem overwhelmed or even greatly inspired by what he saw. For she was never asked to dance with the Ballet Russe.

The horrible thought occurred to her that she might be on the decline.

There was no solace in the fact that *this* was referred to as the "year of miracles": the year of Cubism's triumph, Stravinsky's *Rites of Spring*, Proust's *Swann's Way*, Apollinaire's *Alcools*, the return of Valéry, *Lafcadio's Adventures* by Gide . . . , when all the arts flourished in the hothouse of culture that was Paris in 1913, like those flowers that gardeners cause to bloom exorbitantly, just before they perish, by cutting away the roots.

Her own art seemed on the verge of perishing. For her there were no rites of rejuvenation, no intoxicating triumph, no return, and certainly no season of miracles. She began to have fewer and less exclusive bookings of late. And these were no longer in great theaters but in music halls. Perhaps she should vary her repertoire, for a whole crop of self-styled "Eastern Dancers" had begun to imitate her style. Even Loïe Fuller had gotten into the act, performing "A Thousand and One Nights" with a troupe of Arab dancers now.

She turned to Spanish dances for her engagement at the Folies-Bergères and read with some satisfaction the accounts that appeared in the newspapers:

Mata Hari performs in the costume of Spain . . . retracing the old dances of Andalusia . . . lascivious and captivating, in which the body assumes feline poses . . . It is the power of feminine charm at its greatest which she succeeds in expressing in these dances.

But the return of Isadora Duncan was a threat to her. Her assurance was gone. She began to feel the humiliating stings of decline. Even the appearances she made in the homes of wealthy friends and admirers, such as the Marquis de Givenchy, seemed to her now almost like consolation prizes given to a loser. Her pride would not allow her to show her wounded self-esteem. She masked the gnawing fears by smiles, the wrinkles in her skin by makeup, the graying hairs by dye. Only now and then a letter to a friend revealed her anguish. She wrote to L. Dumur, a writer she knew: "Protect me from the *many, many things which hurt me* and take away my desire to work. . . . I want to work again and forsake my life of ease for all the worries that glory necessarily brings with it; I want to feel there is honor in what I do."

She turned to old and faithful friends in an attempt to find a way of renewing her work. Emile Guimet, with his knowledge of religions and arts, might be able to help her prepare for the launching of an Egyptian ballet. He knew experts in the field all over the world and could suggest how she could get authentic documentation. It turned out to be a wise move, for he recommended her warmly to a renowned friend, Professor Erman, at the Museum of Egyptology in Berlin. Thus, she decided to go there, remembering also that the Germans had always received her enthusiastically on her previous visits, honoring her as an "esthetic" dancer rather than considering her only a high-class stripper fit for music halls, as the French had recently seemed to do.

In the summer of 1914, the newspapers announced: "Mata Hari, the principal character dancer of La Scala in Milan, the Grand Opera in Monte Carlo, and the Odeon Theater in Paris, has just signed an engagement with the Berlin Metropol."

She had liquidated much of her property in Paris for this new move, ready to leave the fickle French for her more faithful Teutonic admirers. And she left for Berlin in hope of new victories. It was a campaign that might lead to a comeback likely to be more successful than Napoleon's return from the island of Elba.

July found her Unter den Linden, which, she decided, was every bit as lovely as the lanes of Paris, lined with the *tilleuls* that Proust had made famous with his *petite Madeleine*. Her first appearance at the Metropol was scheduled for September 1, 1914.

Except for the unfortunate incident at Sarajevo, on August 3, 1914, she might have triumphed there. But her reconquest of Europe was halted abruptly when a far greater battle began.

She was able to make one entry into her notebook on that day only: "WAR—left Berlin—theater closed." With those words, she disappeared from sight.

She was seen one last time as a dancer, after the outbreak of the war in circumstances that were definitely not triumphant, by Misa Sert and Boni de Castellane, the well-known playboy, in a private performance that the former described in terms that are far from laudatory:

The car took us for quite a long way [from the *Meurice*] before it stopped outside a sordid-looking house in the Paris suburbs. We were asked to go to the first floor, to a bedroom that reeked of poverty. Four little Hindus in turbans were squatting on the floor, picking at guitars. As last, dressed in three triangles of jewel paste, the expected wonder appeared . . . Alas! . . . she was a trite night-club dancer, whose art consisted in showing her body. The musicians frantically twanged at their guitars. The whole thing was grim, miserable and rather nauseating.

The ten-year-long reign of Mata Hari the dancer had come to an end. Her conquest of Europe had finished in exile far less glorious than the last sojourn of Bonaparte. The rise and fall of her empire had been accomplished. She might have vanished without a trace had there not also been the demi-monde over which she could continue to rule.

12 The Highroads of the Demi-Monde

"Listen. I know everything. There are some grown-ups who go to bed in the daytime. The men are called *lapins* and the women are called *cocottes*," Cocteau's little cousin explained. Young Marcel, Proust's hero, had made a similar discovery when meeting the "Lady in Pink" at the house of his uncle, who certainly qualified for the title of *lapin*. It all happened once upon a delightfully decadent time in a world of affluence and indolence, luxury and *luxure*, comfort and confidence, before the conflagration of a world war, before the society in which it flourished crumbled. During that *belle époque*, great queens of pleasure reigned in the demi-monde, fondly referred to as *Les Grandes Horizontales*. Sisters of the *hetaerae* of ancient Greece, the glorious courtesans of the Italian Renaissance, the famed geishas of Japan, these women of talent and beauty, skilled in the arts of all the senses, held court in Paris.

Their names are now only a nostalgic echo of days gone by. Their faces appear in the faded photographs of Reutlinger, the now-forgotten portraits of Namur, the yellowed pages of old magazines. Less fortunate than Phryne, forever preserved in marble by Praxiteles, their loveliness would be lost were it not for word paintings by those who saw them during their lifetime and wrote of them in their diaries.

Thus, we can still see the great Otéro through Colette's eyes:

A sort of caryatid, sculpted in the style of her epoch . . . her Greek blood showed in the strong neck, the stubborn profile often found in statues . . . Amidst the clusters of her thick tresses, her low lamb's forehead remained pure. The nose and mouth . . . were models of simple form. From the heavy eyelids to the gourmand's chin, from the velvety tip of the nose to the famous gently rounded cheeks . . . Mme Otéro's face was a masterpiece of convexity . . . .

Or watch her move, caught in Paul Klee's attentive gaze:

She did a Spanish dance. That's when we saw the real Otéro. Haughty and provocative, not a gesture that did not accentuate femininity, anguishing and exhilarating as tragedy . . .

After the first part of the dance she rested. Suddenly, disconcertingly, moving as if of its own will, one of her legs appeared, bathed in a new world of color—an incomparably perfect leg . . . The dance is about to begin again. Take care. The intensity of enjoyment is so terrifying that one almost loses consciousness during its orgiastic climax . . .

Cléo de la Mérode is also preserved for us by Klee, as sharply as if the painter had fixed her image with brush strokes:

She is, without doubt, the most beautiful woman to be seen anywhere. Everyone knows her head. But one must see her neck in real life: slim, quite long, smooth as bronze, not too mobile, with fine tendons, especially those near the sternum . . . Her belly is tightly swathed and harmonizes perfectly with the naked parts of her body. Unfortunately one cannot see her hips. It is frustrating for, due to the virtuosity of her movements, she must achieve singular effects there when . . . she switches her weight. As if to make up for this, she offers us her naked legs and feet . . . Her arms are classical in shape but perhaps more delicate and capable of a greater variety of poses, since this statue is alive . . . Her dance consists of gentle body movements. There is no soul in it, no temperament, nothing but absolute beauty . . .

And Cocteau creates a joint portrait of the great courtesans during one of the best-known rituals, dinner in the private rooms of one of Paris's famous restaurants (in which bidets were tactfully disguised as flower vases):

It was no small affair. Armour, escutcheons, carcans, corsets, whalebone, braids, épaulières, greaves, thighpieces, gauntlets, corselets, pearl baldricks, feather bucklers, satin, velvet and bejeweled halters, coats of mail, these knights-at-arms, bristling with tulle, rays of light and eyelashes, these sacred scarabs armed with asparagus holders, these Samuraïs of sable and ermine, these cuirassiers of pleasure who were harnessed and caparisoned early in the morning by robust soubrettes, seemed incapable, as they sat stiffly opposite their hosts, of extracting anything from an oyster beyond the pearl.

The splendor of these creatures was not easily attained. In order to join this elite, one had to meet strict and numerous requirements. Beauty, charm, and fame were of course mandatory. Besides, one needed prestige acquired through a series of illustrious lovers, duels fought for one's sake, preferably a suicide or two, sumptuous jewels and toilettes, villas or mansions, racehorses, carriages, familiarity with aristocratic ways, connections with the powerful and the sought after, the art of making carefully staged appearances at Maxim's, the Ritz, the Opera, Longchamps, the Bois de Boulogne. In the late afternoon, the Palais de Glace on the Champs Elysées was the place to be seen, for "its sky-blue plush round the draped mirrors, the rosettes and the canopies of the surrounds, the light ironwork of the alcazars round the little alcoves, the slender columns of the arcades" perfectly complemented the beauty of female forms. It was at five o'clock that the ritual entrance of the *grandes cocottes* described by Cocteau took place:

Named Liane this, Liane that . . . all these lianas wound themselves round the olive green instructors. Lowering their muffs, they launched out, bent and rose again, imitating the noble curves of the *métro* entrances, and lowering their eyes, they crossed the rink. During the intervals, their silver skates secured to their Louis XV heels, they limped towards the cloakrooms or lay, in dry dock, round the tables . . . .

While in the late mornings, one might appear in one's carriage, being driven through the Bois de Boulogne and creating visions as magnificent as that remembered by Proust's Marcel upon seeing the former Odette de Crécy pass by:

I saw . . . a matchless victoria, built rather high, and hinting, through the extreme modernity of its appointments, at the forms of an earlier day, deep down in which lay negligently back Mme Swann, her hair now quite pale . . . girt with a narrow band of flowers, from which floated down long veils, a lilac parasol in her hand, on her lips an ambiguous smile in which I read only the benign condescension of Majesty, though it was pre-eminently the enticing smile of the courtesan, which she graciously bestowed upon the men who bowed to her . . . .

These living monuments to desire dwelt in a world of splendor to which few women could aspire.

But Mata Hari would reign in the kingdom of the demi-monde as triumphantly as in the domain of the dance.

She decided to pursue this double road to conquest almost instantly after her debut in 1905. Whether to make up for the years spent chained to an aging, ailing man or to "avenge herself on other men by dragging them behind her chariot on her triumphal path, breaking hearts and devouring fortunes," she launched her campaign when she made her first appearance. The Musée Guimet opened its own as well as many other doors to her. Her talent and seductiveness were public knowledge within hours of her debut, for all the newspapers reported her genius for portraying "tragic coquetry, and cruelty rendered beautiful."

"She demands the life of a man in exchange for a kiss," one ecstatic critic wrote about *The Legend of the Black Pearl* she had performed at her debut, "and she demands it with diabolical joy, relishing the most cruel sensations. But she has a genuine flame of passion which hallucinates and captivates." Evidently, men lusted after such sensations, for their reactions were fraught with desire.

To add to her prestige, she soon managed to be the apex of an amorous triangle that ended in a *crime passionnel*. Nothing could have been better publicity than this. It brought droves of reporters to her door—among them, a young journalist named Georges du Parcq who had connections in all the best places and was quite attractive as well—and scores of admirers who had decided that any woman who could inspire such uncontrollable passion must be indeed exceptional.

Du Parcq promised to procure her a contract at the Folies-Bergères, and she vowed she would reward him with a silver statuette of herself if he succeeded. The other admirers did more than make promises. She was soon able to move from her boarding house to a lovely flat at 3 rue Balzac and purchase a piano of her own, something she had long craved. She received jewels and acquired magnificent clothes not only for the sense of luxury they gave her but also because they were the necessary tools for success, the armor needed in this particular campaign. And she continued to train herself through amorous jousts with numerous opponents. For she remembered the teachings of the *Kamasutra* well:

The characteristics of a courtesan are to be beautiful and pleasing, with a taste for riches and, insofar as sexual prowess is concerned, as indefatigable as a man; intelligent, well versed in all the arts of love and concomitant skills . . .

And while she knew that most of these traits were already hers, she was determined to excel at them all.

She carefully reread the text and came to the conclusion that the advice it gave concerning the choice of men best suited to the double pursuit of wealth and pleasure was excellent indeed. The list was quite explicit:

Members of the police force. High officials at court. Astrologers and soothsayers. Scholars. Men of great influence in government or courtiers. Aristocrats. The rich and generous. Those whom it would be dangerous to slight or to offend.

She smiled as she studied the type of men the *Kamasutra* counseled a courtesan to avoid:

Men who suffer from consumption; those who have a sickly disposition. A man who has worms in his mouth; one whose breath smells of human excrement. A man who loves his wife; one who speaks harshly; one who is always suspicious. Misers. A man with no pity. A thief. A bore.

A man drawn to sorcery; one who does not care about being respected. A man who can be bought with money. A prude.

It seemed to her exceedingly wise counsel. In 1905–1906 she proceeded to do what the book advised: allowed the Prince de Drago to give a fete in her honor; the Chilean ambassador to view her limbs as she danced; Maître Clunet, the great lawyer, to pay her court; the directors of museums and famous orientalists to feel her gratitude; journalists to be dazzled at interviews, patrons of the arts to patronize her; the rich and generous to contribute to her support. She encouraged the stories that described her as an expert in the sixty-four rites of lust practiced in Hindu temples, the rumors that she had studied love philters, incantations, and amulets with aphrodisiac powers. It all served to fan the flames of desire. Legends could only add to her mystery; the exotic was her best ally.

But it was also agreeable to hear people say that she was "a natural in the art of pleasing men, of seducing and holding them . . . of lighting a fire of desire that was never quenched . . . capable both of interesting men by her wit and drugging them with her beauty." (Shades of Cleopatra, she thought. "Age cannot wither her, nor custom stale her infinite variety. . . .")

It all paid off in more sumptuous jewels, more magnificent clothes, a move to a fabulous suite at the Palace Hotel on the Champs Elysées, even a carriage of her own, something she had long dreamed of ever since the loss of her *bokkenwagen*.

She flitted from man to man—ambassadors, diplomats, bankers, aristocrats, politicians, industrialists, composers, impresarios, journalists—partly out of restlessness, partly because she always remembered that the *Kamasutra* taught:

The duty of a courtesan consists of having affairs with the right men, to obtain the wealth of the men involved with her, and to get rid of them after having despoiled them of their riches.

Perfidiousness was obviously part of the game and only added to one's attractiveness. Men were drawn like night moths to such a consuming flame.

To excite desire continued to intoxicate her. It affected her in a way similar to applause. She read the descriptions of her charms that appeared constantly in the newspapers with the eagerness of a nubile virgin. One of her favorite passages read:

She danced, her little breasts covered with chiseled brass cupolas, with glittering bracelets on her wrists, arms, and ankles. The rest of her was fastidiously bare, from the nails of her fingers to the tips of her toes.

She smiled, judging the value of such words for inciting sensuality. The *Mercure de France*, with its usual gravity, might well pronounce: "Mata Hari's art is chaste." She knew better than that and preferred the newspaper accounts that dwelled on her "voluptuous attitudes and lascivious gestures, feverish quiverings . . . and suppleness so great that she seems like a serpent."

She decided to increase her clientele by giving "special performances," which, she knew, would be greatly appreciated by connoisseurs. There was just enough of the clandestine about them to add the spice that their frequently jaded palates needed. She ordered the doors of the theater closed at the end of a public performance and allowed a specially invited, small audience to remain for certain numbers that she gave entirely nude, watching the eyes of the men whose hands had caressed her body.

Some of the critics chided her, of course, for sensationalism and a betrayal of her art; others merely wondered how she managed to get away with such acts at a time when the Paris courts were severely repressing naked dancing and sentencing other performers to fifteen days in prison, while she seemed beyond the reach of the law. Mata Hari was grateful once more for the *Kamasutra*'s wise advice to have friends in high places. In public she dropped hints to her adversaries that she was, after all, not in the league of other naked dancers, but descended from the Devadasis, the sacred temple dancers for whom art and eroticism were inextricably linked and, she might have added, prostitution was a form of worship, an act of communion with the divinity.

To heighten this legendary aura, she decided to acquire a tattoo depicting the *Uroboros*. Then she watched, with great exhilaration, people's reaction to the mysterious image engraved on her flesh. They were more credulous than she had anticipated: "She took from her left wrist the large metal bracelet she wore," one of them wrote, "and we could then see a thin natural bracelet, tattooed in blue on the pale gold skin, which represented a snake swallowing its tail." They apparently swallowed the enigma more eagerly than the serpent his tail. Without being in the least aware of the ancient symbol's meaning.

The god Kama certainly seemed to be on her side. She was now a living monument to luxury as well as *luxure*. Writers dwelled on every detail of her physique, down to her kneecaps, which one of them described as if they were jewels of rare origin: "Amber-colored, they seemed plated with gold-leaf that had rosy reflections . . ." In 1906, at the age of thirty, when most women of her day were worn out by childbearing, husbands and endless household chores—or had been chopped to pieces, that seeming to be a favorite French pastime, as news items continually revealed—she was at the height of her powers, free, and very much in one piece. If anything, she was constantly expanding her erotic horizons and her revenues.

Travel proved to be an excellent opportunity for both these pursuits. The list of her conquests grew more international: Jules Cambon, the ambassador, Spain; the composer Massenet, Monte Carlo; Herr Kiepert, a wealthy industrialist, Berlin; Mynheer van der Linden, Amsterdam . . .

She was now considered to be "the most costly delicacy on the menu of continental night-life."

But Mata Hari remembered that according to her favorite book courtesans were meant to receive sexual pleasure as well as material gain from their commerce with men. She found, however, that after the first years of exhilaration, which important conquests provided, she often tired of the elderly, paunchy diplomats, the self-indulgent men of state, the smug judges, the pompous bankers, the jaded sensualists aroused only by women much bruited about, the impotents who excelled in verbal seduction only.

She began to think of the excitement she had felt in her youth when the sight of young men in uniform made her senses leap, when warriors ready for adventure, risk, and death had seemed to her a special race, far above ordinary mortals. How strong and sure they had seemed, their lithe bodies outlined against the sea of Scheveningen or dancing in the evening at small cabarets. Unfortunately, she had then been too awkward and unsure to enjoy them. She did remember, however, that she had had feverish dreams about them at night in which they secretly entered her room—betrayed only by the swish of their sabers against the trouser legs, the slight squeak of their boots on the wooden floor that separated her bed from the door—and seized her in their arms, hardened by the trials of maneuvers and battlefields, until she swooned in her sleep. Now there was no need for such imaginings or the pursuit of solitary pleasure for lack of the real thing.

Not that she regretted not having fallen in love, a pitfall that all good courtesans must avoid. But having assured her sustenance, knowing full well that she could have any man she pleased, she could allow herself the luxury of indulging her penchants without thought of gain. The young men in uniform beckoned—now as then—varied in color according to the country they served; of delightfully different complexions, build, and size; diverse in the ways they had in bed; speaking of pleasure in many tongues.

She began to intersperse these private pleasures with her more public affairs—the ardent, slim-hipped boys who could engage in hours of amorous combat with the flabby, round-bellied "leaders of men" who rapidly slackened and had to be aroused by artifice in order to salve their self-esteem.

But Mata Hari continued to play to her audience. She posed for photographs wearing fashions that the well-kept woman will wear —such as an "ermine coat, trimmed in white fox, by Ramillon"— in 1908; appeared at all the horse shows; rode in the Bois de Boulogne in a *cavalière* outfit that molded each curve of her body; bemoaned the demise of the horse-drawn carriage but also audibly craved one of those new machines called automobiles; occupied a large suite at the opulent Meurice.

Her worldly triumphs multiplied. Whole cities were moved by her whims and moods. Luxury trains and liners transported her prized body across land or sea. Now that they had begun to travel the air—the great "Zeppelin" made its appearance, and Captain de Koepenick and the aviator Blériot were honored like demigods— she wondered how soon she would be the precious cargo of the flying machines (or have a brave pilot steer her to bed).

And yet she spent much time musing over the cry: *"Faites des enfants!"* that rose from all the newspaper headlines. (Queen Wilhelmina, as if in answer to the call, produced an heir to the Dutch throne the next spring.) At first, she had laughed to think she was free of such bondage, although she had to spend a great deal of time seeking the best birth control means and read widely on the subject (finding that the Arabs inserted date pits into their camels' wombs, Cleopatra used half a lemon, Japanese prostitutes were partial to seaweed). But then she cried as she thought of the loss of her son, ten years ago now, and the near loss of her daughter, who lived in a distant town.

Perhaps she simply needed a change from the mundane life, the bustle of cities, the constant demands of admirers, the curtain calls and stagedoor lovers. She began to think with nostalgia of the countryside, of long shady lanes, the sound of the wind in the treetops at night, sunflowers slowly turning on their stalks as the day makes its round.

So that when in 1910 the banker Rousseau suggested they repair to a small castle at Esvres, where they could ride horses and lead an idyllically clandestine life, she accepted instantly. Let Paris wonder where she had gone. The absence would make them yearn for her return.

It was not hard to adapt to the life of the landed gentry. They dined in the garden, took their *digestif* on the terrace, fragrant with flowers, rode their steeds far and wide in the countryside, galloping over the swelling hills, ambling along narrow lanes, stopping by swift-running streams to water their mounts and refresh themselves on the cool banks.

If only he had been a young cavalry officer, the retreat would have been ideal. Under the circumstances, she preferred the weekdays when he left her to do his duty as paterfamilias and husband, when she was free to roam alone. Her fantasies then had full reign, aroused by the stallion's flanks against her thighs, the strong heaving motion of his gait, the play of the muscles in the neck—so reminiscent of the long lines in a youthful back—the mane that touched her face, as thick and fragrant as a young man's hair. On weekends, when Rousseau returned to their "love-nest," she claimed weariness, complained of vapors, spring breezes, even migraines (that ploy of frigid women that she had always held in disdain). But he seemed to grow all the more infatuated as she held him at bay. He offered to return to Paris, buy her a house there, stock her stables with racehorses and her rooms with objets d'art, if only she would not send him away.

The Villa Rémy at 11 rue Windsor in Neuilly was the outcome. It stood nestled among trees, a delightful house in Normandy style —valued, incidentally, at one million francs—complete with racehorses, and art treasures, and gardens in which she could dance. Moreover, she could once more compete with Isadora Duncan, who had a house not far away. And welcome visitors with the stained-glass inscription which read "*Sois le bienvenu*" that she had placed over the door of her room.

At first, not many guests availed themselves of that invitation, for the winter of 1911 was one of the harshest that Paris had seen. In January, the floods were so great that the *zouave* of the Pont d'Alma had the waters of the Seine come all the way up to his chest. Half of Paris was immersed in muddy brown seepage from the river. The bears in the Jardin des Plantes were saved from the fate of being drowned, but the populace feared that the crocodiles would escape from their flooded pools in the zoo. The sewers broke, and cellars were covered with offal. Rats fled through the boulevards. On the principal avenues, wooden bridges were built for pedestrians, who maneuvered across them as cautiously as if they were walking tightropes. Pillaging began to happen everywhere; criminals crept from the underworld as boldly as the rats left their sewer retreats. The crowd grew furious and meted out its own justice by throwing the robbers into the swollen waters of the river. For the Seine had become a wild, raging stream. Gone was the lethargic flow of lazy summer afternoons when fishermen sat for hours angling in the river and never catching anything. Now it carried along trunks of trees, debris of broken sheds, and drowned bodies. Once, the carcass of a bull was spotted with the cadaver of a young cowherd still clinging to his yoke.

Spring finally came however and with it the select crowd whom Mata Hari welcomed in her new home. Her dance soirées were once more a coveted attraction in town. Although quite another woman had won the Nobel prize that year, she did not feel completely outdone. Let Madame Curie watch over her test tubes; in her own field, she still reigned. The brilliant and famous gathered in her gardens; she had her own Indian orchestra to provide the musical accompaniment for her rituals. Soon they all flocked to her door as they had done in 1909: the diplomats, statesmen, rulers, and marquis, along with at least one secret service chief.

It still amused her to wield her power over these men, to play them like an expert angler, hooked by the bait of her exotic art. The newspapers again spoke frequently of her sacred vocation. A famous journalist even agreed to make an introductory speech at one of her performances, and proclaimed:

Born on the banks of the Ganges, Mata Hari shares her time between her ardent homeland and a small villa in Neuilly, where she isolates herself in a Brahmin communion with animals and flowers . . .

While it was not quite true that she lived in isolation or that she communed with animals and flowers only—there being more tempting objects in her vicinity—it sounded perfect for the occasion and projected an image the audience wished to perceive.

The summer months were especially suited for staging these outdoor festivities. She danced to celebrate the Moon Goddess at the time of the harvest moon and was so successful with this ritual that the news even spread across the Channel, where it was known that Lady Mc Leod (as she was cleverly billed in the British Isles) praised the mother of earthly fecundity in the suburbs of Paris.

Her own fecundity, however, was beginning to wane. She noticed that her waist was not as slim as before, that the flesh sagged slightly when she bent, and that she had to dye her black hair more frequently. Middle age seemed to be approaching rapidly, and she sometimes thought with terror of the fate of aging courtesans. Now and then, also, a disparaging note crept into the chorus of general praise that the public lavished upon her. By 1913 some voices dared to suggest that Paris had transferred its enthusiasm to other stars and was beginning to relegate her to the shadows. She retorted haughtily to these accusations and assured everyone that she need only to invoke her admirers to silence any slight on her powers of seduction. Who but a queen of the demi-monde could boast of a list of lovers that included the Duke of Brunswick, the Marquis de Givenchy, the crown prince of Germany, the head of the French Secret Service, one of the most powerful journalists, and lately, also, General Messimy, the French minister of war, and Herr von Jagow, the foreign minister of Germany?

The last two men intrigued her especially. It was exhilarating to juxtapose them, and it pleased her sense of gamesmanship to pit against each other two powerful figures who were bound to be adversaries, to move them like pawns on the chessboard of desire. Besides, each man was interesting in his own right. Messimy, despite being a rather "strange-looking man, short and dark, with quite stupendous mustaches, . . . married, with a reputation for domesticity and most inexperienced in dealing with worldly women," had a history of daring and unconventionality. He had defied the old-line generals when he became minister of war in 1911 by ordering these rheumatic gentlemen, who should have been retired long ago, to conduct their maneuvers on horseback. She liked his spirit and liked even more being able to dominate him in spite of it. Von Jagow, on the other hand, "was a typical Prussian junker, sanguine and energetic, strikingly handsome after the military model" she had always admired. She liked to remember how she had won him over when he was still the chief of the German police and had visited the theater in which she performed, ostensibly to censor her costumes, only to succumb to her spell.

Now both of them were in her power. Considering the growing animosity that was developing between the two countries that they served, there was bound to be good sport in creating an amorous rivalry between them as well.

Perhaps she was somewhat bored during this winter of 1913–1914. She sensed that she needed stronger sensations than before to keep her satisfied. Mere seduction was no longer a game she enjoyed. There was no challenge left since she knew she could have any man she desired; the maneuvers were too familiar, the prey too easy to bring to its knees, the kill too certain for her to be entertained.

She remembered, with some fondness, a role of temptress–destroyer she had danced long ago, that of the Princess Anuba, whom she had portrayed at her debut, and reread the description of her pantomime:

The princess Anuba knows that at the bottom of the sea there is an oyster shell containing a magnificent black pearl. She attempts to seduce the fisherman Amry, promising herself to him as a reward if he will dive for the pearl. Terrified by this proposal, the fisherman replies that what she asks is madness, because the oyster shell is guarded by a monster who devours any creature that approaches him. But she insists; she cajoles; she intoxicates the man with her amorous glances; and finally Amry plunges to the bottom of the sea. He returns in a dying condition, mutilated by the monster—but he hands the pearl to the princess. Then, as she caresses the blood-stained gem, the princess Anuba dances—dances—until she sinks to the ground in a delirium of joy.

She determined to enjoy far crueler sensations, demand far greater sacrifices, and multiply the number of pearl divers sent to the bottom of the sea. The highroads of the demi-monde had led her to a plateau from which she felt she would relish watching the conflict of armies, the clash of lances, the onslaught of horses—a vast joust in which the knights of both sides wore her colors on their sleeves.

It was no longer a time for temple dancers and sacred prostitutes, for Venus, Cleopatra, or Salomé, but for Kali the Destroyer, to whom the gods themselves must submit. She would emerge from the demi-monde and grind the world beneath her feet.

13 Suddenly One August

Something was in the air that summer of 1914: a kind of electricity, tension mingled with a strange calm, as of forces gathering that would soon be unleashed, an impalpable change in the atmosphere (not unlike the signs that announce the cataclysms of nature). As though an entire civilization approached its inevitable downfall, as though the hothouse of prosperity had produced exorbitant plants that must flower into evil.

Mata Hari had first sensed it in Paris. It was perhaps at the root of her need to revive the *Sacred Flower Dance* with its haunting message, "everything must die"; of Diaghilev's furious banishment of Nijinsky, his greatest star; her superstitious terror when she dropped a jade bracelet on the floor; her liquidation of everything she owned and her departure from the City of Light.

But even when she arrived in Berlin, the sense of foreboding continued. She saw it mirrored in the tight faces of the young men, taut as cats ready to spring; in the harassed air of the officials, who hurried along the steps of the Foreign Office at all times of day; and heard it echo in the endless movement of trains throughout the long summer nights. The saber scars on the cheeks of Prussian youths seemed whiter than before; the women had an anticipatory look of mourning in their smiles; only the children seemed unconcerned, playing with tin soldiers as they had done for centuries.

Two words seemed to be on everyone's lips: *"Krieg"* . . . *"Gefahr."* It was this then that she had sensed: the danger of war. Except that she could not identify it.

She knew this sentiment. It seethed in the breasts of those who saw in it a chance for glory and an escape from the narrow confines of everyday life; an antidote for boredom to those who had long vegetated in peace and prosperity; a rallying point for the estranged and isolated. It was the same drive that had created the colonial armies.

But now it threatened to bring on a great wave of chaos and destruction in which all Europe might be swept along. The upheaval had already begun. Obscure countries suddenly loomed large in the newspapers: Serbia, Latvia, and Herzegovina occupied the headlines at the end of July. Ultimata raced from one capital of the continent to another, demanding satisfaction, participation, neutrality. Instructions to ambassadors arrived after events had already taken place; wires crossed; schemes backfired. A carriage ride in Sarajevo ended in a tragedy that shook the Old World to its very foundations.

On July 31, 1914, the Kaiser declared *Kriegsgefahr*. The two words, murmured separately before, were proclaimed jointly now in one long, ominous-sounding compound noun. The streets were filled with the sound of the word passing from mouth to mouth. It seemed to gather momentum as it was intoned, until it rose, like a vast tidal wave, threatening to engulf the whole of Berlin.

Von Jagow insisted that Mata Hari have dinner with him that evening. But he seemed so tense, having worked constantly during the preceding nights—demanding neutrality from Belgium, preparing instructions for the German ambassador to Paris—that she had difficulty keeping him from being preoccupied while they served the caviar. When at noon the next day the German ultimatum to Russia expired without a reply, the challenge had to be met. At five o'clock, the Kaiser declared general mobilization. At five-thirty, it was reported, "Chancellor Bethmann-Hollweg, absorbed in a document he was holding in his hand and accompanied by . . . Jagow, the Foreign Minister, hurried down the steps of the Foreign Office and sped off to the palace." The conference with the Kaiser must have led to new decisions, last-minute maneuvers, schemes of strategy, for that very night Jagow was known to have "rushed off a telegram to his ambassador in Paris, where mobilization had already been declared at four o'clock, instructing him helpfully to 'please keep France quiet for the time being.'"

The two opponents were now mobilized. Mata Hari knew that it would be hard to keep the French and especially their minister of war quiet. For Messimy was known as an "exuberant, energetic, almost violent man." Besides, he was not afraid of opposition, even when he found it in his own camp. She remembered the story of his decision that the blue coats and red trousers of the French soldiers must be changed to protective gray-blue or green, where he confronted the howls of protest from the conservatives and a violent outburst from the former minister of war, who shouted: "Eliminate red trousers? Never! *Le pantalon rouge c'est la France!*" Surely, he would now raise his round head on his thick neck and glower, his bright peasant's eyes, which not even spectacles could dim, flashing, his loud voice making impolite suggestions as to what the German ambassador could do.

In Berlin, patriotic fervor had already reached a high pitch. Cars raced along Unter der Linden that night, with officers standing upright, shouting, "Mobilization!" to which the people responded with screams and cheers, as if the call were the summons to a new crusade, one that turned instantly not against the Sarazens but against swiftly elected scapegoats. The madness of crowds had begun. A number of suspected Russian spies were trampled or pummeled to death.

It seemed inevitable that war would be declared. It was a matter of hours or, at most, days. Europe stood on the brink of destruction, teetering for an instant before the final plunge. But everyone sensed that there was no turning back now, any more than a throw of the dice can be reversed in midair.

Mata Hari questioned her feelings in this matter as she sat in her luxurious suite in Berlin, wondering where her loyalties lay, if any-where. She had no real roots in any land. Holland, the country of her birth, had become a prison to her when she last lived there; France, after adopting her, had discarded her when her heyday was over; the other participants in the coming battle were simply hosts by whom she had been well, or less well, received. A stranger, she owed no allegiance to anyone; nor did she profess patriotic feel-ings for any nation. If anything, she considered herself Javanese; and Java had no part in this struggle.

But she did feel a sense of exhilaration at the dangers that lay in store. For if Holland remained neutral (as was to be foreseen), she would be able to move freely in the theater of war in which brave men in flamboyant uniforms engaged in battle, reckless and magnificent, not knowing whether tomorrow would come. It was a spectacle she planned to enjoy thoroughly.

She thought for a moment about Messimy when the French newspapers announced the assassination of Jaurès. She knew that this spelled the end of an era and wondered how he fared in the midst of the consternation that this upheaval was bound to bring.

But she forgot about him when, on August 3, war was declared.

Berlin was in a joyous uproar at the news. The bellicose spirit gripped the entire populace. Young men were leaving for the front, singing. Flowers were thrown by cheering crowds sure of a speedy victory. Officers were acclaimed as they passed through the streets; the mass of civilians separated as they approached, as if they were royalty.

Von Jagow asked Mata Hari to drive with him in his official car, accompanied by an escort of mounted police. They went from one end of the city to the other, to the railroad station from which trains left for the front, to all the public gatherings. She felt that she shared a triumphal chariot, as though she were his consort. The crowds that cheered the representative of war seemed to be cheering her also. Playing Venus to his Mars, she enjoyed the sense of glory, the power of the voices raised in unison, the heady sensa-tion of victory.

In Paris, she heard, the mood was a far darker one. When Jaurès was buried on August 4, it seemed to many that the bells that tolled for him also tolled for France. When Messimy opened the Cabinet meeting the next day, he began "with a speech full of valor and confidence," it was reported, but "broke off mid-way, buried his head in his hands, and sobbed, unable to continue"—a most unbecoming spectacle, most people thought, in a minister of war of a country at war. From then on, he went downhill, becoming gloomier and gloomier and appearing to be near despair. Such defeatism could hardly be tolerated in someone constantly in the public eye. It was no surprise to anyone when, by the end of the month, his removal was demanded urgently—and granted speedily. The last news that she heard of him was that he had rejoined the army to serve at the front.

Paris itself had now become an entrenched camp. By the last days of August the City of Light had turned into a shadowy place. Almost deserted (for most inhabitants had fled), torn by bombings, its great boulevards empty, the sumptuous Hotel Meurice (where she had spent such delightful days) converted into a hospital in which the wounded lay in the corridors, moaning, begging for water, brandy, or chloroform, its former lighthearted spirit had been replaced by a somber mood.

The harvest that summer would not be one of grapes, wheat, or jasmine from the slopes of Provence but of blood. The cannons boomed in the countryside; rockets tore the night sky; trenches were cut in fertile fields. In less than a month the war in Europe had become general. It would not end before an entire generation of young men had been killed, mutilated, or maimed in mind or body.

Mata Hari left Berlin at the end of August with the sound of firing in her ears. It seemed to her that each roar of a cannon, each volley of rifle fire, each shouted command to a patrol, punctuated the end of an era, put a final stamp on a chapter in her life. She knew that she was moving into a new phase and that from now on she would be playing on a stage far more dangerous than any she had known before, in which every role could lead to death, and to forget one's part had fatal consequences, for she was entering the theater of war.

Part 4

Voici le temps des Assassins.
—Arthur Rimbaud

14 The Second Oldest Profession

While the great battles of 1914 raged at Namur and Charleroi, Ypres and La Marne, while barbed-wire trenches filled with blood in Flanders, Picardy, and Champagne, as von Kluck opposed Joffre in slaughter after slaughter, another war was waged underground— silent, invisible, but just as deadly as the grim confrontations of troops on the battlegrounds of Europe that took place in sunlight, among fields of poppies and vineyards laden with grapes. Fought by a subterranean foreign legion, as intrepid as that which rallied above ground but far more lonely and unsung, it was a fierce struggle in a world apart. Its champions were despised by those who employed them, hated by those who hunted them, abandoned if they were caught—a race doomed to sewers, dungeons, and firing squads: the secret agents.

Yet theirs was an ancient trade. For they have existed ever since war began. "The second oldest profession" is as old as recorded history: The Egyptians, 5,000 years before Christ, already practiced "the great secret science" amid the sphinxes and pyramids. Among the Hebrews, Jehovah himself instructed his prophet to send spies into Canaan; Joshua triumphed with their help (and that of a

trumpet) at Jericho. The great war of Troy was won with the aid
of intelligence agents who devised the ruse of the wooden horse.
The Roman emperors used them frequently; ancient Athens and
Sparta availed themselves of their skills. In fifth-century China, the
great sage Sun Tzu devoted an entire chapter of his *Art of War* to
secret and double agents.

Nor would Europe be outdone in this matter: From Ganelon,
who betrayed the armies of Charlemagne and was drawn and quar-
tered for his perfidy, to the artful web of espionage spun by the
Borgias and the Medicis, to the voyages of Marco Polo, the secret
service created by Sir Wolsingham for Queen Elizabeth, the spy
system of Cardinal Richelieu and Mazarin, the famous Chevalier
d'Eon, who spent half his life disguised as a woman, Joseph
Fouché's modern espionage service devised for Napoleon, to the
Duc d'Enghien, kidnaped and shot in the fortress of Vincennes, to
Lawrence of Arabia, scores of spies, traitors, and informers line
the pages of the history books.

In this famous and infamous company women have often played
star roles. Tracing their lineage to perfidious Circe, Lilith, or
Lorelei, they have haunted man's imagination throughout the ages
and in every culture known. As Astarte, Rahab, Judith, Delilah,
Morrigan, and Valkyrie, Le-hev-hev, Kali, or Xochiquetzal, they
have dwelled in the myths of men, in which orgasm is linked to
dying (as the Elizabethans well knew), in which the devouring
womb joins the sarcophagus, and death is the companion of desire.

But they have also changed the course of history: sometimes in
the role of pawns, mere "dolls of flesh" or "voluptuous punching
balls," easily discarded or sacrificed in a game whose rules and aims
they did not know; sometimes as lucid, conscious heroines who
chose and accepted the dread consequences of their acts with the
resourcefulness of a Judith, the humanitarian motives of a Rose
Greenbow, the audacity of a Louise de Keroualle, the technical brilliance of a Fräulein Doktor, the tenacity of La Chatte . . .
whether raised to legendary status by the popular imagination or,
as is more often the case, known only to their disdainful spy mas-

ters, they are creatures of mystery, their motives for entering the world of espionage at least as puzzling, strange, and fascinating as those of their male counterparts.

Whether driven by the exhilaration of the chase, the disdain for traditional loyalties, the pleasure of hoodwinking dupes or outwitting brilliant opponents, love of secrecy, disguise and deception, or an incurable thirst for power, these strangers and outlaws, these *Übermenschen* beyond good and evil, these lethal conjurors, have reflected the dark side of humanity throughout history. But ever since the "Great Torment" began, their complexity, their alienation, and their profound sense of the absurd have made them the shadow image of modern man.

By one of the numerous ironies with which history is filled, the peaceful little country of Switzerland became the center of espionage in 1914. In this haven of neutrality, well-being, and cuckoo clocks, in which major disasters consisted of charred *Rösti* or a change in the decimal point of a seven-figure bank account, the jungle of international society thrived. Spies swarmed as in an anthill, mingled with informers, double agents, and counterfeiters. The columns of different species converged here, relayed messages, exchanged information, met head on, tripped over each other, went their separate ways (having acknowledged or feigned not to recognize their adversaries' markings and destination). For all the belligerent nations had their agents here. A babel of tongues was heard in all the principal cities. Furtive glances were cast by everyone at everyone since one could not be sure that even the most innocent-looking of stout housewives did not conceal a code book in her bosom or maps of enemy movements in the diapers of her sturdy offspring. Caution was much exercised since all agents had instructions from their governments to mistrust everyone with whom they dealt: enemies (because they might denounce them to the local authorities), friends, and allies (because they might attempt to gain information or contacts).

Travel in and out of this cloak-and-dagger paradise was much facilitated by the fact that documents did not require photographs and also by a special service located in Zurich (allegedly run by Jews of Polish descent but international outlook) that manufactured false identification papers, besides having its own set of secret agents who collected information that was then classified and offered to interested powers (sometimes three or four different military attachés at a time) to ascertain the highest bidder.

Surrounded by all the surface tranquility, the neat chalets and sparkling, snowy slopes, no mere visitor would have suspected that there dwelled in the shadows a vast octopus whose tentacles reached out to every part of Europe to suck fresh victims into the murky domains of espionage.

Nor would the naïve traveler have had the slightest suspicion about the notoriety of the passengers who occupied a luxury compartment in a train that sped through the spectacular Swiss countryside in the last days of August 1914.

True, they seemed to be an oddly assorted group, quite obviously of different nationalities and all of them foreigners; they appeared deeply absorbed in the contemplation of the plush upholstery or the changing panoramas outside and made no attempt to communicate or exchange the kind of commonplaces that fellow travelers often do; they avoided looking at each other in daylight, but as soon as the advent of a tunnel darkned the windowpane and turned it into a mirror that clearly reflected the compartment's occupants, they engaged in surreptitious mutual scrutiny. Something about their appearance suggested that they were all disguised. And despite the fact that no one spoke, an acute observer might have surmised—mostly from their gestures, the way they smoked and blew their noses, or presented their tickets to the conductor of the train—that they were German, French, English, and Russian by origin.

The only passenger more difficult to place was a tall, lithe woman of indeterminate age with blonde hair (which looked dyed, perhaps because of her dark eyes) and elegant clothes that might have come from any fashionable shop on the continent. Her gestures were so unusually graceful that she could have been a trained dancer. Her accent, detected when she said a few words to the official who inspected her papers, was impossible to pin down and might have been due to a superimposition of several languages. She was obviously a polyglot and so cosmopolitan in her ways that one could not possibly guess her nationality.

Yet there was something vaguely familiar about her face that left the onlooker with the disturbing feeling of déjà vu without being able to place the sensation in any known context or seize the fleeting memories that flitted across his mind. She herself gave one no clue at all, but simply leaned back in her seat after the official had departed and contemplated the others with a superior smile from under slightly lowered (and probably artificial) eyelashes.

They, in turn, made no attempt to engage her in conversation or to determine who she was. For (being spies) they were accustomed to respect the rules of the game: Whenever agents of different nations confronted each other (as in this case), they did not denounce one another, but merely recognized each other's presence and proceeded on their predetermined course. It was quite obvious to her fellow travelers that she was one of them, for there was an indefinable quality about her that they had learned to recognize. But they did not know her identity or for which side she was working in this war.

With the camaraderie that exists among professionals or the gallantry typical of certain British gentlemen, one of them simply leaned forward to light her cigarette. She acknowledged the courtesy with a slight nod of her head, blew fragrant clouds of Turkish tobacco smoke at the ceiling, and proceeded to contemplate the tidy countryside. The others continued to study her while carefully attempting to conceal their curiosity. As the lighting changed, and various angles of her face were revealed, one or the other had a partial reminiscence, a nagging memory that could not be clarified, a tantalizing half image seen somewhere . . . someplace . . . before. But where? In a magazine . . . on a kiosk . . . beyond footlights? It was impossible to be sure. She remained an enigma in this company of enigmatic faces.

They would no doubt have been greatly surprised to discover that the woman was none other than Mata Hari.

The travel document she carried would have given them no clue. For there she was described as Margaretha Geertruida Zelle, the former wife of a man named Mac Leod, thirty years old, born in Leeuwarden but residing in Berlin, of Protestant faith, five feet eleven inches tall, with blonde hair and brown eyes; the Dutch government, whose stamp the papers bore, requested the Swiss authorities to grant her passage and extend every courtesy to this citizen of a neutral nation. The document, despite its pleasant falsification concerning her age (she was close to forty) and her hair color (recently changed to blonde either to cater to Teutonic tastes, cover white roots, or act as a disguise), gave no hint of a masked identity. Nor did anyone but insiders know that she now had a new alias and had become a German secret agent.

Her fellow travelers would not necessarily have approved of the choice made by the *Geheimdienst*. Their objections, however, would probably have varied considerably. The old-timers among them would certainly have been skeptical, arguing that she was far too well known, far too much in the public eye to be a successful spy, whose first prerequisite is to pass unnoticed. The German would have extolled the superior powers of the elderly *"Tante,"* who succeeded where younger, more flamboyant beauties failed. The Frenchman, while fondly remembering the successes of ladies of "small virtue," would have frowned upon the fact that she seemed far too independent in her ways. The Englishman, while thinking with wry humor that she was much less likely to muff a mission by stuttering, as one of his famous countrymen, Somerset Maugham, had done in Switzerland, regretted to see a "lady" engaged in such unladylike endeavors. The Russian would have sighed deeply, believing that no woman is immune to the "bacteria of love'" and foreseeing that she was destined to a tragic fate.

The house at Voorstreek 33 in which M'greet was born in 1876. *(Courtesy of the Tourist Association of the Province of Friesland and the City of Leeuwarden)*

STANDING, RIGHT: Margaretha Zelle (the future Mata Hari) in Leeuwarden, with her grammar-school classmates. *(Van Rhijn-Viollet)*

The house on the Groote Kerkstraat (presently in the process of being restored), where M'greet lived until her father's bankruptcy. (*Courtesy of the Tourist Association of the Province of Friesland and the City of Leeuwarden*)

The young Margaretha, probably shortly after her marriage. (*Harlingue-Viollet*)

From a handwritten letter by Mata Hari in which she says: "My husband won't get me any dresses because he's afraid that I will be too beautiful. It's intolerable. Meanwhile the young lieutenants pursue me and are in love with me. It is difficult for me to behave in a way which will give my husband no cause for reproaches." (Probably written during her stay in the East Indies.) (*Van Rhijn-Viollet*)

The Musée Guimet in Paris, on the Place d'Iéna, where Mata Hari made her debut. This is how the building appeared in 1975.

Mata Hari dressed for one of her Indian roles.   (*From the Collection Viollet*)

The statue before which Mata Hari danced
at her debut: an eleventh-century bronze from
Southeast India of Shiva dancing. (*From the
Catalogue of the Musée Guimet, Paris*)

Mata Hari as a Spanish dancer.
(*Harlingue-Viollet*)

LEFT: Fräulein Doktor, spy for the Germans during the war of 1914–18. (*From the Collection Viollet*) RIGHT: Commandant Georges Ladoux, head of the French counter-espionage service during World War I. (*From the Collection Viollet*)

26 rue Jacob, Paris, the secret headquarters of Monsieur Delorme (alias of Commandant Ladoux).

The head nun of Saint-Lazare
prison, who accompanied
Mata Hari on the morning of
her execution.   (*Roger-Viollet*)

Prison photograph
of Mata Hari in 1917.
(*Harlingue-Viollet*)

The execution of Mata Hari in Vincennes.   (*Harlingue-Viollet*)

Bronze statue of Mata Hari erected
in her native Leeuwarden. Sculptor:
Mrs. Suus Boschma-Berkhout. A bronze
plaque affixed to the statue reads:
    Magaretha Geertruida Zelle
    Born August 7th 1876 in Leeuwarden
    Died in Vincennes on October 15th 1917
    On the occasion of the 100th anniversary
      of her birthday.
(*Courtesy of the Tourist Association of the
Province of Friesland and the City of Leeuwarden*)

Mata Hari herself had not quite decided what she thought of her latest escapade. Certainly it was flattering that Berlin headquarters considered her sufficiently audacious and intelligent to be entrusted with secret missions. But then she remembered a sentence she had read in some nineteenth-century dictionary of conversation: "Women are also used in espionage because, like members of the clergy, they arouse fewer suspicions and run less risks," which did not please her nearly as much. At any rate, she had taken the step now. It seemed a second debut, more daring than the one at the Musée Guimet and well suited to her catholic taste for adventure. She turned her various aliases around in her mind—Mata Hari, Baroness von der Linden, H 21—and enjoyed the many masks as if she were choosing to wear them at a costume ball. The risk implied thrilled her, for there was little else left to explore that did not smack of redundancy. She also suspected, however, that a certain weariness had prompted her choice, a weariness due to her years. She would soon be forty, a ripe old age for a dancer or a courtesan (despite the inspiring example of Ninon de Lenclos, who had saved the last of her youthful lovers for her eightieth birthday to savor like some frosted angel cake). Or perhaps it was simply boredom, from which high-voltage exploits could save her. Or yet another bid for fame, more lasting and far greater than any she had known: To be the most celebrated spy of all time was certainly a way to go down in history.

She smiled at the prospect as she allowed the man opposite her to light her cigarette and went on musing. There was no guilt or remorse to mar her victory. Without allegiance to any country or loyalty to either side, she would not be weighed down by inner struggles or pangs of conscience. She was as free as those birds outside that hopped from wire to wire on the telegraph poles.

The only thing that gave her pause was the momentary panic she had felt when the inspector asked for her papers. Although she knew that none of her terror had showed (for her hands had been quite steady as she held out the document), she knew that she would need rigorous training for her new career. Certainly it took as much practice to be a dancer as a spy, and she was willing to do her exercises. Having already mastered other, equally difficult arts in the past, she would surely acquire expertise in this realm, which seemed somehow related to sleight-of-hand tricks, hieroglyphics, and the acts of conjurers.

She inhaled the smoke of her Turkish cigarette deeply, remembered the ancient Persian proverb "The walls have mice, the mice have ears," and began to daydream about invisible inks and cryptographers, maps committed to memory or traced on postage stamps, passwords and safe houses, poisons concealed in sticks of kohl, secret staircases, airplanes made of glass, suitcases fit for magicians, disguises more elaborate than for any mardi gras, speeding cars and dazzling getaways, and handsome men who moved in the shadows or died gallantly.

As she contemplated the placid Swiss landscape with its doll-like houses and smug peacefulness (so reminiscent of Holland), a sardonic smile played across her face. She would return to the land of tulips and beldams, gather her forces, and leap—from this unsuspected springboard—with one swift bound into the realm of the Red Tiger and of espionage.

15 The Red Tiger versus The Red Dancer

Excitement in Antwerp was a rare commodity. It was confined mostly to the waterfront; ships arrived there from many ports of call or were lowered, in the great locks, into the sea. Sailors from far lands crowded the ocean-front bars, chattering in a dozen tongues, accompanied by exotic pets (and somewhat less exotic women). They gestured or grunted to order the local beer, or stronger spirits, to drive the dampness of the night away. Now and then joviality was marred by a drunken quarrel or a fist fight, but peace was soon made. The booming cannons that in the rest of Europe had become as common as the thunderstorms of late summer did not create even a faint echo in this part of the world.

The inhabitants of the town actually longed for some danger to put a dash of spice into their lives. The young blades, especially, felt somehow neutered by their country's neutrality. Although they swaggered through the district in which whores sat in showcases offering proof of manliness to anyone—for a price—they yearned for more hazardous exploits: if not battles with armor and crossbow, barbed wire and bayonet, at least the pursuit of glamorous spies or the capture of a secret weapon site—something to break the monotony of this overripe summer and provide a harvest of violence.

Oddly enough, what they so eagerly sought existed right under their eyes. For danger lurked on a quiet street, and deadly maneuvers were plotted in a house that seemed to doze in the long hours of sunshine. Located in the center of town, modest in appearance, and indistinguishable from its neighbors, it would not have attracted the attention of the passerby. True, it had two entrances (one at 10 Seminary Road, the other at 33 Harmony Lane), but while this was somewhat unusual, it was by no means unique. Except for the fact that it was known to be inhabited, although all its windows always remained shut despite the heat, and the drapes were drawn at all times of day, it was just another house in a row of houses. If one chanced to dwell on its air of seclusion or secrecy, the charming façade could assume an almost ominous air. But since habit tends to dull perceptions and conjectures, after a few weeks no one even noticed this peculiarity.

Had it not been for a neighbor who sat at a window directly across the street (perhaps from sheer boredom or being an invalid), the unusual scene that took place on a splendid autumn day would have passed unseen: A limousine, its blinds lowered, approached the house from the direction of the railroad station. The chauffeur, the visor of his cap pulled over his eyes, circled the block as if to announce his arrival, passing the entrance on Harmony Lane and drawing up at the gate on Seminary Road. He did not blow his horn but switched his headlights on and off (despite the bright sunshine) as if according to some prearranged plan. Then, pulling the cap even lower over his eyes, he got out of the car to open the door for his passenger. Long, silk-clad legs emerged from the back seat, followed by the rest of a tall, lithe body. The woman's face was veiled beneath her stylish hat, and a long feather boa concealed her figure. Yet there was something familiar about her gait as she strode up to the door. She rang the bell with a carefully timed series of staccato jabs. The heavy oak panels swung open. She disappeared so swiftly inside that it seemed as if she had been pulled into the dark interior. The door slammed shut behind her—of itself—as though operated by a hidden mechanism.

Then the façade resumed its anodyne air. It revealed nothing of what had just taken place. The limousine had vanished without making a sound. Even the keenest observer would have doubted his eyes and begun to question what he had just seen. The neighbor, being not too keen, began to wonder if the scene had happened at all, then pondered over the rumors that had lately been spread about the house without being able to decide which to believe. For some said it was a high-class brothel catering to government officials and royalty; others thought it the headquarters of a mad scientist; a few jokers suggested that it was a finishing school for female impersonators.

In actuality, it was one of the best spy academies in Europe. Formerly run by Major Groos, it had the finest technical staff in the German army and boasted of the bold and curious situation of maintaining itself in an essentially hostile environment. Already notorious for its exploits in espionage circles of the *Vaterland*, it had become especially prestigious since the arrival of its new directress, Fräulein Doktor. The "Walkyrie of Espionage" was actually a brilliant young woman named Elsbeth Schragmüller, who, although only in her twenties, had completed her doctoral studies at the University of Freiburg in economic history and at the outbreak of the war, for patriotic reasons, had offered her services to German Intelligence. Having convinced the famous Colonel Nicolai to engage her in the *Nachrichtendienst*, she had to content herself (being a woman) with nonhazardous work at the Brussels censorship bureau until she was singled out for the precision and brilliance of her work by General Von Beseler (who, naturally, assumed her to be a man).

A rigorous training period began for her then. She studied at Lörrach under the spy master Friedrich Grüber and at Baden-Baden under the well-known Major Joseph Saloneck, learning the technical skills of her trade and the strict discipline necessary for its dangerous tasks. After being made the only woman officer in the German army, she was assigned the post of directing the Antwerp spy academy.

When small, blonde Elsbeth Schragmüller arrived, she realized that her pupils were hirelings, renegades, and malcontents who had been bribed, enticed, or blackmailed to risk their lives for Germany. Had there never been a war, she would undoubtedly have been a *Schuldirektorin* at some first-rate Lyceum for girls. Now, however, she was faced with unruly, fierce, and often dangerous apprentice spies who sneered at being commanded by a frail young woman. Since her physical presence was far from imposing and gave no hint of her extraordinary will and intellectual powers, she realized that she must rule by fear. She set out to create a legend about her that would serve both as armor and constant threat to rebellious spirits. There could be no genteel dispensing of knowledge; training here must be achieved through iron discipline, perfectly designed rules, and the threat of dire consequences if orders were disobeyed. Most of all, the head of this organization must inspire terror, mystery, and awe.

She began by stalking about the academy in her officer's uniform, playing with the butt of the Browning she always kept in the pocket of the uniform or the handle of a riding crop stuck in one of her boots; never repeated an order more than once; learned to use her deep-blue eyes to shoot piercing glances at anyone who questioned her; allowed rumors about "fool-spies" to circulate, which let it be known that she would sacrifice anyone who had outlived his usefulness or proved inept with as much indifference as others chop off the heads of barnyard fowl. The more intelligent of her pupils began to admire the fluency with which she spoke French, English, and Italian; others marveled at the self-discipline that caused her to work twenty hours a day; but only the most advanced could appreciate the brilliance of her analyses and the innovations in espionage theory she continued to produce.

Within a few months she was known as "the terrible Fräulein Doktor," or "Tiger Eyes," and compared (by the more erudite students) to Mesmer, Luther, Macchiavelli, and Joan of Arc. Other titles were conferred upon her by the enemy secret services who had heard of the "Blonde of Antwerp": *Princesse Jeanne* . . . Miss

Rennmüller . . . Captain Henrichsen . . . The Sorceress of the Scheldt . . . Frau Hauptmann Christiansen . . . The Red Tiger . . . Great beauty was added to her other legendary traits (which pleased her, no doubt) and exploit upon exploit attributed to her, making it appear that she could move with the speed of light or create an astonishing number of selves. All of it served to increase the awe of her students and allow her to rule them without fearing mockery or insubordination. The more closely they thought she resembled a she-devil, the more efficiently she could run her academy. She continued to cultivate an aura of terror and mystery in public. In private she spent long days in her study working on new psychological techniques for outwitting the enemy and long nights in the laboratory creating invisible inks, concocting poisons impossible to trace, and checking the reliability of the latest aphrodisiacs. Not that she approved of the latter. She had a deep disdain for siren–spies (perhaps because she could not have excelled in that category) and far preferred training "vertical" to "horizontal" operators. But now and then an apprentice of the latter variety was sent to her, such as the newcomer now waiting in the vestibule. It was for the honor of the Kaiser and Germany that even such creatures must be tutored perfectly.

She pulled herself up to her full height and prepared to meet the woman whom they called "the Red Dancer," smiling contemptuously as she remembered that she herself bore the title "the Red Tiger." The question was whether the tiger could make the dancer cringe.

In the vestibule, the woman stood in the semidarkness when the door had slammed shut behind her. Two men waited beside her, dim as shadows. She slowly removed her hat and veil and loosened the feather boa wrapped around her as she turned toward them. It was Mata Hari.

One of the men instantly ordered her to face the wall. Pulling a mask from his pocket, he handed it to her, indicating by gestures that she was to cover her face. It looked much like the dominoes worn at mardi gras, concealing the eyes and the upper part of the nose. Mata Hari seemed somewhat amused by this masquerade. But she stopped smiling instantly when she felt her arm grasped rather roughly and was led into the dark interior of the house. They passed intersecting corridors with a large number of closed doors. On each of the doors a small card had been tacked. The beam of her guide's searchlight lit up the cards one by one. None bore a name. All she could see was a letter followed by one or two numbers. There was no clue to their meaning. They continued their walk in total silence. As they advanced, she read: E 7 . . . S 24 . . . I 13 . . . D 46 . . . They stopped at a door marked H 21 and led her inside.

The room was cell-like. It somewhat resembled the one she had occupied long ago in the convent school at Leyde. The furnishings were sparse, even Spartan, evidently designed to dictate the occupant's pasttimes: a cot with an army blanket, a night table full of texts, a small wardrobe that could hold only one set of clothes, no paintings but a map of Europe with a variety of markers, a full-length mirror, which seemed somewhat incongruous considering the rest of the accommodations. The window was shut and bolted; the heavy drapes had been drawn. It seemed certain that the outside shutters were locked also, allowing the occupant no view of the street or escape route.

She turned to glance at her two guides. Their faces were expressionless under their masks, their mouths tight and unsmiling. Before leaving, one of them recited the rules of the house in a toneless voice: Apprentices remained in their rooms for three weeks; meals were brought to them at regular intervals; masks were to be worn whenever there were group meetings—at lectures, in the library, or in the laboratory; she no longer had any identity other than the code number tacked on the door and would always be addressed thus; she could soon expect Fraülein Doktor. When he had finished, both men turned on their heels and were gone.

Mata Hari lay back on the narrow cot and stared at the ceiling. The fatigue of the voyage made her close her eyes, but the last words kept echoing in her mind: Fräulein Doktor . . . Tiger

Eyes . . . She must have dozed off, for it seemed to her that the room was suddenly filled with a heavy scent, half animal, half musky perfume, and towering above her stood a blonde woman with eyes of such intense blue that she felt her will dissolve and heard herself mumbling something about fool–spies. A groan came from her lips as she fought against the nightmare. When her eyes opened, she saw the doorknob turn and had to fight down the terror that made her want to cower under the sheets.

A second later, a small, rather plump woman with a youthful face, round cheeks, and a mouth that somehow resembled the rear end of a fowl, wearing a German officer's cap and a string of pearls around her throat, was staring at her fixedly. Mata Hari almost guffawed aloud. So this was the famous Sorceress of the Scheldt, the Brünnhilde of espionage!

The feeling changed instantly, however, when the woman fixed her with her steely eyes. They held her fast, as though she were an insect about to be impaled by a skilled entomologist. It was no use trying to wiggle from under that gaze. Her limbs felt paralyzed. She thought she was back in her dream.

"Fool," Fräulein Doktor said contemptuously as she looked at Mata Hari's sumptuous clothes and her painted face, contorted into the mimicry of a smile. "Your femme fatale outfits will cut no ice here. This is an academy, not the Green Villa in Berlin or a brothel passing as a safe house. Get on some work clothes and be downstairs in five minutes . . . I never give an order twice." The jeweled hand went into the gun pocket of her uniform, and practically clicking the boots of her heels as she turned, she stalked out of the room.

Mata Hari took off her finery, regretfully exchanging her silk dress for a dark outfit of rather rough material that concealed the body lines, her delicate pumps for flat rubber-soled brogues, her boa for a severely cut blouse that buttoned at the neck, the stylish hat for a drab scarf that covered the hair. Donning her mask, throwing one last look at her disguised self in the tall mirror, H 21 left her room.

A long staircase led to the floor below. She followed the hum of voices into a large parlor that had been turned into a library. Its academic air surprised her. All the walls were lined with shelves on which books were arranged most methodically according to title, subject, and call numbers, dealing with every scientific field related to espionage. On stands at various points in the room she could see color plates representing the uniforms of enemy soldiers as well as engravings of warships of every known model. Huge atlases were displayed in racks, and magazines dealing with economics, chemistry, ballistics, as well as such occult fields as animal magnetism, homeopathy, and ancient lore, were set out on the tables.

The library was lit by a series of lamps with green shades, each throwing a circle of light on the table at which the bent shoulders and masked face of a reader created a strange silhouette. There were about thirty of these shadowy figures, some deeply involved in the pages before them, others conversing in low tones that contained a note of expectancy. It was obvious that they were all waiting for something to happen or someone to appear.

A sharp rap on the lectern at the far end of the room made them all look up in unison. Fräulein Doktor had entered the library soundlessly and now stood before them, striking the wooden stand with her riding crop and looking ferociously at the student body of her academy. All murmurs stopped instantly, and something like an electric current seemed to run through the audience. Even the most thuglike figures appeared to shrink into themselves, the slyest of smiles froze; nonchalant stances turned into martial poses, cockiness into subservience, and daring into fear.

"Today's program," the voice behind the lectern said, "will consist of the usual sections of the advanced course of study—cryptography; laboratory science, camouflage; methods of sabotage, espionage theory; applied psychology; language immersion; martial arts; military history. Disperse and go to your sections at once. Report to the lecture hall this evening at eight o'clock. Dismissed."

Before leaving, Fräulein Doktor turned to H 21, who had attempted to remain inconspicuous by standing behind some atlases,

and barked: "Follow me to my study. We shall see what your quali-
fications are. And then decide what to do with you." The words
had a threatening ring, and had there been a way of escape, the
Antwerp spy school would most assuredly have lost a prospective
pupil. But since all doors were locked and well guarded, the only
path led to Fräulein Doktor's office, which, at the moment, seemed
to H 21 decidedly like a tiger's den.

She remained standing before the large desk, which looked like
that of any schoolmistress, and felt absurdly like a delinquent pupil called to account for her misdeeds. The blonde head remained
for a long time buried in a sheaf of papers, which obviously contained accounts of H 21's background, achievements, and creden-
tials. Now and then a few scribbled words or a nod accompanied
the perusal. After what seemed like an endless deliberation, the
Red Tiger looked at the Red Dancer and said cuttingly: "All I can
see to recommend you is your knowledge of languages. Is it true
that you speak Dutch, French, German, English, and Javanese?"
When H 21 nodded silently, she suddenly shot out a number of
questions in French, German, and English and listened to the answers critically. She looked slightly less harsh, however, when she
heard the languages spoken with great fluency. In this linguistic
battle, H 21 had evidently not lost the first round.

"Of course, any parrot can be a polyglot," the spy mistress
snapped, the moment her student looked slightly relieved. "You
have a lot to learn. The first rule being, that if you have any talent
for languages, you must hide it so that the enemy will speak more
freely in your presence, not flaunt your gifts and thus waste them."
H 21 lowered her head, impressed, despite herself, with the superior reasoning of this woman. Before she could begin, however, to
further appreciate the powers of Fräulein Doktor's mind, she was
dismissed in summary fashion and sent to her room.

She found herself waiting for evening, restless because she had
not yet been assigned a course of study and curious to see what else
this woman's penetrating mind had in store. The lecture hall was
obviously a converted dining room whose formal chandelier clashed

sharply with the rows of folding chairs that had been set up for the audience. By now it was no longer strange to see a whole roomful of masked spectators and to hear them address each other by letters and numerals. She took her seat near the back, noticing that she was one of very few women in the crowd. She had the only pleasant sensation of that day when she thought that this made her part of an elite. But the pleasure was short-lived, for at eight o'clock sharp the double doors at the end of the room opened, and Fräulein Doktor appeared.

The lecture topic was highly technical, and she only occasionally understood a few concepts. Most of the others were busily taking notes, looking, except for their weird attire, very much like any group of students who had come to hear an illustrious professor speak. The subject in question dealt with informers and methods of dealing with them in order to obtain the best possible results. The psychological insights of Fräulein Doktor were diabolically clever. An opponent such as she must indeed strike terror in the hearts of the enemy and give even those who were her allies some cause for worry in case she decided to use her skill against them. H 21 remembered one bit of counsel particularly because it was so devious and yet so true. Long after she had gone back to her room, she heard the incisive voice say: "When you want to obtain information by direct bargaining, lead your informant as far from his house as possible, and to a spot removed from your usual place of operations. Try to give him a wild-goose chase, preferably at night. A weary informant is less prudent and suspicious, more relaxed and expansive, less inclined to lie or to bargain skillfully . . ."

After being sequestered in her room for the probation period of three weeks, H 21 began the actual training period. She realized now with what solid, Germanic scholarship Fräulein Doktor ran her academy. Spy competence was not considered achieved before the end of a fifteen-week stint of intensive work, which included labs in codes, ciphers, communicative dodges, the study of chemicals (their use and manufacture), memorization of maps, charts, and photographs, as well as models of enemy arms (always in the process of revision and elaboration), the scientific analysis of every exercise in furtiveness and guile (rather than the reliance on the usual elementary resources of animal cunning), as well as long tirades to inculcate German patriotism.

The classes were fascinating. And the pride that the directress took in her school managed to communicate itself to the students. They knew that when they graduated from this particular institution, they would be masters at their craft with whom enemy practitioners would have a hard time competing. True, there were already some imitators (such as the French spy school at Dijon and the London academy), but they could not match the Antwerp alumni. Even the sluggards were infused with fervor by the end of their training period, feeling a sense of superiority not unlike that of Oxford, Heidelberg, or Polytechnique graduates.

H 21 was no exception to this rule, except that she was perhaps somewhat more smug than the rest. She began to glory in the fact that Fräulein Doktor had survived two attempts to dynamite her office (shooting, the rumors said, the intruding foe) and that the Antwerp headquarters scored heavily against its diverse opponents, forcing the Allies to compound all their arts of guile and vigilance to blind the spy system now inflicted on them. To be a member of such an elitist organization, which scorned danger and outwitted its enemies, gave her the sense of power she had always found intoxicating. The early days of trials and humiliation were forgotten. She now considered herself a full-fledged master spy.

By the end of her stay she felt triumphant. She had once again overcome heavy odds and was launched on a career that promised to be more glamorous and exhilarating than any she had known before.

Fräulein Doktor must have been well aware of these tendencies. For on the day of her departure, calling her in for the usual admonitions she gave her candidates upon completion of their training, she fixed her piercing eyes upon her and said: "H 21, you have received one of the finest educations in the field of espionage. Use it to serve your masters well. And beware of your pride. It might well be your downfall. Far greater than you have ended tragically due to that flaw . . . Remember also that if you fail or betray us, I shall sacrifice you as ruthlessly as if you were a pawn in a chess game. Do not become a fool–spy . . . Our paths may not cross again, but my eyes will follow you wherever you are . . . Go now and do honor to the *Vaterland* and the cause you serve."

Thus ended the encounter between the Red Tiger and the Red Dancer, which would have consequences notorious in history.

16 Double or Nothing

Paris seemed to have aged in the year and a half since Mata Hari had seen it last. By winter of 1915 the war had deeply marked its face. The lines of fear and sorrow were visible wherever one went. What had once been *La Ville Lumière* was now a dim mass of houses after nightfall. People scurried across streets instead of strolling along the boulevards, as if they were hoping to reach the opposite sidewalk before the next artillery barrage. Motorcars had almost vanished, and the bicycles that had taken their place plodded wearily along the cobblestones. Many women were dressed in black, not for the chic, as they had been before, but in deep mourning, orphaned, widowed, or both.

Even the pre-Christmas season did little to bring cheer to the atmosphere. People hurried along the dismal streets with bundles under their arms that did not have a festive look but were probably black-market foods or wool to knit into socks for men who shivered in trenches that icy winter. Their faces were grim, reflecting the deprivations of this changed world: the meager fires, the scarcity of young men, the prospect of a Spartan *Reveillon*.

She sensed that one had to walk carefully in this city, as though each step were mined or snipers waited in every tree. Aliens and neutrals were looked at with a suspicious eye. It would take only the slightest of incidents to fan resentment into fierce hatred. For these were cruel times. The Allies could not forget that Edith Cavell had recently been shot by the Germans; the Germans could not forget that Alexander Szek had gone over to the British side and revealed their diplomatic code, only to disappear without a trace in Holland during the same year; a French war widow had almost been lynched by her own countrymen because she seemed mysterious to some villagers. A new type of witch-hunt was on in which the war cry was: "Kill the spy!" Mata Hari shuddered when she thought that one had only to fit the description of spies given by a young officer—"They are pretty . . . easy to approach, and impossible to understand"—to end up in a moat at Vincennes with twelve bullets in one's hide.

But she shrugged off such dismal thoughts and allowed the exhilaration of being back in Paris to drive them out of her mind. For, despite the gloom, the city of her first triumphs had a tonic effect. Besides, The Hague, with all its ease and luxury, her aristocratic lover, the diplomats and officers, the dance recitals, left much to be desired. Even a short stay at the Grand Hotel in Paris (where the war seemed to have been carefully kept at bay, so that the morning croissants remained unchanged, and the coffee had hardly more chicory in it than in peacetime) was preferable to her lovely house on the Nieuwe Uitweg, or the visiting cards that sported a crown above her name. And even a few nights spent with charming Frenchmen such as the Marquis de Beaufort (who lived up to *both* parts of his name) provided more excitement than months of being kept by Baron van der Capellen in The Hague.

She contacted her friends, accepted invitations, put her affairs in order, and recovered her effects from the Villa Rémy (which she had stored before leaving for Berlin in the summer of 1914), informed Gabriel Astruc in a letter that she would consider bringing her "new and rather strange dances" to Diaghilev "not for the money . . . but as a matter of interest, and for the prestige," walked blithely through the streets, ordered dozens of pairs of shoes from her personal shoemaker at the "Smart" shop, and visited a fortuneteller, who evidently did not foresee the future clearly in her crystal ball.

For while Mata Hari—by virtue of naïveté or arrogance—thought of herself as a "free lancer," an artiste in every field (including espionage) and wended her way gaily through war-torn Europe, using diplomatic pouches to carry her mail, dodging in and out of embassies, entering ministries through back doors traditionally reserved for glamorous ladies, her downfall was being prepared behind the scenes:

British Intelligence, that paragon of patient, methodical, and diabolical sleuthing, had begun to suspect her moves. Either due to a report sent by an M.I.6 agent in Holland (who had seen her associate with the German consul at The Hague) or the work of the British Censorship Bureau (which signaled names or phrases that conveyed secret information to Germany even in letters going in and out of neutral countries), she was now on the list of "undesirable continentals"—a long step down from being "the most costly delicacy on the continental menu" a few years ago. The hawk eyes of Sir Reginald Hall were upon her. That "genius of espionage," sitting watchfully in Room 40 O. B., could "hear intrigues hatching everywhere in the war" and, by dredging the hidden depths of intrigue, could succeed in "catching everything in his net: Indian Revolutionaries and Irish Rebellions, Sir Roger Casement and Mata Hari." In this, the "cryptographers' war," Hall "the best and most famous of all . . . experts in . . . cipher and espionage," had begun to spin his web of words and numbers, codes and decodings, around his unsuspecting victim, who fluttered foolishly about, attracting attention by her brilliant markings and inability to remain still.

In Paris, also, where she already daydreamed of being Diaghilev's new star and planned to masquerade on both sides of the footlights, laying traps for men in at least three domains, it was her own trap that was being sprung. For by 1915 British Intelligence had, in accordance with a new "Register of Suspects" established by the

Inter-Ally Bureau, signaled her to the Deuxième Bureau. Another hunter waited for her there, watching her every move, the tracks she left as she walked, the terrain she frequented, with all the patience of a deer stalker and the single-minded intensity of a trapper observing his prey sniffing the bait.

But she returned to Holland in the winter of 1916 feeling triumphant and renewed, promising herself that the next trip to Paris would be a longer one and bring to fruition all the plans she had begun during this one. Nothing appeared to warn her. She seemed blind to all danger and when the time came to return did not even pause to wonder over the difficulties she had in obtaining a passport to go to France a second time or the problems she encountered in crossing the border into that country from Spain. For she did manage to embark on the Dutch ship *Zeelandia* after some delay in getting her papers and took a train from Madrid to Paris in the summer of 1916. When the train stopped at Hendaye, however, she was detained by the French officials and not allowed to enter France. Furious at such treatment, she contacted her old friend Jules Cambon (now secretary-general of the Foreign Office) and was finally allowed to pass. Pulling strings was evidently to her liking, and she appeared to think that she was an endlessly successful puppeteer.

A strange sense of invulnerability must have cloaked her, for when she arrived in Paris that spring of 1916 she saw only that it was in full bloom. Not even the war, it seemed, could stop the chestnut trees from sending out their exorbitant blossoms, like hundreds of ardent candles, to glow among the leaves. The Tuileries appeared bright with the figures of children who sailed their toy boats around a jet of water and resounded with their high, clear voices and bubbling laughter. The Guignol gave its performances every afternoon; the puppets addressed the rows of eager faces in Parisian slang and asked advice when pursued by villains, resuscitating from apparently fatal blows, as gaily as if there were no death in the world.

Yet the shadow of death was everywhere: in the cafés, emptied of young men; in the wounded, who dragged their bodies into the sun despite bandages and missing limbs; in the haunted eyes of women, who sat staring into space, tattered letters in their laps; in the reports of the Russian Revolution and of mutinies beginning in the armies of France.

But to Mata Hari there was a tragic beauty in the silhouettes of the warriors who came and went, with the backdrop of battle always giving greater perspective to their movements. They had become lean through exercise and deprivation, tanned by the sun and wind, and held their heads high as they stalked through the crowd. They had the proud stance of conquerors.

One young officer in particular exceeded all others in looks, charm, and nobility. A member of the First Russian Imperial Regiment, Captain Vadime de Massloff was also an aviator and, as she tenderly told herself, twenty-four years old. She smiled when he paid her court but realized, much to her horror, that she was in some danger of falling in love.

It was absurd, she thought, besides being dangerous. For neither courtesans nor spies could afford such gross sentimentality. Yet for once she seemed powerless. Having always ruled in this domain and laughed when others spoke of *"coup de foudre,"* she felt weak when he approached and rooted to the ground as if indeed struck by lightning. She began to wonder where it would all lead and felt almost relieved when he was called back to his airfield at Contréxeville, near Vittel.

As soon as he had left, she worked to regain her equilibrium. She would not let this mere boy get the better of her. Reminding herself of the rather vulgar but effective French proverb, *"Un clou chasse l'autre,"* she proceeded to see other men. One of these, Jean Hallaure, whom she had not seen since her appearance at the Cirque Molier before the war, she met by coincidence in the lobby of the Grand Hotel, where she was staying. He must have seen her cross the lobby, for he had a porter bring her his card. She joined him at his table in the dining room, and while they sipped their coffee, she spoke to him with the frankness that comes from having once been lovers and now only friends. The conversation turned quite naturally to the war. "No way to smash the Germans. They are unbeatable. They're going to bring out some terrifying new weapons . . ." she said. Jean suggested that, having such valuable information, she might give the Deuxième Bureau the benefit of her superior knowledge. But his tone was bantering, and she, with equal lightness, let the suggestion pass, going on to speak of how bored she was in Paris during this dead month of August and confiding in him that she only stayed because she awaited an important visit. She also intimated that her resources were running low but that she expected large sums earned in the Nordic countries and in Germany and was also about to launch a sensational "sketch" for which she needed a musician. Jean introduced her to the friend with whom he had been lunching when she arrived, who happened to be exactly what she sought. He was hired on the spot, and they decided to meet in order to prepare the work that Mata Hari hoped to present at the Casino de Paris.

During rehearsals she often sat down herself at the piano. Being an excellent musician, she demanded or suggested cuts, additions, revisions, and found the two men admiring and compliant accomplices. Jean, however, seemed preoccupied with the difficulties of the times. Mata Hari, gaining confidence, admitted that she had not paid her hotel bills for two months, that she expected a large sum of money from Holland that seemed to be slow in arriving, and that she needed desperately to sign a contract with the Casino de Paris. Jean suggested laughingly that espionage was a gold mine, besides being good "sport" for those who wished to play for high stakes. He himself had been asked to work in the field at Bern but had refused, out of some silly scrupulousness, a fact that the French secret service held against him, especially a man named Ladoux, who, he implied, was probably corrupt and certainly highly overrated. The name seemed to stir up memories in her mind, but she could not place it for the moment, probably because she was too preoccupied with Vadime de Massloff, who had been bombarding her with letters from Contréxeville. Try as she would, she could not seem to forget this man. It was no use resorting to her usual cynicism, to formulate variations on well-known proverbs—*"la nuit, tous les matous sont gris"*—to impose silence on the absurd clamor of her heart. She could not even hold her tongue, but found herself asking Jean about Vittel and how she could possibly obtain permission to go there for a "cure."

He seemed obliging enough, and although he teased her about the restorative virtue of the "waters" she sought, he advised her to go to the Military Bureau for Foreigners located ,at 282 Boulevard Saint-Germain. She thanked him profusely and did not stop to question why he seemed confused, embarrassed, and even a bit guilty as the result of her effusions. Could it be that she had forgotten all the lessons learned from Fräulein Doktor? For she appeared to suspect nothing Jean said and to walk without hesitation straight into the trap he and his superiors had prepared.

For every step in the maneuver that would land Mata Hari at French counterespionage headquarters had been carefully planned, in a manner not unlike that of hunters who beat the bushes in a wooded terrain to flush out their prey: Jean Hallaure, a lieutenant in the dragoons since the war, had recently entered the French secret service. When Colonel Goudet, its chief in 1916, spoke of the frustrations encountered in the surveillance of Mata Hari's movements and correspondence (because she seemed to cover all her tracks perfectly), he bragged of his past encounters with her as her accompanist in the dances she performed in the Cirque Molier and assured Goubet that he would, in the space of a week or so, have found the means of introducing him to "Lady Mac Leod." Knowing that she was staying at the Grand Hotel, Hallaure went to lunch there with a musician friend in the hope of encountering Mata Hari. As luck would have it, she passed through the lobby just at the moment coffee was served. He had his card brought to her and lured her to his table. During the encounter that followed and in the days to come, Hallaure undertook the delicate task of encircling his victim by psychological means, drawing her out, intimating that he had been tempted by espionage and was in disfavor with the French secret service, playing on her love of danger, her need of money, sabotaging the contract with the Casino de

Paris, watching her infatuation with de Massloff grow until she could no longer control her yearning to see him at Vittel, then steering her to the place where the trap was located: A house at 282 Boulevard Saint-Germain, headquarters for both the Military Bureau for Foreigners and, secretly, the French Bureau of Counter-Espionage. Commandant Georges Ladoux lay in wait for her there, eager to tighten the snare around her, but biding his time until the moment was right.

Thus, in late summer of 1916, Mata Hari drew up before the house at Number 282, along the lovely tree-lined Boulevard Saint-Germain—very much as she had drawn up on Seminary Road in Antwerp about a year ago—and was directed by the porter to what she thought was the office that would grant her a permit to go to Vittel but that was actually the den of Commandant Ladoux.

As soon as she opened the door, she realized why the name had been familiar when Hallaure had mentioned it in passing: Ladoux had been one of the visitors to the Villa Rémy before the war and had attended her dance recitals in the garden, along with other dignitaries. She recognized his prewar mustache, his indifference to decorum, the way he flattened the ashes of his cigarette instead of brushing them off his coat, the sharp, shrewd eyes behind his pince-nez. As soon as she had put the various pieces of the puzzle together in her mind, however, she realized where she was and—recalling her training in Antwerp—conducted herself with outward ease and nonchalance, treating the interview as though it were an everyday occurrence in her life.

Not so Ladoux, who, fifteen years later, remembered every word and gesture of this momentous encounter:

I can still see her, as though it were yesterday, despite the summer weather, in a suit of dark cloth and a straw hat with a wide brim and floating grey feather.

She strode into my office with that easy gait which actors have, being used to walking on stage. But she had, besides, that slight swaying of the hips characteristic of dancers, that provocative "salero" . . . of the Andalusian gypsies.

When I did not hasten to offer her a seat, she took a chair, brought it over to my desk and sat down familiarly, as though she were part of the establishment.

"What do you want of me?" she said in perfect French, only slightly marred by a guttural inflection that went quite well with her oriental type.

I said that I knew she wanted to go to Vittel and was ready to give her a pass to do so.

"In that case," she pursued, "do me a favor and tell those cops downstairs who stick to me like my own shadow that, since it's very hot, you give them permission to have a drink to my health in the *bistro* across the street."

I made believe that I did not know what she was talking about.

"I'm followed wherever I go . . . they even take advantage of my being out of the hotel to search my luggage . . . When I return, everything is upside down . . . and you know I don't have the means to give extra tips to the chambermaid."

I asked myself, seeing her tranquil self-assurance and control . . . if British Intelligence which swamped me with notes about Mata Hari for over a year now, was not wrong in affirming, without any proof moreover, that she must be a German spy, a fact which she seemed quite aware of and spoke about freely.

"But," she added, "now this idiotic game has to end. Either I am dangerous, and in that case, you must expel me from France, or I am just a nice little woman who, having danced all winter, would like, now that summer has come, to have some peace of mind."

I asked her for a photo to put on the pass for Vichy. To which she retorted that she had two and would give me one for myself.

I felt I had to warn her that there was an airbase near Vittel. At the mention of this, she grew coy and even appeared shy. She admitted that she was in love with someone.

"Masloff?" I asked.

She smiled mysteriously.

And then the strange creature walked out, with an even more supple gait than when she had entered.

I asked my secretary, Taté, to bring me the Mata Hari file.

Thus ended the first meeting between these two adversaries. Obviously, Mata Hari had come out on the winning side. Her charm had acted on Ladoux. For the moment she held the better hand in this game. She knew that he would be examining a file containing intercepted letters, putting them to every available laboratory test, and that he would find nothing except some vaguely suspicious meetings with foreign officers and the infatuation of a middle-aged (she winced somewhat at the word but forced herself to face its reality) woman with a younger man.

She hurried away from the Boulevard Saint-Germain, her steps light with exhilaration. Vichy was no longer a forbidden zone, an inaccessible Eden; now she could fly to meet Vadime there. Already she imagined it as that "Garden of Delights" that had always captured her imagination on museum walls. Let French espionage headquarters discover that the army planned to bomb German factories from the airfield nearby. The risk only enhanced the excitement of her assignation.

When she returned two weeks later, she was radiant. All who saw her remarked about the glow of happiness that illuminated her features, rejuvenated a beauty that had begun to fade, and gave her the look of triumph that was unmistakably that of a woman fulfilled in love.

True, she had never been so pleasured in her life. But it was more than that. The blood seemed to course differently through her veins; she reacted to everything more intensely, yet more tenderly; felt as uncertain and vulnerable as if she had never been with a man. Moods of wild exultation alternated with spells of weeping, the desire to dominate with that of being subdued. The only constant was a terrible longing to be near this man, coupled with the certainty that she could never get her fill of him. Could it be love? she asked herself fearfully. It had been one thing to have a delightful fling, a passionate escapade, or even to toy abstractly with the idea of falling in love. But this was real, devastatingly real, and its power was frightening. For she felt ready to abdicate her freedom, to make desperate moves, even to take measures that could not be undone and might be her undoing.

Two days after her return from Vittel, she decided to pay a

second visit to Ladoux, now passing as Monsieur Delorme, in his new headquarters at 26 rue Jacob. She was unaware of the emotional state she was in, for she was like a woman possessed. But he did not lose a single detail of her appearance or behavior and long remembered every word of their interview:

She wore the same outfit as before, but her beautiful face seemed paler and her features were rather drawn.

"I must see my friend again . . . He's perhaps the only love of my life," she murmured.

"Well, then you must marry this Malzov [*sic*]," I retorted.

"He won't have me . . . He comes from a noble family," she sighed. There was a long silence.

"Ah, if only I had a great deal of money.

There we are—I thought.

"How much do you need?

"A million . . ." She paused. "If I became the mistress of the German Kronprinz, would you give me that million?"

"It would be really he who should give you the money then."

Another silence.

"I've already been his mistress and it's only up to me to see him again. The Germans adored me and treated me like a queen, whereas to you I'm nothing but a whore . . . Ah, if you had seen our orgies in Berlin! . . . When they were lying on the floor, fawning over my naked feet . . . and I unleashed their animal desires. They all obeyed me . . . Do you want me to try?"

She was standing now, trembling with emotion . . . a marvelous artist who created a role and played it as ideas occurred to her, changing her poses and even the tone of her voice to suit them . . . She was gaining ground on me, using the only weapon with which she could attain me . . . my love for France and the passion for my work. But I played my game well, saying:

"But nobody can get you to see the Kronprinz at Stenay."

"Oh yes," she retorted, "'only one man can do it and he has also been my lover . . . Craemer . . .'"

(The name hit like a bullet . . . Craemer was one of the most important agents of Fräulein Doktor, who recruited spies in Holland.)

"Do you really want to enter our secret service? Watch out, it's dangerous work."

"I have no doubts about that."

"We have no agent in Holland . . . and you could be valuable to us. Do you know how to use sympathetic inks?"

"No, but I'll learn . . . Sympathetic inks, what a pretty name!"

"Yes, but if one is caught . . . it's the firing squad."

"No one catches Mata Hari. She knows how to take care of herself."

"Mata Hari," I said, looking her straight in the eyes, "listen to me. I am certain . . . absolutely certain that you are a German agent, but what I don't know yet, is why you have just made me a proposition which is going to make you betray either the Germans or us. You're a gambler, Mata Hari . . . but this time, it's your own life you are gambling. Red or Black . . . Red, that's us . . . Black, is your German friends. I warn you, Red wins, Black loses. Think hard before you place your bet. Tomorrow will be too late . . ."

"I've already thought about it. I'll play the Red. I'm a gambler it's true, but I'm also superstitious. I know that I will have luck . . . Let me tell you my big secret: My birth sign is that of the Serpent . . . Look at my wrist. Do you see that blue, undulating line? That's my emblem. Snakes that are sleeping, arise at my approach . . . Well, this morning, after having spent the night gambling, I went to see them at the menagerie . . . and, this time, they did not stir."

"Just one last warning then. If you betray us, Mata Hari, you will answer for it before a military court."

She left Ladoux's office, less blithe than after their last interview, and strolled along the rue Jacob, lost in thought. As she passed a house just a few doors away, she realized that it was there that she had danced for the "Amazons" during her first year in Paris, which now seemed ages ago. What a long road she had traveled, and how weary she suddenly felt. She knew nothing of where it would now lead. Only that she had just signed her life away for the second time. For there was no more terrible profession than that of the double agent—caught between two fires that could, at a moment's notice, change to the gunfire of a rifle squad—alone, totally alone, and exposed to the hatred of both sides in this worldwide slaughter.

She shuddered as she approached the Seine. Was it the evening wind that blew more sharply near the water or the long shadows thrown by the lampposts that evoked gallows or the wooden stakes to which the condemned are fastened before execution by a firing squad? For a moment she thought of turning back. But then she lifted her head, clenched her fists, and strode forward across the Pont Neuf.

Tomorrow she would leave for Spain to dance the desperate *paso doble* for which she had just signed an unwritten contract on which, she hoped, her signature was traced in sympathetic inks rather than blood.

17 Last Tango in Madrid

The November winds lashed the waves in the port of Vigo, so that the water rose high along the hulls of anchored ships, and the shutters of the taverns on the waterfront banged loudly against their stone walls. When a large liner appeared on the horizon, it seemed like a ghost ship, and one fully expected to see *The Flying Dutchman* sail into view.

The vessel turned out to be the S.S. *Hollandia,* sailing from South America to her home port in Amsterdam but stopping in Spain to pick up some passengers along the way. Her battered sides spoke of the storms she had weathered during the long journey from the other side of the world, and the strained faces of the crew of the constant vigil against mines and submarines.

The tall, regal figure of a woman, as well as the elegance of her traveling clothes, stood out among the passengers waiting on the dock to board ship. She smiled enigmatically as a naval officer escorted her up the gangway and allowed her gloved hand to linger on his arm even when they had reached the deck. When she turned her face to look back at the land, the other passengers recognized the profile: It was Mata Hari.

She sat at the captain's table in the dining room, reclined in her deck chair, wrapped in furs when the weather was clement, emerged from her cabin in the evenings in all the splendor of her Paris gowns to dance away the night with the ship's officers. The whole voyage was made glamorous by her presence, and the passengers on board seemed to forget the German headquarters that the ship passed at San Sebastian and the abandoned pleasure resort of Biarritz as the vessel moved along the coast. It was not until they reached the English Channel that they seemed to become aware of the sea, its moods and hazards. There the waters turned rough, guardrails were put up around the tables in the dining room, and many passengers turned green when the food appeared or vanished altogether at meal times. Even the polite British journalist who had been regaling Mata Hari with stories of his exploits excused himself from time to time, rapidly disappeared in the direction of the ship's rail, and then returned to finish his sentence out of sheer gallantry.

She, not being plagued by seasickness, remained on deck enveloped in shawls to watch islands glide by and the coast of Cornwall come into view. It loomed high and forbidding in the distance, conjuring up the rites of Druids and practices of human sacrifice. One could also imagine Yseut setting forth from these cliffs, leaving her father's castle to become King Mark's wife, armed with a magic potion that would be the death of her. As the ship swung into Falmouth, the wild landscape seemed more awesome still. It was indeed land's end in this region, the outer reaches of the earth, especially as the fog rolled in and figures climbed the rope ladders leading up the sides of the ship with all the stealth of warlocks.

One of these figures emerged from the mist and approached Mata Hari, standing on deck. He intoned a strange-sounding formula that she could not understand, but in the clipped, rapidly pronounced sentences, a name appeared—"Clara Benedix"—which, for some reason, the speaker seemed to apply to her. When repeated slowly and a number of times, his pronouncement translated into the surprising statement that she was to be taken into custody.

When she objected that there must be some mistake, another

figure—female, and resembling some harpy in the uncertain light—pushed her into her cabin and proceeded to search her bodily. She was so outraged that she could hardly speak. The pair flashed papers at the captain, who looked dismayed and allowed them to take her off the ship. Escorted down the gangway like some common criminal while the shocked passengers watched, she was rushed to the train station and embarked on a journey whose destination she did not know.

All through the long night the couple watched her as they sat in their special locked compartment in the train that sped through the darkened countryside. And all the while the comedy (or tragedy) of errors continued: They insisted on calling her "Benedix," while she insisted that they had made a mistake, that she was Lady Mac Leod, which, under the circumstances, sounded suspiciously like Lady Macbeth, she realized.

She wondered how to soften her captors' hearts. Obviously, there was no use applying her charms to the woman. But the man might fall under her spell. Tears were often effective, and she knew that she looked loveliest with a melancholy expression on her face. And so she applied herself to playing a sad role, which was not difficult, given the nature of her situation. By morning, she knew that her powers were undiminished and that she had made another conquest, for she heard the man whisper to the waiter in the dining car (where she had left her breakfast untouched to foster the impression of dismay) that she was "one of the most charming specimens of female humanity he had ever set eyes on."

This did not prevent him, however, once they reached London—which, it turned out, was their destination—from taking her straight to Scotland Yard.

London was tense. One could feel it even through the glass windows of the car that whisked them through the streets. Probably because it had been the bloodiest year of the war for the Allies. The battle of the Somme alone had claimed thousands upon thousands of their lives. There was much talk of total submarine warfare. And the disease named "espionitis" had swept through Britain with the devastating power of a plague. While their French allies suspected Maggi bouillon cubes, insisting that the shape of the bull's horns on their wrappers contained German messages in code, the British suspected one of the chiefs of their own Secret Service and imprisoned and beat him because the headlights of his car produced strange beams. The madness of crowds had reached such proportions that the Yard had to find a dramatic solution to its plight, for thousands of supposed enemy agents were signaled by the zealous citizens and left them no time to deal with real dangers when they arose. An imaginative inspector thought of inventing an extraordinary character—who was christened Von Burstorph and made an agent of the Kaiser—with fantastic powers of omnipresence and omnipotence. When he was in turn denounced by a righteous citizen, the Yard pretended that it had shot him dead. This greatly enhanced its prestige and pacified the populace for some time.

Mata Hari had begun to wonder whether such was to be the fate of the—to her—imaginary character, Clara Benedix. Did they need a female effigy to burn now, she mused as the car entered Scotland Yard.

But apparently the head of British Intelligence, Sir Basil Thomson, into whose offices she was now ushered, was more concerned with nonimaginary acts. He began to probe, pry, and interrogate, grilling her with questions that, at first, she managed skillfully to evade or answer in such a way that he had to conclude that she was innocent. But as the days wore on, this became more difficult an attitude to maintain. She then reminded him that as a Dutch citizen she was a neutral; but he was adamant, accusing her of "unneutral acts" and intimating that he knew that she was a German agent. She countered, insisting that she be allowed to write to her country's legation in order to clear up this case of mistaken identity and the "terrible accident" that had befallen her. He grudgingly agreed, but her country seemed indifferent to her fate, for there was silence in answer to the request to come to her aid. She inwardly cursed her countrymen, who, once again, had taken a cautious, neutral stance letting their sense of outrage at her life style provoke what they considered "proper" treatment of her case.

When she saw that there was no way out of the dilemma, she thought rapidly and decided on a ploy that might overwhelm Sir Basil by virtue of its element of surprise. "Yes," she finally said, acting as though he had wormed the truth out of her by his expert questioning. "I have come to England to spy." She paused to see the effects of her confession. "But not for the Germans, as you think, but for the ally of Britain, France!" With the typical restraint of an Englishman, Sir Basil did not react. He simply left the office and remained away for a while. She knew that he would contact the Deuxième Bureau in Paris; Ladoux would inform him that she had been engaged as an agent by the French Secret Service. She had only to bide her time, sit back, and smoke one of her cigarettes.

When she was released shortly afterward, she concluded confidently that her ruse had worked.

What she could not know was that Sir Basil's query to Ladoux had been answered quite differently than she imagined. Ladoux's reasons were complex, based partly on a case of professional rivalry with British Intelligence; partly on the growing conviction that she was a German agent; partly on the fact that he felt foolish in having engaged an agent whom the British had warned him about and whom they had now discovered to be in his employ. When he received the message from London, indicating that she had been arrested there, only to claim to be a member of the French Secret Service, he answered, in response to a request for instructions in dealing with her; "Do not understand a thing. Send Mata Hari back to Spain." Thus he had revenge on her for having exposed him to ridicule. He was also sure that she was in a place in which she would be easier to supervise than in Holland and could be followed in the hope of revealing her accomplices.

Mata Hari, unaware of the danger, breathed a sigh of relief as she registered at the Savoy, her favorite hotel in London, there to await the return of her passport. Despite its plush accommodations and the sense of ease that palm courts tend to create, the Savoy was far from tranquil or exempt from attacks of "espionitis." Just recently, the chambermaid informed her as she unpacked her bags, a Swiss busboy had been arrested as a spy because he was seen drawing a map (of the tables he was expected to clear, it later turned out). She wondered what they would do if they knew her story and shuddered slightly when she thought of being driven out into the raw, damp winter of London pursued by an angry mob.

But she was determined to enjoy her stay and proceeded to pursue her usual way of life: accepting invitations from admirers, dining out, attending events at theaters and concert halls, living for the moment while she waited for Scotland Yard's decision on what was to become of her.

One of her most amusing encounters involved two young men, one of whom she found particularly interesting. He had introduced himself as Louis-Ferdinand Destouches (the man who would become the world-famous writer Céline), joked about his horrendous experiences in the French army and his war wounds, and spoke warmly of his passion for dancers. What fascinated her most were his eyes, a piercing blue when one was caught in his direct gaze but otherwise veiled with reptilian cunning. She appreciated his expert appraisal of her legs; besides, he worked in the Passport Bureau of the Allies and could be useful in obtaining her visa. She therefore invited Destouches and his friend Geoffroy to lunch with her at the Savoy. She watched the former closely as they talked. There was something about him that made her feel a kinship, despite their being total strangers, that she could not explain. Perhaps it was a sense that what awaited him in life was an unusual fate.

When her papers arrived a few days later she attributed it to this charmed encounter (little knowing that the two young men had orders to issue her papers after having made her "dangle" for a while).

And so she triumphantly prepared her baggage and got ready to bid damp London adieu. But to her surprise another official communication was delivered to her room. It was from Sir Reginald Hall, requesting her to appear in Room 40 O. B. She wondered what this address in code might be but discovered that it was nothing more mysterious than the abbreviation of "Old Building." Sir Reginald was another matter. This was the man about whom the American ambassador in London had said: "Neither in fiction nor in fact can you find any man to match him . . . All other secret service men are amateurs by comparison . . . Hall can look through you and see the very muscular movements of your immortal soul while he is talking to you. Such eyes as the man has!"

When she arrived, expecting to be transfixed by his gaze, she found a small ruddy man with a disarming smile and twinkling eyes, looking out from under bushy eyebrows, who suggested a kindly Mr. Punch. She felt momentarily reassured. He looked like the traditional benevolent uncle whom, as a child, one waited for at Christmas time because he was sure to arrive with bundles of presents. But suddenly his expression changed. His brilliant blue eyes now seemed to blaze and the tufts of white hair to bristle around the bald pink head until he looked like a demonic Mr. Punch in uniform.

"I have been watching you," he said as she stood before him.

She noticed now that he had an intermittent eyelid twitch (which is why, she had heard, he had been nicknamed "Blinker Hall") that contrasted disconcertingly with his piercing gaze.

"Watching you for quite a while," he continued, his speech a staccato series of utterings, reminiscent of machine-gun bursts on the battlefront.

It seemed to her that she was doomed to be observed by sharp blue eyes to the end of her days. First, Fräulein Doktor and now, Sir Reginald. This master of espionage who was rumored to live in a cottage called "Hawk's Nest," hovered over her like a bird of prey. She felt as exposed as a small animal in an open field, sensing the circling shadow of a giant predator high in the sky. What chance did she possibly have, facing this legendary figure, a lord in the kingdom of spies, whose super Inter-Allied service watched over neutral countries as well as enemy territory?

But then she remembered that she had also heard that he was an Englishman of the old school, with all the chivalrous habits of that breed. She decided to take advantage of this knowledge and to exploit her recently proved status as a "charming specimen of female humanity." Her first ploy was to throw herself on his mercy by offering all the information she had about Section IIIb of the German General Staff. When this did not seem sufficient, she added facts about Section N of the Kaiser's navy. But it was useless, too, for he seemed to know it all from far more reliable sources than she. He silently took down her confession but did not yet seem moved to magnanimity.

It was probably best to look tearful, for she had noticed that Englishmen could not bear to see a woman in those particular straits (which Spaniards, for example, seemed rather to enjoy). She began to weep delicately into a scented handkerchief and noticed that he was about to yield.

"I shall release you," he said, "but only on condition that you never set foot in France again. If you do, you will most certainly be caught and executed."

She wept even harder at those words, and he, apparently feeling that his words had been too harsh, softened the tone of his voice and added, with a fatherly note: "Give up this awful profession, my dear lady, before it is too late."

As she was leaving, his words—more an admonition, such as a kind and worried father might give his wayward child, than a threat —echoed in her ears. She knew, as she walked down the steps of the Old Building, that she had encountered one of the last surviving gentlemen. Not that she had any intention of mending her ways, but it was touching that someone was concerned about her fate. It had been a long, long time since she had felt anyone care in this way. Maybe not since the day her mother died. All the forgotten tenderness rushed back to envelop her; to her surprise, she found herself weeping (in earnest this time) as bitterly as when she was a mere girl.

The next day her papers arrived. But they did not permit her to enter Holland and were accompanied by orders to return to Spain. She realized that she would have to alter her plans due to this unexpected turn of events. And for the first time she felt very much alone, for there was no one to turn to who could explain the mysterious change or share her puzzlement. Holland would have been far safer, she knew. In Madrid, the eyes of the French, Germans, and British would all be on her. She did not know whether Fräulein Doktor, Ladoux, or Hall was the most to be feared. The last was, perhaps, despite his avuncular airs, the most awe-inspiring. She vowed to heed his warning and stay out of France.

Spain beckoned. She fondly recalled her early triumphs there, when she had taken Madrid by storm, and decided that she would rule again, although in a somewhat different domain. When she set foot on shore in the port of Gijon, she felt suddenly free. She was on neutral soil. No one could touch her here. Madrid was as active a hornet's nest of international intrigue as Zurich or Bern, and she believed she had shaken the bloodhounds of both her employers. (In reality, however, a French secret agent attached himself to her from the instant she stepped on Spanish soil and never let her out of his sight.)

As she walked down the gangway to enter the same country she had left only a few weeks before, the episode in England seemed no more than a bad dream.

Once in Madrid, where she arrived toward the middle of December 1916, she decided to work seriously at her espionage. She needed money, and although she had heard that Diaghilev was now performing in Spain, she could no longer even hope to be engaged by him, for he had studiously ignored her advances in recent times. Not that spying would be easy, for she would have to compete with younger, prettier (she had to admit her looks were fading despite her careful attention to every part of her body and all possible vigilance), and more talented operators. There was one woman agent in particular whom she had heard rumors about, who particularly worried her and incited her spirit of rivalry: a double agent named Marthe Richer or Richard, a/k/a "L'Alouette." She had never encountered her in her travels, but since she was reported to be operating somewhere in Madrid, she knew she would inevitably run into her along one of the paths in that treacherous network of espionage in which they both were trapped.

The Ritz, however, cured her of such dismal ruminations. For there great luxury reigned; even the butlers looked haughty and noble (as only Spaniards know how); and high society mingled with international aristocracy (such as Prince Ratibor, who had become the German ambassador to Spain), making appearances with all the pomp and glitter of a world that war had passed by. A new dance had taken the country by storm and reigned in the great ballroom night after night. It was called the tango and had all the passion and elegance that suited her mood. She danced until dawn with lean men, their bodies taut as bows, their moves supple and gliding as those of serpents. The dance was so intoxicating that she might have allowed herself to be drugged by it and forget the world, as pipe dreamers do in opium dens. But she remembered why she was in Madrid, and desperation (as carefully concealed as the wrinkles on her neck when she prepared for a night out) twisted her innards, driving her to seek out those whom she must beguile and betray.

The first of these was Colonel Denvignes, the military attaché of the French Embassy. After the usual preliminaries, he suggested as her first mission for the Allies a visit to General von Kalle in order to obtain information from him concerning the submarine landings of armaments made in Morocco by the Germans. She decided to move to the Palace Hotel, in which Denvignes resided, in order to make contact more easily with him (also to be able to watch his activities, which she could then describe to her other employers), and succeeded in getting a room that was only two doors away from his.

She did not pay much attention to her next-door neighbor on the other side, a blonde young woman who spoke with a decided French accent. The latter, however, did not lose one detail of Mata Hari's moves. For she was Marthe Richard, the young war widow, now operating as a double agent in Madrid under Ladoux's orders. When she noticed the woman, whom she described as "tall and proud," in the room next to hers, she inquired of one of the chambermaids (those invaluable sources of information who know all the gossip worth repeating) who the lady might be. "Lady Mac Leod," said the chambermaid. Lady Mac Leod, Marthe Richard remembered, was Mata Hari, who, according to her latest information, was on a mission here also. Their destinies were going to cross in Spain. The same chambermaid, looking suddenly very sly (much more so than was usual for her calling), pulled a letter from her pocket and held it out for Marthe to read. The letter was short and cryptic: "Meet me after midnight. At 5, Calle Orfila." It was signed with the initials "V. K." (which instantly suggested von Kalle to agent Richard). When she dropped the paper on the table, the chambermaid seized it, saying, "We must leave nothing lying around. The chief's orders," and threw a look of complicity at L'Alouette, tearing the paper into minute shreds.

Mata Hari hurried to the contact point after midnight had struck on the elaborate clock that stood in the lobby of the Palace Hotel. Calle Orfila was at the other end of Madrid, and her driver had some difficulty in locating the address on the wintry night since the inhabitants who reveled into the early hours when the weather was warm had all retired to escape the cold.

When she arrived, she found von Kalle in an intransigent mood. None of her cajoleries seemed to have any effect on him. Neither coyness nor lasciviousness softened the harsh line of his chin or the relentless rhythm of his walk as he paced the floor before her in his boots (which she had not succeeded in getting him to take off). "I have instructions to order you back to France," he barked. She moaned softly when he had uttered these words and remembered Hall's warning with new urgency. But von Kalle would not tolerate any sign of insubordination. "You must obey orders, H 21," he pursued, "for we have no room for questioning in our occupation." She sat mutely in her chair now, her head bowed as though under a sentence that she could not appeal. "You will be paid well," he continued, "an installment of 15,000 pesetas will await you in Paris . . . payable through a friend of yours in the Dutch legation." She knew that meant Kremer, yet felt only slightly reassured. The interview ended rapidly, and she drove back to the hotel, feeling somehow that vast forces had gathered against her that she could not combat. All the rest of that night she tossed restlessly in her sleep, subject to nightmares from which she could not awaken.

Von Kalle did not enjoy peaceful sleep, either. For although he had toughened himself in the course of his long military career, it was not exactly easy to obey orders such as he had received: to liquidate this woman, for whom his country had no further use, like some outworn luxury that one discards without a thought or an aging hunting dog that can no longer run with the pack.

He might have felt less responsible for Mata Hari's fate if he had realized that the trap into which he had just sent her was not only that of his masters but had been set by the French as well. For Ladoux also had a hand in all this and was as set on her downfall as the *Tiergarten* in Berlin. Indeed, both sides of the mighty espionage world had joined forces to catch this prey in their snares.

She stayed in bed late the next day. From her windows she could see the snowy roofs of Madrid, which seemed like a gigantic white shroud ready to envelop her. She no longer knew which way to turn. The French surely suspected her, for Ladoux must have had her shadowed by his men; the British assured her that if she reentered France, she would be caught and executed; the Germans no longer seemed to want her services in Spain and ordered her back to France. If she disobeyed orders and remained here, she was not safe, either, for the long arm of Fräulein Doktor could reach her wherever she was. There was no place to hide and no neutral territory for double agents, whom everyone hated and despised.

Christmas had passed (that feast of children and family merriment) here, making her feel suddenly childless and bereft. Non was in a far-off land. And even if she were here, she would not want a mother who had sunk into such depths of depravity. Now Saint Sylvester approached, when lovers came together to welcome in the new year. And Vadime was on some icy airfield in the Vosges or on leave in Paris (filled with hundreds of lovely young women hungry for the arms of men). The fierce yearning took hold of her again. It had been ages, it seemed to her, since she had seen him. Money awaited her in France. Perhaps she could still realize the wild dream of sharing his life.

She began to daydream, forgetting the vicious gossip of the guests in the hotel at Vittel, their whispers about the "ill-matched couple," a handsome young officer and an aging belle, even Ladoux's man who had attempted to tail them by hiding behind a potted palm in the lobby. She only remembered the leap of her whole being whenever Vadime came into view, the desire to caress him endlessly, the knowledge that she had never loved before. Let him be the first, then, and the last. She decided that she would return to France.

On the eve of the New Year she danced the whole night with an abandon even she had never known before. The faces of the dancers who held her seemed vague, floating before her in a shadowy array, reminiscent somehow of all the men she had known: Rudolph as he appeared in the Rijksmuseum, Emile Guimet, du Parcq in the early Paris days, Rousseau at Esvres, Messimy and von Jagow, Canaris, who had just crossed her path . . . But all of them somehow merged, and as her head turned from the wine and the dizzy round of the dance, it seemed to her that they faded away into the past. When the last partner led her across the floor in the last tango, she realized it was dawn. The light that filtered through the heavy drapes looked ashen, the faces of the dancers haggard. Empty bottles were strewn all about; the streamers that had decorated the ballroom ceiling hung limply from the extinguished chandeliers.

The year 1917 had come. She had a strange premonition that she would not see its end and that her pas de deux with life was almost over.

Part 5

The bloody mathematics that
command our fate.
—Albert Camus

18 Back to the Menagerie

France seemed in a state of exhaustion; the past three years of bloodletting had left it completely drained. Its youth had been decimated—not only by the enemy but by its own officers, as mutiny spread through the ranks, resulting in executions of deserters, of those accused of having practiced "voluntary mutilation," even of those who were deemed insufficiently brave, to "set an example" for their comrades—and demoralized. France sought desperately to hide this state of affairs from its allies and looked within its own boundaries for those responsible. Pacifists and defeatists were attacked in the government, but the country staggered under these interior blows. Inflation had assumed alarming proportions, and an economic crisis threatened to add to the woes. The enormous and futile hecatomb of Verdun had given the final blow. When Mata Hari returned to France, half of its population was starving or sickening or dying.

Luxury still pretended to reign in certain places—such as the Plaza-Athénée, where she decided to stay—but it had the same desperate air as the greed with which some condemned men devour their last meal or inhale the smoke of the cigarette offered by the executioner before the axe falls. Somehow she sensed that this was all in harmony with her own mood and circumstances. For she had come here to wait for Vadime to return from the front; for the money von Kalle had promised she would receive; perhaps even for a miracle that would allow her to leave the dreadful roulette game in which she had placed her chips on both the red and the black. To wait as a condemned man waits for a reprieve when almost all hope is gone.

The days were hideously slow in passing. Never had she had such a feeling of time stretching endlessly. It was as though she were forever frozen in a forward pose, attempting to reach the next hour, the next mail, the night, the morrow.

Not a word came. Not a sound broke her vigil. The tray on which messages usually awaited her lay empty. As did her bed. For she found it impossible to distract herself with dalliance. And Vadime was absent, still absent, and totally silent.

The day set for his arrival had long passed without so much as a sign from him or news of his fate. She searched the newspapers, read the lists of war casualties, attempted to get news from various friends in the military, but to no avail. One could not travel through the war-torn land, and she had no hopes of obtaining another permit to go to Vittel. Her torments became such that she could no longer sleep at night, but sat staring at the wall, imagining all possible disasters with such vividness that she lived every nightmare as though it were real: He had been killed or gravely wounded; he no longer desired her and had left her for another; he had learned of her exploits and hated her for her infamy.

(The last of these was closest to the truth, for de Massloff, about to go on leave, had been called before his regiment's commanding officer, warned about the "dangerous adventuress" with whom he was involved, and ordered to have nothing more to do with her. Frightened and trained in military discipline, he obeyed. It would have taken far greater love or courage than his to disregard a warning of this kind in those hazardous times.)

She continued to wait. Her nights were filled with fears, her days with doubts of a different nature. There was no word from the Germans who had ordered her to return to France. The promised sum did not arrive. She went to the Dutch Embassy to inquire but realized that she was being tailed and had to resort to her old ruse of using the building's secondary exit in order to leave unseen. She dodged through the streets, continuing to feel that she was being shadowed. It must be, she thought, that the Deuxième Bureau, having recently come under much criticism for not doing its job efficiently, had redoubled its efforts. Not that it had been idle before, for she had heard that about 500 spies (or suspected enemy agents) had been arrested since the start of the hostilities and at least half of them executed. But that was apparently not enough, for in times such as these, only a constant flow of blood would satisfy the angry populace's need for human sacrifice.

Perhaps it was best to go straight to the source and brazen it out. She went to Ladoux's headquarters with that in mind. But she left in a state of total uncertainty, having been shunted off to inferiors and completely avoided by Ladoux. When she finally got in to see him after repeated efforts, he was noticeably cold and so evasive that she could not conclude anything from his attitude. Hearing that Denvignes was in town, she tried contacting him in the hope that he could be appealed to in order to convince the French secret service of her devotion while on mission in Spain. But when she finally caught up with him, in the Gare d'Austerlitz ready to board the train for Spain, he almost fled from her, stopping only long enough to whisper surreptitiously in her ear that she was under suspicion by the French.

She would have turned to the Germans, but they frightened her now as much as the French. It was known that they either abandoned their agents if they were suspected by the enemy—as did all secret services—or betrayed them if they proved their uselessness. She remembered the "fool–spies" of Fräulein Doktor and realized with horror that the two whom she had already sacrificed were both Dutch: Hoegnagel (whom she had purposely given a code known to the French so that he would be caught and executed) and van Kaarbeck (whom she set up to be arrested by the French police and shot at Vincennes).

Even if she did not have to fear both her employers, she knew that she must dread the times. It was the season for scapegoats. As in ancient times, when plague or mass misfortunes struck, men looked for victims to carry the blame. Thus, to distract the attention of the populace from defeats on the front, the failure of the economic system, and the defeatist tide that swept over France, spectacular arrests and sacrifices of a public nature were needed. To combat the psychosis of fear and hatred, hatemongers-turned-analysts pointed to hidden causes for the existing traumas or disasters: either the Jews (as Daudet had done), the Masons, or aliens, especially if they were suspected of spying. It had happened once in recent times—in Dreyfus's case—and could certainly happen again, only on an even larger scale..

When the people screamed for blood, and there were no royal heads to roll, then famous victims must be found. She realized with horror that despite her status as amateur, an experimenter in espionage who had dabbled in the art and then cheated to magnify her exploits, she was a perfect target. And the best candidate for the role of prima donna scapegoat.

She suddenly felt an icy indifference come over her. Perhaps, she thought, this was what was known as despair. She was so tired of running, of waiting in vain. She felt old and could not imagine herself turning into a crone gracefully. Vadime was gone. The moments they had spent together were already past, a relic enshrined in the memory. When she looked into the mirror, she saw an aging woman who would live out her days alone or, worse still, become one of those grotesque *cocottes* who had to pay some simpering fool of a gigolo.

The words *taedium vitae* echoed constantly in her mind—was it the Latin of her school days?—but she also expressed her ennui and weariness in other ways. To Priolet, the commissioner of police she met one day, she found herself saying: "You know, it's time I settled down. This adventurous life is fatiguing me." It was a euphemism for feeling washed up, she realized.

The sunless days of February seemed to mirror her mood. They gave the gray streets a grimness that made Paris resemble one gigantic prison yard in which the chimney pots stood like sentinels against the colorless sky. And although she had moved to the Elysée Palace, she felt no better for the change, nor any closer to the Elysian Fields. If anything, more hell had broken loose. Unrestricted German submarine warfare had begun. The mutinies among the French had spread, and there were rumors that two-thirds of the army was ready to desert. She had also heard it whispered in German circles that Mexico was ready to join the war against the Allies. The atmosphere in Paris was more frenzied and close to panic than ever before.

She decided, having finally received the check from Kremer, to cash it as quickly as possible and make one last, desperate effort to escape. She spent the night of February 12 sorting out the various dismal possibilities but was unable to decide which path to take. Her sleep was fitful and disturbed by a series of nightmares, all of which centered around her own running figure, surrounded by multiple shadows instead of a single one, which rose from the ground to enclose her with the hideous snap of a steel trap.

On the morning of the next day, while she was still dozing, finally at peace with the coming of dawn, there was a loud knock at the door of her room. She pulled the covers up to her chin and called out to ask who her visitor was. For one wild instant she thought it was Vadime. But when the door opened, she saw five men in uniform. With typical French courtesy (which makes them observe a pecking order when entering *pissoirs*), they introduced themselves as Inspecteurs Marcadier, Curnier, Des Logères, and Quentin. Behind them stood the well-known figure of the commissioner of police, Priolet.

They informed her that they had orders for her arrest and read her the *mandat d'arrêt*, indicating that she was accused of espionage, in all the convoluted formulas of legal speech.

She gasped but thought it best not to speak. Being naked in her bed, she excused herself, got up, and dressed in the bathroom. Without a word she followed them downstairs to a waiting police car, her face veiled from the crowd that had instantly gathered, her hands protected from the stinging cold by a large fur muff, with which she also fended off the arms stretched out to seize her before the police could whisk her away.

Saint-Lazare prison loomed up ahead, that monument in the tradition of Dumas *fils*, which had held many famous women criminals in the past, among them Mme Caillaux, Mme Steinheil, and Marguerite Francillard. She would join them now. The terrible irony of it was, it occurred to her, that even in this domain she would probably attain great fame, far greater than any of her predecessors.

But there was no time to speculate about this dubious grandeur, for as soon as the car entered the courtyard, and the prison gates swung shut, she was roughly pulled from her seat and, flanked by armed guards, marched along dim, winding corridors. When they had reached the far corner of the edifice, a cell door was opened, and she had just enough time to read its number to know that she was in the Menagerie.

19 Invisible Inks and Aphrodisiacs

It seemed to Mata Hari that her whole life had passed before her sleeping eyes that night (as it is said to happen to one drowning). When she awoke the next morning, she did not know where she was or in what year. She only heard a loud, harsh noise: iron against iron. It seemed to be shortly after dawn. She opened her eyes and did not recognize the ceiling or the walls. Her body ached; she felt rough wool against her skin and an odd, burning sensation at the nape of her neck.

Suddenly it all came back. It was 1917 and Saint-Lazare prison. She sat bolt upright, and the full horror of the scene returned: the leprous walls, the horse blanket and the straw pallet, the sound of scurrying rats, the vermin that attacked the tender spots of skin. And beyond the Judas window in the door, those who would torment her for a long time before her execution. For she was certain that it would be like a trial of heretics and that the inquisitors were already gathering.

All the victims of witch-hunts crowded her imagination: the feebleminded girls and senile hags whose bodies had been racked and burned because a cow's milk turned sour or a man claimed they cast a spell on his cock; mad Joan and her voices; la fille

Mathieu, who had bitten the hand of Deibler *père* as he pushed her under the blade of the guillotine; and the last occupant of this cell, Madame Steinheil, that "expert at shaking men's loins" who had ended in the Menagerie for performing *fellatio in extremis* on one of France's presidents.

The clanking noise came closer. Was it the executioner's helpers or merely the jailer's keys hitting the iron bars of the cells to awaken the inmates?

The sound had reached her door. She cowered in a corner of the cell. The Judas window slid open, and an eye peered inside. Then the key turned in the lock, and two armed guards entered.

"Our orders are to bring you before Capitaine Bouchardon," one of them barked.

The Grand Inquisitor, she thought, remembering that he was the chief investigating officer of the military tribunal. She began gathering together her clothes in order to prepare for the journey, but they gave her no time to attend even to her most elementary needs—not that there were any such facilities in this cell—and marched her as she was, unwashed and disheveled, along the long resounding corridors.

Obviously, the first trial was to be one of humiliation, for the vehicle that was to transport her to the Chancellerie for interrogation was not a closed car but the *"panier à salade"* in which common criminals were conveyed. The guards pushed her up the steps, once they had reached the edifice, and she was soon standing outside the captain's door. One of the men tapped the glass discreetly with his knuckles and waited.

In the moments before there came a response to his knock, she composed her features (and her thoughts), having decided it best to play the role of outraged grande dame, although she fully realized the difficulty of the part, considering her present dismal appearance and reduced state.

A gruff voice bade them enter. She was suddenly confronted with a middle-aged man with a thin mustache, high forehead, arched eyebrows, and rather thin face—very much the officer type. He was walking up and down in the room, tapping the glass of the window-pane and compulsively biting his nails. The last detail she found somewhat reassuring, for he seemed less able to control his nervousness than she. In one corner of the small office she noticed a clerk of some sort who held a pad and pencil in readiness, evidently to take down her statements. The office was well heated, she noted with pleasure, and created a welcome contrast to the icy cell from which she had just come.

Capitaine Bouchardon inspected her closely as she came forward but did not utter a word. She decided to launch into her role instantly (without the benefit of a cue) and pour forth the first words that came to her mind—name, marital status, date and place of birth—followed by a long tirade pronounced in the haughty tone of an important personage who had been treated abusively and unnecessarily disturbed by being arrested as she was getting out of bed, intimating that surely there had been some mistake.

When she had finished, she looked at Bouchardon to see the effect of her monologue. He said nothing and proceeded to bite his nails. For an interrogator he certaintly seemed singularly mute. For one wild instant she thought she had won and would be released. But then she saw a malevolent flash in his eyes as he allowed her to reach the door, which, when it was opened, revealed the same two armed guards who would lead her back to her prison cell.

As she descended the stairs, she could hear his laconic voice dictating to the clerk, whose pen moved with rapid squeaks across the paper:

February 14, 1917. First interrogation. I saw a tall woman with thick lips, dark skin and imitation pearls in her ears, who somewhat resembled a savage . . .

Although the rest was lost when she turned on the landing, she realized that she was dealing with a far shrewder adversary than she had at first thought. He was obviously willing to wait, let her spin her yarn, do her histrionics, let her entangle herself in the web of her own words, hoping she would be caught, stung, paralyzed, and put to death. He had all the time in the world. And his offices were well heated and comfortable. She would have to play against an opponent who had no handicaps in a game in which the dice were already loaded.

The next confrontation was of a different kind. For when she returned to her cell, she was told to prepare for a visit from the prison doctor. Here, perhaps, was someone who would show some sympathy. She planned to appeal to him concerning the hideous conditions in which she was forced to live. In order to present the picture of a woman used to better days, she attempted to smooth her tangled hair and the disorder of her clothes but found, to her dismay that it was more urgent to scratch her head filled with lice (the way she had seen primates do in the zoo).

The door of the cell opened, and Dr. Bizard appeared, accompanied by a grim-faced nurse who eyed her disdainfully. "What a great mare!" the woman hissed audibly. "She has a restless air!" she said, as though she had come to look over the occupant of a stable. The doctor's gaze also was cold as he looked her up and down. She could see that he analyzed her with the pitiless precision of a surgeon, noting impressions as for a case study in a medical text. She could almost guess what his description would sound like:

The features of Mata Hari . . . gave no impression of beauty. She was of Asiatic type, with lots of long, black, sleek hair . . . a low forehead, prominent cheekbones, a wide mouth with lascivious lips, large eyes, a large nose with wide nostrils . . . features not at all delicate or feminine . . . A being without physical charm . . . a savage . . . a proud and wayward woman . . .

In other words, a typical criminal type.

She saw that here there was no hope of appeal or sympathy. His only conclusion was that she was not the suicidal type, that they could dispense with precautions while she awaited further interrogation in solitary.

The interview resulted in nothing more than this, except that her clothing was confiscated, as well as all of her personal effects (some of which had been put under seal at the moment of her arrest), and she was given regular prison garb to wear.

The transformation was now complete. The elegant woman had vanished; instead of her, there was only prisoner Number 721 44625, dressed in rough cloth, her graying hair tied back according to regulations, her skin blotchy from cold and neglect, her body covered with vermin, sluggish from lack of exercise and giving off a strong stench, for there was no means of bathing.

Alone in her cell for weeks during the unpredictable intervals between interrogations, she was alone also in the uneven battle she fought with Bouchardon, for no lawyer was allowed except at the first and last sessions of the investigation. Her arrest had been kept secret, and she knew that almost nobody was aware of her incarceration or her whereabouts. The feeling of isolation and hopelessness sometimes threatened to overwhelm her totally. She sank into a state of apathy so complete that she resembled catatonic patients at La Salpêtrière or Bedlam, only to fly into states of frenzy and almost uncontrollable rages.

But when she was called to face Bouchardon again, the animal instinct of self-preservation returned, and she fought with the only arms at her disposal: masks, pantomime, imitations, and all the tricks of illusion she had learned in various theaters. Torrents of words poured from her lips, however (perhaps in reaction to her long weeks in solitary), and she delivered endless soliloquies, while Bouchardon sat there silently, listening, watching, waiting. Like some great mustached spider, she thought, lurking in the background as she paced the floor, gesticulated, mimed actions of epic proportions much in the manner of the shadow puppets in the Javanese plays that had enchanted her so many long years ago.

Suddenly, however, he thrust the handbag at her that had been confiscated and put under official seal at the time of her arrest. Its contents now stood on his desk: a whole array of jars, flasks, tubes, vials, sticks of rouge and *kohl*, as well as pillboxes and bottles of medicine. She blanched slightly at the exhibit but feigned great surprise at seeing her intimate belongings thus displayed, saying, with a coy smile:

"You have discovered all my beauty secrets, Captain. And know now that I resort to aphrodisiacs."

"It is not beauty which you are after," he countered with an ogrelike tone in his voice, "but the transmission of secrets."

She put on her most puzzled face and waited for an explanation.

"We put the contents of your bag into the expert hands of one of the topmost specialists in secret service techniques. He found two objects particularly interesting." He pointed to a bottle of lotion and a metal tube, while referring to notes that obviously described the chemical composition of their contents.

"It just so happens that they contain chemicals which—one by simple dilution, the other by solution—produce sympathetic inks which are very new and are even considered to be the latest development in this domain."

She passed over the lotion lightly, insisting that it had been prescribed by her physician, Dr. Vergne, for medicinal reasons and filled by the Pharmacie Roberts, which had the authorized order on file. As for the tube of oxycyanide of mercury, she whispered to Bouchardon with a confidential and somewhat embarrassed air:

"You know, Captain, a woman in my profession must protect herself, for men do not wish to be bothered with such details as venereal disease or pregnancy. The chemicals it contains were given to me by a doctor in Madrid not only as a disinfectant but with the recommendation that, when used as a douche, it was the best contraceptive to be found in Spain."

He seemed to be nonplused by her answers, but she did not know whether to attribute her momentary triumph to her presence of mind or to male repugnance for what men liked to refer to as "female plumbing." Whichever the reason, he dismissed her almost instantly.

There followed a lull in the interrogations, and although she felt some relief, the days in prison became even more intolerable than before. More than anything, she suffered from the silence and the sense of stagnation. It was as though the world had forgotten her in her dungeon and she were already dead and buried. Or, worse still, buried alive. None of her so-called friends came to her aid, her nation seemed to ignore her fate, her lovers had evidently forgotten her. Most painful of all was Vadime's continued silence. At times, she was certain that he was dead.

When she could bear it no longer, she turned to her inquisitor for help. Anything was better than this uncertainty. She would beg Bouchardon to give her news of Vadime. Addressing him with a title more flattering than the one she gave him privately, she wrote:

I would be grateful, your Honor, if you would give me some news of Captain Massloff. I am worried and weep such a great deal. Please be kind enough to search for him in the hospital at Epernay. I beg of you. I am in so much pain at the thought that he is perhaps dead and that I was not able to be near him. He might even have thought that I had forgotten him. You do not know how I suffer. Get me out of here, I cannot bear it anymore . . .

(But the only result of her entreaty was to convince Bouchardon that the sole passion of this woman of forty had been a young Russian officer of twenty-five and to incite him to interrogate de Massloff about Mata Hari, an interview that ended with the latter's renunciation of her.)

Her cry for help remained unanswered. The days continued to pass with nothing to mark them, blank spaces in a world without time. It occurred to her that she was losing her mind.

Certainly she had already lost her looks. The harshness of prison life had undermined her health as well as her sanity. She dared no longer look into the primitive mirror she had used at the start of her stay, the underside of a metal plate. But one thing was sure, she said to herself with a bitter laugh (for she had lately begun to speak her thoughts aloud): She could no longer bank on her seductiveness or hope to count on French gallantry.

This was confirmed when next she was called in to face Bouchardon. He was studying her passport as she entered, and as he looked up, she knew that he compared her ravaged face with that of the charming young woman in the photo affixed there. It seemed to her that she could read his thoughts:

Had she been pretty? Without a doubt, from her passport photo. But the woman . . . in my office . . . had suffered many affronts from time. Eyes big as eggs, protruding, yellowish and full of red striations, a bulbous nose, chapped skin, a mouth that touched the ears, the swollen lips of a negress, teeth as big as plates with a gap in front, graying hair no longer covered by dye, she hardly resembled the dancer who had bewitched so many men . . .

Shocked into lucidity by his appraisal, she realized that it would be difficult to convince a man who saw her in this light that her meetings with numberless diplomats and military men had been solely for amorous purposes and not to elicit information, that the large sums of money she had received over the years were the wages of sin rather than espionage. Thus, when Bouchardon turned to her meeting with "von K." in Madrid, she insisted that she had seen him only on the orders of Denvignes. But Bouchardon seemed convinced that the contrary was true, although it appeared impossible to prove anything conclusively.

She sensed that he had something up his sleeve or was waiting for further information. And also that he had arrived at the conclusion that she was a spy and would not be shaken from his conviction. Even slight suspicions sufficed to confirm him in his belief. Besides, what hope was there in a world in which even Dreyfus himself, grown old, insisted, upon hearing that someone had been accused of spying on the basis of slight evidence, retorted: "Well, you know, there's no smoke without fire."

Her fears were realized on the first of May. Bouchardon, after months of interrogation, which proceeded in circles and resembled a pursuit on a moving carousel, decided to shut himself up with his prey. The next time the armed guards came for her they led her to an underground chamber, a sort of cellar far from all intruders. For an instant she thought that it was a torture chamber, and she looked for the thumbscrews and the rack. But it was another kind of torment she was about to be subjected to. Bouchardon held several pieces of yellowish paper in his hand as she entered that he' raised in the air like a player who holds trump cards.

She recognized the color and format and knew that they were telegrams.

"The game is over, H 21," he screamed. "I have the evidence to damn you!"

She turned very white, and shivers ran over her body. The jig was up. They had to be telegrams sent by von Kalle receiving and giving instructions concerning her, written in a code that the French could decipher and that they had managed to intercept. Either the cryptographers of the Allies had been working overtime, or the Germans had decided to make her a fool–spy. In both cases, she was lost.

Her faintness was not feigned this time. She had to be almost carried back to her cell, in which she lay for many days in something resembling a delirious state. She developed a high fever, which, from the snide remarks she overheard, the others attributed to· what the French called the "Neapolitan malady" and to which other nations, returning the compliment, gave the name *"Morbus Gallicus."* Mocking her frantic request for water, which she downed like an animal whose thirst takes gallons to be slaked, they spread the rumors among the inmates that—aside from her other repugnant characteristics—she had syphilis.

As soon as she had slightly recovered, she was confronted with Ladoux. A new battle was about to take place. She knew that they would play with each other as cat and mouse and prepared herself for the duel. His opening words were calculated for their dramatic effect:

"I warned you, Mata Hari. But you insisted on playing the Black. You will now be condemned. It's all over." He paused for an instant. "I see only one way for you to save yourself. Tell me the whole truth, and I give you my word of honor that I will do everything I can to keep you from the firing squad."

She thought rapidly, realizing that he was hoping by this promise to entice her to reveal her contacts and accomplices, and said (putting every remaining ounce of strength into her voice):

"Give and take, Captain. You give me your word as a soldier that my life will be spared, and I tell you everything." At this, Ladoux became evasive and said that only the judge could make such a promise. But obviously the latter was not willing to enter into such a deal. For when she was called into Bouchardon's office, Ladoux had to admit his impotence. She looked at her opponents with a defiant air and announced:

"Very well, then. I shall not say another word. Take me back to prison."

They did as she had asked and left her there while spring turned to summer. She could hear vague sounds of birds outside her cell and at times even catch a glimpse of the tender blue sky. But in the world outside (as she heard from bits of the jailers' conversation) there was neither warmth nor tenderness. The mutinies had reached their paroxysm, and the numbers of those involved had risen to 40,000; Pétain blamed spies for this state of affairs; the army just ordered massacres. Paris was paralyzed by strikers, of whom 100,000 were massed in the streets; there were rumors of troops marching on the city. It was a moral Verdun, almost as hideous as the battle of the same name that had cost half a million lives. And to top it all, Nivelle's offensive had failed.

She knew what all this meant for her. She was a sensational capture, and if built up with the right publicity, she could provide a diversion important enough to hide the fatal errors of the military and bear the guilt they were so eager to unload.

There was no hope left. The only faint remaining possibility was to do what she had refused in the bargain proposed by Ladoux, to tell Bouchardon everything in exchange for an attempt on his part to save her life. On May 21, she thus offered to "confess."

The story she offered Bouchardon (in the hope that it would pay the ransom for her life) dealt with von Kremer—whom she identified simply as the German consul in Holland, neglecting to mention that he belonged to Section IIIb of the Kaiser's secret service—who, she said, had come to see her in May 1916 to ask her to procure information that interested the German military during her next visit to France. He had offered her 20,000 francs as a first installment and promised her a great deal more if she succeeded.

She became so engrossed in her tale that she did not see the gleam of triumph in Bouchardon's eyes as soon as she mentioned Kremer's name.

She went on to say that she had pretended to accept the offer (to avenge the loss of her furs in Berlin at the start of the war, which had been Kremer's fault). When she had taken the 20,000 francs, she claimed, Kremer said with a smile: "Now you are agent H 21. When you have some information you wish to communicate to me, use these three flasks." And he gave her the flasks, which were numbered 1, 2, and 3. Numbers 1 and 3 contained a white liquid, while the liquid in Number 2 was green. He wet the paper with the first, wrote with the second, and made the writing disappear with the third. "These are secret inks," he said. "Write with them between the lines of an ordinary letter and send it to me at the Hotel Europe in Amsterdam."

She finished her story by saying: "When Kremer left, I pocketed the 20,000 francs and threw the three flasks into the canal in Amsterdam which empties into the sea. Then I forgot all about Kremer and the German espionage service."

When she fell silent, waiting for the effect her confession had produced, Bouchardon got up suddenly and advanced toward her. His face had a leer on it as he said: "Now I have all I want to know. You can go back to your cell. We have come almost to the end of this affair."

She left with the uneasy feeling that somehow a turning point had been reached. The pieces of an unknown puzzle must have somehow fitted together for Bouchardon to have such a triumphant air. And she had, without meaning to, supplied the missing piece.

Weeks went by. It was now the time of the summer solstice, when violence reigns, and the red sun stands at its zenith, a time of sacrifice in old religions, a time when fires burned and consumed human victims.

On June 21, she was called before Bouchardon for their last meeting, with which the hearings would close. She found herself trembling as she climbed the stairs. For she knew that his judgment would really decide her fate. She had been told that her lawyer could be present and had contacted her old friend (from the Musée Guimet days) Maître Clunet, who, although quite old now, was the only one she felt she could trust to undertake her defense.

The summer heat made the small office stifling. The drone of voices, endlessly reiterating all the accusations and denials of the past four months, began to sound indistinct, and she had the strange sensation that the voices came from another world. She felt utterly exhausted and faint. Seeing Clunet through a haze of heat, she found him bent, obsequious, and rather grotesque. The knight in shining armor who was to fight for her honor looked ready for the grave. And might well lead her to her grave, she thought, but was too weary to object. Both men seemed somehow to be in league against her, but perhaps that was just an illusion or a mirage produced by the heat.

She felt ready to collapse, but the meeting was about to end. She heard one phrase only. But that one with the clarity of ringing steel: "To sum it all up, it's . . . a case of *flagrant délit*." Which meant that he considered that she had been caught red-handed and that there was no longer any question of her guilt. The verdict of Bouchardon was that she was guilty. The rest, she knew, was pure formality. She would now pass before a military court and be judged and sentenced as foreseen.

A black hole of despair seemed to engulf her as she descended the stairs, assisted by Maître Clunet, who babbled foolishly about the high hopes of the case, the brilliant defense he planned, and ended his tirade by nodding his head in senile fashion and repeating in a high, whining tone (reminiscent of a tearful child): "No, no,

Poincaré will never allow your body, formed by the hand of the Graces, to return to clay."

Mata Hari suddenly laughed. She drew herself up with the pride of an injured lioness, looked about her, and shook her head as if to free herself from torpor. She was not ready yet to lie down and have them butcher her submissively. She would fight to the end. And, as always, unaided and alone.

20 The Trial

"THE HUNTING SEASON HAS OPENED," she heard the newsboys cry as she sat in the Concièrgerie on July 24, waiting for her trial to open. She looked about the ancient edifice (resembling medieval castle and dungeon combined) and at the thick walls, which, some said, were smeared with the tears and blood of prisoners over the centuries. Its cells had held many royal captives—Marie Antoinette among them—who, during the French Revolution, were incarcerated there, awaiting the carts that were to take them to meet "The Widow" just across the Place Dauphine. The rabble had greeted them with the same bloodlust that they now welcomed the hunting season.

"1080 DAYS OF WAR TODAY. FIERCE FIGHTING ALONG THE CHEMIN DES DAMES," another news-seller cried. And she thought that she would also fight a battle today, not like a lady but for one woman's life. The men she had to face were her enemies, as surely as the foe that soldiers meet in trenches. Only she had no arms except her wits. Victory or defeat would come not under the open sky but in a shut arena devoid of spectators. For her trial was to be held "*à huis clos*," that threatening, ancient phrase evoking all the terror of subterranean chambers and secret tribunals without appeal.

A military escort suddenly arrived. Surrounding her as though they were the bodyguards of a high personage, they escorted her to the courtroom. There were sentinels posted outside, holding back the crowd and allowing no one to approach the doors or come within thirty feet of the room. When the portals had closed after her, not a sound penetrated from the outside. The world was now out of reach. She stood in a narrow circle of hell, alone with her would-be executioners.

The judges sat before her on a raised dais, looking stern and resplendent in their uniforms, covered with medals and decorations, bearing their titles of Colonel, Capitaine, and Lieutenant with righteous dignity. They looked down upon her, in the box of the accused, attempting to pull herself up to her full height as she faced them. She stood there, very erect, elegantly dressed for the occasion (they had allowed her to change from her prison garb into a dark blue, rather low-cut dress and a tricornered hat), and raised her large, burning (and carefully madeup) eyes to look at Colonel Sempron, Lieutenant Mornet, and Capitaine Bouchardon.

She waited attentively for their attacks to begin, knowing that they would be swift and that her life or death would be decided in a matter of hours. She knew that she must answer them with speed and precision, for the military does not tolerate hesitation or bad memory. (Men had been shot for an instant's procrastination or the faulty enunciation of a password.) All the control of her body that had gone into her dancer's art must now be exercised over her thoughts and words.

The first to speak was the President of the military tribunal, Colonel Sempron. His voice was hard as he proclaimed:

"You have been under surveillance since June 1916. Our reports show that you were always accompanied by military men. Exclusively military men. The wealthy men who frequented the Grand Hotel at that time did not interest you. You had to have uniforms. The rank, the branch, the nationality, did not matter. What you wanted were soldiers. Is that usual for a courtesan who is not interested in military secrets?"

Her voice was clear and strong when she answered; but despite all her efforts at control, it trembled somewhat:

"I don't know if it's usual, but I do know that I have always loved officers. Ever since my childhood, nothing seemed to me more seductive than an officer. I love men whose profession is dying. They have other needs than those who vegetate until they reach the grave. I am a woman who gets paid for her favors, but I have never hesitated between a rich banker and a poor officer. It was the latter I always chose. Always. My greatest pleasure was to sleep with them without there ever being a question of money involved. You can ask all those who sought me out. They all left me feeling contented, and without my ever having spoken to them about the war, nor having asked them anything indiscreet."

Sempron made no comment after her reply. He went on to pursue another tack: her trip to Vittel to visit de Massloff. In an accusing voice, he stated that she had told Ladoux that she was in ill health at that time and yet written to her Dutch lover Van der Cappelen that she was in fine shape. Then seemed to pause triumphantly, as though he had caught her in a trap.

She smiled a worldly smile and said:

"I told Captain Ladoux that I was ill because that was the excuse that permitted me to go and meet Massloff. And to my lover, I said that I was well because men who pay do not like sick mistresses. They want women who are merry, always ready for feasts and pleasure, scantily dressed in lace, not wrapped in flannel and wool blankets."

The judges looked embarrassed, coughed, and seemed somewhat at a loss on how to continue. Captain Bouchardon bent and whispered in his neighbor's ear:

"What picturesque French, and so full of savory expressions . . . what suppleness of mind! What irony! And what fittingness in her replies! To think that French is not even her native tongue!"

Sempron retreated and let the attorney general, Lieutenant Mornet, take over the next charge: He concentrated his barrage on the money she had received from Germans. She used her "favors" as camouflage. He pursued, suggesting that 20,000 francs was a high price and surely paid for more important services. She resisted, claiming that a woman as rich and sought after as she could not have been approached by an admirer for a lesser sum.

But Mornet proclaimed loudly, with the voice of a histrionic preacher spreading the gospel truth, that she had received those 20,000 francs for services rendered to the Germans during a visit to France in 1915. At that point, she gave in to one of her great rages. Screaming at her persecutor, she cried out in a voice that echoed from the walls: "Mephistopheles!"

He ignored her outcry and went on to attack methodically from another side, reproaching her with the fact that she claimed to be a débutante in espionage and yet demanded one million francs from Ladoux.

She returned to her former line of defense:

"It was my contacts I was selling him. And I assure you, those were worth much more than a million."

When Mornet saw that he could not prove her guilt with his first tactics, he began to bombard her line of defense by pointing out its inconsistencies. Why, for example, did she say nothing to Ladoux about her meeting with Kremer, or about being H 21, or about the mission she was sent on—which she had revealed in her confession to Bouchardon on May 21—while to von Kalle she had explained that she had pretended to have joined the French Secret Service.

"Whom were you betraying?" he screamed. "And whom are you serving? The answer is self-evident."

As the questions ripped into her like so many bullets in an artillery charge, she suddenly stretched out both her arms, pointing at him, and cried in a voice shrill with violence:

"That man is evil!"

But she controlled herself instantly (when she saw the threatening looks of the judges at her outburst) and continued in a calm, logical tone:

"Perhaps the answer is self-evident, if one wishes to make a desired truth plausible! But the *natural truth* is quite different. To admit my meeting with Kremer would have aroused Ladoux's suspicions, and I would have risked losing my million . . . With von Kalle, on the contrary, I was on a precise mission. I wanted information; passage to Belgium via Germany, since I could not enter England; money, since Captain Ladoux left me without means. How could I have gotten all that without a stratagem? . . . Only one tactic was possible: to give the Germans the impression that I worked for them, while it was the French who had the upper hand."

Now that she saw that she might succeed, she pursued lucidly what she had begun to suggest, taking advantage of every possible argument in her favor:

"The proof that I am telling the truth, is this: If I had felt guilty in the slightest, would I have come back to France, knowing that I was under suspicion?"

She seemed to be winning the day. The admiring glances of some of the jury told her that they appreciated her intelligence and skill at reasoning (qualities which the French, at least since Descartes, have had an exaggerated respect for).

But just as she began to feel that she had won a minor victory, the witnesses for the prosecution were brought in. The most violent and the one whose judgment would undoubtedly have the greatest weight was Colonel Goudet, the head of French counterespionage. His pronouncement was short, but it had the impact of a charge of dynamite and the finality of the trumpet of doom:

"I have studied the case of the accused with extreme care and have arrived at the conviction that you have before you one of the most dangerous spies which the German Intelligence Service has ever used."

There was a terrible stillness in the air when he had spoken. The judges drew themselves up until they appeared like giants on their dais and loomed over the figure of the accused. The jurors sucked in their breath sharply and seemed to look at her in a different light, as though someone had changed the illumination and she now appeared in lurid colors (such as the figure of the villain in the horror plays of the Grand Guignol).

She heard a faint, cracked voice from a corner of the room as Maître Clunet, fumbling with his papers and consulting her dossier as though he were seeing it for the first time, announced:

"The defense will now proceed to present its witnesses. . . . The innocence of my client shines with such radiance. . . ."

Colonel Sempron did not allow him to finish his naïve diatribe.

"Bring in your witnesses," he ordered.

They were Jules Cambon, the ambassador, Henri de Marguerie, the diplomat, her manicurist, the fortuneteller who had warned her of her fate . . . The court did not seem impressed by their testimony. Even the most important (such as that of Cambon) was lukewarm and would not have convinced anyone to do more than hire her as a governess. Lieutenant Hallaure and Adolphe Messimy had stated that they were unable to appear. (She noticed that when the latter's name was mentioned, the court instructed the stenographer to record only the first and last letters of his name: M———y.) She wondered why, but was instantly recalled from her musings when she heard a letter read that came from his wife stating that her husband was unfortunately suffering from rheumatism and could not leave his room; and anyway, she went on, her husband had surely never known the woman in question.

The jury guffawed, and Mata Hari laughed for the first and only time during the trial. "That's a good one! He hasn't known me! He's got some nerve!"

But she stopped laughing instantly when she heard the name of Vadime de Massloff pronounced. She looked wildly around the courtroom, half expecting to see his tall, slim figure approach and the face she had so longed to touch appear in the witness box. She had begged Maître Clunet not to call him, writing: "You must understand: I love this man more than anything in this world. Therefore, he is the only one I do not have the strength to see again!"

But the court announced that he had been unable to appear. She sank back with a feeling of relief so great that she felt almost faint. Mornet, however, held out a sheet of paper from which he read the text of an interrogation of de Massloff by the police commissioner of Rennes. She listened anxiously, wondering whether he had been in danger, raising her hands as if to shield him from the harm that might have come to him because of her. Mornet's voice became louder as he read: "Captain de Massloff went to the Elysée-Palace on March 3, 1917, and asked for Madame Zelle, also known as Mata Hari, despite the orders to the contrary from his commanding officer." She smiled at this rash and courageous proof of his love. The courtroom seemed to fade away. She only thought of Vadime's eager face as it would have bent over her on that day if only she had not been rotting in prison. And of the radiant hours that would have followed.

Instantly, however, the sharp voice of Mornet cut into her reveries: "Captain Massloff then went on to state: 'The sole purpose of my visit that day was to *break off* my liaison with Madame Zelle.' "

A gulf suddenly opened beneath her feet. She fell a long distance, without ever seeming to reach the bottom.

The court noted that the prisoner had fainted and ruled that the proceedings were suspended until the next day.

Already, in the early morning hours, the newsboys called out in the streets: "MATA HARI TO BE JUDGED TODAY" . . . "TWO SPIES EXECUTED" . . . And the crowd gathered outside the courtroom, hoping to catch a glimpse of her as she passed with her armed escort.

In the corridor, they crossed Maître Clunet, draped in his robes, which, too large on him or badly fastened, dragged on the floor and swept the dust that lay on the marble surfaces. His head rocked back and forth grotesquely as he confided to one of his colleagues that he had high hopes. And the file he carried under his arm slipped now and then and had to be readjusted by an assistant to keep it from falling to the ground. Mata Hari had the sinking feeling that the rumors she had heard about him were right, that he had never wanted to consult her dossier, refusing to hear of the charges against her, and that his lack of awareness and "sublime" naïveté would lead her straight to the firing squad. But it was too late now to seek a remedy, too late for almost anything but a last-ditch stand of her own.

She walked into the courtroom where the members of the court-martial now stood in full regalia, awaiting the public prosecutor's speech. Lieutenant Mornet proceeded to ask the eight vital questions of the military tribunal. Is the accused guilty of:

1. Having, in December 1915, entered the entrenched camp of Paris, in order to obtain documents and information in the interest of Germany, an enemy power?

2. Having, in Holland, during the first part of 1916, procured for Germany, an enemy power, in the person of Colonel Kremer, documents and information likely to harm the operations of the French army or to compromise the safety of military installations or locations?

3. Having, in Holland, in May 1916, had intelligence with the enemy nation of Germany, with the aim of furthering the enterprises of this enemy?

4. Having introduced herself, in June 1916, into the entrenched camp of Paris in order to procure documents in the interest of the enemy power, Germany?

5. Having, in Paris, since June 1916, had intelligence with Germany, with the aim of furthering the enterprises of this enemy power?

6. Having, in Madrid, in 1916, had intelligence with the enemy power of Germany, in the person of the military attaché von Kalle, with the aim of furthering the enterprises of the enemy?

7. Having, in the same place and at the same time, procured for Germany, in the person of the military attaché von Kalle, documents and information liable to harm French army operations or to compromise the safety of its installations or locations?

8. Having, in Paris, in 1917, had intelligence with the enemy power of Germany, with the aim of furthering the enterprises of the enemy?

The jury looked sterner than ever and seemed to drink in every word of Mornet, as if mesmerized by the repetitious and pernicious phrases. Maître Clunet looked shattered and seemed to grow smaller, as if each word were a hammer blow.

The president called on the accused, asking her if she had any statements to make before the jury entered into its final deliberation. Mata Hari stepped to the very edge of the accused's box and said slowly:

"I admit that I am H 21 and have received money from von Kalle, a German spy-master. But he was my lover and paid me out of official funds, putting me nominally on his spy roll.

I . . . I am telling you it was to pay for my nights of love. It is my . . . my price."

Her speech had faltered, for she had seen the dubious expression of the jury. She realized that hers was only one small voice in the whirlwind of violence and fear that the war had created. And that it was not likely that she would be heard by the ears that had become deafened by the thunder of cannons and the sharp crackle of machine-gun fire.

But she would make one last effort to break through the barrage of Mornet's artillery. Drawing herself up with all the majesty she had left from the old, bygone days, she proclaimed:

"I call upon you to note that I am not French and that I reserve the right to cultivate any relations that please me. The war is not a sufficient reason to stop me from being a cosmopolitan. I am a neutral, but my sympathies are for France. If that does not satisfy you, *do as you will.*"

The jury filed out silently. She was removed from the courtroom, while the jurors deliberated and the verdict was publicly announced. Only then would she be called before the tribunal again to receive her sentence.

The ten minutes that elapsed before the end of the deliberation seemed to last eons, yet fly with the swiftness of a bullet that finds its mark. Suddenly she was again before her judges. She noticed absentmindedly that Clunet was crying and that a group of soldiers stood awaiting orders at one side of the courtroom.

The presiding officer, Colonel Sempron, read her the verdict: *Yes, to All Questions Unanimously*.

The platoon of soldiers shouldered their rifles.

"Present arms!" ordered the adjutant.

The sentence was death.

They were waiting for her outside. A milling crowd, larger than any that had lingered around the stagedoors of theaters, craned its necks to catch a glimpse of the seductress–betrayer condemned to die. It was not every day that one could catch such a show.

Finally, she appeared. "Tall and erect, she dominated the police who accompanied her by at least a head. Looking very elegant in a floating blue coat, she passed through the crowd with her supple dancer's gait, her head held high and a smile on her lips—her last smile to her last audience!" one observer noted.

The onlookers dispersed quickly, once she had been whisked away in the police car. The drama was over. And they went home, feeling the same salutary emotion as after a good tragedy.

But for Mata Hari a season in hell was about to open.

21 The Theater of Execution

The inmates called it "The Slaughterhouse." The death cell at Saint-Lazare prison smelled of centuries of dread (the way a bullring retains the odor of blood long after the *corrida* is past). Since 1683, when it was built, thousands of condemned had spent their last days here, dreamt their nightmares, awaited each dawn with hearts pounding like terrified animals, until one morning they were led away to perish under the knife, on the gallows, or ripped apart by a dozen bullet holes.

Being the last residence of Saint-Vincent-de-Paul, this human stockyard had, however, a religious flavor to it (solace to some, an irony to others), for it was presided over by nuns and priests who entreated the doomed to repent their sins and accompanied them to their final ordeal.

The death cell itself was at the end of a long corridor along which rats galloped continuously, dimly lit by a gas lamp, on the first floor of the leprous prison, across an overpass nicknamed "Le Pont d'Avignon" (because everyone had to cross it to reach any part of this labyrinth). In it stood three iron bedsteads that were so close that they almost touched each other, giving the cell the appearance of a pen or cage (with a few concessions to its human occupants).

The condemned were thus never left alone but had to endure the company of their fellow sufferers, or perhaps illustrate the old cliché that misery loves company. To compensate for the shortness of their days, it seemed, or because fatted cattle are more suitable for slaughter, the occupants of death row were fed superior food, served wine with their meals, and allowed to indulge the vice of smoking and reading.

It was into this setting that Mata Hari was introduced by Sister Léonide, the old nun in charge, whose unnaturally tranquil face showed nothing of the numberless agonies she had seen. Her speech had been colored by her long association with outcasts and desperados, for she swore most colorfully and used blasphemies on the slightest occasion (for which she must have won absolution easily, considering the harshness of her tasks).

"Make yourself at home," she chuckled. "It's your last one, so you might as well live it up." The other two prisoners attempted to join in the joke, but something in their eyes belied the smiles on their lips.

Mata Hari drew herself up haughtily and faced the nun. "I do not want to feel too much at home," she said. "My appeal has been made, and I am certain to gain a reprieve."

"Sure, dearie," one of the other women cackled, "that's what they all say. But when they go out of here, it's to keep their date with 'Monsieur de Paris' or a platoon of Zouaves."

"You do not seem to know whom you are speaking to," Mata Hari pursued. "The Queen of Holland will intervene in my behalf. And probably the Pope also."

"There have been queens in these walls who lost their heads," her companion chimed in, "and even a bishop or two. So get off your high and mighty. And join the crowd."

There was no use lording it over them, Mata Hari decided. But somehow the exchange had cheered her, and their gallows humor lightened the atmosphere. She began to look at these two women, who had had none of her triumphs, adventures, or privileges, and felt a sudden rush of feeling, a sense of companionship she had never known. Their simple, homely faces had seen agony as great as hers; their flesh was as vulnerable, their thirst for life just as intense, and, in their matter-of-fact tones, their offer of warmth was more moving than most she had known.

July passed. She had a few visits from Clunet, who, with a weepy expression, informed her that her appeal had been refused. As if to make up for this, he had brought her a bouquet of flowers and several boxes of candy.

Mata Hari smiled bitterly when he had left, gave the flowers to Sister Léonide for her altar and the candy to her prison companions (who marveled at the fancy wrappings and gorged themselves on the contents). Then she turned to her readings. She had begun to review the newspaper accounts of her trial and condemnation, hoping to find a clue that might be used for a possible appeal. Turning habitually to the rubric entitled "Chroniques des Tribunaux," she found numerous articles devoted to her court-martial in which the phrase "CONDEMNED TO DEATH" leaped out at her repeatedly. Some dwelled on the "mechanical smile" on her lips as she faced her audience after the condemnation; others, on the fact that she held her head high, or showed no emotion. But all of them seemed to agree that she was guilty and should receive capital punishment. Nothing was said about any of the statesmen or military leaders who had provided the information she was accused of selling to the enemy: Messimy was safe behind the shield of dashes that carefully hid his name; the others were passed over completely. Instead, the journalists concentrated on the hundredth anniversary of the death of Mme de Staël, attacking the work De L'Allemagne, which, they decided, had exercised "the most pernicious influence." Evidently scapegoats could be exhumed after a century to receive chastisement. But there were also living beings galore who bore the brunt of this need to heap guilt upon and provide diversions for the country's defeats and failures: D. H. Lawrence was looked upon as dangerous in Cornwall because he wrote and had a beard and a German wife; Thomas Mann was suspected in London because he carried a sketch of the seating arrangement at a dinner that Goethe once gave in his house; Diaghilev had to throw the letters she had written him out of the window of a moving train when leaving Spain in order to free himself of the suspicion of being her accomplice. And she herself, it seemed, was the sacrificial beast par excellence.

Who would reach out a hand to keep her from dying? The Queen of Holland, who had been implored by van der Linden to sign an appeal, firmly refused, either because the lady had heard about the lovers so abundant, and the dance costumes so scanty, or because Holland was now under the vigilant eye of the Allies and dared not make a move so compromising to its neutral virtue. The Pope, on the other hand, had attempted to intervene for clemency. (Which made her feel somewhat more kindly disposed toward Sister Léonide—perhaps, underneath that impassive exterior, she did actually have a heart and some human emotions.)

Another month had gone by. One could almost smell the chestnuts ripening outside on the trees. She wondered, in anguish, whether this harvest season would bring about not only the reaping of corn and crushing of grapes in the wine press but also the cutting down of her own life. It seemed to her, in her nightmares, that she could hear the sharpening of scythes, the flail descending on the threshing floor, the grinding of millstones, the screams of slaughtered pigs.

Her time was drawing near, she knew. And she had not even written a last will and testament. It was at this moment that a visitor was suddenly announced. She looked expectantly at the door, having seen no one except old Clunet and a portrait painter who had come to immortalize her notorious traits for weeks now. It was Georges du Parcq, her reporter friend from happier days.

He still had the debonair airs of the journalist and the easy charm she had once known. She saw in his eyes that he found her much changed and attempted to assume a light tone to cover her confusion.

"So, the crime reporter has come to see the criminal," she joshed.

Then, taking his hands in hers, she looked into his face (hoping that she could thus revive some memories of her former appeal) and said in a cajoling tone:

"Georges *chéri*, I want you to write my *souvenirs*, my memoirs. I will tell everything . . . *everything* . . . and then they will be sorry they sentenced me to death."

She could see that the idea appealed to him as a newspaper man. However, he hesitated for a moment and said that he would have to think it over. But she was certain that the bait was too strong for him to refuse and that he would return, take down her amazing story, and publish it—after her death. It would be some form of vindication. At least she would not go silently to her grave. And her last will and testament would appear on all the front pages. A legacy of revenge, for she would name all those who had—wittingly or unwittingly—conspired with her, who were guiltier than she: the people in high places, those whose names were household words and revered by the righteous of the world. She would die, it is true, but not without company.

As she had wagered, du Parcq returned within a short space of time. He seemed more eager than before. Promising that every word she spoke would be published without alteration, he sat and for three hours took down in dictation the story of her affairs with the men she had known. He gasped now and then when she came to a particularly illustrious name but never paused or stemmed the tide of her outpourings.

When she had finished, she felt as if a great weight had been lifted from her. Her pent-up feelings were somehow alleviated by this document, which would outlive her and speak for her when she was mute. (What she did not suspect was that even this one apparently friendly act was a betrayal, for her memoirs would be handed over to intelligence headquarters by du Parcq and never see the light of day.) She had attained an end and made some sort of quietus within herself by means of these words. A great stillness came over her. She almost felt she would be ready to face them if they came for her on the next morn.

But this was not to be her fate. The end of September arrived, and she still saw the sun rise to its zenith every day. She grew fat and sluggish on prison food and lack of exercise. Her hair turned grayer, and she felt so greatly aged that they might take her for an octogenarian when they finally tied her to a stake at Vincennes. Her forty-first birthday had passed without her even having noticed. Besides, such numbers had no meaning in the world without time in which she now lived.

There was a moment's elation and a recall to the realm of men when she spotted a news item from an American paper that reported that "Mata Hari, in her cell in Saint Lazare prison, has been engaged in writing her memoirs . . . Paris is waiting to discover whether a certain French deputy furnished . . . the secret of the 'tanks.'" But this also passed from her, and she found herself musing about matters of another world.

She had begun to read Buddhist texts, returning to the solace she had found long ago, after the death of her son in the East Indies. She thought of him often now, not as he lay in his death throes in her arms but with the tranquil face of a young Pharaoh (such as she had seen on funeral masks in Egypt). And while the prison chaplain, M. Darboux, came to see her from professional duty (having heard she was a Jew converted to Protestantism), she preferred talking with an old Catholic almoner, the Abbé Doumergue, whose face—old and soft as the linen of certain shrouds—brought her tranquility. She liked to hear him use the phrase "World without end," which had an almost songlike cadence, to have him place his hand silently upon her head in benediction before he left the cell, and to address him as "Father."

Toward the end of the second week in October, she received a call from the prison photographer. She, who had been photographed so many times in her life in the most sumptuous robes and seductive poses, standing on marble pedestals or seated on precious antique *bergères*, was now roughly thrust against the prison wall, her face aligned to confront the camera and snapped, in the harsh glare of a flashbulb, to preserve her criminal features for posterity.

She knew that this meant that the end was near and that the only other picture still to be taken would be of her facing the firing squad.

When du Parcq came to visit her again that day, he found her seated among her possessions, musing. She seemed preoccupied with a small object, which she hid under the blanket as soon as he approached.

"I'm going to ask you something I would not ask any other man," she began. Then she paused and looked away toward the window. Her once-beautiful face cupped in her hands, she seemed to be gazing into an unseen distance through the bars. Then she continued in a low voice:

"I have a child . . . a little girl . . . I shall never see her again . . . I wonder, when the war is over, whether you would go . . . and give her this." She took the object from under the bedclothes. It was a portrait of her, in a frame of tiny pearls, made by Fossard, a famous Swiss miniaturist.

Autumn had come. The cold October winds were blowing, and the sound of the hunting horns was heard more often now in the woods. Fallen leaves lay on the ground; the chestnuts had burst and were lying, their innards exposed, on the wet soil.

But the prison was peaceful on that Sunday. The inmates of death row slept soundly until after dawn, for it was the only day of the week when there were no executions. Mata Hari had risen from her cot beside her sleeping companions and watched the sun rise high above the horizon through the iron bars, remembering that long ago, in a time so distant that it seemed like another life, her name had signified the Eye of Dawn. Before she was reduced to a cipher and finally to a number in the warden's files.

Her thoughts were interrupted, however, because a visitor was announced. She turned and saw Clunet edge his way into the cell. He had a sly look on his old face and beckoned her to come toward him, as though ready to impart a secret that would shake the world.

"I have thought of a way to save your life," he whispered.

She shrugged and looked at him unexpectantly.

"In my lawbooks," he continued, undaunted by her skepticism, "I found a clause which states that pregnant women cannot be executed. All you have to say . . ." His voice became even lower as he spoke into her ear.

Mata Hari guffawed. So loud was her laughter that her cell mates stirred uneasily in their sleep.

"With whom?" she said between fits of hysterical merriment. "There hasn't been a man near me for seven months . . . Except you! . . . And you don't suggest . . . Oh, no! . . ." She held her head, and continued to laugh uncontrollably.

Maître Clunet retreated, backing out of the cell with the look of an offended child. And Mata Hari went back to watch the sun rise until it had reached its zenith.

Toward sundown, as the day was drawing to an end, the inmates chatted on their beds, the prison fare served on Sundays and the wine having produced a state resembling that of well-being, joined now by Sister Léonide, who celebrated the Day of the Lord by good deeds, such as talking with her charges.

"Dance for us, Mata Hari," one of the women suddenly said. "Yes, Zelle," Sister Léonide chimed in, "we've never seen how you bewitched all those audiences." She looked down at her bloated body and the rough prison clothes. "I don't know . . ." She faltered. But they would not let her off, clapping their hands now like an impatient public that cannot wait for the curtain to open. Seeing their poor, eager faces and the hands that would soon be joined in a funerary pose, she rose. Loosening her robe slightly, arching her back, and holding her head high, she began to move with the sinuous undulations of the past. As the spirit of the dance pervaded her, the prison walls seemed to sink away; she felt only her body, long unused, assume its rightful poses and the blood course through her veins as it had ages ago when she first had moved thus in the sunshine of Java. Nothing else seemed to matter now except the feeling of being still, terribly and vibrantly, alive. Every fiber of her being was in this dance. She was—and would never cease to be—Mata Hari.

When she had finished, she sank exhausted on her cot and slept that night, dreamless and serene.

Just before dawn, on October 15, a small procession of men climbed the staircase of wood and chipped bricks that led to the first floor of the prison. Crossing the "Pont d'Avignon," they followed a long corridor where rats scurried beneath their feet, illuminated by a weak gas jet. A nun preceded them and stopped at the door of the last cell.

The door swung open, and Capitaine Bouchardon, Capitaine Thibaut, Lieutenant Mornet, Pastor Darboux, and Maître Clunet —lagging behind the others—saw three women sleeping there in metal beds.

"Which one is it?" one of the men asked.

"The one in the middle," the nun answered, pointing to what looked like an old woman with gray hair at her temples, wrinkled and wilted by the pitiless passage of time.

At the sound of the voices, the other two prisoners awoke. Seeing the men, they began to weep. Sister Léonide knelt in one corner of the cell and prayed silently. One of the officers advanced and shook the figure in the center bed.

"Zelle, be brave!" he called.

She opened her eyes and stared wildly about her, uncomprehending at first, then encompassing the whole horror of the scene. Taking her head in her hands, as if it were too heavy to bear, she murmured in a toneless voice:

"It isn't possible . . . it isn't possible . . ."

Maître Clunet suddenly forced his way through the assembled group and threw himself, sobbing, around her neck. He kissed her cheeks frenetically, filling the cell with grotesque, smacking sounds.

"Come on," one of the soldiers said with a coarse laugh. "She was only condemned to death . . . not torture!"

Mata Hari suddenly drew herself up to her full height, looking like a fallen queen. She towered over the men in uniform. The wan light illuminated her noble, ravaged face. The two women prisoners fetched her clothing and helped her dress, like ladies-in-waiting to some royal personage. She put on fine linen and her dark blue suit, shivering slightly in the damp, drafty cell.

"It is cold," she said absently, addressing no one in particular. "Why do you execute at dawn? . . . In India . . . it takes place at high noon."

She then asked for her delicate shoes, powdered her face, and began to fasten her hat with long jeweled pins.

"Hat pins are strictly forbidden," one of the officers snapped.

She smiled bitterly at this precaution, tied a veil around her hat, and drew on a pair of kid gloves. Handing some letters to Maître Clunet, who received them with trembling hands, she turned to the others.

"I am ready, gentlemen," she said in a firm voice.

Only when the chief warder seized her arm to lead her into the corridor did her eyes flash with sudden fury. She shook off his hand and said in cutting tones:

"I am not a thief! What manners are these?"

At a sign from Bouchardon he desisted, and she walked, free of all restraint, between the rows of officers.

In front of the prison a group of people and several cars stood waiting. Evidently the journalists had gotten the scent of blood, and the spectators, who in other days would have bought ringside seats for the execution, had come to see her off on her final ride.

The air was raw before dawn. The trees had begun to lose their leaves. But the sky seemed an enormous expanse, now that it was no longer framed by prison bars. And the avenues looked endless, stretching toward the horizon. A sudden feeling of freedom came over her, so strong that for an instant she thought that the car with lowered blinds that awaited her would take her on a journey to another land or for a drive into the countryside. But a loud, raucous voice cut into her thoughts.

BUTCHERS OPEN TODAY! it cried.

She jumped and, turning, saw the figure of a newsboy, waving a paper in the air, repeating his cry as he ran along the street.

The two nuns had already seated themselves in the waiting car. Pastor Darboux took her arm and led her toward it. She entered without a word. The door was slammed shut. An officer climbed in next to the driver and announced their destination.

"To the *théâtre d'exécution*," he said.

The car moved away from the prison, followed by the others, in single file. They might have been taken for a wedding procession by onlookers if the hour and the expressions of the passengers had been less grim. Once they had reached the outer boulevards, the cortege moved swiftly, passed the Porte de Vincennes, and crossed the large wooded area that surrounded the chateau.

They stopped at the castle dungeon to observe the first part of the ritual. For military executions are full of pomp and must be carried out with all the attendant ceremony. An armed guard waited at the door of the car. Mata Hari descended. They presented arms. Acknowledging their salute, as though she were reviewing her troops, she passed through the gate.

The path to the Polygon was difficult. The recent rains had turned the terrain into a kind of marsh, full of deep ruts made by the wheels of cars. But she advanced so lightly over the muddy soil that her feet, leaping over crevices and puddles with dancer's grace, hardly appeared to touch the ground.

When they had arrived, she saw a thin wooden stake at the far end of the clearing. This was the spot, then, where she would die. The drums began to sound behind her as she walked toward it, flanked by the prison chaplain and Sister Léonide, who murmured prayers as she walked. Once there, a soldier tied her hands behind her. Another advanced with a blindfold. She refused it with a majestic toss of her head.

She looked straight at the twelve Zouaves who presented arms, then readied their rifles and aimed them at her body.

She smiled, as if to acknowledge the salute. Then nodded, either to acquiesce or order them to fire.

The twelve shots rang out. She fell.

(Yet the firing squad had aimed badly. Only three bullets reached their mark. But one of them went through the heart, and death was instantaneous.)

There was no need for the coup de grâce, but since tradition demands it, one of the officers approached discreetly (like the *cachetero* who puts the finishing touch to a bullfight) and emptied his gun into her ear. The weapon, being an ancient model using heavy lead bullets, left a hideous hole where her face had been.

Dawn broke.

It was the end of Mata Hari.

Epilogue

When you shall these unlucky deeds
relate, Speak of me as I am . . .
—William Shakespeare

Post-Mortems

The amphitheater was crowded. Medical students, now that the academic year had begun once more, rushed to their seats expectantly, awaiting the anatomy lesson that was about to begin. A hum of eager voices filled the air.

"Here comes the '*pièce anatomique*,' " one of them called. The cadaver was wheeled in and placed on the slanted autopsy table. The chief surgeon appeared. He motioned to his pet disciples to approach so that they formed a circle around the body, then raised his hand, about to make the initial incision.

"Shades of Rembrandt," one of the students murmured in the amphitheater.

The anatomy lesson had begun.

Thus ends the story of Mata Hari. For it was her once-famed and desired body that lay on the dissecting table. No one having claimed it for burial, it was sent, as was customary, to a medical school. Flayed, disemboweled, dismembered, it would disappear when there was no longer anything worth studying. And all trace of her would be wiped away. Or so it was thought.

But this was not to be her fate. For as soon as Mata Hari died, legend claimed her. The mortal woman, already shrouded in mystery, was now replaced by a figure, larger than life, whose deeds and attributes partake of the realm of mythology.

Transformed, fictionalized, and glorified, she would reappear in novels, plays, and films, be reincarnated in Garbo, Dietrich, and Moreau; lend her name to dance teams; even be portrayed by a female impersonator and in an animated cartoon. Her name, exalted by some, played upon by others, subject to allusions and puns, continued to echo through the decades until finally it has become a figure of speech.

For the drama of Mata Hari continues to be played in the imagination of generations, her ghost haunts their dreams, her enigmatic fate continues to tantalize. Nor will the enigma be resolved for some time to come. For the year 2017 will have arrived before everything is known and the historians are able to vie with the mythmakers.

This is not true for the minor characters in this drama. Their stories, less tragic for the most part and seldom as mysterious, are often forgotten. But for the sake of irony or poetic justice, they deserve some mention in this tale:

Antoine—the famous director whom Mata Hari had sued for breach of contract in her heyday and against whom she had won a favorable judgment—would, after her execution as a public enemy, demand a refund for the fine he had paid.

Fräulein Doktor, after having disparaged Mata Hari as a spy by calling her "a dud" (Ein Versäger), vanished for years without a trace. Exhumed by the Nazis, decorated as a national heroine, and used for propaganda purposes by the Third Reich, she died in the 1940s in her native Germany.

Sir Reginald Hall, after continuing his brilliant career in cryptography and succeeding, by means of the Zimmerman telegram, in involving the United States in World War I and perhaps winning that war as a result, would die without being allowed to publish a factual autobiography.

Commandant Ladoux would himself be arrested as a spy only a few months after Mata Hari's execution, be interrogated by the same Bouchardon, and spend six months in the prison of Cherche-Midi. After being liberated, he would become inspector of cures and tourism in a small French spa and die of a mysterious illness, allegedly poisoned by Fräulein Doktor.

Jean Hallaure would feel some guilt at having ensnared Mata Hari and attempt to hand in his resignation to Ladoux after her execution. Years later it was evident that he still felt some twinges of conscience and could not forget her.

Marthe Richer (a/k/a Richard, a/k/a *L'Alouette*) would continue her work as a double agent but have a happier fate than Mata Hari (a/k/a H 21), for she would become a French national heroine, decorated with the Légion d'honneur, go on to write successful accounts of her exploits, champion attacks against houses of prostitution, and live to a ripe old age. As a matter of fact, she is well and living in Paris at this date.

Capitaine Bouchardon and Lieutenant Mornet would go on to interrogate and condemn other spies, only to state quite smugly— many years later, in a radio interview during the 1950s—that Mata Hari was a "mediocre" spy who probably did not deserve to be executed.

Malvy and Messimy would, for political reasons, be confused in the mind of the public (by referring to the guilty man associated with Mata Hari simply as M———y). The former would be deposed, after a dreadful incident in the Chamber of Deputies, and exiled as a result of the latter's crimes. The latter would only rectify this "error" by making a public confession eight years later, without, however, having to suffer any consequences for his acts.

None of the important political or military figures who had supplied Mata Hari with information and were therefore at least as guilty as she were prosecuted.

Mata Hari's only daughter, Non, would die mysteriously at the age of twenty-one (August 9, 1919) while on her way to the Dutch East Indies to become a schoolteacher.

The French government would sell all of Mata Hari's possessions at a public auction after her death in order to "defray the cost of her trial."

Almost sixty years later, on the hundredth anniversary of her birth, the Dutch government would decide to erect a statue of Mata Hari in her native city of Leeuwarden and to restore the house she lived in on the Groote Kerkstraat, thus making her a national heroine.

And Mata Hari would be reborn once again as one of the great legends of our time.

A Note from the Biographer

Biographers are an odd breed: half scholars, half detectives. Their research must be meticulous and done in the best academic fashion, in libraries, archives, newspaper files, and documentation centers, yet—if the biography is to be readable—this groundwork must disappear or, at least, give no hint of the effort required. The same is true for the detective work involved: the unearthing of clues, the cross-checking of various accounts, the sorting of bits of information and elimination of misinformation, the hunch followed, the lead which does (or does not) pay off, the questioning of witnesses, the ferreting out of truth.

Perhaps, however, the biographer is most closely akin to a creature of another kind for he must be willing to meet informants in odd places and at strange hours; have an eye for detail, fittingness, and incongruity; distinguish sincerity from hypocrisy; draw out all manner of people, be the perfect listener, ask leading questions; change his appearance, approach, and personality to suit the occasion; tolerate delays, frustrations, and complications; ignore his own bodily needs; charm, ingratiate, coax, impress, or threaten in order to gain information; fit the pieces of puzzles together; eavesdrop, pry, engage in a bit of voyeurism; be versatile, cunning, and ruthless in his pursuit—in other words, have all the attributes of a good spy.

While the sources of information used by the spy are secret, those of the biographer are not. The bibliography which follows attests to that fact. It contains a large number of items of unequal importance and purpose and thus needs some clarification. The first being the several major categories of sources used: background material such as historical and political studies, works on espionage theory and practice, travel books, works on religion, dance, erotic doctrines, etc.; journals or memoirs written either by observers or participants; newspapers and periodicals of the time; factual, as well as fictional, treatments of Mata Hari's life; related material concerning either minor incidents or characters or material necessary for establishing the atmosphere of the narrative; documents in the archives of the *Service Historique de l'Armée Française*.

In the first category the most valuable background sources were Lambert's *The Making of the Dutch Landscape*, Baedeker's *Belgium and Holland*, Torchiana's *Tropical Holland*, the studies on espionage by Pastor-Petit and Houbart and Rankovitch, Rawson's article on the myths and erotic art of India, Tuchman's *The Guns of August* and *The Proud Tower*, Pedroncini's *Les Mutineries de 1917*, Roger Shattuck's *The Banquet Years*—all of which are outstanding contributions in their field.

The memoirs and journals of greatest interest in the second category were those of Cocteau, Colette, Klee, and Misia Sert for the period in Mata Hari's life in which she was a dancer and courtesan, and those of Marthe Richer (alias Richard), Ladoux, du Parcq, Maunoury, and Bauchardon for the period concerning her spy activities, imprisonment, interrogation, trial, and execution.

Newspapers and periodicals of the times, which constitute the third category—preserved in the archives of the *Bibliothèque Nationale* in Paris—all provided valuable insights into events of the period as well as into the mentality of the reading public. They included all the major Paris dailies from 1905 to 1918 and ranged from the literate and dignified *Le Figaro* to the sensationalist *Le Gaulois* which specialized in lurid accounts and detailed descriptions of violent acts.

Of the factual accounts, the fourth category, dealing with Mata Hari's life, by far the best and most complete is Waagenaar's *Mata Hari* (flawed only by the author's constant intrusion and his desire to whitewash Mata Hari and free her of the accusation of being a spy); neither Heymans' *La Vraie Mata Hari, courtisane et espionne* nor Coulson's *Mata Hari: Courtesan and Spy* can compare to it in accuracy and are only useful if cross-checked with other accounts. The four-part article by Presles and Brigneau provides quite valuable and, for the most part, accurate material dealing with Mata Hari's capture and trial. Fictional works such as those by Tucker and Masson are interesting for insights into flights of the imagination provoked by the Mata Hari legend but, of course, do not provide useful facts—any more than do the films with Garbo and Moreau.

In the category of related material the most fascinating sources are Hall and Peaslee's *Three Wars with Germany*, Rowan's *The Story of Secret Service* (for the most reliable account of Fräulein Doktor), Tuchman's *The Zimmerman Telegram,* and Massard's *Les Espionnes à Paris.*

There is no doubt that the most valuable items in the sixth category, in the file of intercepted telegrams for the year 1916 (File 5 N 83 of the *Service Historique de l'Armée Francaise* at Vincennes), are the two telegrams quoted in the Note on page 247, which prove unquestionably that Mata Hari was a double agent.

A number of libraries were used to gather the research material listed in the bibliography: the New York Public Library at 42nd Street; Bobst Library of New York University; Lincoln Center Library for Performing Arts, also in New York; *La Bibliothèque Nationale* and *Les Services de Documentation de la Fondation Nationale des Sciences Politiques,* both in Paris. My thanks to the latter for special permission to consult their materials.

I also wish to express my gratitude to Elaine Brody, Patrick Chabrier, Jean-Pierre Favarger, André Kaspi, George Kooijman, Gerald Krefetz, and Michel Roudevitch for expert counsel in their respective fields.

Notes

The Woman in the Menagerie

Page

1   "Espionitis" — term used to designate hysteria concerning spies: Richer, 4, 11–22; Silber, *AI*, 125; Lacaze, 87; *Les Espions* . . . , 62; *L'Espionnage* . . . , 295.

Unusual cold wave. Fuel crisis: *Le Journal*, 2/5–13/1917.

2   New laws passed against deserters. Unrestricted submarine warfare: *Le Journal*, 2/13/1917; Silber, 168.

Woman arrested for selling laxatives: *Le Temps*, 2/9/1917.

Waiter accused of drawing plans: Silber, 126.

Old man and pidgeons: Lacaze, 87.

Headlines listing restrictions concerning restaurants, pastry shops, chocolate, butter: *Le Journal*, 1/23, 2/2, 2/12, 2/13/1917.

3   Battle of the Somme — historic battle of 1917.

Le Chemin des Dames — famous pass, hotly fought over especially at the start of 1917.

Headlines listing restrictions concerning theaters, newspapers, announcing crises of marriage and coal: *Le Journal*, 1/7, 1/14, 1/23; 2/7, 2/10/1917.

Xenophobia in France at this period: Maunoury, 24.

Need for scapegoats; unity in hate: Maurice Barrès, quoted, Domenach, 126.

Frequent executions by firing squads at Vincennes: accounts in *Le Figaro*, *L'Echo de Paris*, *Le Journal*, *Le Matin*, *Le Gaulois*, and *Le Temps* during early 1917.

Deibler — official executioner of Paris at this period, the son of Deibler, Sr., who was executioner before him.

Saint-Lazare prison, location and description: Morain, 218.

4 "The Menagerie": Waagenaar, 179.

Madame Steinheil, Marguerite Francillard: Bouchardon, 302. For details about Madame Steinheil's crime, see Chapter "The Theater of Execution."

Prisoner No. 721 44625: Bouchardon, 87.

Margaretha Geertruida Zelle — real name of Mata Hari.

Lady Gresha Mac Leod (or Mc Leod) — one of the stage names used by Margaretha Zelle at the start of her career: Heymans, 119; Ladoux, MS, 139; see Chapter 11, "The Conquest of Europe" for details.

"The Red Dancer" — name frequently used to refer to Mata Hari: Locard, 6; Coulson, 1; Morain, 227; Hall and Peaslee, 5.

H 21 — Code name of Mata Hari as a German spy: reported by Ladoux, CE; Bouchardon, Coulson, and others.

"The woman Zelle . . ." — text of accusation against Mata Hari read at time of her arrest: Morain, 218.

5 Description of cell: Bouchardon, 312. For more details, see Chapter 18, "Back to the Menagerie."

Clothing worn by Mata Hari on her arrival in prison: Bouchardon, 305; Priolet, quoted, Montardon, 8.

February 13, 1917 — date of Mata Hari's arrest.

Room 131, 103 Champs Élysées — address of Mata Hari at the time of her arrest: Presles and Brigneau, II, 10.

Thirteenth Arcana of the Tarot — death. Mata Hari had consulted a fortuneteller, Madame Soreuil on 1/26/1917, who predicted, "You will be shot, Madame": Presles and Brigneau, II, 10.

The sign of Leo — Being born on August 7, Mata Hari's sign of the zodiac is Leo, characterized by pride and ambition.

The Eye of Dawn (Mata Hari, or Matahari, in Malay) — chosen at the time of her debut at the Musée Guimet, designates the sun.

Mata Hari's serpent tattoo: Ladoux, *CE*, 243; Morain, 212.

Bokkenwagen (goat cart in Dutch): Waagenaar, 45. See Chapter 1, "Childhood's End" for more details.

PART I

1. *Childhood's End*

Page

9   History of Frisia and the Frisians: Lambert, 34–38, 127; Roberts, 3; Baedeker, 359.

"It is difficult to say . . .": Gaius Plinius Secundus (A.D. 47), quoted, Lambert, 45.

St. Amandus "much abused . . ."; St. Boniface murdered: Lambert, 127–128.

Exploits of the Frisii in various wars: Lambert, 129–130.

Treaty with Charlemagne: Baedeker, 358–359.

10 Frisian language: Baedeker, 359; Goudsblom, 28.

Description of Leeuwarden: Lambert, 139, 239, 282, 295; Baedeker, 358–359.

Facts regarding the childhood and adolescence of M'greet are scarce and often unreliable because of Mata Hari's embellishment or fabrication of her background. The most reliable source for the early part of her life remains Waagenaar. Some additional facts can be gleaned from Coulson, Roberts, and Heymans. Unless otherwise indicated, factual information concerning M'greet and her family is provided by Waagenaar, 5–20.

"An orchid miraculously dropped . . .": Roberts, 3.

Possible Jewish or Javanese ancestry: Roberts, 3–4.

11 Leeuwarden museum, and its name: Baedeker, 358.

Adam Zelle's gift to his daughter: Waagenaar, 4.

12 Description of Hofplein (Royal Square) and Stadhuis (town hall) of Leeuwarden: Baedeker, 358.

13 Education of Dutch children in the nineteenth century: Goudsblom, 98.

14 Description of the Willemskade and surroundings: Baedeker, 358.

16 Customs and mores of Dutch society: Goudsblom, 17, 30, 49, 128, 138; Capek, 84.

Antje Zelle (née van der Meulen) died on May 10, 1891 when her daughter was fourteen. Funerals such as the one described were current in nineteenth-century Europe and can still be seen in small villages today.

The Stadtuin and its function: Baedeker, 359.

19 "It was the pain I felt . . .": friend of M'greet, quoted, Waagenaar, 9.

2. *The Bride Wore Yellow*

Page

20 Description of Sneek, Holland: Baedeker, 359.

"Nice, neat, sensible . . .": Capek, 84.

"Like a toy shop . . . its living rooms . . .": *ibid.*, 99, 103.

21 School at Leyde for the training of kindergarten teachers — Margaretha is variously reported as having attended such an institution and a convent school; to have seduced or been seduced by the headmaster or priest in charge, whereupon she was sent home to her relatives in disgrace: Waagenaar (who mentions primly that the headmaster was "in love" with her), 10–11; Heymans, 22; Roberts, 3; Coulson, I, 61; Newman, 179; *Life*, December 9, 1939.

22 "As regards the Dianas and Venuses . . .": Capek, 76–77.

"*Petit capital*" (term used by French girls to designate their virginity): de Gramont, 410.

Life at the Hague in the 1890s: Baedeker, 304.

23 Description of Scheveningen and "the custom of promiscuous bathing": Baedeker, 288, 290.

Family origins and military career of Rudolph Mac Leod: Waagenaar, 12; Heymans, 7; Newman, 179.

24 Café Américain — location of, in Amsterdam: Baedeker, 305.

There are two versions of the matrimonial ad, placed either by Mac Leod or his friend. Version a: Waagenaar, 15; version b: Newman, 179.

25 Passionate letters of Margaretha; Rudolph's comment that she "seemed to be quite a girl": Heymans, quoted, Waagenaar, 15.

Description of Rijksmuseum, Amsterdam: Baedeker, 320, 322.

26 Description of Margaretha at eighteen: Coulson, I, 60; Heymans, 27. See also photograph taken at about this time.

Descriptions of Rudolph at thirty-nine vary: Waagenaar, 16; Heymans, 28. Photographs bear out the former (which is here used).

27 "Young, but good-looking . . .": Norman Mac Leod, quoted, Waagenaar, 18.

According to Dutch law, a woman could marry at sixteen with parental consent, but only at thirty without it: Goudsblom, 43.

Margaretha's yellow wedding dress: Heymans, 32; Waagenaar, 21.

28 Descriptions of Rudolph as a brutal drunkard, vicious satyr, ruthless libertine: Rowan, 585; Newman, 181; Roberts, 3; May, 106; Coulson, I, 60.

"Do whatever you want . . ." (Letter from Margaretha to Rudolph): quoted, Heymans, 30.

3. *Love's Labors*

Page
29 German "lemmings": Lambert, 356.

Gezelligheid (Dutch for homely coziness): Goudsblom, 38.

Location of Leidschekade, Amsterdam: Baedeker, 306.

30 Drunkenness, brutality, and neglect of his young wife by Rudolph Mac Leod: May, 106; Coulson, I, 62; Newman, 181–182.

31 January 30, 1897 — actual birth date of the son of Margaretha (née Zelle) and Rudolph Mac Leod, erroneously reported by a number of sources (e.g., Newman, 180) as January 30, 1896, thus giving the impression that the child was conceived out of wedlock. Corrected and documented: Waagenaar, 19.

Reception given by the Queen Regent Emma of Holland during the first year of the Mac Leod's marriage: *ibid.*, 22.

32 Norman John was named after his paternal grandfather, John Van Brienen Mac Leod, and his great-uncle Norman (whom Margaretha had met before her marriage).

4. A Passage to the Indies

33 His home leave was drawing to a close — Rudolph Mac Leod had two years' leave to spend in Holland and thus had to return to his military duties by the summer of 1897.

"Insulinde" ("Island India") — name for the Dutch East Indies: Torchiana, 15.

34 *"Oost-Indisch Archipel"* — Dutch name for the same region: *ibid.*, 16.

Volcanic eruption of Krakatau in 1883, description of: *ibid.*, 18.

Departure of the Mac Leods for Ambawara, Java, on the S.S. *Prinses Amalia*, May 1, 1897: Waagenaar, 23.

PART II

5. Scorpions and Birds of Paradise

Page
39 Descriptions of Java — its fauna, flora, landscape, customs: Torchiana, 25–27, 94, 217, 218, 239, 247, 257, 281, 284–285; Freeman 551, 553.

Sawahs — rice fields; *dessas* — native villages; *caraboes* — water buffalo; *weddana* — regent of village; *sarongs, kabayas* — native clothing for women, cloth wrapped around the body: Torchiana, 217–218.

Pasars — markets.

40   Children of Java: Torchiana, 207.

Increase in population during the nineteenth century: Hyma, 187.

Description of fish ponds at Garut: Torchiana, 283.

Temples of Djokjakarta and Boro-Budur, descriptions and history: *ibid.*, 44–48.

41   Rudolph's comments on the natives, reflecting common attitude of colonialists: Torchiana, 174; Day, 346; Furnivall, 189.

Invasions of moths, termites, flying ants (mentioned in letters by Rudolph Mac Leod to his wife): quoted, Waagenaar, 30.

Caution to be exercised concerning scorpions: *idem.*

42   *Wayung* — shadow puppet play (traditional entertainment of Javanese nobles): Torchiana, 42.

Ushas — temptress of Hindu legends (also, the female Dawn), who, by causing the seeds of the gods to gush forth, was instrumental in the creation: Rawson, 135.

Hindu influence in Java: Van Gils, 601; Torchiana, 42–45.

"Bitch" — insult to Margaretha by Rudolph Mac Leod, witnessed by Dr. Roelfson, who knew the couple in Java: quoted, Waagenaar, 32.

Drunken rages of Mac Leod; mistreatment of his wife, including physical brutality, threats to her life, etc.: Rowan, 585; Newman, 181; Roberts, 15; May, 106.

Description of a visit to the temple of Boro-Budur: Torchiana, 47–48.

43   Climate of Java — seasonal changes; monsoons, etc.: Torchiana, 23–24.

44   History of Java during the Roman period and the early centuries of the Christian era; Javanese epics; forerunners of *wayungs: ibid.*, 42–44.

Margaretha, who already spoke Dutch, German, English, and French began, during this period, to learn Javanese: Rowan, 585.

Margaretha's motive for murder: Rowan, 585; Newman, 182.

Insulin shock — since Rudolph suffered from diabetes (as mentioned in Chapter 2).

45 Officers and rank and file in Dutch colonial army: Freeman, 552; Torchiana, 282; Day, 270.

May 2, 1898 — birth of the daughter of Margaretha and Rudolph Mac Leod in Toempoeng, Java. Named Jeanne Louise (after Rudolph's sister): Newman, 184; Waagenaar, 23–24.

Opium and its widespread use: Furnivall, 336, 412.

Nonah — young girl in Malay. Abbreviated to "Non" — the name by which the Mac Leod's daughter became known.

6. *The Dead of Summer*

Page
46 *Baboe* — Malay for native nursemaid employed by Europeans: Torchiana, 288.

Rudolph Mac Leod was transferred to Medan on the east coast of Sumatra at the end of December 1898; he deposited his wife and children at the home of Mr. van Rheede, the comptroller, after having sold his furniture at auction. They remained there until May 1899: Waagenaar, 24–25.

47 Goods for export read like an alchemist's catalogue: Furnivall, 336.

Description of Medan (in a letter from Rudolph Mac Leod): quoted, Waagenaar, 25.

48 "A girdle of emerald . . .": Multatuli, quoted, Furnivall, 1.

Residence of Mac Leod as garrison commander; activities of Margaretha at this time: May, 106; Heymans, 56.

"Jan Pik," "Fluit" (nicknames for his son and daughter) used in a letter by Rudolph Mac Leod in 1889: quoted, Waagenaar, 27.

49 On June 27, 1899, both children of the Mac Leods were poisoned by one of the natives. Norman died, but Non survived. The causes of the murder have never been elucidated but are generally attributed to a desire for revenge for Rudolph's mistreatment of a native. Descriptions of the event: Newman, 182; May, 106; Roberts, 15; Heymans, 60.

7. Rites of Initiation

Page

50 Transfer to Banjoe Biroe — soon after Norman's death, Mac Leod was transferred from Medan to this dismal outpost. He attributed this change to the antipathy of his superior officer, General Biesz. Description of Banjoe Biroe in a letter by Mac Leod: quoted, Waaggenaar, 29–30.

51 Margaretha's questions concerning the poisoning are based on the various stories recounted — (a) Rudolph's beating of a native soldier, whose mistress then avenged her lover: Waagenaar, 28; (b) a servant killed for intervening in a bloody quarrel between the Mac Leods, avenged by his wife: May, 106; (c) a Malaysian woman who had been Rudolph's concubine seeking revenge: Heymans, 72.

Rudolph aged overnight and became almost mad with grief; descriptions of his suffering and the accusations against Margaretha: Waagenaar, 28; Newman, 182; Roberts, 15.

Margaretha's interest in and study of Indian epics, sacred texts, and erotic cults: Rowan, 585; May, 106; Roberts, 15.

52 *Puranas* — Hindu epics transmitted to Java and still read in the nineteenth century: Miller, 23–24; Torchiana, 41.

Anangaranga; Kokashastra; Rahaysa Kalolini; Kamasutra — Hindu sacred erotic texts: Rawson, 85.

Devadasis (or "slave girls of god") — dancer–prostitutes of Hindu temples: *ibid.*, 91–93.

Apsaras — divine incarnations of beauty and desire depicted on Hindu temples: *ibid.*, 65–68.

Surya — Hindu sun god who rides in the celestial chariot of love: *ibid.*, 134.

Kali — the Great Goddess of India in her destructive aspect: Rawson, 164–167; Neumann, 150–153.

Shiva — principal Hindu divinity, creator of the universe by means of dance, personalized representation of the sexual, creative vitality in the universe, traditionally represented *urdhvalinga* (in a state of erection): Rawson, 33, 94.

Typhoid fever of Margaretha, lasting from the middle of March to the end of May 1900. Rudolph's remarks about the cost of milk, Margaretha's state (letter from Mac Leod to his cousin): quoted, Waagenaar, 29.

Description of the worship of *Shiva*: Rawson, 39.

53 Metamorphosis of Margaretha's personality: Rowan, 585.

Description of Javanese dances, still performed according to the Hindu tradition of their origins: Roberts, 14, 15; Van Gils, 601–602; Carson, 320; Craig, 432; Torchiana, 171.

Matahari — name that, according to one source, was already adopted by Margaretha in Java and that she would later make world famous as Mata Hari: Roberts, 15.

Transformation during which "Margaretha Zelle vanished and the Java-born artiste emerged": Rowan, 587.

8. Farewell to Sindaglaja

Page

55 Sindaglaja, Java — small mountain village in which the Mac Leods lived after Rudolph's retirement from the army on October 2, 1900: Waagenaar, 30–31; Roberts, 15; Heymans, 79.

Europe at the turn of the century: Tuchman, *PT*, 268–270; Shattuck, 8, 16–18, 25.

56 Miss Tinguette, later known as "Mistinguette": Shattuck, 26.

Rudolph's angry utterances concerning Margaretha's interest in Paris: quoted, Waagenaar, 32.

57 Return of the Mac Leods from the East Indies to Holland in March 1902 (after almost five years in the colonies): May, 106.

PART III

9. Toward the City of Light

Page

61 Paris during *la belle époque*, compared to a stage: Shattuck, 5–6, 9, 354.

Décor of Paris: Tuchman, *PT*, 268; Shattuck, 11, 56.

The Bois de Boulogne as the "Garden of Woman": Proust, *SW*, 597.

Costumes of the day: Shattuck, 6; Cocteau, *PA*, 66, 75.

62   Skating instructors in "caviar toques . . .": Cocteau, *PA*, 64.

Grandes cocottes — great courtesans of the period.

Demi-castors — elegant middle-class ladies.

Lalique jewelry, description: Cocteau, *PA*, 76.

Monstres sacrés — the greatest stars of the stage.

Sarah Bernhardt "like some Venetian palace . . .": Cocteau, 110.

Grandiose gestures of the day, examples of: Shattuck, 6–18; Tuchman, *PT*, 173; Tuchman, *GA*, 4–5.

Jarry, "like a wild animal . . .": Shattuck, 194.

63   Proust, "with his strangely luminous . . .": Painter, 12.

Anna de Noailles, "the most sensitive . . .": Cocteau, *PA*, 162.

Colette, "thin, thin . . .": *ibid.*, 69.

Apollinaire in 1903: Shattuck, 260.

Satie, description of: *ibid.*, 133.

Mistinguette, "with her big, cheerful . . .": Cocteau, *PA*, 96–97.

Otéro's face: Colette, *MA*, 25, 28.

Cléo de la Mérode, "in her golden . . .": Cocteau, *PA*, 89.

Isadora Duncan "wanted to live . . .": *ibid.*, 109.

Loïe Fuller "discovered the dance . . .": *ibid.*, 89.

Footit and Chocolat; Rastelli (performers in the New Circus of the period): *ibid.*, 52, 54.

Les Frères Lumière (The Brothers Light) who first introduced the "*cinématographe*": Shattuck, 12.

"Wild Miss Barney" (Natalie Clifford Barney) — the leader of the "Amazons" (Ida Rubinstein, Renée Vivien, and others; see Chapter 10): Painter, 406–409; Colette, *MA*, 210.

Ida Rubinstein, "thin, long, glaucous . . .": Cocteau, *DE*, 47.

64 Margaretha was beaten and deserted by her husband on August 27, 1902, and her daughter was taken away by him: Waagenaar, 33; May, 106; Heymans, 86; Roberts, 15.

Court ruling in Margaretha's favor, August 30, 1902.

Refusal of Rudolph to pay support: Waagenaar, 33; May, 106.

Text of ad placed by Rudolph Mac Leod: Waagenaar, 33.

Accusation of desertion made by Mac Leod. Pronouncements that Margaretha had "broken his heart": Roberts, 15, May, 106.

65 Attempts by Margaretha to find work; to study acting. Residence in the red-light district of Amsterdam: Heymans, 91; Waagenaar, 34; May, 106.

Destitute condition of Margaretha: Bouchardon, 213.

66 Failure of Margaretha's first trip to Paris: Roberts, 16; Waagenaar, 34-35.

Rudolph's threats: Roberts, 16.

Margaretha's stay at Nijmegen (North Brabant) in the winter of 1904: Waagenaar, 35; Roberts, 16.

Text of letter by Margaretha from Nijmegen, January 1904: quoted, Roberts, 16.

67 Margaretha's second trip to Paris, probably at the end of January 1904; her arrival there with half a franc in her pocket and a revolver, etc.: Waagenaar, 36-37.

10. *Among Buddhas and Amazons*

Page
68 News items concerning German crown prince, grand duke, Mme Otéro, Sarah Bernhardt, Eleonora Duse, the Dreyfus case, Baron Rothschild, de Max, Jules Verne, Rockefeller, the Salon des Indépendants, Gabriel Fauré, Anatole Deibler, the *Potemkin*: Paris daily, *Le Journal*, February 5-June 30, 1905.

News items concerning Chaliapin, Duse's appearance in *The Lower Depths*, Sardou's *L'Espionne* (*The Spy*), the Grand Guignol's program: Paris weekly, *Le Cri de Paris*, February 5-September 17, 1905.

Einstein: Tuchman, *PT*, 270.

Richard Strauss and *Salomé: ibid.*, 323.

Fauve exhibit; "wild animal cage . . .": Shattuck, 61; Tuchman, *PT*, 336.

March 13, 1905: début of Mata Hari at the Musée Guimet: Waagenaar, 36; *Crapouillot*, 39. *Note:* The Musée Guimet, on the Place d'Iéna in Paris, began as the private collection of Emile Guimet (1836–1918), a wealthy industrialist from Lyon who had traveled around the world on a scientific mission for the French Ministry of Public Education to study various religions. He brought back numerous art objects and documents and founded a museum of history of religions, first in Lyon and then in Paris (the latter inaugurated in 1888). The museum was to serve as a center of study for orientalists and had an excellent library, which, at the outset, comprised 13,000 volumes. The museum also published specialized journals and sponsored public lectures and performances: *Petits Guides des Grands Musées*, 4–5.

This information contradicts the statements made by Waagenaar (38–39) and others that Emile Guimet was not an expert in Asiatic art and religion and was therefore easily misled by the future Mata Hari into believing that her dances were authentic. Since he was, on the contrary, eminently suited to judge her dances and the religious meaning they contained, his decision to have her perform at the Musée Guimet bears out the affirmations made by Rowan, May, and Roberts that Margaretha Mac Leod had devoted herself to the study of Hindu art and religion while in Java and had acquired a thorough knowledge of both.

Description of spectators, number of invitations, etc., at Mata Hari's début at the museum: *Crapouillot*, 39; *The Gentlewoman*, March 25, 1905, 5.

69   *"Le gratin"* — colloquial term for "the cream" of society.

"The rotunda had been transformed . . .": Waagenaar, 40.

"[Then] sounds of a strange music . . .": Svetloff, 193.

70   "Her undulating body . . .": quoted, Massard, 15.

"The spectators — both male and female — . . .": Colette, 213.

"Come to honor the museum . . .": speech quoted, Morain, 211.

"My dance is a sacred poem . . .": letter from Mata Hari to a friend (unidentified), quoted, Massard, 16–17.

71 Translation of her speech by Mata Hari into English, Dutch, German, Javanese, after delivery in French: Bouchardon, 310.

Misspellings of Mata Hari's name — for example, "Mata Kari": *The Gentlewoman*, March 25, 1907, 7.

"Tall and slender . . ." (with grammatical errors): quoted, Morain, 211.

Reported name of her father: May, 104.

Birth in the south of India, etc.: Morain, 210.

72 "My mother was a glorious temple dancer . . .": quoted, May, 104. *Note.* It is interesting that Margaretha transformed her mother, as well as the time and circumstances of her death.

Defiant resolve as the basis for her metamorphosis: Rowan, 587.

Lady Mac Leod, widow of Sir George Mac Leod: *The Gentlewoman, op. cit.,* 7.

"This is different from anything we have in Paris . . .": *Crapouillot,* 39.

73 Unerring instinct for showmanship, imagination; beginning of an obsession: Rowan, 587.

"Before a portable altar . . .": Colette, *MA*, 212.

Performance at Mme de Loynes "for women only": *Crapouillot,* 39.

"Suddenly, from behind a screen . . .": Colette, 212–213. *Note:* Colette, dancing herself at this time, might have been motivated by envy.

The "Amazons," led by Natalie Clifford Barney — to whom Rémy de Gourmont had addressed his famous *Lettres à l'Amazone* — were a group of artistic women who preferred each others' company to that of men. The group included such well-known figures as Renée Vivien, Evelina Palmer, Mme Clermont-Tonnerre (Proust's friend), the British feminist Anna Wickham, etc. It was frequented by such great courtesans as Liane de Pougy and

Emilienne d'Alençon, as well as by such famous women writers as Colette and Anna de Noailles. Other friends and visitors included Proust, Gide, Valéry, Saint-John Perse, Ezra Pound, T. S. Eliot, and d'Annunzio. For detailed descriptions of these "Amazons," see, especially: Painter, II, 406–409.

74 Mata Hari's second appearance at Miss Barney's occurred at the latter's house at 20 rue Jacob: Colette, 214.

Le Temple de l'Amitié, an eighteenth-century garden pavilion that Proust erroneously (and repeatedly) referred to as "Le Temple de l'Amour": Painter, II, 408–409.

Appearances at the Trocadéro; bookings by Gabriel Astruc to perform at the Olympia, beginning August 1905 in Le Rêve (The Dream): Waagenaar, 54–55.

Only six months after her debut (in early September), Mata Hari appeared at the most prestigious theater in Paris, the Olympia.

11. The Conquest of Europe

Page

75 First appearance of Mata Hari outside of France: Central Kursaal, Madrid, January 1906. Offers to dance in London, St. Petersburg, Berlin, Vienna, Rome, Monte Carlo: Waagenaar, 62–71.

76 "This spoiled darling, upon whom destiny . . .": F. Namur, quoted, Coulson, MH, 48.

77 "She's got flat feet . . .": Rudolph Mac Leod, quoted, Waagenaar, 3.

Handwriting analysis by Edouard de Rougemont communicated by Louis Dumur; text quoted, Massard, 20–23.

78 "Isadora Duncan is dead . . .": Neues Wiener Journal, December 23, 1906.

A war that divided the city (often referred to as "the war of the tights") and took place in Vienna due to Mata Hari's appearance there.

Rudolph had succeeded in getting a divorce on April 6, 1906, in Arnheim (a very difficult thing to do in Holland) on the grounds cited: Goudsblom, 132; Bouchardon, 306; Heymans, 98.

Book published by Adam Zelle, *The Life of Mata Hari — The Biography of My Daughter and My Grievances Against Her Former Husband*; exposé written by G. H. Priem (Rudolph's lawyer), *The Naked Truth about Mata Hari*: Waagenaar, 74–75.

"Mata Hari" cigarette: *ibid.*, 75–76.

79   "The famous Hindu dancer . . .": Indian snake number: Roberts, II, 23.

"She has renounced Shiva and his cult . . .": *Crapouillot*, 39.

80   Explanation of the "Sacred Flower Dance": letter by Mata Hari, quoted, Massard, 16–18.

"She danced like Salammbô . . .": *Le Gaulois*, March 17, 1905.

"Iokanaan's head, made up . . .": Tuchman, *PT*, 323.

81   "Salomé pouring out her hot erotic plea . . .": *ibid.*, 320.

Mata Hari's encounter with the famous director Antoine; the ensuing lawsuit: Bouchardon, 308.

"Wrapped in a bunch of rugs . . .": Cocteau, DE, 48.

Around 1910 Mata Hari acquired the "Villa Rémy" at 11 rue Windsor in Neuilly: Massard, 14.

Dances performed by Mata Hari in her garden: *The Tatler*, September 24, 1913.

"*Gros légumes*" (literally, big vegetables) — French slang, equivalent of "big shots."

"In the temple of Vishnu . . .": *La Vie Heureuse*, September 15, 1913.

82   "*Una creatura adorabile*," judgment of director Tullio Serafin: quoted, Waagenaar, 92–93.

Performance of *Salomé* at the home of Prince di Faustino: *ibid.*, 96.

Mata Hari's attempt to kidnap her daughter: *ibid.*, 90–92.

83   Troupe of the Ballets Russes "in which all the fever and fecundity . . .": Tuchman, *PT*, 337.

Description of Ida Rubinstein as Cleopatra, of Bakst's sets and costumes: *ibid.*, 338–340.

Nijinsky in *L'Après-midi d'un Faune;* in skin-fitting tights painted in animal spots: *ibid.,* 340; Cocteau, *DE,* 47.

84 "He seemed to wear the smallest hat . . .": Cocteau, *DE,* 46–47.

Diaghilev "seated in the back . . .": Cocteau, *PA,* 54–55.

85 Letter to Astruc from Mata Hari: quoted, Waagenaar, 99.

1913 — frequently referred to as the "year of miracles" (see, e.g.: Shattuck, 28).

Loïe Fuller in "A Thousand and One Nights": *La Vie Heureuse,* May 20, 1913.

"Mata Hari performs in the costume of Spain . . .": *Comoedia Illustré,* March 1913, 961.

86 Appearance at the "Villa Turquoise" of the Marquis de Givenchy: *Match,* January 8, 1964.

"Protect me from the *many, many things* . . .": Letter from Mata Hari to Louis Dumur: quoted, Massard, 19.

"I want to work again . . .": *ibid.,* 19–20.

Recommendation from Emile Guimet to Professor Erman of the Museum of Egyptology in Berlin: Waagenaar, 108.

Germans honored Mata Hari as an "esthetic" dancer: Roberts, II, 23.

"Mata Hari, the principal character dancer . . .": *London Bystander,* June 10, 1914.

87 *Unter den Linden* (Under the lime trees) — famous and elegant section of Berlin.

Tilleuls (lime trees) line many of the walks and boulevards of Paris. Also, the trees that provide the blossoms used in making lime tea, the beverage into which Marcel, the hero of Proust's *Swann's Way,* dips the *madeleine* in the most famous episode of the author's work.

Entry in Mata Hari's notebook on the day that World War I was declared: quoted, Waagenaar, 114.

"The car took us for quite a long way . . .": Sert, 114.

12. *The Highroads of the Demi-Monde*

Page
88 "Listen, I know everything . . .": Cocteau, *PA,* 49.

Marcel's meeting with the "Lady in Pink": Proust, SW, 105–110.

Demi-monde (literally, half world) — French term for the world of the courtesans.

Les Grandes Horizontales — term frequently used to designate the famous courtesans, implying that their fame was achieved in a horizontal position.

Reutlinger — renowned photographer of the period who did portraits of all the well-known women on the Paris scene (including a number of Mata Hari).

Namur — a portrait painter of the period who has now fallen into oblivion.

89 "A sort of caryatid . . .": Colette, MA, 22–28.

"She did a Spanish dance . . .": Klee, J, 86.

"She is, without a doubt . . .": ibid., 94.

90 Bidets, disguised as flower vases, in the cabinets particuliers (private rooms) of the great restaurants of the period: de Gramont, 373.

"It was no small affair . . .": Cocteau, PA, 63–64.

Palais de Glace — famous ice-skating rink of the period, located on the Champs Élysées.

"Its sky-blue plush . . .": Cocteau, PA, 61.

"Named Liane this, Liane that . . .": Cocteau, PA, 65–66.

91 "I saw a matchless victoria . . .": Proust, SW, 600.

"Avenge herself on other men . . .": Bouchardon, 306.

"She demands the life of a man . . .": quoted, Roberts, II, 22.

Mata Hari, at the apex of an amorous triangle resulting in a crime passionnel: du Parcq, 60–61.

92 Mata Hari's move to her first Paris apartment at 3 rue Balzac: Waagenaar, 62.

Readings of the Kamasutra by Mata Hari: Rowan, 595.

"The characteristics of a courtesan . . .": Vatsayana, K, 230–232.

"Members of the police force . . .": ibid., 227–229.

93 Prince de Drago; the Chilean ambassador: Roberts, II, 23.

Maître Clunet — the lawyer who would later play a fateful role in defending Mata Hari at her trial for espionage.

Stories describing Mata Hari as an expert in the "sixty-four rites of *luxure* (lust)," etc.: Morain, 214.

"A natural in the art of pleasing men . . .": Roberts, II, 22.

Move to the Palace Hotel; a carriage of her own: *idem.*

"The duty of a courtesan . . .": Vatsayana, 249.

94 "She danced, her little breasts covered . . .": Morain, 211.

"Mata Hari's art is chaste": *Le Mercure de France*, April 26, 1906.

"Voluptuous attitudes . . .": quoted, Morain, 213.

"Special performances" given by Mata Hari; reactions of the critics: Roberts, II, 22.

Repression of naked dancing by Paris courts; prison sentences of fifteen days for performers such as Sarah Brown, while Mata Hari seemed exempt from court action: Svetloff, 194.

Uroboros — ancient symbol of origin, totality, the joining of opposites; the "Great Round"; also, chaos. For details; see Neumann, 18 *et passim.*

95 "She took from her left wrist . . .": Dumur (minor writer of the period): quoted, Morain, 212.

"Amber-colored, they seemed plated with gold-leaf . . .": Morain, 212.

"The most costly delicacy . . .": Rowan, 597.

96 Fashion photo of Mata Hari wearing "an ermine coat, trimmed in white fox . . .": *La Vie Heureuse*, February 1908.

Disappearance of horse-drawn cabs in 1908: Tuchman, *PT*, 395.

97 Appearance of "Zeppelin"; Captain de Koepenick, Blériot celebrated in Paris: *Le Journal*, April–June 1909.

"*Faites des enfants!*" ("produce children"): Headlines in leading French newspapers, January–February 1909.

Birth of Wilhelmina-Emma, daughter of Queen Wilhelmina of Holland: announced in *Le Journal*, April 30, 1911.

Retreat with the banker Rousseau at Esvres, description of: Waagenaar, 84–89.

98   "Villa Rémy," description of: *La Vie de Paris*, June 1930; value of: Roberts, II, 24.

"*Sois le bienvenue*" ("Welcome," or "Be my guest", m.): *La Vie de Paris*, June 1930.

Floods in Paris during the winter of 1911: Painter, II, 198–199.

99   Nobel Prize awarded to Eve Curie: *La Vie de Paris*, October 8, 1911.

"Born on the banks of the Ganges . . ." (speech made by the journalist Paul Olivier on December 24, 1912): quoted, Morain, 210.

Dances to celebrate the Moon Goddess: *La Vie Heureuse*, September 15, 1913.

100   Across the Channel, *The Tatler* reported on September 24, 1913: "Lady Mc Leod Dances in the Light of the Moon to Her Friends," showing photos of the performance.

Paris's enthusiasm transferred to other stars: Svetloff, 194.

Duke of Brunswick, et al.: Roberts, II, 24.

The head of the French Secret Service (Deuxième Bureau), Georges Ladoux, who was later to play a fateful role in Mata Hari's life.

Messimy, the French minister of war, a "strange looking man . . .": Roberts, II, 24.

Messimy's defiance of the old-line generals: Messimy, *MS*, 93.

Von Jagow, "a typical Prussian junker . . .": Roberts, II, 24.

101   "The princess Anuba knows that . . ." (pantomime described by a spectator): quoted, Roberts, II, 21–22.

102   *Kali* — Hindu goddess known as "The Destroyer."

13.   *Suddenly One August*

Page

103   "Sacred Flower Dance" revived by Mata Hari: *La Vie Heureuse*, September 15, 1913; description of, see note, Chapter 11.

Diaghilev's banishment of Nijinsky: Tuchman, *PT*, 345.

Mata Hari's terror at dropping jade bracelet — story recounted by Namur: quoted, Massard, 28.

104   *Krieg* — war; *Gefahr* — danger.

Kriegsgefahr declared by Kaiser: Tuchman, *PT*, 72.

Von Jagow's insistence that Mata Hari have dinner with him: Roberts, II, 24.

"Chancellor Bethman-Hollweg . . .": Tuchman, *PT*, 73.

105   Jagow "rushed off a telegram . . .": *ibid.*, 80.

Description of Messimy and his decision: *ibid.*, 36–38.

Suspected Russian spies trampled to death: *ibid.*, 74.

106   Mata Hari's lack of loyalty and her tendency to consider herself Javanese: Rowan, 587.

Death of Jaurès: Tuchman, *PT*, 489.

Mata Hari's ride through Berlin on the day war was declared (which would have fatal consequences for her in 1917): Roberts, II, 24.

107   Messimy opened Cabinet "with a speech full of valor . . .": Tuchman, *PT*, 264.

Removal of Messimy; his rejoining the army: *ibid.*, 351.

Paris — an entrenched camp during the last days of August: Tuchman, *GA*, 74.

Mata Hari left Berlin almost immediately after war was declared for destinations unknown. Some sources claim that she spent the first year in various parts of Europe and re-entered Paris in 1915 (Morain, 215); others state that she went to Holland, England, and thence to France (Roberts, II, 24).

PART IV

14. *The Second Oldest Profession*

Page

111   Von Kluck, Joffre — most important German and French generals, respectively, during the early part of World War I.

Namur, Charleroi, Ypres, La Marne, Picardy, Flanders, Champagne — sites of the most important battles at the start of the war.

"The second oldest profession" (espionage): Ind, 11.

"The great secret science": Altavilla, 7.

112   Sun Tzu's study of spies: Wise, 288.

Marco Polo's voyages undertaken for purposes of espionage: Pastor-Petit, 20.

Secret service created by Sir Francis Wolsingham: *Les Espions et le monde secret*, 47.

Spy system of Cardinal Richelieu and Mazarin: *idem.*

The Chevalier d'Eon: *ibid.*, 48.

Joseph Fouché; Duc d'Enghien: *ibid.*, 49, 50; Pastor-Petit, 23.

Lawrence of Arabia: Pastor-Petit, 320.

Astarte, Artemis, Aphrodite, Rahab, Judith, Delilah, Morrigan (Celtic), the Valkyrie (Germanic), Le-hev-hev (Melanesia), Kali (India), Xochiquetzal (Aztec) — various forms of the terrible goddess, the enchantress–destroyer that appears in almost all mythologies. For details, see: Neumann, 80–81, 164–165, 174, 196–197.

"Dying," in Elizabethan parlance, means to reach orgasm.

Sarcophagus (Greek, literally, devourer of bodies). In Egyptian burial rites, the goddess Nut, represented on the floor of the sarcophagus, embraces the dead man: Neumann, 163–164.

Women spies as pawns, "dolls of flesh," "voluptuous punching balls," falling into the category of "horizontal" agents: Houbart and Rankovitch, 9, 182.

Lucid, conscious heroines, or "vertical" spies: *ibid.*, 9.

Rose Greenbow, famous woman spy during the American Civil War who fought for the abolition of slavery; *ibid.*, 266.

Louise Renée de Keroualle, double agent working for both Louis XIV and Charles II. Probably the highest paid spy of all time, having earned ca. 12 million francs in the year 1681 alone: *ibid.*, 283.

Fräulein Doktor (Elsbeth Schragmüller), notorious German spy mistress whose academy in Antwerp Mata Hari attended: Buchheit 323–326; Rowan, 557–564; Ladoux, *EE*, 8, 9; Wighton, 87; Maunoury, 73; Ind, 128; Houbart and Rankovitch, 282. For details, see Chapter 15 ("The Red Tiger versus the Red Dancer").

La Chatte (Lily Carré), double agent for France and Germany during World War II. Condemned to death in 1949; sentence commuted to life; freed in 1954: Houbart and Rankovitch, 250–253.

113 Motivations, characteristics of spies: Felix, 36; Wise, 289; Dulles, 18; Altavilla, 95; Gibson, 13.

"The Great Torment" (*"La Grande Tourmente"*) — term used to refer to World War I: Lacaze, 7.

Switzerland became the center of espionage during World War I (as it would again in World War II): Lacaze, 139, 141, 144.

Spying — "jungle international society": Sparrow, 16.

114 Zurich — center for the manufacture of false papers: Lacaze, 16.

Comparison of espionage to a vast octopus: Felix, 43.

115 Rules of the game observed among spies: Lacaze, 144.

Presence of Mata Hari during the latter part of August 1914. Contents of travel document she carried at this time: Waagenaar, 116–117.

116 *Geheimdienst* or *Geheimnachrichtendienst* — German secret service bureau: Erasmus, 88–89.

Probable opinion of German concerning women spies: Altavilla, 86.

Of Frenchman: Pastor-Petit, 211, Lacaze, 156.

Of Englishman (concerning stuttering of Somerset Maugham): Altavilla, 194; unladylike acts: Rowan, 591. Of Russian (concerning "bacteria of love"): Buchheit, 317.

117 "Women are also used . . .": Corbelle, 133.

"Baroness von der Linden" — pseudonym allegedly used by Mata Hari during her stay at the famous Maison Verte (Green Villa) located Unter den Linden in Berlin: Felix, 55.

New alias — H 21, code name of Mata Hari as German spy. There is much disagreement among authorities concerning the exact date at which she acquired the classification. See, for example: *Crapouillot*, 41; Rowan, 591.

Mata Hari's "catholic taste for adventure": Rowan, 587.

Mata Hari's age and related motives: Franklin, 81–83.

Ninon de Lenclos (1620–1705) — brilliant, celebrated, emancipated, aristocratic woman of seventeenth-century France, of whom this anecdote concerning her eightieth birthday is frequently related.

118 "The walls have mice . . .": quoted, Ind, 56.

15. *The Red Tiger versus the Red Dancer*

Page
119 Holland's role in World War I: Pastor-Petit, 223.

120 Descriptions of the German spy academy in Antwerp: Houbart and Rankovitch, 284–285; Rowan, 561; Kremer, 42.

Arrival procedures at the academy: Rowan, 567; Kremer, 42.

121 Her doctoral dissertation is actually available at the 42nd Street New York Public Library. Listed under "Dr. Schragmüller, Elsbeth," it is entitled *Die Bruderschaft der Borer und Balierer von Freiburg und Waldkirch* (Karlsruhe: G. Braunsche, 1914) and deals with an aspect of German economic history: the medieval guilds of stone-cutters and polishers in the region.

History of Elsbeth Schragmüller's career in the secret service before her appointment to direct the spy academy at Antwerp: Houbart and Rankovitch, 282–288; Rowan, 557–564; Buchheit, 323–326; Ladoux, EE, 8–11; Wighton, 87–90; Kremer, 39; Bouchardon, 214; Pastor-Petit, 245; *Crapouillot*, 41.

123 "The Red Dancer" — name often used to refer to Mata Hari: Locard, 6;

Mata Hari's training by Fräulein Doktor at Antwerp: Wighton, 87; Ind, 128; Maunoury, 73; Buchheit, 323; *Crapouillot*, 41.

125 "Fool-spies" — invention (often credited to Fräulein Doktor) by which cowardly, mistrusted, or treacherous agents were deliberately

sacrificed to the enemy: Rowan, 565; Houbart and Rankovitch, 289.

The Maison Verte in Berlin, where Mata Hari is reputed to have operated, was devoted to catering to perverse sexual practices of important government or military officials in order to establish records of their perversions for purposes of blackmail: Felix, 55–56; Coulson, 64.

"Safe house" (frequently a brothel) — a contact place used by secret agents: Felix, 55.

Description of program of studies at the Antwerp spy academy: Rowan, 565–573; Houbart and Rankovitch, 285–286.

127 "If you have any talent for languages . . .": quoted, Houbart and Rankovitch, 286.

128 "When you want to obtain information . . .": quoted, *ibid.*, 287.

Length of training period at the Antwerp school: Rowan, 568.

129 Attempts to dynamite the office of Fräulein Doktor: *ibid.*, 569.

130 Consequences of meeting of Mata Hari and Elsbeth Schragmüller: see Chapters 18 and 20.

16. *Double or Nothing*

Page
131 Winter of 1915, Mata Hari's first trip to Paris after the beginning of the war (December 15–January 1): Waagenaar, 130.

Reveillon — traditional grand dinner eaten after midnight on Christmas and New Year's Eve.

132 Edith Cavell, executed as a British spy in Brussels in 1915: Silber, *AI*, 111.

Alexander Szek and his mysterious fate: Boucard, 73–75.

French war widow almost lynched; description of spies, given by young officers: Marthe Richer (alias Richard), *MVE*, 11–14, 22. *Note:* Marthe Richer, a/k/a Richard, was a famous double agent during World War I whose career has some parallels to that of Mata Hari, with the important difference that she was not executed but decorated with the Légion d'honneur and considered a heroine by the French.

Mata Hari's stay at the Grand Hotel in Paris; encounter with Marquis de Beaufort; house on Nieuwe Uitweg; kept by Baron van der Capellen at the Hague: Waagenaar, 133–134.

Beaufort lived up to *both* parts of his name: *beau* — handsome; *fort* — strong, also skillful.

"New and rather strange dances" proposed to Diaghilev via Astruc, "not for the money . . .": Letter from Mata Hari to Gabriel Astruc, quoted, Waagenaar, 134.

133 Shoemaker at "Smart" shop; fortuneteller: *ibid.*, 131.

Mata Hari, a "free lancer": Dulles, xii.

British intelligence suspected her . . . due to report sent by M.I. (military intelligence) 6 agent: Silber, 80.

Associated with German Consul at The Hague: Franklin, 78.

British Censorship Bureau; list of "undesirable continentals": Silber, 30.

"The most costly delicacy on the continental menu": Rowan, 597, *op. cit.*, Chapter 12.

Hawklike nature of Sir Reginald Hall: Boucard, *GR*, 16.

Hall "that genius of espionage" in Room 40 O.B. who could "hear intrigues hatching . . .": Tuchman, *ZT*, 16.

This "cryptographers' war": Gibson, 232.

Hall "the best and most famous of all . . .": *idem.*

British Intelligence had, in accordance with a new "Register of Suspects" established by the Inter-Ally Bureau, signaled her to the Deuxième Bureau (French Secret Service): Ladoux, *CE*, 203–205.

134 Difficulties in obtaining passport for a second visit to France; problems in entering France; detained at Hendaye; appeal to Cambon: Presles and Brigneau, I, 19.

Her old friend Jules Cambon: see Chapter 12, "The Highroads of the Demi-Monde."

Tuileries — famous French park, near the Louvre.

Guignol — puppet shows for children in Paris, to be distinguished from the Grand Guignol (specializing in horror shows).

135 Russian Revolution; mutinies in French army in the summer of 1916: Presles and Brigneau, I, 17.

Captain Vadime de Massloff (whose name is often misspelled and appears as Malsoff, Malzov): Ladoux, CE, 234, 236; Maroff: Rowan, 589; Morov: Locard, 17. Description of: Waagenaar, 141–143; Presles and Brigneau, I, 19; III, 15.

Falling in love with Vadime de Massloff. *Note:* This episode in Mata Hari's life, although true, has been much exaggerated; as, for example, in the famous film with Greta Garbo.

"Un clou chasse l'autre" — "One nail drives out another."

Jean Hallaure — his association with Mata Hari before the war, meeting with her in the Grand Hotel, and subsequent conversations: Ladoux, MS, 141–144, 210; Presles and Brigneau, I, 17–18. *"La nuit tous les matous . . ."* variation on *"La nuit tous les chats sont gris"* — English equivalent, "All cats are gray at night."

137 Vittel — Spa in the Vosges region, specializing in cures for kidney ailments.

Preparation of trap by Hallaure in conjunction with French Secret Service: Ladoux, MS, 14–143; Presles and Brigneau, I, 18. Late summer of 1916, first meeting of Mata Hari and Ladoux: Maunoury, 74.

138 Description of Ladoux and his habits: Richard, EGP, 94–95.

Interview between Mata Hari and Ladoux: quoted, Ladoux, CE, 231–234.

140 Intercepted letters . . . find nothing: Maunoury, 74; Ladoux, MS, 140; CE, 235.

"The Garden of Delights" — famous painting by Hieronymus Bosch, depicting earthly (erotic) pleasures.

Army plans to bomb German factories from airfield near Vittel a few days before Mata Hari's trip: Ladoux, CE, 236.

Mata Hari, "woman fulfilled in love" — inscription by Mata Hari on photo taken at Vittel, indicates that she had "spent some of the most beautiful days in her life" with de Massloff there: quoted, Waagenaar, 140.

Abdicate her freedom (definition of life of spy or double agent): Marthe Richard, *EGP*, 210.

141 Ladoux, under the assumed name of Monsieur Delorme, was now operating on the top floor of 26 rue Jacob: Richer, *MVE*, 37.

Contents of second meeting between Mata Hari and Ladoux: quoted, Ladoux, *CE*, 236–244.

Craemer [sic] — Frenchified version of Kremer, Johann von, ex-member of Service III b (German Secret Service), whose book *Le Livre Noir de l'Espionnage* (Paris: Editions Fleuve Noir, 1955) is used in this study: See, for example, Chapter 12, "The Red Tiger versus the Red Dancer."

142 Sympathetic inks — another name for invisible inks.

A house just a few doors away (on 20 rue Jacob) where she had danced for the "Amazons" in 1905. See Chapter 10, "Among Buddhas and Amazons."

Description of the plight of the double agent; "caught between two fires . . .": Richer, *MVE*, 1.

143 *Pont Neuf* (New Bridge) — oldest bridge in Paris, connecting Left and Right banks and leading in the direction of the Place des Grèves where public executions used to take place.

Mata Hari to leave for Spain on the orders of Ladoux: Ladoux, *CE*, 244. See Chapter 17 for voyage to Spain.

17. *The Last Tango in Madrid*

Page

144 Mata Hari embarked on the S.S. *Hollandia* at Vigo ca. November 10, 1916, after having crossed from France into Spain on November 6: Waagenaar, 151; *Crapouillot*, 41.

145 German spy headquarters at San Sebastian: Boucard, *DAS*, 110–112; Richer, 80.

Clara Benedix episode: Waagenaar, 155–156; Presles and Brigneau, II, 10 (who give a variation of the name — Clara Benedikt).

Note: The episode has never been explained. It might simply be a case of mistaken identity or a ruse used by British Intelligence or the German Secret Service, which had knowledge of her betrayal in becoming a double agent and wished to liquidate Mata Hari.

146   "One of the most charming specimens . . .": George Reid Grant, quoted, Waagenaar, 153.

For the Allies, 1916 — the most bloody year of the war: Tuchman, ZT, 122.

Cases of "espionitis" in France (Maggi cubes) and England (*von Burstorph*): *Les Espions* . . . , 64–66; Thomson. In: Greene, 200.

147   Sir Basil Thomson, the head of British Intelligence. . . . : Locard, 18.

Letter by Mata Hari to Netherlands Minister in London; quoted, Waagenaar, 159.

148   "I have come to England to spy . . .": Rowan, 591.

Sir Basil's query to Ladoux and Ladoux's answer: Ladoux, CE, 50, 52, 256. Ladoux's revenge: Waagenaar: 163. Mata Hari easier to supervise in Spain: Presles and Brigneau, II, 10.

149   Attack of "espionitis" at the Savoy (busboy): Silber, 126.

Encounter of Mata Hari with Louis-Ferdinand Destouches, later to become the famous French novelist Céline; orders to keep her "dangling": Geoffroy, 11–12; Ostrovsky, VV, 20–21.

O. B. — Old Building (40 O. B., famous cryptography center run by Hall during World War I): Tuchman, ZT, 16; Ind. 85.

150   "Neither in fiction nor in fact . . ." — letter from Ambassador Page to President Wilson: quoted, Hall and Peaslee, 3.

Descriptions of Sir Reginald Hall — (1) as kindly Mr. Punch: Hall and Peaslee, 5–6; (2) as demonic Mr. Punch in uniform: Tuchman, ZT, 8; (3) traditional benevolent uncle: Wighton, 46; "Blinker Hall": Boucard, DAS, 11.

Cottage of Hall named *Hawkes Lease* (or Hawk's Nest): Boucard, GR, 16.

Inter-Allied service in neutral countries: Boucard, DAS, 12, 58.

151   Chivalry and magnanimity of Hall; warning to Mata Hari: Boucard, DAS, 16–17; Hall and Peaslee, 5–6.

152 Arrival of Mata Hari in Spain (port of Gijon) on December 11, 1916: Waagenaar, 165; Franklin, 82.

Followed by French secret agent: Perlès, 3.

Diaghilev performing in Spain: Sert, 144.

Compete with younger, prettier, and more talented operators: Franklin, 81.

Marthe Richard, a/k/a Marthe Richer, a/k/a "L'Alouette" (The Skylark) — French spy who posed as double agent; she survived World War I, was subsequently made into a heroine, and decorated with the Légion d'honneur. She has written several books about her exploits and is, at the present date, still alive and well in Paris. History of: *Crapouillot*, 41; Richer, 26–90.

153 Mata Hari's stay at the Ritz: Presles and Brigneau, II, 10.

Prince Ratibor, German ambassador: Richer, VE, 180.

New dance — tango: Presles and Brigneau, II, 10.

Colonel Denvignes (sometimes spelled Danvignes: Presles and Brigneau, II, 10), military attaché: Ladoux, CE, 171.

Von Kalle: Rowan, 591; Maunoury, 71. *Note*. Von Kalle is also erroneously referred to as Von Kralle (German, claw): Widder, 39; or von Kalley: Richer, 116.

Mata Hari's stay at the Palace Hotel; incident involving Marthe Richer, a/k/a Richard, a/k/a "L'Alouette": Richer, MVE, 104–106.

154 Von Kalle's instructions to order Mata Hari back to France in order to liquidate her: Franklin, 83; Rowan, 591; promises of payment: Rowan, 591.

Orders to return to France — trap by Ladoux: Maunoury, 75.

155 Kremer, spelled Craemer by Ladoux (friend in a neutral [Dutch] legation): Ladoux, CE, 246.

Tiergarten — espionage headquarters located in this section of Berlin. *Tiergarten* (German, zoo): Boucard, 163.

156 Comments about "ill-matched couple"; inspector behind palm tree at hotel in Vittel: Presles and Brigneau, I, 19.

Canaris (famous German agent, extremely handsome) who was in Madrid at this time and with whom Mata Hari is rumored to have had an affair: Ind, 188; Clark, 74–75.

Georges du Parcq — young journalist whom Mata Hari had met in 1905 and who was in Madrid, working for the French Army Intelligence at this time. She feigned not to recognize him, and he was warned at the French embassy that she was "a dangerous woman": du Parcq, 61. For their next encounter, see Chapter 19, "Invisible Inks and Aphrodisiacs."

1917 would indeed be the year of Mata Hari's death. See Chapter 21, "The Theater of Execution."

PART V

18. *Back to the Menagerie*

Page
159 In early January (ca. January 3) 1917, Mata Hari returned to France: Presles and Brigneau, II, 10; Rowan, 591.

France in a state of total exhaustion: Tuchman, ZT, 106.

Mutiny in French army: Pedroncini, 132–194; Réaud, 25, 55, 127.

"Voluntary mutilation," punished by firing squad, often extended even to those wounded by the enemy: Réaud, 320.

Attempt to hide mutinies from Allies: Pedroncini, 306.

Pacifists blamed for state of affairs (among them, Malvy, Minister of the Interior): Pedroncini, 260, 264, 309.

Defeatism in France at this time: Rowan, 594.

Inflation and economic crisis: Ratinaud, 44, 47.

Half the population of France (and Europe) starving, sickening, or dying: Tuchman, ZT, 106.

Plaza-Athénée (elegant hotel in Paris), where Mata Hari stayed upon return from Spain: Rowan, 592; Presles and Brigneau, II, 10.

160 Vadime de Massloff warned about Mata Hari and ordered to stay away from her: Presles and Brigneau, II, 10.

Ruse of using second exit to leave Dutch embassy: Maunoury, 48, 73.

161   Criticism of Deuxième Bureau for not doing his job efficiently: Ratinaud, 117.

500 spies arrested since start of hostilities and more than one-half of them executed: Ladoux, *CE*, 220.

Ladoux's coldness and evasiveness: Maunoury, 77. *Note:* Ladoux, who at this time had accumulated proof that Mata Hari was a German agent, was just waiting for orders to arrest her: Ladoux, *MS*, 147 and *CE*, 245–247.

Behavior of Colonel Denvignes toward Mata Hari: Presles and Brigneau, II, 10.

Betrayal of their agents by Germans: Widder, 39.

"Fool–spies" (both Dutch) sacrificed by Fräulein Doktor: Houbart and Rankovitch, 290.

162   Psychosis of fear and hatred: Richer, 5.

Léon Daudet's attacks on the Jews is contained in the book *L'Avant-Guerre. Etudes et documents sur L'espionnage Juif-Allemand en France* (Paris: Nouvelle Librairie Nationale, 1914).

Xenophobia and hatred of aliens: Maunoury, 24.

Amateur in espionage: Buchheit, 323.

Experiments in espionage: Rowan, 584.

Cheating by magnifying exploits: *Crapouillot*, 41.

Perfect target: Franklin, 85.

Famous victim: Silber, 125, Richard, 211.

Scapegoats: Rowan, 594; de Launay, 20; *Les Espions* . . . , 68.

She felt old: "Nearly forty, in an age where there was nothing glamorous about being forty": Franklin, 81.

Cocotte — slightly derogatory term for a courtesan.

Taedium vitae felt by Mata Hari: Locard, 19.

"You know, it's time I settled down. . . .": Priolet, quoted, Montardon, *Marianne*.

163 Move to Elysée Palace, Room 131, 103 Champs Elysées: Presles and Brigneau, II, 10.

Unrestricted submarine warfare began February 1: Tuchman, *ZT*, 7.

Two-thirds of French army ready to desert: Pedroncini, 309.

Mexico ready to join war against Allies: Tuchman, *ZT*, 158.

On the morning of the next day (February 13, 1917) — arrest of Mata Hari by inspectors Marcadier, Curnier, Des Logères, Quentin, and Commissioner Priolet: Presles and Brigneau, II, 10.

Official statement read at arrest: for text see Prologue, "The Woman in the Menagerie."

Being nude in her bed . . .": Maunoury, 77. *Note:* This is the opposite of usual descriptions given (e.g., Massard, 46) that state that she wore a nightgown but stood nude before the police to seduce them.

164 Description of Mata Hari's clothing at time of arrest: Priolet, quoted, Montardon, *op. cit.*

Saint-Lazare prison, monument in the tradition of Dumas *fils*. . . .": Rowan, 591.

Mme Caillaux; Mme Steinheil; Marguerite Francillard: see explanation of their crimes in Prologue, "The Woman in the Menagerie."

Far greater fame — Mata Hari would indeed achieve far greater renown than any of these women criminals.

Cell known as the Menagerie and description of that cell: see Prologue, "The Woman in the Menagerie."

19. *Invisible Inks and Aphrodisiacs*

Page
165 Conditions in Saint-Lazare prison: Morain, 218; Bouchardon, 218.

166 Fille Mathieu, description of crime and execution: *Le Gaulois*, October 16, 1917.

Madame Steinheil, that "expert at shaking men's loins" who performed *fellatio in extremis* on one of France's presidents, Félix

Faure, who died "clutching Meg Steinheil's curly head to his groin," a story that General de Gaulle still liked to joke about. For details, see: de Gramont, 390–391.

Bouchardon was the *rapporteur militaire* (investigating officer) of the military police in Paris at the time.

The *Chancellerie* where Bouchardon had his office was in the center of Paris, connected to the Palais de Justice: Waagenaar, 186.

"Panier à salade" (literally, "salad basket" used by French to shake water from lettuce, made of wire mesh)— colloquial term for police wagon ("Black Maria" or "paddy wagon"). Mata Hari having to travel in this manner: Bouchardon, 320.

Description of Bouchardon: Waagenaar, 185; his habits, office, and clerk *le greffier* Baudouin: *ibid.*, 186.

167 First statements and attitude of Mata Hari; Bouchardon's reaction and description of Mata Hari: Bouchardon, 305–306.

168 Attitudes and statements of Dr. Bizard and his nurse: quoted, Morain, 219.

Judgment of Dr. Bizard that Mata Hari was not suicidal and that padding of cell was unnecessary: Morain, 218.

169 No lawyer allowed (except at first and last sessions of the interrogation): Presles and Brigneau, III, 16.

La Salpêtrière; Bedlam — famous insane asylums of Paris and London, respectively.

Theatrical means used by Mata Hari to defend herself: Presles and Brigneau, III, 16; Bouchardon, 315.

Contents of Mata Hari's bag; lotion for which indeed prescription by Dr. Vergne was found on file at the Pharmacie Roberts in Paris and about which M. Edouard Bayle, assistant chief of Judiciary Identity Bureau and expert in these matters, stated that "the simple possession of these products could be explained by medical reasons," while at the same time functioning as sympathetic or invisible inks; tube of oxycyanide of mercury, indeed useful for contraceptive purposes and known at that time: Franklin, 85; Presles and Brigneau, III, 16.

171　Letter from Mata Hari to Bouchardon concerning de Massloff: quoted, Bouchardon: 307.

De Massloff's renunciation of Mata Hari: Waagenaar, 249. See also Chapter 20, "The Trial" for more details.

Comparison of the prisoner Mata Hari with her passport photo: Bouchardon, 309.

Hopes of counting on French gallantry: Lacaze, 194.

172　Meetings of Mata Hari with *"von K."* — It will be remembered that Marthe Richer (106), had seen a message signed "von K." that she took to be an abbreviation of von Kalle, the German military attaché in Spain. Some confusion arose, however, between von Kalle and von Kron (also spelled von Krön [see, for example, Massard, 44] von Kroon, von Krohn, von Kröhn) who was the naval attaché in Madrid, whose mistress Mata Hari was also reported to be, but who disclaimed any association with her: Richer, 220–222.

Bouchardon waiting for further information — Bouchardon was indeed waiting for permission from Lyautey (minister of war at that time) to use telegrams sent by the Germans concerning Mata Hari — or H 21 — and intercepted by the French Secret Service. See notes on page 173 for further details. On Lyautey: de Launay, 29.

Remarks by Dreyfus in old age, "Well you know, there's no smoke . . . ": quoted, Sir Basil Thomson. In: Greene, 212.

Bouchardon decides to shut himself up with Mata Hari in a sort of cellar for interrogation on May 1, 1917: Bouchardon, 315.

173　Telegrams from Spain to Germany and answers from Germany to Spain. There is a great deal of controversy concerning the contents of these telegrams dealing with agent H 21 (considered to be Mata Hari). Various and somewhat contradictory versions are given by Ladoux and Maunoury. Ladoux (CE, 247) gives the text as: "Agent H 21 has just arrived in Madrid. She has succeeded in being engaged by the French Secret Service, but has been sent back here by the British. She asks for instructions and money. She has given me the following information [there followed the positions of a certain number of French regiments at the front, which were not all exact] and the news that a certain

French statesman, X . . . [the name is deleted by Ladoux] has close relations with a foreign princes . . ."; as well as the answer, which he states arrived forty-eight hours later from German army headquarters: "Tell agent H 21 to go back to France and to continue her mission there. She will receive a check of 5,000 francs to be drawn by Craemer [sic] on his account."

Maunoury (*PG*, 75–76) states, however, that he remembers the text read to him by Ladoux as soon as it was deciphered and that this text does not correspond entirely to the one given by Ladoux in his book. Maunoury's version is: "H 21, an excellent agent before the war has given us nothing important since the war . . . (Tell H 21 to go back to France. . . .)," thus adding an important sentence, which seems to exonerate H 21 as far as activities during the war are concerned. Maunoury also states that the political and military information that Ladoux includes in the text of the telegram was contained in a postcard sent by Mata Hari and does not appear in the first German telegram at all. His version does, however, give evidence of German dissatisfaction with the work of H 21, which might reinforce the notion expressed by certain authors (Gribble, 155; Wighton, 79) that the Germans purposely sent telegrams in a code known to the French in order to get rid of "fool–spies." It is also known that the Allies had succeeded in breaking the German code by this time (Maunoury, 76; Tuchman, ZT, 168), a fact that may or may not have been known by the Germans.

There is a third version of the intercepted telegrams, however, which the author discovered while doing research for the present book. It was found in the folder containing intercepted telegrams for the year 1916 in the archives of the *Service Historique de l'Armée* and reads as follows: "Agent H 21 of the Information Service Center in Cologne, sent to France for the second time in March, has arrived here. She pretended to accept the offers made to her by the French Intelligence Service to work for them and to make two trial trips to Belgium in their interest. She wanted, with the agreement of the French secret service, to go from Spain to Holland on board the *Hollandia*, planning to profit from this trip in order to make contact with Cologne. Even though she had French papers, she was arrested in Falmouth on November 11 . . . She furnished me with very complete reports on subjects which I shall transmit to you by letter or telegrams. She received

5,000 francs in Paris at the beginning of November and is now asking for 10,000." (The telegram is dated December 13, 1916 and was sent by the German military attaché in Madrid to Berlin. It was intercepted by the French on December 14.) The answer seems to have been slow in coming, for the military attaché in Madrid sent a second telegram, dated December 26, which was intercepted on December 27, to German Army Headquarters, which reads: "Despite the request I sent you to provide me with a rapid conclusion to this matter, by pointing out the danger to H 21 in the case of delay, I have received no instructions after 13 days. As I fear that H 21 might not want to undertake her trip to France if it is postponed to a still later date, I am remitting her 3,500 pesetas." (Reference for both these telegrams: *Service Historique de l'Armée*, 5 N 83.) It should be noted that they clearly indicate that Mata Hari (H 21) was a double agent.

173 Mata Hari accused of suffering from *"La maladie napolitaine"* (syphilis) because she had a high fever and drank enormous quantities of water: Bouchardon, 315.

Mata Hari's confrontation with Ladoux: Ladoux, CE, 249–251.

174 40,000 mutineers in French army in the spring of 1917 (May): Pedroncini, 308.

Pétain blamed spies for this state of affairs: Ratinaud, 16, 49.

100,000 strikers in Paris: de Launay, 37.

"Moral Verdun": Pedroncini, 12.

Mata Hari — sensational capture for the Allies: Richer, 222.

175 "Confession" of Mata Hari to Bouchardon (which was actually a false confession): Presles and Brigneau, III, 16; Bouchardon, 316.

Mention of Kremer — turning point (since Bouchardon had information that Kremer was a member of IIIb Secret Service of the Germans): Bouchardon, 319.

176 June 21, 1917 — last meeting with Bouchardon; hearings would be closed after this: Waagenaar, 252.

Presence of Maître Clunet as her lawyer: Presles and Brigneau, III, 16; Bouchardon, 321; Massard, 49.

Summing up Bouchardon — *"flagrant délit"*: Bouchardon, 311.

"No, no, Poincaré. . . .": Clunet, quoted, Bouchardon, 323. *Note:* Poincaré had recently become the president of the French Republic.

20.   *The Trial*

Page
178   Headline: "The Hunting Season . . .": *La Presse* (Paris daily), July 24, 1917.

La Concièrgerie — famous French prison, located not far from the Place Dauphine and the Palais de Justice, in which many of the nobility were incarcerated during the French Revolution before being guillotined. Mata Hari had been moved from Saint-Lazare prison to the *Concièrgerie* on July 20, 1917, in order to be closer to the court proceedings, which were held in the Palais de Justice: Morain, 218.

"The Widow" (*"La Veuve"*) — slang term for the guillotine.

Headline — 1080th Day of War Today": *Le Temps* (daily), July 24, 1917. "Fierce Fighting along the *Chemin des Dames* (Road of the Ladies), famous battle site during World War I: *idem.*

Trial of Mata Hari to be held *"à huis clos"* (archaic phrase meaning. literally, behind closed doors): *Le Matin* (Paris daily), July 24, 1917.

179   Sentinels do not allow crowd to come within thirty feet of courtroom: Massard, 32.

Clothing and appearance of Mata Hari during trial: *ibid.*, 36.

Statements of Colonel and Sempron and answers by Mata Hari: Presles and Brigneau, IV, 15.

180   Exclamations of Bouchardon — "What picturesque French . . .": Bouchardon, 310.

181   Rage of Mata Hari; and Mornet called "Mephistopheles": Bouchardon, 323.

Further accusations by Mornet: Presles and Brigneau, IV, 15.

Cry of Mata Hari: "That man is evil!": Rowan, 393.

182 Intelligence of Mata Hari and mastery: Bouchardon, 323; Massard, 36.

Witnesses for the prosecution and statement of Colonel Goudet: Presles and Brigneau, IV, 15.

183 Maître Clunet's fumbling, etc. — The defense lawyer of Mata Hari has been described by various witnesses of the trial as ineffectual, although well-meaning. For example, Massard (49–51) states that he had "a noble, old man's head, wore the Military Medal of 1870 . . . his plea was full of warmth but totally unconvincing."

Witnesses for the defense: Waagenaar, 276; Presles and Brigneau, IV, 15.

The Marquis de Messimy (former minister of war) had been Mata Hari's lover, it will be remembered. In the reports of the trial in the newspapers, his name was given only as M———y, a fact that led to confusion and the accusation of Malvy (minister of the interior), who was a Leftist, the enemy of Clemenceau, Daudet (Rightists) and of the Deuxième Bureau, and such men as Ladoux, who was actually the former orderly of Messimy (Maunoury, 4–8). Malvy, of whom Clemenceau wrote: "I have a friend in the police, like everyone else except, I'm afraid, M. Malvy" (letter quoted by Sancerne, 342), would be exiled in 1918. Only about nine years later (1926) would Messimy confess: (Maunoury, 78); For more details, see: Malvy, MC; Rowan, 598–599; also Epilogue, "Post-Mortems."

Mata Hari's statement concerning Messimy: Bouchardon, quoted, Waagenaar, 275.

Letter from Mata Hari to Maître Clunet concerning Vadime de Massloff: quoted, Presles and Brigneau, IV, 15.

184 Text of de Massloff's statements when interrogated in Rennes: *idem.*

Trial proceedings suspended until the next day, July 25, 1917: *Le Temps,* July 26, 1917.

Headlines: *Le Temps,* July 25, 1917; *L'Echo de Paris* (daily), July 25, 1917; *Le Matin.*

Description of Maître Clunet; suspicions; naïveté: Bouchardon, 321, 323.

185　Questions asked by Lieutenant Mornet (which the jurors simply answered with "yes" or "no"): Presles and Brigneau; *Le Gaulois*, July 26, 1917.

186　Mata Hari's final statements: Hinchley, 95–96; Rowan, 594. *Note.* Marthe Richer had made an identical claim (being paid for her "favours" by being put on the spy roll in order to subvert official funds), which, in her case, was believed.

187　Description of the reading of judgment: *Le Gaulois*, July 26, 1917; *Le Figaro*, same date; *Le Temps, ibid.*

Unanimous judgment of "guilty" is reported by almost all sources, although several (including Mornet, quoted, Presles and Brigneau, I, 19 and *Crapouillot*, 41) state that this was not justified and that Mata Hari was brought to trial not to be judged but to be condemned (Rowan, 591) or that her activities did not warrant a death sentence (Maunoury, 61). One authority, however — Bouchardon — states that the judgment of "guilty" was *not* unanimous and that if there had been one more voice in her favor, she would have been freed: Bouchardon, 77.

Description of Mata Hari's last appearance outside the courtroom: *Le Gaulois*, July 26, 1917.

21.　*The Theater of Execution*

Page
188　"The Slaughterhouse" ("L'Abattoir") — French prison slang for death cell.

History of Saint-Lazare prison: Morain, 218.

Location and description of Mata Hari's death cell: Bouchardon, 325.

189　Conditions and rules for death-cell inmates: Morain, 223.

Description of Sister Léonide: Bouchardon, 325.

"Monsieur de Paris" — title given to executioner: *Le Gaulois*, October 16, 1917.

Appeal made by Mata Hari immediately after condemnation: *L'Echo de Paris*, July 26, 1917.

190　Visits and presents from Maître Clunet: Massard, 51.

"Condemned to Death": *Le Temps,* July 27, 1917; *Le Gaulois,* July 26, 1917.

"Mechanical smile" on Mata Hari's lips after judgment: *Le Figaro,* July 26, 1917.

"Held her head high": *L'Echo de Paris,* July 26.

"Showed no emotion": *Le Matin,* July 26, 1917.

Nothing said about statesmen or military leaders: see Rowan, "Who Was Guilty?" 596–600.

One hundredth anniversary of the death of Mme de Staël (famous writer of the eighteenth century and author of *De l'Allemagne,* a work of literary criticism) and attacks upon her (which distort the meaning of her work): *La Presse,* page 1, July 26, 1917.

Scapegoats bear the brunt of, and provide diversion from, defeats and failures: *Les Espions* . . . , 63, 65; Franklin, 85.

D. H. Lawrence looked upon as dangerous: Basil Thomson. In: Greene, 203.

Thomas Mann suspected: *ibid.,* 205.

191 Diaghilev had to throw away Mata Hari's letters: Sert, 144–145.

Mata Hari, sacrificial beast par excellence: Hinchley, 98.

Reasons for the Queen of Holland's refusal to sign an appeal: Rowan, 594.

Holland under the vigilant eye of the Allies at this time: Silber, 149.

Pope intervenes: Lacaze, 189.

Visit by Georges du Parcq to Mata Hari while in prison: du Parcq, 62–66. *Note.* Du Parcq states that this was made possible by his father who had an important position in the ministry of war. When she asked him to take down her memoirs, he was torn between his journalist's inclination and his position as an officer in the French army and its intelligence department. When he spoke about this matter to his superior, Comte de Lesdain, and indicated that Mata Hari wished to implicate highly placed French and British officers, he was ordered to proceed, promise

Mata Hari that her memoirs would be published, but to give the transcription of the notes dictated to him by her to intelligence headquarters. This was done as planned. As du Parcq himself states: "Mata Hari's souvenirs lie today in the archives of the war ministry in Paris. They will never be published." (p. 66)

193 "Mata Hari, in her cell in Saint-Lazare . . .": *New York Times*, September 29, 1917.

Mata Hari's reading of Buddhist texts: Morain, 223.

Prison chaplain; Abbé Doumergue: *idem.*

Mata Hari — a Jew: Massard, 61.

Prison photo of Mata Hari (see illustration) taken two days before her execution (on October 13, 1917): Wighton, 85.

194 Visit of du Parcq shortly before Mata Hari's execution and her request to give her portrait to Non after her death: du Parcq, 66–67.

Sunday — the only day on which there were no executions: Dr. Bizard, quoted, Morain, 224.

195 Maître Clunet's suggestion was that Mata Hari claim pregnancy as a last resort, for according to Article 27 (now Article 17) of the first chapter of the French Criminal Code, if a woman is pregnant, she cannot be executed until her child is born. However, it did not apply — which again confirms Clunet's incompetence — since Mata Hari came under French Martial Law which makes no distinction between men and women condemned to death and therefore has no provision for pregnancy.

Mata Hari dances for her fellow prisoners and Sister Léonide: Morain, 224.

197 Hat pins forbidden: Massard, 74.

Letters handed to Maître Clunet: Massard, 76; *Le Figaro*, October 16, 1917.

198 Headlines — "End of meatless days! Butchers open today!": *Le Gaulois*, October 15, 1917.

Occupants of car in which Mata Hari rode: *L'Echo de Paris*; *Le Temps*, October 16, 1917.

Silence of Mata Hari: Svetloff, 197.

Théâtre d'execution ("The theater of execution") — military term for place of execution: Massard, 79.

Ceremony of entering dungeon; pomp of military execution (presentation of arms; drums, etc.): *L'Echo de Paris*, October 16, 1917; Massard, 80).

Descriptions of Mata Hari's execution: Bouchardon, 325–328; Presles and Brigneau, IV, 15; Morain, 225; Rowan, 594.

Although some authorities claim that it was Mata Hari's show of nobility that intimidated the firing squad so that nine out of the twelve riflemen missed their mark (Morain, 225), there are others who quote legends, such as her wearing only a fur wrap or a toga, which she dropped at the strategic moment so that the soldiers, dazzled by her naked body, would miss; that the rifles were loaded with blank bullets, and that her death was a sham: Hinchley 97; Pastor-Petit, 320.

199 In actuality, Mata Hari died at 6:15 A.M. on October 15, 1917, just after the sun rose.

EPILOGUE

Post-Mortems

Page
203 *"Pièce anatomique"* ("anatomical piece"): Heymans, 294.

Although some sources (Svetloff, 197; *Le Temps*, *Le Figaro*, October 16, 1917) state that Mata Hari's body was buried in a nameless grave in Vincennes cemetery, it appears that this was a sham (Massard, 83–84) and that, in actuality, the body was given to a medical school for dissecting purposes: Morain, 226–227; Presles and Brigneau, IV, 15; Massard, 83–84; Clark, 41.

204 Mata Hari in novels: *The Eye of the Lion*, by Lael Tucker; *Pavane pour une espionne*, by René Masson; as well as in a libretto: *Ballad for a Firing Squad* by Edward Thomas.

Plays about Mata Hari: *Silk Stockings*; the recent off-off-Broadway *The Dance of Mata Hari*.

Films: *Mata Hari* (1931) with Greta Garbo, Ramon Navarro, Lionel Barrymore; the more recent *Mata Hari, Agent H-21* with Jeanne Moreau in the title role; the take-off on the Mata Hari legend, *Dishonored*, with Marlene Dietrich.

The dance team *Mata and Hari* (Ruth Mata & Eugene Hari), which has appeared extensively on American TV; female impersonator Kenneth King appearing as "Mater Harry" (see photo in *Village Voice*, 1/5/1976). Animated cartoon by Tashlin, *Plane Daffy* (1944), featuring pidgeon se-duck-tress "Hatta Mari" (see photos in *Film Comment*, January–February 1969).

Figure of speech: "Mata-Harism" (*Crapouillot, op. cit.*, 39–40); statement such as "She's no Mata Hari," made by ex-husband of "JFK Mystery Woman" (*New York Post*, 12/22/1975); the term "male Mata Hari," used to describe homosexual seducers trained by Japanese espionage service in the East Indies for use in Java: Seth, 173.

Mata Hari's ghost haunts Villa Rémy: statement in *Il Matino* (Naples), July 27, 1932, fifteen years after her death.

Enigma of Mata Hari to last until the year 2017 — despite some authors' assurances to the contrary, Mata Hari's *Memoirs* remain unpublished (du Parcq, 66); the official files of the Mata Hari case are classified information (probably because of the large number of diplomatic personalities involved) and will remain so until 100 years have elapsed — making it A.D. 2017. (See letter to the author from General Guinaud of the *Service Historique* of the French Army at Vincennes.) Some of the material has also been either destroyed or scattered, and it is difficult to know whether, even after 100 years of silence, the full truth will come to light.

Antoine asking for refund: Waagenaar, 83.

Fräulein Doktor calls Mata Hari "ein Versäger": quoted, Ladoux, *CE*, 251; disappears during World War I: Rowan, 573; exhumed by Nazis and made national heroine, etc.: Ladoux, *EE*, 10. *Note.* A film, transforming the Fräulein into a legendary heroine, has been made: *Fräulein Doktor* (Dino de Laurentiis, 1969) starring Suzy Kendall and Nigel Greene.

Sir Reginald Hall and the Zimmerman telegram: Tuchman, *ZT*.

205 Commandant Ladoux arrested and interrogated by Bouchardon,

incarcerated at Cherche-Midi prison: *Le Figaro*, March 20, 1918, p. 1; *ibid.*, March 21, 1918; Boucard, GR, 8; Richer, *EGP*, 7; Ladoux, *MS*, V.

Ladoux, Inspector of Cures and Tourism (in 1932): Ladoux, *CE*, 8; Ladoux poisoned by Mlle Docteur (Fräulein Doktor): Ladoux, *MS* (Introduction by his widow), V–VI.

Jean Hallaure, guilt feelings: Ladoux, *MS*, 147–148; Richard, *EGP*, 6.

Marthe Richer (a/k/a Richard...) decorated, author of books used in this study, attacks against houses of prostitution: *Crapouillot, op. cit.*, 41–44.

Bouchardon and Mornet, radio interview and views on Mata Hari: *ibid.*, 41.

Confusion of Malvy and Messimy, reasons for: Rowan, 598–599.

Incident in Chamber of Deputies — Malvy was interrupted by hostile spectators while making a speech there, by cries of "Mata Hari! . . . Mata Hari!" He is reported to have pitched forward in a faint and lain insensible on the floor of the rostrum: Rowan, 598. Exile of Malvy: Malvy, *MC*; Maunoury, 77–78; *Le Figaro*, March 18, 1918. Confession of Messimy: Maunoury, 77–78.

None of the political or military figures . . . prosecuted — with one exception, General Denvignes is reported as having been brought before a military court for having "forgotten important documents in a taxi" (*Le Figaro*, April 14, 1918) but is not reported to have been prosecuted or convicted for this.

Mysterious death of Non — attributed by some to a "cerebral hemorrhage": Waagenaar, 296.

206 Mata Hari's possessions sold to "defray costs . . .": *ibid.*, 295.

Statue of Mata Hari and reconstruction of house: *New York Times*, January 23, 1976 ("Travel Section").

Bibliography

BOOKS AND ARTICLES

Altavilla, M., *The Art of Spying*, New York: Prentice-Hall, 1967.

Auboyer, Jeannine, *Petits Guides des Grands Musées* (Le Musée Guimet), Editions des Musées Nationaux, Paris.

Baedeker, K., *Belgium and Holland*, 11th ed. Leipsig: Karl Baedeker, 1894.

Barzun, Jacques, "Meditations on the Literature of Spying," *The American Scholar*, Spring 1965.

Bergier, Jacques, and Delaban, Jean Philippe, *L'Espionnage straté-gique*, Paris: Hachette, 1973.

Berndorff, H. R., *Diplomatische Unterwelt*, Stuttgart: Verlag Dieck & Co., 1930.

Boucard, Robert, *Les Dessous des Archives secrètes*, Paris: Les Editions de France, 1929.

―――, *La Guerre des renseignements*, Paris: Les Editions de France, 1939.

Bouchardon, Pierre, *Souvenirs*, Paris: Albin Michel, 1953.

Brissaud, André, *Canaris*, Paris: Librairie Académique Perrin, 1970.

Buchheit, Gert, *Secrets des services secrets*, Paris: Arthaud, 1974.

Čapek, Carel, *Letters from Holland*, London: Faber & Faber, 1933.

Carson, Sylvia, "Raden Mas Jodjana and His Javanese Dancers," *The*

261

Dancing Times (London), July 1931, 320–321.

Cendrars, Blaise, *La Main coupée*, Paris: Denoël, 1946.

Clark, Ronald W., *Great Moments in Espionage*, London: Phoenix House, 1963.

Cocteau, Jean, *Journals*, New York: Criterion, 1956.

———, *La Difficulté d'être* (Coll. 10/18), Monaco: Editions du Rocher, 1957.

———, *Paris Album, 1900–1914*, London: W. H. Allen, 1956.

Colette, Sidonie Gabrielle, *Mes Apprentissages*, Paris: Ferenczi, 1936.

Corbelle, Danielle, "Roman d'Espionnage et Science Politique" (Unpublished doctoral thesis: University of Paris, Faculté de Droit et des Sciences Politiques, 1964).

Coulson, Major Thomson, *Mata Hari: Courtesan and Spy*, London: Hutchinson & Co., 1932.

———, "Mata Hari—the 'Red Dancer,'" *The Forum*, LXXXII, No. 1, 1–4, 60–64.

Craig, Gordon, "The Rarest Dancing in the World," *The Dancing Times* (London), January 1932, 429–432.

Crapouillot, Special Issues: "Les Mystères de la Police Secrète," May 1936, 1–72; July 1936, 73–168.

———, Special Issue: "Les Femmes et l'Espionnage," No. 15 (1955).

Daudet, Léon, *L'Avant-Guerre: Etudes et documents sur l'espionnage Juif-Allemand en France depuis l'Affaire Dreyfus*, Paris: Nouvelle Librairie Nationale, 1914.

Day, Clive, *The Dutch in Java*, Oxford University Press, 1966.

de Gramont, Sanche, *The French: Portrait of a People*, New York: Putnam, 1969.

de Launay, Jacques, *Secrets diplomatiques*, Brussels: Brepols, 1963.

Domenach, J. H., *Barrès par lui-même*, Paris: Editions du Seuil, 1954.

Dulles, Allen, *The Craft of Intelligence*, New York: Harper & Row, 1963.

———, *Great True Spy Stories*, New York: Harper & Row, 1968.

du Parcq, Georges, *Crime Reporter*, New York: Robert McBride, 1934.

Erasmus, Dr. Johannes, *Der geheime Nachrichtendienst*, Berlin: Musterschmidt Verlag, 1952.

Espionnage et contre-espionnage pendant la Guerre Mondiale d'après les archives militaires du Reich (transl. L. Lacaze), Paris: Payot, 1934.

Espions (Les) et le monde secret (Transworld Publication, Rome, 1973), No. 18–1, 34–41, 42–68.

Felix, Christopher (pseud.), *The Spy and His Masters. A Short Course in the Secret War*, London: Secher & Warburg, 1963.

Franklin, Charles, *The Great Spies*, New York: Hart Publishers, 1967.

Freeman, Lewis R., "The Dutch in Malaysia," *Contemporary Review* (1914), vol. 105, 548–555.

Furnivall, J. S., *Netherlands India*, New York: Macmillan, 1944.

Geoffroy, Georges, "Céline en Angleterre," *L'Herne*, III (1965), 11–12.

Gibson, Walter, *The Fine Art of Spying*, New York: Grosset & Dunlap, 1965.

Goudsblom, Johan, *Dutch Society*, New York: Random House, 1967.

Greene, Graham (ed.), *The Spy's Bedside Book*, London: Rupert Hart-Davis, 1957.

Gribble, Leonard, *Stories of Famous Spies*, London: Barker, 1964.

Hall, Sir Reginald W., and Peaslee, Amos J., *Three Wars with Germany*, New York: Putnam, 1944.

Heymans, Charles, *La Vraie Mata Hari, courtisane et espionne*, Paris: Editions Prométhée, 1930.

Hinchley, Colonel Vernon, *Spy Mysteries Unveiled*, London: George Harrap, 1963.

Houbart, Jacques, and Rankovitch, Jean-Michel, *Guerres sans drapeau*, Paris: Julliard, 1966.

Hyma, Albert, *The Dutch in the Far East*, Ann Arbor, Mich.: George Wahr, 1942.

Ind, Colonel Allison, *A History of Modern Espionage*, London: Hodder & Stoughton, Ltd., 1965.

Jung, Carl C., *Man and His Symbols*, New York: Doubleday, 1964.

Klee, Paul, *Journal*, Paris: Grasset, 1959.

Kremer, Johann von, and B-9834, *Le Livre noir de l'espionnage*, Paris: Editions Fleuve Noir, 1955.

Lacaze, *Aventures d'un agent secret français*, 1914–1918, Paris: Payot, 1934.

Ladoux, Commandant, *Les Chasseurs d'espions: Comment j'ai fait arrêter Mata Hari*, Paris: Editions du Masque, 1932.

————, *L'Espionne de l'Empereur*, Paris: Editions du Masque, 1933.

————, *Mes Souvenirs*, Paris: Les Editions de France, 1937.

Lambert, Audrey, *The Making of the Dutch Landscape*, London: Seminar Press, 1971.

Lebrun, Mathilde, *Mes Missions*, Paris: Fayard, 1921.

Locard, Edmond, *Mata Hari*, Lyon: Editions de la Flamme, 1954.

Malvy, L. J., *Mon Crime*, Paris: Flammarion, 1921.

Massard, Emile, *Les Espionnes à Paris*, Paris: Albin Michel, 1922.

Masson, René, *Pavane pour une espionne*, Paris: Presses de la Cité, 1965.

"Mata Hari": *Match*, January 8, 1964.

Maunoury, Henri, *Police de guerre*, Paris: Editions de la Nouvelle Revue Critique, 1937.

May, Antoinette, "The Mata Hari Mystery," *MS*, March 1975, 105–107.

Miller, Harry, *The Story of Malaysia*, London: Faber & Faber, 1965.

Miquel, Pierre, *L'Affaire Dreyfus*, Paris: Presses Universitaires de France, 1973.

Montardon, "Mata Hari et sa légende," *Marianne*, November 2, 1932, 14–16.

Morain, Alfred, *The Underworld of Paris: Secrets of the Sûreté*, New York: Dutton, 1931.

Nadaud, M., and Fagé, A., "Mata Hari," *Le Petit Journal*, July 16, 1925, 13–19.

Neumann, Erich, *The Great Mother*, 2nd ed., Princeton, N.J.: Princeton University Press, 1963.

Newman, Bernard, *Inquest on Mata Hari*, London: R. Hale, 1956.

Ostrovsky, Erika, *Voyeur Voyant. Portrait of Louis-Ferdinand Céline*, New York: Random House, 1971, p. 21.

Painter, George D., *Marcel Proust*, 1904–1922 (vol. II), Paris: Mercure de France, 1956.

Pastor-Petit, Domingo, *L'Espionnage*, Paris: Julliard, 1973.

Pedroncini, Guy, *Les Mutineries de 1917*, Paris: Presses Universitaires de France, 1967.

Proust, Marcel, *Swann's Way*, New York: Modern Library, 1956.

Perlès, Alfred (ed.) *Great True Spy Adventures*, London: Arco Ltd., 1956.

Presles, Alain, and Brigneau, François, "Le Dossier secret de Mata Hari," *Le Nouveau Candide* (3/1/1962), I, 18–19; (3/8/1962), II, 10; (3/15/1962), III, 16; (3/22/1962), IV, 15.

Ratinaud, Jean, *1917 ou la Révolte des poilus*, Paris: Fayard, 1960.

Rawson, Philip, In: *Erotic Art of the East* ("India"), New York: Putnam, 1968, pp. 29–188.

Réaud, R. G., *Les Crimes des conseils de guerre*, Paris: Editions du Progrès Civique, 1925.

Richard, Marthe, *Espions de guerre et de paix*, Paris: Les Editions de France, 1938.

Richer (alias Richard), Marthe, *Ma Vie d'espionne au service de la France*, 2nd ed., Paris: Les Editions de France, 1935.

Roberts, Adolphe, "The Fabulous Dancer," *The Dance Magazine*, July 1929, 13–16; August 1929, 21–24.

Rowan, Richard Wilmer, *The Story of Secret Service*, New York: Doubleday, 1937.

Sancerme, Charles, *Les Serviteurs de l'ennemi*, Paris: Fayard, 1917.

Schragmüller, Dr. Elsbeth, *Die Bruderschaft der Borer und Balierer von Freiburg und Waldkirch*, Karlsruhe: G. Braunsche, 1914.

Serano, Marcel, "Aux Folies-Bergères, Nouveaux Débuts," *Comoedia Illustré*, March 1913, 961.

Sert, Misia, *Misia and the Muses: The Memoirs of Misia Sert*, New York: John Day, 1953.

Seth, Ronald, *Anatomy of Spying*, London: Arthur Barker Ltd., 1961.

Shattuck, Roger, *The Banquet Years*, New York: Vintage Books, 1968.

Silber, J. C., *Les Armes invisibles. Souvenirs d'un espion allemand au War Office, 1914–1919*, Paris: Payot, 1933.

Sparrow, Gerald, *The Great Spies*, London: John Long, 1969.

"Speaking of Pictures," *Life*, December 9, 18, 1939, 34–35.

Svetloff, Valérien, "The Execution of Mata Hari," *The Dancing Times* (London), November 1927, 193–197.

Torchiana, H. A. van Coenen, *Tropical Holland*, Chicago: University of Chicago Press, 1921.

Tuchman, Barbara, *The Guns of August*, New York: Macmillan, 1962.

———, *The Proud Tower*, New York: Macmillan, 1968.

———, *The Zimmerman Telegram*, New York: Macmillan, 1958.

Tucker, Lael, *The Eye of the Lion*, Boston: Little Brown, 1964.

Van Gils, Henrietta, "Javanese Dancing," *The Dancing Times* (London), February 1927, 601–602.

Vatsyayana, *Kama Sutra*, Nonexpurgated Edition, Toulon: Les Editions Provincial, 1959.

Waagenaar, Sam, *Mata Hari*, New York: Appleton-Century, 1965.

Weltkriegsspionage (Die), Munich: Verlag Moser, 1931.

Widder, Arthur, *Adventures in Black*, New York: Harper & Row, 1962.

Wise, David and Ross, Thomas B., *The Espionage Establishment*, London: Jonathan Cape, 1968.

Wighton, Charles, *The World's Greatest Spies*, London: Odham's Press, Ltd., 1962.

Il Matino, July 27, 1932.

La Presse, July 24, 26, 27, 1917; October 15, 1917.

La Vie de Paris, May–December 1911.

La Vie Heureuse, April 2, 1905; February 12, 1908; May 20, 1913; September 15, 1913.

Le Cri de Paris, February 5, 26, March 19, April 2, October 8, December 17, 1905.

L'Echo de Paris, July 25, 26, 1917; October 16, 1917.

Le Figaro, July 26, 1917; October 16, 1917; February 15, 1918.

Le Gaulois, March 17, 1905; July 26, 1917; October 16, 1917; March 20, 21, 1918; April 14, 1918.

Le Journal, February 4, 1905–May 27, 1905; April 1, 30, 1909; May 31–July 27, 1909; July 27, 1917; October 16, 1917.

Le Matin, July 25, 26, 1917; October 16, 1917.

Le Mercure de France, April 26, 1906.

Le Temps, March 21, 1907; July 21, 23–27, 1917; October 16, 1917.

London Bystander, June 10, 1914.

New York Post, December 22, 1975.

New York Times, September 29, 1917; July 2, 1934; January 23, 1977.

New York Tribune, June 15, 1905.

The Gentlewoman, March 25, 1905.

The Tatler, September 24, 1913; October 24, 1917.

Index

Crécy, Odette de, 91
Curie, Mme Eve, 99, 232
Curnier, Inspecteur, 163, 245

d'Alençon, Emilienne, 63, 227
d'Annunzio, Gabriele, 227
Darboux, M., 193, 196, 198
Daudet, Léon, 162, 244, 251
Debussy, Claude, 63
de Gaulle, Charles, 246
Deibler, Anatole, 3, 68, 166, 214,
    224
de Laurentiis, Dino, 256
Delorme, Monsieur. See Ladoux,
    Georges
de Max, 62, 68, 224
de Milloué (museum director), 72
Denvignes, Colonel, 153, 161, 172,
    242, 244, 257
Des Logères, Inspecteur, 163, 245
de Staël, Mme, 253
Destouches, Louis-Ferdinand (later
    Céline), 149, 241
Deuxième Bureau, 134, 136, 148,
    161, 232, 238, 244, 251
Diaghilev, Sergei, 63, 74, 83, 84,
    103, 132, 133, 152, 191, 229,
    233, 238, 242, 253
Dietrich, Marlene, 204, 256
Doktor, Fräulein. See Schragmüller,
    Elsbeth
Doumergue, Abbé, 193
Drago, Prince de, 93, 231
Dreyfus, Alfred, 62, 68, 172, 224,
    247
Dumur, Louis, 85, 227, 229, 231
Duncan, Isadora, 63, 78, 80, 86, 98,
    223, 227
du Parcq, George, 91, 92, 156, 191,
    192, 194, 208, 243, 253
Duse, Eleonora, 62, 68, 224

Edward VII, King of England, 62
Einstein, Albert, 68, 225
Eliot, T. S., 227
Erman, Professor, 86, 229

Faure, Felix, 245–46

Fauré, Gabriel, 68, 224
Faustino, Prince di, 82
Fokine, Michel (choreographer), 84
Footit (clown), 63, 223
Fossard (miniaturist), 194
Fouché, Joseph, 234
Francillard, Marguerite, 4, 245
Freud, Sigmund, 55
Fuller, Loïe, 63, 80, 85, 223, 229

Garbo, Greta, 204, 209, 239, 256
Gauguin, Paul, 56
Gide, André, 85, 227
Givenchy, Marquis de, 85, 100, 229
Gorki, Maxim, 68
Goudet, Colonel, 137, 182, 251
Gourmont, Rémy de, 226
Greenbow, Rose, 112, 234
Greene, Nigel, 256
Groos, Major, 121
Grüber, Friedrich, 121
Guilbert, Yvette, 63
Guimet, Emile, 63, 69, 70, 72, 74,
    86, 156, 225, 229
Guinaud, General, 256
Guitry, Sasha, 78

Haanstra, Wybrandus, 21, 22
Hall, Sir Reginald ("Blinker"), 133,
    149, 150, 152, 154, 204, 238,
    241, 256
Hallaure, Jean, 135, 136, 137, 183,
    205, 239, 257
Hari, Eugene, 256
Hoegnagel ("fool-spy"), 161

Inayat Khan, 81

Jarry, Alfred, 62
Jaurès, Jean Léon, 106, 107, 233
Java ("Spice Islands"), 33–34, 39,
    41, 218, 219
Joffre, General, 111, 233

Kalle, General von, 153, 154, 155,
    160, 173, 181, 182, 185, 186,
    242, 247
Kendall, Suzy, 256

Keroualle, Louise de, 112
Kiepert, Herr, 95
King, Kenneth, 256
Kiréevsky, Mme, 63, 72
Klee, Paul, 62, 89
Kluck, General von, 111, 233
Koepenick, Captain de, 97, 231
Kremer, Johann von (a/k/a/
    Craemer), 141, 155, 163, 174,
    175, 181, 185, 242, 249

Ladoux, Georges (pseud., Monsieur
    Delorme), 136, 138, 139, 141,
    142, 148, 152, 153, 155, 156,
    161, 173, 174, 180, 181, 182,
    205, 208, 232, 239, 240, 241,
    244, 247, 251, 256
La Goulue, 56
Lalique, 72
Laurencin, Marie, 63
Lawrence, D. H., 190, 253
Lenclos, Ninon de, 117, 236
Léonide, Sister, 189, 190, 191, 195,
    196, 198, 252, 254
Lesdain, Comte de, 253
Linden, Mynheer van der, 95, 191
Loynes, Mme de, 73
Lyautey, Minister, 247

Mac Leod, Jeanne Louise ("Non")
    (Fluit) (daughter), 45, 47, 49,
    51, 56, 64, 65, 66, 76, 78, 82,
    205, 220, 254, 257
Mac Leod, John Van Brienen
    (father-in-law), 218
Mac Leod, Louise (sister-in-law),
    26, 27, 29, 31
Mac Leod, Margaretha Zelle (née
    Zeele; also Lady Gersha Mac
    Leod), 72, 100, 214, 215, 226,
    232. See also Mata Hari; Zeele,
    Margaretha Geertruida
Mac Leod, "Non." See Mac Leod,
    Jeanne Louise
Mac Leod, Norman John (Jan Pik)
    (son), 26, 32, 35, 46, 49, 218,
    220
Mac Leod, Rudolph (husband), 23,

24, 25, 26, 27, 29, 30, 31, 33,
    34, 35, 41, 42, 43, 44, 45, 46,
    47, 48, 49, 50, 51, 52, 53, 55,
    56, 64, 77, 78, 83, 156, 217,
    218, 219, 220, 221, 222, 224,
    227
Malvy, Minister, 205, 243, 251, 257
Mann, Thomas, 190, 253
Marcadier, Inspecteur, 163, 245
Marguerie, Henri de, 183
Massenet, Jules, 78, 95
Massloff, Captain Vadime de, 135,
    136, 138, 139, 140, 141, 155,
    156, 160, 162, 163, 171, 180,
    183, 184, 239, 240, 243, 246,
    251
Masson, René, 255
Mata Hari (a/k/a Baroness von der
    Linden; "Clara Benedix"; H 21;
    "Red Dancer")
  imprisonment, 4–5, 165–77, 188–
    96
  origin of name, 44, 54, 72–3, 215,
    222
  Paris début (1905), 69–74, 225
  as "Star of Dance," 79–80
  as Salomé, 80–82, 228
  decline and end of career, 83–87
  as demi-monde, 91–102
  Neuilly estate, 97–100, 228
  as secret agent, 114–143, 235,
    236, 237
  as double agent, 141–42, 151–56,
    161–63, 248–49
  arrested as "Clara Benedix"
    (1916), 145–48, 240–41
  arrested in Paris (1917), 163–64,
    214
  trial (1917), 178–87, 250, 251,
    252, 253
  execution (October 15, 1917),
    196–99, 254, 255
  legacy and legend of, 203–204,
    206, 255, 256
  See also Mac Leod, Margaretha
    Zeele; Zeele, Margaretha
    Geertruida
Mata, Ruth, 256